A Beacon in the Dark

The Tanners, Book 2

Pamela Ann Cleverly

CLEVER INK, LLC,
Mentor, OH

Copyright © 2018 Pamela Ann Cleverly
All rights reserved.

ISBN-13: 978-0-9970522-2-0
Library of Congress Control Number: 2018912578

This book is dedicated to my family who tried their best
to keep me focused on finishing the book.

Happy reading!
Pamela Ann Clews

1

Limousines still represented death, so when one parked off to the side, behind the contractor's vehicles, Olivia Bentley couldn't ignore the sense of dread rising up in her throat. She glanced at her watch. He'd said one o'clock, and here he was, right on time. She pulled the heavy wool shawl more tightly around her shoulders. She shuffled her feet in the light dusting of snow and, with some trepidation, waited on the newly repaired front steps. Only the front door was good enough for Lionel Montgomery.

Once inside, Olivia stood on her toes to kiss his cheek. "Your call was quite a surprise. I assumed you would at least let me finish the renovations before you felt the need for an inspection." She paused for a beat. "I'm so excited, Uncle Lionel. This is the perfect house and location for a bed and breakfast." He wore his poker face. Something was wrong. "I'm afraid you're going to tell me I'm throwing my money away on this old relic. It's going to be fabulous. Trust me."

Uncle Lionel laughed as he took off his black cashmere overcoat and handed it to Olivia. He was still an incredibly handsome man, even if his hair seemed a little thinner and perhaps a little more gray had crept in around the temples. His tall, athletic frame and air of confidence commanded attention wherever he went, whether he was wearing a two-thousand-dollar suit or a turtleneck and jeans. His gaze took in the large entrance hall. He smiled at the massive staircase then his gaze followed it to the stained glass window on the landing. "Very impressive."

Olivia beamed with a sense of pride at the look of approval on Uncle Lionel's face. The sounds of hammering and table saws combined with loud rock music drifted down from the floor above. The smell of sawdust permeated the air. "I would give you the grand tour, but I don't believe that's the reason for your visit."

"Olivia, is there somewhere a little quieter where we can talk?"

Familiar feelings of panic washed over her. She hadn't talked to Uncle Lionel since he'd transferred the funds from her investment accounts to pay for the house. He'd added a generous amount to cover the renovations. With the money sitting in a savings account, Olivia figured she would have enough to carry her for the next three years or so. By then the house should be making a profit. But she knew, all too well, that life's road is unpredictable.

"This sounds serious, Uncle Lionel, I hope you're not going to tell me I'm broke."

"No. Quite the contrary."

"In that case, I think you will like the morning room."

Mother Nature came through with one of those rare, beautiful winter days in January. She had covered Marblehead, Ohio in a thick blanket of fresh snow with the dark, bare tree branches standing out against a clear azure sky. Uncle Lionel entered the room with large windows on three sides framing the view beyond. Olivia paused in the doorway, her left hand clutching the doorknob for support. The intricate scrollwork pressed deeply against her palm. With hands clasped behind his straight back, Uncle Lionel gazed out upon the frozen Lake Erie. Its blanket of white was in sharp contrast to the large, black rocks anchoring the base of the lighthouse.

"I can see how you could fall under the spell of this wonderland," he said without turning.

"Enjoy the view while I get us some coffee."

Olivia slipped into the kitchen for the fresh pot that waited on the counter. She poured the hot coffee into the ornate sterling silver coffee pot then placed it on the matching tray. Her mind wandered back to a happy, carefree time when she and Brian had found the treasure in a small antique shop in London. But that was the past, now she needed to deal with the present. The sturdy handles gave her strength for what was sure to follow. Uncle Lionel didn't make social calls. She re-entered the morning room. He still stood with hands clasped behind his back.

He turned to face her. "Olivia, I really don't know where to begin. There is so much about your mother's past that you don't know." He moved to stand next to the table. "All I ask is that you listen and be objective."

She had learned long ago how to hide feelings of panic and appear calm. She took her time setting the tray on the sideboard and carefully poured steaming coffee into the two cups. Olivia maintained steady eye contact as she handed Uncle Lionel his cup, hoping he wouldn't notice the slight trembling of her hand. The large, oak pedestal table with the lion-paw feet took up the major portion of the room. It had been one of the family treasures she'd inherited from her grandmother Thompson. He pulled out a chair and set the cup and saucer on the table, then placed a briefcase in front of him and sat down.

Olivia watched as he reached for his tie then adjusted the knot. Next, he tugged on both shirtsleeves then studied his cufflinks. Olivia sat with folded hands noting his movements. Could he be stalling? He'd driven an hour and a half to talk about her mother? She'd died twenty years ago. What could he possibly have to say that required her to be objective?

"Your grandmother, Olivia McLeod, has passed away." His voice sounded reverent, as if he'd actually known her. "She named you as her sole heir."

Whatever she'd been expecting, it wasn't this. Jumping up from the table, Olivia went to the window then turned. "Died? I didn't know she was still alive. I want nothing from her. She didn't care about my mother or me, and I don't care about her." What the hell was he thinking, coming here like this? "Uncle Lionel, how could you think, even for one minute, I would take anything from her?"

"Olivia, you don't know the facts."

"Yes, I do. My mother told me what happened, and how her father disinherited her. She never heard from her mother again. Does that sound like a loving grandmother to you? I want *nothing* from her." The hammering above stopped. They'd heard her. She'd been shouting. Olivia took a deep breath. She couldn't lose her cool over some petty inheritance.

"Look, I never knew her or anything about her. Give it to some charity."

"She was an extremely wealthy woman."

The hammering on the floor above continued. "So am I, at least that's what you tell me."

"I mean *real* money, Olivia . . . *old* money." He'd put his hand out, palm up, as if he were pleading his case.

She sat back down. Her body trembled with suppressed anger. "*You* have *real* money, Uncle Lionel."

"Olivia, the Montgomerys—as a family—may be the wealthiest in Ohio, but your grandmother was one of the wealthiest women in the *country*."

"She didn't care about me. Did I ever get a birthday card? No. Did I ever get a Christmas card? No."

Uncle Lionel opened the briefcase that until now had remained closed. "That's not true Olivia, she cared very much right up until the day she died. She knew you better than you think."

He pushed a large manila envelope across the table. Olivia picked it up with shaking hands. She removed newspaper articles and photos covering every part of her life from the time she was born. It all lay in front of her like a documentary—the happy times and the tragedies.

"I don't understand. How did you get these? Shouldn't her attorney be giving me these, or someone close to her?"

Uncle Lionel hesitated for just a moment. "I'm the executor of your grandmother's estate."

This bit of news hit Olivia like a punch to the gut. She shook her head slowly back-and-forth as if in defeat. "Executor? Even *you* have betrayed me. Uncle Lionel, you're my Godfather. Shouldn't your loyalty me to me?"

"I'm sorry, Olivia. It's what had to be done." He pushed a blue envelope toward her.

Olivia picked it up. There was just a wisp of a floral scent. It looked personal and Olivia hesitated before her trembling fingers pulled apart the seal. She removed several pages of pale blue stationary. The penmanship was bold with beautifully formed letters, and most certainly was written with a fountain pen.

My Dear Olivia,

I can only imagine the hurt you are feeling as you read this. But I assure you that if there had been any way for me to be a part of your life, I would have been from the day you were born. You are strong willed and stubborn like your mother and grandfather, but I beseech you to continue to read. And listen with your heart.

Your grandfather was the product of his ancestors. His Scottish blood ran deep. Once he made a decision, he stayed true to his word, regardless of the consequences. I believe he later regretted his actions toward your mother, but his stubborn Scottish pride would not allow him to back down.

I loved your mother more than life itself. She was the center of my world, and I looked forward to growing old in her shadow, with her children at my feet. A big part of me died the day she walked out of my life forever, but I've never blamed her for her decision to follow her heart.

Your grandfather forbade me any personal contact with Maureen. In the beginning, we corresponded by letters. I shared in her uncertainty of being a wife and running a household on her own and then her joy when she realized she was expecting her first child. I looked forward to her letters and checked the hall table each day in anticipation of reading another narrative of her life.

Angus came home early one day and happened to see a letter addressed to me in his daughter's distinctive handwriting. He was livid and waved the unopened letter in front of me and then as I reached for it, he tossed it into the fireplace. His anger terrified me. His face turned beet-red and his whole body shook. He told me if I ever tried to contact Maureen in any manner, I would be disinherited as she had been. I was sure he meant every word and I dared not cross him.

I know my strong, beautiful Olivia, you would have walked out and gone to your daughter, but I could not. We are from different generations and live in different worlds. I had given my word to obey my husband. My life no longer had meaning, but I could live for Maureen's children. I plotted and planned and finally, with the help of Lionel Montgomery, I found a way.

Your mother often wrote about Lionel, telling me what a good friend he was and how much he had helped her and Fred. She told me about the new finance company he wanted to start in Cleveland. I contacted him and offered to invest in his company, if he would in turn help me. That began our long relationship and I value him as a friend. Lionel forwarded Maureen's letters, keeping me informed of her life, until her death. He buried the letters in the financial and Board of Directors reports. He also made arrangements for me to be at the funeral of your parents and brothers. You were so brave and poised and grown up, just like your mother. It was as though I were watching a young Maureen standing on the steps of the funeral home. And then at the cemetery, my heart ached for you. I wanted to hold you in my arms and take away your pain. But I could not, and I watched you reach the place where I had stood. I blew you a kiss from the car as we drove away.

Years later while you were married to Winston Montgomery III, Lionel brought me to you once again. I stood at your side in the hospital as you fought for your life and the life of your unborn child. It broke my heart to leave you, but I had no choice. I would have been with you at Brian's funeral, but I'm an old woman and my health would not permit the trip. But my thoughts and prayers were with you.

You are a strong woman, Olivia, and now I need your strength, your honesty and your dedication to what you believe in. You are part of a proud and noble family and my only heir. My absence from your life has assured that your place is secure. I know you must hate me, but if you do not accept your inheritance, then the worthless sons of Angus' partner will control the company, which your ancestors began three hundred years ago. Something is very wrong here Olivia. I am too ill to get to the truth and fight for the rightful outcome. McLeod blood flows through your veins. If you do not come and take your place, then all my sacrifices were for naught and I will have lived my life in vain.

I have always loved you, my darling Olivia.

Sincerely,
Olivia Maureen McLeod

Olivia choked back overwhelming emotions of sadness for her grandmother. But it was too late to change anything. Her tear-filled eyes met those of Uncle Lionel. "The lady in black. I remember seeing her at the funeral. I felt drawn to her then suddenly she was driving away. I saw her again in the hospital. Everything seemed foggy, and later I thought I must have been dreaming." Olivia took a deep breath. She needed to calm the raging emotions rushing through her like an inferno. "I was cheated out of an important part of my life . . . my family. Why didn't you tell me, Uncle Lionel? My whole life has been a lie. I'm not prepared for this."

Shaking his head, Uncle Lionel looked contrite. "I couldn't. I'm sorry. I know this is a shock."

Olivia's chest heaved with anger. "I need time to think about this."

"I'm sorry, Olivia. There are some unusual circumstances, and unfortunate delays. You need to make a decision before I leave."

2

"Dammit, Uncle Lionel! If you had waltzed into my life nine months ago, when I was burying my husband, and the home I loved was being stripped and pulled out from under me, I would have rejoiced! I've spent my whole life hating my grandmother for abandoning my mother and me. Now, she's sent me the proof that she sacrificed her own happiness for my future," Olivia took a deep breath, then let it out slowly. "Back then, I would have loved to thumb my nose at those accusing me of embezzlement and the attorneys who took everything but my clothes. Yes, I would have jumped at the opportunity of taking on a new identity—in a new world! But I'm just now getting my life together again—for the fourth time."

Olivia's gaze went to her left hand and the ring on her finger.

"I'm in love with a wonderful man named Travis Tanner and I'm *happy*. You can't just walk in here and tell me to give up my life, as I know it. My grandmother's world is totally unknown to me. And it sounds like she was trying to pull something over on her husband—something like me inheriting."

Lionel Montgomery remained calm during Olivia's tirade. "I'm not telling you to do anything. I'm giving you the facts. And, yes, I did notice the ring. It's beautiful. Congratulations. Have you set a date?"

Olivia twirled the ring. Travis and his mother had been pressuring her for a date. Why was it so difficult for her to look at a calendar and pick a day? "No, I want to get the house finished first. I need to have my life in order before I make the final commitment. Marriage is a big step, and I've already screwed-up twice."

"Sounds to me like you're dragging your feet. Waiting for some sign that this is your mother and father's kind of love. The love you've been searching for."

"Uncle Lionel, I *have* found that love—with Travis."

"Can you really go on now as planned, knowing there is a big black hole in your life? You're at another fork in your road. If you don't at least see what's around the next bend, you'll always wonder if you made the right decision. You can always come back, Olivia. But once I leave, the opportunity leaves with me."

"But why? What's the urgency?"

"There were extenuating circumstances regarding your grandmother's will and her shares in the company. Time's run out, so to speak."

"I think I need something stronger than coffee."

Olivia unlocked the doors to the antique liquor cabinet. Her eyes immediately fell on the very expensive bottle of Cognac. Returning to the table with the bottle and two Waterford brandy snifters, she poured the amount of two fingers into each glass.

The noise upstairs suddenly stopped and was immediately followed by the sound of heavy boots clomping down the front staircase, then the slamming of the side door.

Olivia nodded toward the doorway. "We have the house to ourselves, and I think we need a more comfortable place to talk. These chairs are feeling a bit hard."

Uncle Lionel followed Olivia to the front of the house and into the parlor. Four tall windows glistened in the afternoon sun. The old, oriental carpet in the center of the room, once again showing its ornate pattern after a good cleaning, and the intricately carved marble fireplace beckoned one to come for a closer look. Uncle

Lionel headed toward her grandfather Thompson's leather Club chair. She loved that chair. It fit like a comfortable old shoe. After noting the smoking cabinet, with the built-in ashtray on the top, he pulled a cigar from his vest pocket.

Needing support, both mentally and physically, Olivia chose the stiff-backed Sheraton sofa.

Uncle Lionel puffed on the cigar. Taking in the room, he nodded with approval. "You've done a nice job here, Olivia. This room is warm and comfortable, yet has the elegance this house demands."

"This was the first room I finished after I moved in. I'm using the dining room, at the back of the house, as my bedroom while the upstairs is under renovation. Most of the things in here were my grandmother Thompson's. I hung the drapes the day of the shooting."

That horrible night, last October, was still fresh in Olivia's mind. The night she stood on this very carpet with a gun leveled at her heart. Olivia wiped a tear and watched Uncle Lionel through blurry eyes, beseeching him to change the subject.

"I remember when you were a little girl. You were your Father's pride and joy. Even then, you were strong willed and knew how to get your way. It was unfortunate that your childhood was cut short by disaster, but you seem to grow stronger with each tragedy. Your parents would be proud."

The Cognac trickled down Olivia's throat. She was already feeling its warm, soothing effect. "Fifteen was a tough age to lose my family. I was just getting to know my mother as a woman. Our last weekend together, at the cottage, she began to talk about her childhood, and how she met and fell in love with Dad. Just after the funeral, while I was cleaning out the house, I ran across my birthday present. She had wrapped the small box and hidden it on the top shelf in her closet so I wouldn't find it. It was a diary. A note inside said that on her sixteenth birthday, she had received a diary from her mother, and her mother before her had received one in the same manner. The last time I saw Mom, she told me someday she would give me her journals to read. I found them in a cedar chest in her bedroom. I haven't read them yet."

Lionel swirled the amber liquid in his glass. "Perhaps it's time."

The journals had been in the back of her mind for the last twenty years, but the time never seemed to be right. She loved her mother the way she remembered her, and over the years had raised her up onto a pedestal—Olivia didn't want the unknown to cause an imbalance that would allow her to fall.

Olivia watched the smoky cloud forming in the corner of the room, just as she remembered from her childhood. They were happy times when Uncle Lionel had come to the house and he and her father would sit with a scotch and a cigar.

Uncle Lionel took a sip of Cognac. "The Montgomery Savings & Loan in Cedar Hill was my responsibility and I took it over from my grandfather. Back then I watched our servicemen come home, get married, and start a family, your father included. Up to that time, it had been a society that believed in cash. The depression hurt a lot of folks, and they were leery of lending institutions. But these young families needed to furnish their homes and buy clothes and cars, and they couldn't wait to save the money. Department stores offered credit with their charge-a-plates. I came to the conclusion that there was a need on a larger scale, a single card that could be used anywhere. The rest of the family thought it was just another one of my hair-brained schemes and didn't take me seriously. So after much research and planning, I took my own money and formed the finance company. But I needed a lot more capital than I could raise alone. That's when your mother told me about her family. By then, old Angus had cut off the last ties between mother and daughter. Maureen suggested I write to your grandmother with a business proposition that would benefit both of us."

He paused, looking at the glowing end of the cigar, as if it allowed him to see into the past. "It was springtime when I flew into Virginia. Your grandmother had her chauffeur meet me at the airport and drive me to the house outside of Richmond, not all that far from Williamsburg. That's when I realized what "*old*" money meant. The estate—or farm, as it was known—was part of a historic Virginia plantation along the James River. I was told our Nation's Founding Fathers often met in those very rooms while plotting against King George and making plans for a new country. Of course it wasn't *your* ancestors living there then. The McLeod's bought the house and much of the land in the late 1800s. There's also a townhouse in Norfolk where your grandfather often stayed—so he could be near his business."

Uncle Lionel's description of her McLeod grandparents began to tweak Olivia's interest. A blanket of warm, comforting feelings held her safely, giving her courage—or perhaps it was the effect of the Cognac. "What was the business?" she asked in a soft, lazy tone.

"Shipbuilding. Huge ships—mostly government contracts."

Olivia studied the swirling Cognac in her glass as if gazing into a crystal ball. "I once told my mother, after spending a week at the cottage, how much I loved boats and being on the water. She just laughed and said it was in my blood. I didn't know what she meant at the time."

"This was the heritage your grandmother fought so hard to preserve for you. We struck a deal that day. She became my business partner, and I became her eyes and ears. I kept her informed of her daughter's life—and of yours."

"This is all so overwhelming. I don't understand how I can inherit after everything my grandfather did to prevent it."

"Your grandmother was a smart and determined woman. She hated her husband for what he did and vowed to find a way to win in the end. His last will and testament stated that she would be disinherited should she contact her daughter or any child of Maureen's. His business partner's sons would then divide the estate equally. She fulfilled the conditions and had no contact, leaving her free to name you as her heir. Your grandfather's will never stated outright that no child of his daughter could inherit after his wife's death. I'm sure it was an oversight, but nonetheless it will hold up in court."

Olivia took a deep breath. "Will it come to that?"

"There's no doubt. But the Olivia I know can handle anything thrown at her. This inheritance is your birthright. Ever since that terrible accident took the lives of your parents and brothers, you have been searching for a family. Well, you may have found your family too late, but you have some fine ancestors who are worth getting to know."

The Cognac had worked its magic. Feelings of excitement and a new challenge were beginning to stir. Olivia stood and walked to the center of the room. "Perhaps, you're right Uncle Lionel, and the time has come for me to discover who I really am. I remember the old lady dressed in black. She came to me in my darkest hours. Perhaps it's time I get to know her and the plantation my mother called home."

Lionel got up from the chair and wrapped strong, loving arms around her. "I knew you wouldn't let her down." They strode slowly, arm in arm, back to the morning room. He walked to the table and began closing his briefcase. "Oh, I almost forgot something." Reaching inside he pulled out a small faded blue silk bag and handed it to her.

The bag felt heavy for its size. Pulling open the ribbons at the top, there was a faint metallic sound. Three small keys fell into the palm of her hand. They were the sort of old keys that could open a cabinet or desk. She felt inside and pulled out a folded piece of paper. It was a short note written by her grandmother, but this time with an unsteady hand.

My dear Olivia,
These are the keys to the past.
They will open trunks, well-hidden
and protected in the valley.
Remember, I will always be watching over you.
Look to me for your answers.
Your loving grandmother,
Olivia Maureen McLeod

Olivia's mind, still fuzzy from the Cognac handed the note to Uncle Lionel. "Do you know what this means?"

After he finished reading, he shook his head. "It seems to be some sort of message or clue to something at the farm. I was instructed to give you this bag, only if you agreed to the inheritance." He folded the note and handed it back to Olivia.

"Do you remember a valley near the house?"

"No, but I was only there for one day and I don't remember much of the surrounding area."

After putting the note and keys back into the delicate satin bag, Olivia looked up at the man who had always been at her side, ready to help her through the disasters in her life. He had stepped in to be a father figure when her own father was taken from her. "Does this mean you and I are now business partners?"

He chuckled and kissed her cheek. "No. It means you have inherited your grandmother's shares of stock in my company."

"Thank you, Uncle Lionel, for always looking out for me. I know I haven't always been forthcoming with my gratitude. I do appreciate you always being there, and watching over me."

"It's what your father would want." His look was tender, and his voice soft.

Olivia slipped her arm through Uncle Lionel's. "So, how much is the stock worth?" she asked with a grin and chuckle.

"As of yesterday, about a hundred million."

A hundred million dollars was more than Olivia could fathom. Her smile faded. She tightened her grasp on the little blue bag that was going to change her life . . . again.

3

Olivia's world had changed. Stretching her legs out in front of her, she scooted back against the pillows on the window seat. It wasn't long before Spooky jumped up to join her. She stroked the black kitten's head with her free hand. She'd never had pets as a child. Her mother was allergic to everything on four legs—except horses. Win couldn't be bothered and the subject never came up with Brian. It was nice having the undemanding fury companion. Holding the glass by its fragile stem, she sipped the last of her best bottle of Bordeaux. She could afford to buy many more bottles of expensive wine. She could buy anything she wanted. She should be happy.

Yesterday, her future looked ordinary, and ordinary was exactly what she wanted. She wanted to leave the horrors, the scandal, the tragedy, and the heartache behind. She wanted to walk down a golden path with Travis Tanner. She looked forward to holidays with his large family. They were the family that had embraced her as one of their own. Olivia now had many friends and was an accepted and loved resident of the tiny town of Marblehead, Ohio. The old Captain's house was being transformed into a Bed and Breakfast. She looked forward to filling it with happy guests—and the happy children Travis had promised.

Olivia stared out at the night sky, black and foreboding, only broken by the rhythmic beacon from the lighthouse. How was she going to tell Travis she no longer knew what her future held? She had efficiently run a hospital, but could she even consider running a company that built ships? Her course was now charted to take her into the dark waters of the unknown, and she was terrified. She watched the lighthouse beacon reach far into the night sky. Hopefully, when the time came, that beacon in the dark would guide her back home.

Olivia sat at the kitchen table with a mug of strong coffee and a bowl of steaming oatmeal. The morning news program showed a severe snowstorm moving across Michigan and heading straight for the Lake Erie islands. The accumulation could reach an inch or more an hour. This was her first winter on the lonely peninsula. All the locals had warned her that she was now living on the roughest point on Lake Erie. It was just a few months ago that she had survived her first nor'easter. The monstrous storm had kept her a prisoner for three days in the drafty old house. She would survive this storm as well. This time she would have Travis at her side.

Olivia heard Nick Tanner's diesel truck. She went to the side door to let the big burly man in from the cold. She smiled, remembering the first time she'd met Travis's cousin and thought he looked like Paul Bunyan. Spooky used the opportunity of an open door to dash outside.

"Mornin', Miss Olivia. Listen, I sure hate to bail on you like this, but there's one nasty storm barrelin' down on us. There's a few places around town we need to batten down before the storm hits. This old house will keep you safe, and we're actually ahead of schedule on the work upstairs. The new bathrooms are framed in."

"I'll be fine, Nick. This can't be any worse than everything else I've survived since moving here. Besides, Travis should be coming by this afternoon."

"I'll swing by later this evening and check on you and plow the drive if need be."

Wrapping her arms around herself to ward off a chill, Olivia walked through the rooms on the first floor of the old stone mansion. With the help of Nick and his crew, it was becoming the home she had dreamed of. It would be a happy home, with laughter and Travis's love to guide her into a future free of lies, betrayal, and dangerous jealousies.

A bone-chilling shiver caused her to stop at the large window overlooking the back of the house. The unstable garage was scheduled for demolition in early spring. The building and cave beneath had been the perfect location for smuggling liquor in from Canada during Prohibition. Few people knew about the cave that had been found when the old boathouse was built in 1910. The entrance was sealed and nearly forgotten until the early 1920s, when someone decided it would be the perfect location for smuggling. And someone else decided it would be Olivia's final resting place. Another shiver racked her body.

Olivia couldn't relive the horror of that October day. She wanted warm and cozy thoughts and moved toward the hall that would take her to the front of the house. She paused at the door to the old music room. Her grandmother Thompson's bedroom furniture filled one corner. There were boxes of her brother's toys she had lovingly packed twenty years before after their funeral. Metal racks, hung with plastic garment bags containing her mother's beautiful gowns, lined one wall. The old Chickering Square Grand piano was the only remnant of the once elegant room. Next to it was the small trunk containing her mother's journals. Olivia remembered Uncle Lionel's comment about it being time she got to know her mother.

With hands crammed deep in her pockets, Olivia took a long breath and stared at the trunk. It wasn't just a trunk . . . it was Pandora's box. She loved her mother the way she remembered her, but after twenty years, the memories were beginning to fade. Olivia kept a bottle of Chanel No.5 on her dresser, just so she wouldn't forget her mother's scent. Was she strong enough to open the trunk and see her mother as she really was—or should she just keep the past locked safely away?

4

The storm raged outside, dumping inches of snow beyond the long parlor windows. Inside, Olivia snuggled into the big leather Club chair, her feet resting on the ottoman, an afghan draped over her legs. The crackling fire didn't do much to dissipate the cold draft seeping in around the windows. The now familiar sounds of hissing radiators and banging pipes comforted her as she reached for the first of her mother's journals. There were twenty-one small hardbound notebooks of varying sizes, dating from 1943 to 1964. Olivia had stacked them neatly next to the chair with the oldest on top.

She'd just opened the cover of the first book when she heard someone stomping on the side porch. Jumping to her feet, she tossed the journal onto the seat and raced toward the side hallway. Spooky darted through the door as Travis knocked more snow off his boots then closed the door behind him.

Olivia joined him in the coatroom. "You're early. I didn't expect you until this afternoon."

Travis took off his snow-covered leather jacket, shook it once then hung it on one of the hooks that lined the wall. After running fingers through his hair to dust off the snow, Travis wrapped his arms around Olivia. "Hmm, you're nice and warm." He bent down for a long, possessive kiss that sent shivers all the way down to Olivia's toes.

Olivia let out a moan. "Sex in front of a hot, sizzling fire sounds good to me."

"In case you haven't seen the news, there's one hell of a storm heading our way. If I'm going to get stranded somewhere, I'd rather it be with you. And sex in front of a fire sounds like the perfect way to keep warm."

Olivia took his hand and they walked to the parlor and the warmth of the fire. Travis nodded toward the stack of books. "What are those? They look old. Find another treasure in the house?"

"They're my mother's journals. It's taken me twenty years to build up the courage to read them. It just seemed like that kind of day. You know, a stay-at-home-in-front-of-a-fire-and-learn who-your-mother-was kind of day."

Travis nodded as if it made perfect sense. "You know, I've wanted to rummage through that old trunk of stuff you found in the attic. It looks like it's filled with old newspaper articles and documents about various shipping accidents and disasters that happened in the area."

"Sounds like this just turned into a reading day. The trunk is really heavy. I had Nick's guys bring it down from the attic. It's in the library now. I can bring the journal and join you."

Travis headed toward the library then stopped. "No, I think I'd like to rummage on my own. I'll need room to spread things out."

"That's okay by me. I'll just go back to the chair by the cozy fire."

Olivia threw another log on the fire. "So much for sex-by-the-fire," she mumbled before settling into the leather chair.

She ran her fingers over the old cover, embossed with the year 1943. There was a part of her that wanted to keep her mother's past buried. Her mother never talked about her life growing up. She had walked away from her family. If Olivia was going to deal with her grandmother's estate, then she would need to know what drove her mother away. Olivia took a deep breath and opened the cover. She immediately recognized her mother's distinctive handwriting, although not as flamboyant as it would become with age.

SATURDAY, JANUARY 9, 1943

This is my best birthday ever. Mother gave me this journal to write down my most personal thoughts of the day. She told me her mother gave her one on her sixteenth birthday and it made her feel very grown-up. I feel grown-up too, especially since William gave me a very grown-up kiss. It wasn't the peck-on-the-cheek he has given me since I was a kid. It was a real kiss on my lips and I just wanted to swoon. I wore the beautiful blue dress Mother bought me in New York last week. William gave me a lovely heart-shaped locket on a gold chain and put it around my neck. I think I'll put our pictures in it to remember this special day. Father's gift will arrive tomorrow and he said it's to be a big surprise. I wonder what it is. Perhaps it will be a shiny new automobile. That would be just grand, although Mother will not allow me to drive alone. She is still afraid I'll be kidnapped like the Lindbergh baby. That is silly. I'm sixteen now and too old to be kidnapped. I'm very sleepy now, but I'll write again tomorrow.

SUNDAY, JANUARY 10, 1943

My present is a horse! A beautiful black Arabian, just like Mother's. Father took me out to the stable and made me cover my eyes while the groom brought him out of his stall. I think I'll name him Sinatra, after Frank. I hope Munchkin will understand and not be too jealous. Munchkin is a stupid name for a pony, but they were my favorite characters in the Wizard of Oz. William has gone back to Annapolis. I'll write to him tomorrow and tell him about Sinatra. I still think about his kiss. I wonder if the kiss and the beautiful locket mean he loves me?

MONDAY, JANUARY 11, 1943

Mother has hired a professional trainer for Sinatra and me. Mr. Heinz Linsenhof competed on the German equestrian team in the 1936 Olympics and took a medal in Dressage. He'll be coming to the farm once a week for our lessons. My new clothes arrived from New York today. Mother is not happy with all the baggy sweaters and long pleated skirts, and she hates the ankle socks and penny loafers. But now I'm a real bobby-soxer and I hope someday I'll get the chance to see Frank in person. Mother gave me a new phonograph and all the latest records for my birthday. She loves to spoil me, but I sometimes feel bad for all the other kids who don't get wonderful presents.

Olivia skimmed over the next few months filled with school, friends, war news, and Maureen's riding lessons on Sinatra. Her mother believed in maintaining a low profile by keeping local spending to a minimum and followed the rules of rationing. She helped the war effort by growing extra crops in unused pastureland and giving the fruits and vegetables to the poor. The farm appeared to be fairly self-sustaining, and her grandparents hired many of the local disabled men who were not able to fight for their country. The one thing that continually bothered Maureen was the fact that her mother refused to have the barns and fences painted. Maureen was embarrassed by the shabby look of the farm but her mother was fearful Maureen might be kidnapped if they showed too much wealth during such hard times.

A frown creased Olivia's brow. She had just begun to read, and already there were questions racing through her mind. To have Frank Sinatra as a teenage idol wasn't surprising. But a horse for her birthday and clothes from New York was definitely not normal—especially in those days of rationing.

Travis stopped in the doorway holding an old newspaper. "Hey, Livy, there's amazing stuff in that trunk!" He took a step into the room. "You're frowning. What is it? Is something wrong?"

"It appears my mother grew up on an old farm. I knew Mom had grown up in Virginia. It was always her answer as to where she had developed a Southern accent."

"Didn't she ever mention growing up? I thought all parents told their kids how tough they had it."

"She always avoided stories about her childhood, saying it was just a simple life in the South. From what I've read so far, her childhood was anything but simple."

Travis moved to her side. "Want to tell me about it?"

"Not now. I think I'll just keep reading. You looked excited about something when you came to the door."

"Yeah, I found this newspaper dated April 15, 1912. The front-page article is about the sinking of the Titanic."

Olivia took the newspaper and read the article. "This is amazing. I wonder what else you're going to find."

"Don't know. But I'll be in the library if you need me."

Olivia picked up the journal and began reading where she'd left off.

MONDAY, AUGUST 2, 1943

It's been so dreadfully hot this past week. It was too hot to write in this silly old book and too hot to do more than swim in the pool. Daisy came over every day since she doesn't have a pool of her own. She is my best friend and we promised today to be best friends forever. It's too hot to ride and Mother would not allow me to take out the skiff for fear there would be lazy farm folk swimming in the river. She still worries that I could be kidnapped and killed for Father's money. Last night was the worst. Not the slightest breeze to ruffle the sheer summer curtains. The fan just moved thick, sticky air. I perspired so much my nightgown was soaked. I took it off. The sheet beneath my naked body soon became wet and I rolled to a new spot feeling the coolness, but only for a few precious minutes. I thought about the hill out beyond the old cemetery. There would be fresh air up there and I could breathe again lying in the cool grass. I put on my prettiest nightgown before leaving my room. I was out-of-breath by the time I reached the cemetery. I was sure no one had followed me. The only sounds I could hear were crickets and frogs and the lapping of the water down by the dock. I followed the tree line until I reached the top of the hill and the clearing beyond. I was alone with a million stars above. The air was fresh and I pulled my nightgown over my head and neatly folded it into a pillow. The cool grass cradled my naked body and I drifted into sleep listening to the lullaby of night sounds. The sound of rustling and snorting startled me before dawn and for a minute I didn't know where I was. Three deer stood pawing the ground. I was scared and put on my nightgown before running all the way home. I reached the safety of my room without seeing a single soul. It was a true adventure and I feel wonderful. I think I will try it again.

TUESDAY, AUGUST 3, 1943

I did it again last night and it was so exciting. Daisy came over again today and I wanted to tell her, but I'm afraid she might tell her mom. So it will have to be my secret. I'll only write about it here in my journal so I will never forget, even when I'm old.

WEDNESDAY, AUGUST 4, 1943

I must be more careful. Mother picked a piece of clover out of my hair this morning. This is the most daring thing I have ever done and it feels a little wicked. But I'm sure no one saw me. I'm very careful when I talk to Daisy not to mention anything that might make her suspicious. Mr. Linsenhof was here for our lesson. He got mad and yelled at me because he said I was being nervous and jumpy. I was throwing Sinatra off because he was feeling my anxiety. Mr. Linsenhof stormed off and said I'd better learn how to concentrate before our next lesson. I hope he doesn't tell mother.

THURSDAY, AUGUST 5, 1943

This night was not good. The air was still and hot and not even the river was moving. I heard new sounds and woke many times. Once I dreamed I was being chased across a field by a monster. I was naked and it was laughing at me. I grabbed my nightgown when I woke up and looked around, but it was just an owl hooting up in the tree. The hairs on the back of my neck prickled. I had the feeling some- one was watching me. Bushes rustled, but there was no wind. I got scared and ran back to the house. Was that black shadow I saw next to the tree a man or just the moonlight playing tricks on my mind? I'm sure no one followed me. I don't know if I'll go again.

MONDAY, AUGUST 9, 1943

The heat spell finally broke on Saturday but I stayed in the house. Thoughts of how dangerous my actions could have been still fill my head. I could have been kidnapped, or worse. In church on Sunday I prayed for forgiveness for my sins of disobedience and promised God that I would never again leave my room at night. Hattie came today to do the laundry. She gave me a lecture about how good girls do not go gallivanting about outdoors in their nightgowns, even if it is as hot as blazes. I wonder how she knows? Was someone really up there and saw me? Did they tell her? I'm truly scared.

5

Olivia glanced back at the entries. Three days were missing. Then her mother made reference to being in danger and asking God for forgiveness. Her chest tightened with frustration toward her mother. What happened that she couldn't write for three days? Why the secrecy? Olivia needed to vent, and Travis was only a room away.

She stormed across the hall stopping at the library door. "You're not going to believe this," Olivia waved the diary back and forth. "Three dates are missing," Olivia shouted.

Travis jumped at the sudden outburst, his hand nearly knocking over his mug of coffee. "Calm down. What are you talking about?"

"My mother! My very ordinary mother snuck out during the night to sleep naked on a hill behind the old cemetery!"

"Hmm, sounds like my kind of woman."

"She's sixteen, for Christ's sake!"

Olivia took a long breath to calm down. "On August 5th, 1943, something scared her during the night. She ran back to her room thinking that she wouldn't go back to the hill again. She doesn't write again for three days. Then it picks up again on the 9th when she talks about asking God for forgiveness in church, and the laundry woman gives her a lecture about gallivanting around at night in her nightgown. *What* did she do that was so bad? What happened to my mother that night?"

"I don't know, Livy. But you're overreacting. I think you should stop. I'm hungry. Let's have lunch."

Olivia couldn't believe his lack of concern. "Lunch? You want to have *lunch*? This is about my *mother*! The most daring thing I ever saw Mom do was to ride the roller coaster at Cedar Point."

"I think you're overreaching. That happened forty years ago. Your mother's been dead for twenty years. Does it really matter all that much?"

Olivia's exasperated sigh filled the small room. "Yes, it does—to me. And I'm going to finish this book."

Travis stood and gestured toward his chair. "Here, you sit down and read while I fix lunch. I think I can manage grilled cheese and tomato soup, or maybe even chicken noodle as long as it comes out of a can."

The entries for the next few months were filled with events at The Mount Pleasant Academy for Girls and fears about the war. Each evening, the girls would sit around the radio and listen to Edward R. Murrow's broadcasts. Maureen didn't like school very much except for all the social activities and, of course, riding. She had Sinatra with her at school, and they took a ribbon in every event they entered. She made friends easily, but her mother was fearful of her traveling to unknown areas where she could be kidnapped. Maureen's life appeared to be rather lonely. She stayed at school on weekends while her friends traveled to each other's homes and came back with exciting stories. There was no way in the world Olivia could have abided by the many restrictions placed upon her mother. It certainly was a different world back then.

THURSDAY, NOVEMBER 25, 1943
We had a wonderful Thanksgiving here at the farm. I wore my dark green dress with the wide belt and short jacket with the padded

shoulders and matching suede shoes. It makes my waist look smaller. Several times William told me how lovely and grown-up I looked. The Morrisons always join us. Mother says it is an important tradition to celebrate in a home that was so important back in colonial days. All the servants and hired help and their families set up tables in the building that was the kitchen in the old days. They even cook some of the food in the big fireplaces. I think they have a better dinner than we do. I remember when I was little and Miranda let me watch the womenfolk prepare the food while the men brought in the large tables that would groan with the weight of the Thanksgiving meal. There hasn't been as much food on the table since the war began, but it doesn't seem to matter. I remember when William and I would sneak out back after dinner and join in the fun with the other children. I miss those times.

Olivia set the book in her lap and gazed into the fire. Thanksgiving dinners had always been at her grandparent's house, so had Christmas and Easter. Her mother had offered to host holidays, but Gran always said that it was better if mom stayed out of the kitchen. Olivia looked up at her mother's portrait hanging over the fireplace. "Well, Mom, now I understand why our meals were basic meat and potatoes. Your cakes and cookies were great, but you never did quite master the art of pie making." Olivia chuckled. "Had you ever cooked a meal before marrying Dad?" Olivia flipped through the pages to see what Christmas would bring.

FRIDAY, DECEMBER 24, 1943

We are going to the Morrison's for dinner tonight. I'm so excited. William is home from Annapolis and Mother bought me a new dress on her last trip to New York. It's the most smashing creation ever. I'll wear my lovely locket with our pictures side-by-side. I hope William likes my dress. I hope he takes me in his arms and kisses me on the lips and tells me he loves me. This will be my best Christmas ever.

SATURDAY, DECEMBER 25, 1943

Yesterday was the worst day of my life. I felt so beautiful and grown-up in my new lavender dress, but William kissed me on the cheek like I was his sister. He took my hand as we walked to the library, but only to tell me that he was in love. He's fallen in love with the sister of his new roommate. Jennifer has blond hair and big brown eyes and a fabulous figure. He wants me to keep it a secret since his father will say she isn't suitable. I hate her. I hope Mr. Morrison finds out about her.

Olivia arrived in the kitchen just as Travis set the plates on the table. The perfectly browned sandwiches oozed with melted cheese.

Travis pulled out Olivia's chair with a sweeping motion of his arm. "What happened on the hill?"

"I don't know. I read all the way to the end of the year, but she doesn't say another word about it." Olivia watched as Travis settled in the opposite chair. "Maybe you're right and I was overreacting."

"So how did your mother fair for the remainder of the year?"

"She was feeling love and jealousy for the first time." Olivia took a bite then licked the cheese from the corner of her mouth. "I remember our conversation the week before the accident. She began talking about her past and how she had been engaged to a William Morrison. But, the last entry I read says William is in love with Jennifer. I can't wait to find out how Mom gets him away from Jennifer."

"I thought your father's name was Fred."

"It was," said Olivia, with a tinge of annoyance.

They finished their lunch in silence.

The second book was calling to Olivia. After putting their dirty dishes in the sink, she grabbed a mug of hot tea. "I'm going back to the parlor and start on 1944."

Travis grabbed a beer out of the fridge and followed. "I'll throw a few more logs on the fire for you."

The ticking of the grandfather clock and the crackling fire comforted Olivia's frayed nerves. She snuggled into the large leather chair and rested her feet on the ottoman. Then she reached for the second journal and opened its cover.

SATURDAY, JANUARY 1, 1944

It's noon and Mother is still sleeping. By 3:00 a.m. I had enough champagne, dancing and excessive merrymaking to last me another year and came upstairs to our suite. Saxophones, trombones, and clarinets, still ring in my head. Mother stumbled in around 5:00 singing Boogie Woogie Bugle Boy of Company B. *Half of the ballroom was filled with Mother's family and friends, and she had acted as if she hadn't seen them in years. She certainly takes on another personality when we come to New York. At home she is so conservative and proper, always worried about her image and that of the family. This will be a quiet day until we dress for dinner. I think I'll write to William.*

SUNDAY, JANUARY 2, 1944

Today in church, I prayed this horrid war would end soon so my life can be as it was before. I must be looking rather depressed. Mother said she had been worried about me on the train trip because I was so quiet in our compartment. She thought it was because we have to take the train now instead of taking Father's plane since fuel is rationed. I just didn't feel like talking, my mind was full of William and Jennifer. I could just imagine him kissing her. Mother thinks I should get more involved in the USO and organize scrap drives. All I really want is for William to say he loves me and not Jennifer.

MONDAY, JANUARY 3, 1944

This was a good day. I promised to get active in the USO and Mother promised to take me shopping for appropriate clothes. We had a lovely lunch with Cousin Carrie at her house then went to all of Mother's favorite stores, although we only had time for ready-to-wear. I must leave for school tomorrow, but Mother will stay here for another week. I miss Sinatra and I will have to work extra hard to be ready for the shows in the spring.

WEDNESDAY, JANUARY 5, 1944

I was too tired last night to write. Sinatra and I practiced after classes. I'm a little rusty after being away and the saddle feels harder. There are fewer girls in school than there were before the Christmas break. Miss Porter came to my room while I was changing into my riding clothes and said Josephine would not be coming back. Because of the war, many of the families can no longer afford the expense of private schools. I don't mind. Now I'll have the room all to myself. I'll write to Josephine and tell her not to feel bad because a lot of the other girls didn't come back either.

SUNDAY, JANUARY 9, 1944

I stayed at school for my birthday. I received a card from ER. She's proud of me for helping with the war effort. She says we can't let this war reach our shores. I'll keep this card forever. Father is in San Francisco for a month, and Mother said it was best if I didn't travel. She sent me a new saddle and tack. Our trainer said it's very expensive and she'll keep it locked-up and we'll only use it for shows. Miss Porter had a party for me, but it wasn't the same with so few of my friends here. William sent me a card and a copy of Hemingway's For Whom the Bell Tolls. I guess he's still in love with Jennifer. I hate her!

FRIDAY, JANUARY 28, 1944

I've been too busy and tired to write. It just doesn't seem all that important anymore. Sinatra and I practice everyday. I have also taken on the job of organizing the scrap drives for the school. Charlotte, who took care of all the details for the last two years, didn't come back after Christmas break and Miss Porter asked me to take over. How could I say no? It's my duty and Mother would have been furious, but it leaves me less time to ride.

FRIDAY, FEBRUARY 4, 1944

Tomorrow morning I leave for home. I think I'll sleep on the train. My days have fallen into a routine of classes, followed by hours devoted to the scrap drives and whatever task comes before me to help our country win the war. I find time to study before falling exhausted into my bed, only to wake at dawn and head to the stable for an hour with Sinatra. The first of the USO dances I promised to attend is tomorrow evening. I'm too tired to worry about what I'll wear.

SUNDAY, FEBRUARY 6, 1944

I'm on my way back to school. The dance was a lot of fun. Mother was a chaperone and I wore my lavender dress. I'm so glad Mother stocked up on stockings before the ban on silk. The other girls have to draw lines up the back of their legs to look like they're wearing stockings. There were more servicemen than I could count and I think I may have danced with all of them. My feet had been stepped on so many times they were bruised by the time Mother and I left. This whole USO thing is going to be painful. Mother is leaving for New York tomorrow. I think she's helping ER with something. She'll be back before the end of the month.

6

A gust of wind rattled the window reminding Olivia of the storm raging beyond the thick stone walls of the house. She set the book aside and went to check on Travis. She found him in the library with his feet propped on the edge of the desk, reading a yellowed newspaper.

Olivia leaned against the door-jam. "I thought I'd make a pot of coffee. Can I bring you a cup?"

"Sure," he said without looking up.

Olivia returned a few minutes later with two mugs of steaming coffee and handed one to Travis. "It smells like soot in here. How can you stand it?"

"Just a downdraft from the storm. It's not that bad. How's it going with your mom?" Olivia sat on the opposite corner of the desk. "I guess I never thought much about the war and how it changed peoples lives. Gran talked about rationing and how difficult the times were, but my mother never said anything. I figured it was just one more way for Gran to complain about something. Mom did a lot for the war effort while she was at school, and she was active with the USO when she was home. She mentions someone with the initials ER. I get the impression he or she is important."

Travis set the newspaper in his lap and reached for a book he'd been reading. "I'm learning about the various steam ships on the Great Lakes."

"I don't know much about that period. But if I'm going to live here I need to know the history. I'll check out that book when I get a chance," Olivia scooted off the corner of the desk. "But right now I need to head back to 1944."

SUNDAY, MARCH 5, 1944

I can't believe another month has gone by. Daisy came with Mother and I to the USO social. We had a great time and we both wore blue dresses. Some of the boys are really cute and I danced until my feet couldn't take another step. Besides the scrap drives at school, we are now selling war bonds and I volunteered to organize that, too. Mother is very pleased. She's written to ER to tell her of my continued commitment to the war effort.

SATURDAY, JUNE 3, 1944

This was one of the greatest days of my life! I've graduated from The Mount Pleasant Academy for Girls and received the highest award for Civic Duty and helping to promote the war effort. Sinatra and I received a special award. I'm the only student in the school's history to take a ribbon in each of the events we entered. Mother and Father seemed more pleased with my awards than with my scholastic achievements. Actually, I'm not good with my studies, but there have been so many students who had to leave school before the end of the term. Several of the girls are going on to Vassar and Radcliffe next year and I would like to join them. Father says I don't need to think about that now. I need to concentrate on my duty to the family and the community and what is best for the country. That sounds like a lot of work.

Olivia looked up at the sound of heavy footsteps crossing the hall. Travis entered the room with his arms loaded down with an odd assortment of old newspapers and books.

"The storm is gaining in strength and battering the north side of the house. The hundred years worth of wet soot from the fireplace and the howling wind against the windows is finally getting to me. Do you mind if I join you?"

Olivia set the book aside and stretched. "Not at all. It's warm and cozy in here."

While Travis set the stack on the floor, Olivia stood and went to the long window overlooking the front yard. "It's a white-out. If this keeps up we'll be buried by morning."

Travis moved to her side.

He put a protective arm around her waist. "We'll be fine. This old house has survived many storms worse than this one. I'm learning a lot about the Captain. He cared a great deal about the welfare of the people who worked and traveled on his ships. He would have built this house to take care of his family. She'll take care of us too."

"I know. I'm not worried. But it does seem like a chili kind of day. Want to join me in the kitchen?"

Within minutes Olivia had all the ingredients for a pot of chili on the table and put Travis to the task of chopping an onion. "In the last entry, Mom just graduated from the Mount Pleasant Academy for Girls. She wanted to go on to Vassar or Radcliffe with her friends. Her father demanded that she return home to her duties to the family, community, and the country. She practically ran the school's war effort with little help or sleep."

Travis wiped his watering eyes with his sleeve. "Your mother sounds amazingly mature for her age."

Olivia stirred the ground beef sautéing in the large pot. "I couldn't have lived like that. Every part of my mother's life was controlled by her parents, especially her father. She wasn't even allowed to join her friends for weekends or holidays at their homes for fear she might be kidnapped. No wonder she left. I would have left, too."

Travis added the onion to the pot. "You really haven't mentioned your grandfather much. What did he do?"

The exact nature of her inheritance was not something she was ready to discuss with Travis yet. She wasn't ready to deal with it in her own mind much less try to explain how she was about to become part owner of a company that built huge ships. He needed an answer—a believable one.

"He built boats," she said while adding the rest of the ingredients to the pot.

Travis nodded. "I can relate to that. Building boats is an art, and back in his day it entailed real craftsmanship. He doesn't sound like such a bad guy . . . just busy."

Olivia put the lid on the pot and shook her head. It always amazed her how men band together making even the most bizarre situations appear normal if common interests were involved—in this case—boats.

She followed Travis down the hall to the parlor where he tossed another log on the fire. Olivia curled up in the big chair and opened the journal.

WEDNESDAY, JUNE 14, 1944

Mother cried when we heard on the radio that the Germans bombed London yesterday. She's worried that the Germans will bomb Cliveden and cousin Nancy will lose her beautiful home. Mother and I talked about the times when we traveled to England aboard the Queen Mary. We had such wonderful times visiting Mother's family in England and then going on to visit Father's in Scotland. It was difficult understanding Father's family with their thick brogue. I wonder if any of it will still be the same when we go back? I can't imagine how terrible it must be to live with the threat of bombs dropping.

Olivia set the book aside and absentmindedly stroked the sleeping kitten in her lap. Her mind went back to the trip she'd made with Brian to London several years ago. They had toured the great estates, and she remembered her fascination with Cliveden. Oh, how she had frustrated the tour guide by lingering in each room, holding up the rest of the group as she gazed at the beautiful portraits. Olivia admired Lady Astor and everything she had achieved during such troubled years. She was the first woman to sit in the House of Commons, and during the German bombings in 1941 continued to hold dances in their bombed house in order to keep up the morale of the local citizens. She also organized evacuations and housing for those whose homes had been destroyed. Lady Astor had been born Nancy Witcher Langhorne in Danville, Virginia, and later moved to Richmond. Olivia had felt a certain kinship toward Nancy Astor. Could it be possible that she was actually a relative?

Feelings of frustration and sadness rushed through Olivia. She felt cheated once more of a family she never knew. How different her visits to London would have been if she'd had relatives to visit. She could have been greeted at Cliveden as a relative and not just a tourist. Olivia now understood Uncle Lionel's words when he said that she had some fine ancestors who were worth getting to know. Could her grandmother have been an Astor? Olivia gritted her teeth. Why hadn't her mother told her about something this important?

Olivia gazed up at her mother's portrait through teary eyes. "Who are you? What happened?"

Travis glanced up from his pile of newspapers. "Did you say something, Livy?"

"Just more questions. I think my grandmother was an Astor."

"That's nice."

Travis didn't appear to be listening, but that was a good thing. Olivia wasn't ready to talk. Maybe her grandmother wasn't an Astor. Maybe she was a Langhorne since there was the Richmond connection. And what about Cousin Carrie who lived in New York?

Olivia hoped the answers to the mounting questions about her mother's past could be found in the diaries. She picked up the book and resumed reading.

THURSDAY, AUGUST 31, 1944

I'm just devastated! Daisy's parents are sending her to live with her aunt and uncle in Montana until the war is over. They say it's not safe living so close to Washington. They think the Germans could bomb us. I'm worried that the Germans might try to bomb

Norfolk and destroy our Naval base and Father's shipyard. Father doesn't want me to worry He promised we'll be safe. How is a sweet Southern girl like Daisy going to survive in the harsh Montana climate? I'm so afraid that wolves or bears could attack her. I may never see her again. This is just the worst news ever.

SUNDAY, OCTOBER 1, 1944

Over dinner this afternoon, Mother surprised me with the most wonderful news I have ever had. She has gotten tickets to Frank Sinatra's concert at the Paramount Theater in New York on October 12th. And best of all, she has arranged with Daisy's mother for her trip to Montana to be postponed until the 21st so she can go too. How am I going to get through the next twelve days? I wonder which sweater and skirt I should wear? I'll wear the pearls Mother bought at Tiffany's for my birthday last year.

SUNDAY, OCTOBER 8, 1944

We had dinner at Cousin Carrie's house. After we finished eating, I took Daisy upstairs to the attic where many of Caroline Astor's clothes are stored. Each of us chose one of the beautiful gowns and pretended we were at a ball. It was just like when I was a little girl and pretended I was the Princess of Astoria. Those were happy times. Daisy and I are now in my room at the Waldorf reading magazines and listening to Frank's records. Mother shocked us on the train when she said she had seen Frank years ago when he sang in Tommy Dorsey's band. Imagine that, and I never knew. Since this is Daisy's last visit to New York with us, Mother is going to take us to all the wonderful museums, to the movies in the afternoon, and to the theatre at night. It's going to be my best trip ever.

FRIDAY, OCTOBER 13, 1944

I'm so excited. I mustn't leave out a single thing. We had front row seats at the Paramount. The house was packed and there were thousands more kids outside trying to get in. Our driver took us to the stage door where the house manager met us and escorted us to our seats. Frank was there right in front of us, and I looked up into his beautiful blue eyes. It was like he was singing just to me, and I almost forgot the hundreds of screaming girls behind us. Some actually fainted and others were throwing their bras and panties at him. I find it very difficult to understand how someone could disgrace herself that way. Then, just before he finished, the house manager came and said we had to leave. I was so disappointed until she took us backstage so we could be introduced to Frank. He shook my hand and said how wonderful it is that my family is doing so much to help us win this war. I'll never forget this day as long as I live and I never want to wash my hand. This morning we read in the paper there were over twenty thousand screaming girls mobbing Times Square just to get close to Frank and it took seven hundred riot police to restore order! I'm glad we have our own driver and didn't have to use the front door. Mother said she would never have gotten the tickets if she had known we might be in danger. I assured her that we were safe at all times.

7

Olivia snapped the book shut. "Shit! Who the hell *was* my mother?"

Sitting cross-legged on the floor with his back against the sofa, Travis looked up from the old newspaper. "This sounds bad. I'm ready to hear the juicy news."

"My grandparents apparently had a suite at the Waldorf. I guess that isn't so unusual if my grandmother was an Astor. Mother talks about Cousin Carrie, and it sounds like the famous Caroline Astor might have been Carrie's mother or at least a relative.

"I read something about a Carrie Astor in one of the articles about the sinking of the Titanic. She was the sister of John Jacob Astor IV who died on the Titanic. That would make Caroline their mother."

"But the most interesting thing I've read so far is that mother and her friend Daisy got front row seats to see Frank Sinatra and then met him backstage. Did you know back then girls threw their underwear at him on stage? I thought throwing one's underwear started with the Beatles. I just can't imagine it."

Travis chuckled. "I can't either. Didn't they wear rather large girdles and stuff back then? I can just see some huge cotton bra whizzing past your mother's head and landing at old Frank's feet."

Olivia laughed at the mental image of flying bras. "Mom loved Frank Sinatra's music, but she never mentioned the fact that she actually met him. Frank said something to Mom backstage about her family helping to win the war. I wonder what that was all about?"

"Beats me. I guess you should keep reading."

Olivia nodded and opened the book.

THURSDAY, NOVEMBER 23, 1944

Miranda tried her best, but Thanksgiving wasn't the same. Have we all just gotten older, or is it the war that has dragged the festivities through the mud? William looked dashing in his uniform but he practically ignored me. Immediately after dinner he joined the men in the library for further discussion of the war. Even the servants out in the old kitchen seemed sullen. I hope Christmas will be better.

SUNDAY, DECEMBER 24, 1944

The war is catching up to our families. We didn't go to the Morrison's tonight for our usual Christmas Eve celebration. Mrs. Morrison has gotten word that her brother has been killed in the Pacific and she left to be with her family in Boston. We stayed home, and after dinner we gathered the servants together around the tree and handed out their presents. They were just simple clothes and toiletries, but to those who have so little, they were wonderful gifts to be treasured. Mother and I bought Miranda's gifts on our last trip to New York. She's so much more than our housekeeper. She's like a second mother to me . . . she keeps my secrets.

MONDAY, DECEMBER 25, 1944

Sinatra and I went for an early morning ride, and then Mother, Father, and I spent a quiet day opening our gifts. Mother gave Miranda and the servants the rest of the day off after an early dinner. We listened to the radio and played cards until suppertime when the three of us got hungry. It made me feel really good when I returned from the kitchen with a tray of leftovers fit for a king. I'm thankful for all the years I've spent in the kitchen watching Miranda and the cooks. I liked being alone in the kitchen and preparing a meal all by myself. I bet it's fun being a housewife without servants.

Olivia's stomach growled reminding her of just how long she'd been sitting without food. She stood and stretched her cramped and aching muscles. The fire was nearly out and the sun going down. Travis added more logs, then they followed the spicy aroma of chili which had been simmering for the past several hours.

Olivia pulled a pan of garlic bread out of the oven, then ladled a generous amount of chili into two large bowls.

"Travis, let's eat in the morning room. I think the snow stopped and the view should be lovely with the setting sun."

Olivia placed the food on the table then went to stand at the window. The Marblehead lighthouse stood bathed in shades of orange from the setting sun. The huge rocks at its base were only faint shapes in the deep snow covering everything as far as the eye could see.

Travis wrapped his arms around her, pulling her tight against his chest. "It's really beautiful, isn't it?"

"Yeah, maybe the storm is over." Olivia turned her head toward Travis and kissed him on the cheek. "Let's eat while our dinner is still hot."

Olivia savored the steaming chili with a generous amount of grated cheddar cheese sprinkled on top. Travis was full of stories about the Captain and his adventures and hardships on the Great Lakes. The Lake Erie islands were a major tourist destination at the turn of the century.

"When I was a boy, I played in the ruins of the wineries and the old Victory Hotel on South Bass Island. Now these places are coming alive with the Captain's exciting stories."

Olivia tried to give Travis her full attention, but her mind kept wandering back to the book of 1944. Even though each book seemed to raise more questions, she was eager to begin 1945.

The sound of the snowplow scraping along the drive broke into Olivia's thoughts.

Travis stood and went over to the window. "It's Nick. I'll see if he has time to come in."

A few minutes later the side door slammed. Nick followed Travis to the kitchen, less his coat and boots. "Hmmm, smells like chili. Got any left?"

Olivia went to the stove and heaped a large ladle-full in a bowl and added a slice of warm garlic bread, then carried it to the morning room and placed it on the table. "You look like you could use some sleep as well as food."

"This storm is just giving us a short break. An even bigger one should hit within the hour. There are power outages all over the area."

Nick devoured the chili. Dressed in a green plaid shirt of heavy wool and snow pants, he reminded her of Paul Bunyan.

"You know, Olivia, if you're going to turn this old house into a bed and breakfast, you should consider putting in a generator. The power goes out a lot on the point. And without lights this place could get really creepy," Nick said as he took the last bite of garlic bread.

Olivia shuddered and slipped her hands into the pockets of her jeans. "Thanks, it sounds like a good idea. Go ahead and put it on the list of things to do."

Travis leaned toward his cousin. "Nick, you know the old trunk you brought down from the attic? It's filled with the Captain's notes and newspapers. Even the newspaper about the sinking of the Titanic is there, and you're not going to believe . . ."

"Yeah, well, you're not gonna believe the *disaster* we're gonna have just beyond these walls," Nick handed his empty bowl to Olivia. "Is there anymore left?"

Olivia took the bowl and headed to the stove.

"Just heard that much of Detroit is buried and without power. There's a major pileup on the bridge to Canada and both the police and fire departments are scrambling to keep up," He took his second helping of chili from Olivia and started eating.

"And that's what's coming our way?" asked Olivia.

"Yep."

8

Leaving Travis to his new audience, Olivia returned to the parlor. Dying embers in the fireplace bathed the room in a warm glow. After turning on the floor lamp, she settled into the big leather chair and picked up the book labeled 1945. So far, there was nothing in the journals to justify her mother walking away from her life. Despite the hardships of war, Maureen lived a pretty pampered life. Why had she kept it a secret? The phone rang ending any thoughts of what her mother may be doing.

Olivia got up from the chair and headed to the hall where the phone sat in the little niche in the wall. She caught it on the third ring.

"Nick, it's for you," she yelled.

He hustled in from the kitchen. "I let my crew know I was coming here."

Olivia nodded and headed back to the parlor.

A few minutes went by before Nick yelled from the hall. "I'm leaving."

Olivia and Travis caught up with him as he pulled on the last boot and reached for his coat.

"This storm is doing more than taking down power lines. It's stranding people in their homes without heat. There are lots of old folks who depend on neighbors and family to be able to look in on them." He shook his head while fastening the last button. "This damn snow is coming down faster than we can dig out. Cousin, Patsy and her husband have been called to the hospital. They're bringing in extra staff to handle the emergencies. I dropped off the kids at her parent's house, but the road to the farm is almost impassible. They shouldn't be out there alone."

Olivia didn't understand his urgency. "But it stopped snowing a while ago."

"That first storm was just the prelude to what just hit. Take a look outside," Nick said with great urgency as he opened the side door.

Olivia took a couple steps onto the porch. The icy crystals pelted her face. She jumped back inside. "I can't even see the lighthouse. The beacon is just a faint glow. How does a storm this bad happen so fast?"

"When it comes from the north and west at the same time." Nick chuckled. "You ain't seen nothin' yet."

Travis reached for his coat. "What can I do?"

"Put chains on your tires, and meet me at the police station. We need to come up with a new plan."

Olivia grabbed a scarf off a hook and wrapped it around Travis's neck, then pulled his head down. She kissed him hard with the intensity and feeling of a woman sending her man off to war. "I love you, Travis. Please be careful."

"I'll be fine. Call me if you need help with anything."

"What if the power and phone lines go down?"

Travis hesitated for just a moment. "If you need help, take the big flashlight I gave you and put it in the window at the top of the house. I'll be able to see the beacon from town. I'll tell the police chief it's your distress signal."

The phone rang as Olivia finished washing the lunch dishes. She picked it up on the third ring. "Hello? Travis, is that you?"

"Livy, honey, this is the worst I've ever seen it, and there's no sign of the storm letting up. We've organized a team with snowmobiles to check on the elderly and those with poor access to the roads. We need to get folks to shelters, but it's going to take everyone we have just to see who needs help."

"What about bringing them here? So far I have electricity, and even if that goes out we can keep warm and eat. There's plenty of room. You can start by bringing Patsy's family. The maid's rooms on the third floor still have the old furniture. We can put a lot of cots in the bedrooms on the second floor."

"Lakeside has a bunch of cots in storage. I can swing by the resort later and pick up whatever we need. They should have a lot of bedding, since they're closed for the winter."

"We're also going to need food and more oil lamps."

The realization of the danger involved in rescuing families from the storm's death-grip on the tiny town had Olivia's stomach in knots. She didn't want to think about the hardships he would have to face before the day was done. "Please be careful, Travis . . . I love you."

A dozen families now called the old Captain's house home until the storm passed and utilities could be restored and roads cleared. It was well after midnight when Olivia crawled into the sleeping bag she'd placed on the window seat a few hours earlier. The power had finally succumbed to the storm. Perishable food arrived with the various families, and Olivia had turned the breezeway into a walk-in refrigerator. Travis delivered a truckload of cots and bedding from Lakeside along with a couple stockpots.

It seemed like only minutes had gone by before Olivia woke to sounds coming from the kitchen. She rolled out of her sleeping bag and stood, stretching sore muscles before pushing open the door. "Travis, did you bring someone else?" Olivia glanced at her watch. "It's after two o'clock."

He set a bowl of hot soup on the table and poured a mug of coffee from the old pot on the stove. "I tried to be quiet so I wouldn't wake you."

"I've just been dozing. The window seat isn't all that comfortable."

"Window seat? What's wrong with your bed?"

"Spooky and four little kids are asleep on my bed at the moment. Not enough room for me, too."

Olivia and Travis sat on opposite sides of the table. She folded her arms and leaned forward. Travis dug into the chicken noodle soup as if it were his first meal in days. "I've got three teenagers with sleeping bags camped out at the top of the house. They thought it was cool to have the storm raging around them." Olivia took a deep breath. "The house is filled to the rafters with kids. Thankfully, Angela Simpson taught me how to make hot chocolate."

Travis's eyebrows shot up. "You don't know how to make hot chocolate? Even I know how to do that."

"Mom and Gran made it. I guess I never paid much attention. Opening a bottle of wine is much easier."

Travis finished the soup and leaned back in his chair. "You're an amazing woman. You certainly have more than your fair share of Astor blood running through your veins."

Olivia wasn't ready to forgive her mother and grandmother McLeod for keeping her heritage a secret. She leaned forward speaking quietly. "What are you talking about? I have nothing in common with the Astor's."

"No?" Travis stood and took his dishes to the sink, then returned to stand next to her. "What about the fact that within minutes of hearing that people were stranded without heat or electricity, you opened your home to total strangers? Or the fact that you found a way to get enough food and blankets brought in to make everyone comfortable."

"Anyone would do what I did."

"No, they wouldn't. And you also figured out a way to turn the breezeway into a giant refrigerator so all this food wouldn't spoil."

Olivia helped Travis shrug into his coat and gloves then followed him to the side door. He wrapped his arms around her in a fierce hug. "Lady Astor would be proud of you. So would your mother and grandmother."

"She was only a cousin by marriage—no Astor blood."

"Her actions still count," whispered Travis as he kissed her ear.

Olivia closed the door behind him. She stood alone in the silent hall, his words echoing in her head. But she was too tired to give them more than a passing thought.

The storm raged for two full days, yet everyone pulled together to make the most of a bad situation. The women organized the sleeping arrangements then pitched in to help with the cooking. Meals were served on the old claw-foot dining table in the morning room and folding tables had been set up in the large entrance hall. Once again the house was filled with laughing children who found the many rooms, halls, and stairs a great place to play with Spooky at their heels. There was always a big pot of leftover chili, soup, or stew on the back burner of the stove just waiting for a cold, hungry man or woman who needed a break from plowing or repairs. Hot chocolate and mulled cider was served before the fireplaces in the parlor and library. Thus, a difficult situation was turned into an adventure.

The last folding table had been returned to its owner, and the only sounds were those of hissing radiators. Travis was now checking out the damage done to his own properties. Olivia expected to be on her own for the next day or two. At eight o'clock in the evening, Olivia pulled the last load of bedding from the dryer. She'd spent an hour putting the kitchen back in order. The stockpots were scrubbed and ready to return to Lakeside along with the cots and bedding. Olivia had everything that needed to be returned stacked and ready in the side hall. She took a deep breath. As tired as she was, she made her nightly rounds, checking the doors and windows. Feeling comfortable that the house was locked and secured, she finally succumbed to screaming muscles and crawled under the thick comforter, happy to have the bed to herself.

Thoughts of her mother's journal of 1945 had haunted her for most of the day. Travis had been right in his comment. She'd acted in the true spirit of Lady Astor, even if it was just a snowstorm and not a war. All her life she'd wondered what her mother's family had been like. She remembered the last conversation with her mother. She'd promised to tell Olivia everything when she was old enough to understand. Olivia smiled, with a warm feeling in her heart. She was ready to understand now.

9

The wind howled outside the bedroom window. With the radiator hissing its defiance, Olivia pulled the comforter up as far as she could. She arranged the pillows at her back until they were just right, then opened her mother's journal.

MONDAY, JANUARY 1, 1945

I have a horrible headache. I drank too much champagne, ate too much rich food, flirted with every male even close to my age, and danced all night. I wore my pink taffeta gown with the sweetheart neckline and big puffy sleeves. It was the best New Years Eve, ever! Granted, it hasn't been the same festive night since this dreadful war started, but it seemed grand to me. Father had an important meeting in Washington and was not able to join us. He has been in Washington a lot lately and Mother said we will stay here at the Waldorf until after my birthday.

TUESDAY, JANUARY 9, 1945

I'm eighteen years old today. We celebrated my birthday with cousin Carrie at her house. Mother and cousin Carrie call it a milestone. I hope that doesn't mean more work. I thought I would feel older and more grown-up. Actually, I don't feel any different. But I do see the world around me differently now that I have been following in

Mother's steps this past week. I'm glad we're rich. There is so much poverty, and families are struggling to make a life for themselves. It's so difficult with the men off at war. Women and children are doing the jobs only men did before. ER and mother visited several factories where nearly all the workers were women. Women drive trucks and work construction jobs. Children have had to drop out of school so they can help support the family. I'm very lucky to have this lifestyle, but I also see that there is a big responsibility ahead of me in order to maintain it. Mother says I must not be frightened of my duty to my family and my country, but embrace it as a challenge. I will try.

FRIDAY, FEBRUARY 2, 1945
Another letter came today from Daisy. Poor thing, I feel so sorry for her. She hates Montana and swears she'll either freeze to death or be trampled by cattle. She feels like a prisoner ever since the snow started falling. She hasn't been warm since she left Virginia. I must remember the next time I complain about our hot and humid summers that it could be a lot worse.

FRIDAY, APRIL 13, 1945
The news all day on the radio is about the death of President Roosevelt at his home in Warm Springs, Georgia, yesterday. Mother is just devastated. The whole country is in mourning and wondering if Harry Truman is the man who will end this war. Father telephoned to say he's been called to Washington and may not return to the farm for several weeks. Mother is leaving with him and will be attending the funeral. ER asked that I stay at Fairfield and help with USO and bond drives in Richmond. Ever since this war started we hardly ever see Father. I hope he brings Miranda some coffee and sugar.

TUESDAY, MAY 1, 1945
Adolph Hitler is dead! He committed suicide yesterday. Perhaps the war in Europe will end soon and Mother can stop worrying about

the safety of her family. I received a long letter from Daisy today. She has a boyfriend. He's the only son of a neighbor and her uncle's best friend. He has taught her how to ride western and she's finally beginning to accept the harsh climate and countryside. She wears dungarees and flannel shirts and her uncle bought her a Stetson. I just can't imagine her like that. I'll be glad when this dreadful war is over and she returns home.

Travis called at noon the next day to say the roads were still bad. He was heading over to Kellys Island to help with the cleanup.

Olivia retrieved the journals from the library where she'd put them for safekeeping during the storm. She restacked them next to the club chair in the parlor before heading to the kitchen. She finished the last of the leftover pot roast. The ghosts of her mother's past had crept into her thoughts more than once that afternoon. Now, as she relaxed with a glass of Bordeaux she felt strong spirits pushing her toward the next journal and her mother's life.

The fire blazed, surrounded by cool marble, sending a warm glow throughout the room. She settled into the leather chair, rested her feet on the ottoman, and reached for the book.

TUESDAY, MAY 8, 1945

Germany surrendered today. At last there's victory in Europe. German troops have laid down their weapons. Mother gathered Miranda and the servants around the radio as we all listened to the broadcast. They're calling this V-E Day. Mother is leaving for New York in the morning. Father called from Washington. He said the war will end soon. What a wonderful day this is.

WEDNESDAY, JUNE 6, 1945

The weather in Annapolis has been absolutely dreadful all week. My new hat was ruined in the rain. William looked splendid in his dress whites, and the class of 1,040 graduates was equally impressive. It should have been a happier time. But we all knew that many of these young men would not be returning from their tours of duty. We tried to keep positive, with smiles on our faces, but you could see the concern in everyone's eyes. I felt sorry for the hundreds of mothers who sniffled into their handkerchiefs and dabbed at their eyes. I might lose my best friend and hero to this horrible war. It seems so real here—not like listening to the commentaries on the radio. Maybe the war will end before William has to leave.

THURSDAY, JUNE 7, 1945
Mother and I took the train to New York to shop for the ball which will be given in William's honor at the end of the month. Because of the war and rationing, entertaining on a grand scale has all but stopped, so this is sure to be the event of the year. Mother is determined that I have a new grown-up gown and clothes. Father agreed. I'm so excited. I love shopping and I love New York. Mother and I are treated like royalty here at the Waldorf. I wish I could live here always and not at that dirty old farm, as cousin Carrie calls our home.

FRIDAY, JUNE 8, 1945
Today was wonderful. We spent the morning at the salon of Mother's favorite designer, Mainbocher. My gown will be fabulous and I'll look like a princess. It's made of the softest ivory silk, with a low square neckline and narrow straps set at the shoulders. The tight bodice ends with yards and yards of silk that drape out exquisitely from the waist, and beautiful cabbage roses made from the same fabric cascade down the back. Mainbocher himself designed the gown. He was so excited because V-E Day ended the clothing restrictions. At last he can use silk again, and he'll use yards and yards of the beautiful fabric. Mother demanded that the gown be finished and delivered before the 30th. I believe she is as important in New York as Father is in Washington. I joined Mother and cousin Carrie at her house for dinner. They had spent the day planning a gala event to be held at her house to promote a newly formed charity for single,

working women. Cousin Carrie is amazing. I hope I can achieve as much as she does when I'm eighty-two. You would think she was the Queen of England the way people bow to her every move. Father says by the end of the war, we'll be far richer than the Astor's ever dreamed of. I'm glad we're rich. I would also like to be treated like a queen. Mother doesn't want people to know how wealthy we are, although I think I'm too old now to be kidnapped.

Olivia closed the book over her finger to mark the page, and looked up at the portrait. "Well, Mom, you're still full of surprises, but at least I finally understand about the gown you're wearing and where it came from."

Suddenly the hairs on the back of her neck bristled. She wasn't alone. She needed a weapon . . . anything. The poker wasn't close enough to reach without standing first.

She took a deep breath and turned toward the hallway.

Travis leaned against the door jam, his arms crossed in from of him.

"Travis, don't *ever* do that again! I didn't hear you come in." Just a few months before, she'd been startled by someone standing in this room threatening to kill her. "I think my heart stopped!"

"Sorry, Livy. I wasn't being all that quiet."

Olivia placed her hand over her heart. "What are you doing here? I expected you'd still be over on Kellys Island."

"I thought I'd surprise you," Travis said, entering the room.

Olivia smiled and reached for his hand. "You did!"

"I really am sorry, Livy. What has you so deep in thought that you didn't hear me?"

Olivia glanced up at the painting with a gesture. "That. As a child, I fantasized that I was a princess. Only a princess could have a gown that beautiful. Later, it would become my wedding dress as I walked up the aisle with my veil fluttering behind. They were wonderful visions—it broke my heart when Mom told me her father had it burned."

Travis walked over to the fireplace and added more logs to the fire. He stood back, looking closely at the portrait. "This painting must have cost a small fortune, not to mention the cost of the dress. Why would a man who is obviously very conscious of money burn something that valuable? It just doesn't make sense."

"Beats me. I just know Mom wouldn't talk about it."

The lights flickered just as Travis had the flames roaring back to life. He pulled a long match from the holder on the mantle and lit an oil lamp. "It looks like they're still working on the lines."

Travis moved to Olivia's side. He eased himself down on the floor with his back resting against the chair and his legs stretched toward the fire. He patted the floor next to him. "Come join me."

The power went out just as Olivia snuggled against Travis on the floor of the parlor.

"Hmmm, this is rather nice." He bent down to nibble her ear. "Very romantic." His tongue danced along her neck. "I could get used to this."

Travis pulled Olivia's sweater over her head. His lips on her neck sent shivers racing through her.

Olivia's fingers fumbled with Travis's shirt buttons until she had his chest exposed.

All thoughts of her mother were forgotten. Passion took control and their lovemaking became as intense as the fire before them. An hour later, they lay spent in each other's arms before the smoldering embers.

Travis gave Olivia's ear one last nibble then pulled away. "As delightful as this is, I think we should continue in the bedroom. I don't relish the thought of spending the night on the floor if we don't have to."

Helping Olivia to her feet, Travis pulled the afghan off the ottoman. He wrapped it around her naked body then reached for the oil lamp sitting on the mantle.

Olivia followed Travis down the long hall toward the bedroom. She hadn't made her nightly check of the locks on all the windows and doors. Had Travis locked the side door when he'd come in? Should she send Travis on to the bedroom and make a quick check? Would he think less of her for taking time away from his romantic homecoming? She slipped her hand into his. She'd check it first thing in the morning.

10

The aroma of coffee woke Olivia the next morning. She climbed out of bed and slipped on a white chenille robe before following the enticing scent to the kitchen. Pushing open the pantry door, she found Travis standing at the massive stove with several skillets before him.

He glanced over his shoulder. "Good morning, sleepyhead. I worked up quite the appetite and thought I'd start breakfast. The power is still off, but I think I'm managing quite well. Do you know this is the first time I've had to use this ancient relic on my own? I've found three warming compartments on the top, three ovens, two broilers and six burners. And, I suggest you never attempt to use the wood burning side of this behemoth."

"Yeah, it took me awhile to get used to it. But I love it now." Olivia pointed to the name in large letters on the oven door. "I've never heard the name Glenwood before. One of the women who was here during the storm thinks it dates from around 1918."

"Wow, that's older than I thought."

Olivia, still a little groggy, watched Travis arrange slices of bacon in one of the skillets. He appeared comfortable in his role of backwoods chef. Neither of her ex-husbands would have been able to find their way around a kitchen, much less prepare a meal on an ancient stove. Olivia smiled at the mental image of Win and Brian fumbling with the stove.

"What are you smiling about? I promise I won't burn the eggs. This is a whole lot easier than camping, although I can't guarantee how the coffee is going to taste."

Olivia chuckled. "I'm sure it'll be fine. There's room for two at this stove, so what can I do?"

An hour later, Olivia entered the parlor dressed in jeans and a heavy black turtleneck sweater. "I'm glad the power came back on, I was able to get a quick shower and dry my hair."

Travis sat hunched over an old yellowed newspaper spread on the floor.

"I see you're still finding treasures in that old trunk."

"Yeah, it's an article about the fire that destroyed the Hotel Victory on South Bass Island in August of 1919."

The ruins of the Hotel Victory had fascinated Olivia as a teenager. She'd often find her way there when exploring the island. She wanted to read the article—but not now.

"I can't wait to find out more about my wealthy mother and that beautiful gown."

The phone rang as Olivia picked Spooky up from the chair. "I'll get it." Olivia, still carrying Spooky, raced for the little niche in the hallway.

"Hello?"

"Uncle Lionel. Is anything wrong?"

Olivia returned to the parlor a few minutes later, her stomach in knots. She stopped just inside the door. It was too soon. She wasn't ready yet.

"What did your Uncle Lionel want? You look worried."

Back in her chair, Olivia took her time pulling her legs up and tucking them under her. She took a deep breath before answering.

"He wants to see me in his office tomorrow afternoon. It has something to do with my grandmother's will."

The Ohio Turnpike was clear of snow down to the pavement from Sandusky to Cleveland. The downtown streets were slushy, but nothing Olivia couldn't handle. Even though she'd been coming to Uncle Lionel's office since she was fifteen, her gut told her this trip was different.

Olivia sat alone in the dark paneled conference room. Her heart pounded against the black wool jacket of her suit—the Chanel. This was the suit she wore to funerals and somehow it seemed appropriate as she rummaged through the closet early that morning. She wished Travis were sitting there with her. She needed his strength and support, and most of all his love to assure her all would be well. Together they could handle anything. But Uncle Lionel had been adamant she come alone.

"Good afternoon, Olivia."

Lost in her own thoughts, she didn't hear the tall double doors open and was surprised to see her attorney following Uncle Lionel. She'd first met Stanton, an attorney with the prestigious law firm of Squire Sanders and Dempsey, sixteen years ago when he was assigned to handle her inheritance. His head was slightly bent with his eyes focused on Lionel's back. He was more than a few steps behind. Grandmother Thompson would have said he was dragging his feet. Not a good sign. Both men took seats opposite Olivia, arranging documents on the table in front of them.

Uncle Lionel took a deep breath. "Thank you for coming on such short notice, Olivia. I realize you've been buried in snow for the past couple of weeks, but this couldn't wait." His tone of voice held no emotion—not good, not bad, just . . . nothing.

"Not a problem—although, I would have liked Travis to be here."

"I'm sorry."

"Uncle Lionel, I don't under . . . "

"Stanton is here, Olivia, to discuss the details of your inheritance."

"I guess condolences aren't in order this time since until recently you didn't know you had a grandmother McLeod. Nonetheless, this isn't going to be easy." Stanton had his best attorney's voice on—strong and confident.

She'd known Stanton since the accident—the year her family died and she needed her own attorney. This voice was new to her, not the familiar don't-worry-everything's-going-to-be-fine voice.

"I'm feeling something really bad coming on. So let's just cut to the chase and get on with this."

Stanton nodded, his eyes piercing hers . . . searching. What was he looking for?

"Your grandmother owned half of McLeod and Morrison—shares she'd inherited from her husband, Angus McLeod. The other shares are owned equally by the three Morrison brothers. The eldest, William, is their attorney. His office is in D.C. and runs the large legal department. He is also the Chairman of the Board. The two younger ones, Clive and Wilson, are CEO and CFO respectively."

Olivia nodded. "I believe my mother was engaged to William."

Lionel smiled for the first time. "The only good one in the bunch."

Stanton cleared his throat. "I don't have the exact wording of the will, just what you need to know at this point." He paused for several seconds before continuing. "Olivia, if we were only talking millions this would be easy. They'd probably just buy you out. But with billions and a share in the company at stake, they won't go down without a fight."

Olivia's stomach churned. "Do they know about me?"

Uncle Lionel shook his head and shrugged. "We don't know for sure."

Stanton tapped the folder in front of him. "In order for your grandmother to inherit the shares from her husband, she could have no contact with her daughter or any child of Maureen's. At this time the Morrison's believe your grandmother's shares will be divided three ways and go to them."

"It's only through your grandmother's determination and sacrifices brought about by the hatred she felt toward her husband's injustices that your inheritance is possible," said Uncle Lionel.

"So, let me get this straight. These guys believe they will have all the shares in the company and a hundred percent control. But dear old grandma's pulled a fast one and they're screwed—only they don't know it. Yet."

Lionel Montgomery rested his elbows on the table and pressed his fingers together. "Olivia . . . "

"It sounds like I could have a major battle ahead of me," her voice rose an octave.

Stanton cleared his throat. "Your grandmother's attorney, Horatio Dumbarton, will meet you at the airport in Richmond on Monday."

"Monday? But, today's Friday."

For the first time Stanton looked sympathetic. "We're not talking battles here, Olivia, we're talking war. And we need the advantage of surprise on our side."

"Why the long face, Uncle Lionel? I would think, as my financial advisor, you would be jumping off the table with excitement. Billions, Uncle Lionel!" She was just getting used to the idea of the millions she'd inherit. She'd already scrapped the idea of turning the Captain's house into a bed and breakfast. With billions she could fulfill her dream of honoring her twin brothers by providing healthcare for inner-city children. "We can even build the Angus and Andrew Thompson Memorial Children's Wing at East Side General."

"This isn't going to be easy. And the legal issues may be the easiest of all." Uncle Lionel had the look of a man who could see into the future—and didn't like what he saw.

He pushed a manila envelope across the table. "Your airline ticket, employee bios, and the history of McLeod and Morrison.

I've also included the bios of the staff at the house. I encourage you to study them well."

Olivia removed the contents. "This ticket is one way. Don't you expect me to come back?"

"You'll be returning on your own plane."

She should have been feeling positive—even happy. After all, she'd walked in a comfortably wealthy multi-millionaire and only an hour later was a billionaire. She could take Travis to Paris during Fashion Week. Her money would buy her a front row seat. They could travel the world. What could possibly cause the doom and gloom in Uncle Lionel's voice?

She gave a nervous laugh and smacked the side of her head with the heel of her hand. "Oh, yeah. How could I forget something like my own plane? And, I assume my own pilot."

Stanton brought the file folder around to her side of the table and set it in front of Olivia. He reviewed each section of the documents and had her sign and initial where marked. "That's it for me, Olivia. I've spent a great deal of time talking to Horatio. You can trust him. He's been with your grandmother for a long time."

Stanton took the folder and placed it in his briefcase, then walked to the door. He gave Olivia a smile that didn't quite reach his eyes then closed the door behind him.

Stanton might have been finished, but clearly Uncle Lionel wasn't.

"Okay, Uncle Lionel, out with it. You have the look of a man who has something to confess . . . something that I probably don't want to hear. But hell, this afternoon has just been full of surprises. What could possibly be worse than a war over shares in a company I knew nothing about?"

His eyes held hers with an intense gaze. He inhaled deeply and held it. Then let it out slowly.

"Horatio and I believe your grandmother may have been murdered."

11

She'd been right. She didn't want to hear this little bit of news that he'd waited until the last minute to divulge. Could the day get any worse? "Uncle Lionel, just what do you mean? Why do you think Grandmother was murdered?"

Uncle Lionel hesitated. Olivia could see the wheels turning in his head. He was choosing his words carefully. Why?

"Because *she* believed someone was trying to poison her. Whatever it was it could have been given over a period of several months, based on when your grandmother started complaining about being too ill to leave the house. Although her doctor could find no physical problems other than her heart condition."

"I don't understand. What heart condition?"

"She had Ventricular Tachycardia, or arrhythmia. But it was stable and she took medication that controlled it."

"What about an autopsy? Surely one would have been done under the circumstances."

"Horatio ordered one, but it didn't reveal anything except her heart condition."

"But Grandmother thought she was being poisoned. What about blood tests?"

"Nothing. There was nothing that could be construed as a poison. Her death appeared to be just another old lady passing away in her sleep. Her death certificate listed a heart attack as the cause."

Olivia relaxed and let out a long sigh of relief. "So it's only a hunch that my grandmother was murdered. The rest of the world believes that Olivia McLeod died from a heart condition."

Lionel Montgomery slapped both hands on the conference table and rose. "Yes, Livy, it's just a . . . hunch."

Olivia switched radio stations, hoping to relieve the anxiety consuming her on the drive back to Marblehead. A line from her grandmother's letter haunted her. *Something is very wrong here Olivia, and I am too ill to get to the truth and fight for the rightful outcome.*

So far, only Uncle Lionel and Horatio suspected someone had wanted Olivia Maureen McLeod out of the way—but why?

Mile after mile cold gray pressed against the Mercedes. The gloomy day didn't help alleviate Olivia's growing feelings of anger. It was one thing for her to hate her grandmother for not standing up for her daughter, for not cherishing her grandchildren, and for keeping herself hidden away from the family that needed her. But how dare someone else, perhaps someone she trusted, take her life? Her grandmother's death was quickly becoming a consuming mission—a wrong only she could right. And, damn it, she would find the answer—even if it meant stepping into her mother's world and the life she'd left so many years before.

Olivia checked the rear view mirror. The downtown skyline was only a faint shadow. Cleveland was known for its dreary, gray days of winter, and today was no different. She thought about the winters in Virginia. Did Richmond have snow for Christmas? She now owned the old farm which had been part of a plantation and where her mother grew up—the home that stole her grandmother's last breath. Would the stable where Sinatra lived still be there? Could she find the hill where her mother spent a hot summer night, naked under the stars?

Route 2 turned into the highway that would take her home. Finally a patch of blue sky broke through the clouds in the distance. The journals holding the answers to her mother's past were waiting at home in the parlor.

Travis's Bronco sat in the drive when Olivia arrived home around five. She wasn't sure if this was good or bad. She loved Travis, but she needed more than the hour and a half drive time from Cleveland to sort out her feelings—and she needed to be alone to do it. Her feelings toward her grandmother had changed from anger and frustration to compassion and concern. Olivia wanted to know what drove her grandmother to such extreme sacrifices.

After locking the car, Olivia slapped a smile on her face and climbed the porch steps. The aroma of what could only be a pot roast or stew greeted her at the door. This part, at least, was good.

Travis leaned against the doorframe just as Olivia finished taking off her boots. Damn, he looked good. His dark brown cords, a cream-colored turtleneck and brown cashmere sweater were a huge improvement from his normal ratty jeans and sweatshirt.

"Welcome home, Livy. How did it go?"

"Okay. A lot to think about, but okay . . . I guess." Where could she even begin? That he was now engaged to a billionaire? Or maybe that her grandmother may have been murdered? She needed more time to process the events of the day.

She stood, moving toward Travis. "Something smells good and I'm starving."

He folded Olivia into his arms. She felt the steady thud of his heart against her chest. His kiss was long and slow. It wasn't an erotic kiss that says *I'm-glad-you're-home-we're-going-to-have-sex-now,* but a soft, sensual kiss.

Then his hand reached around her waist, and he guided her toward the kitchen. "I was able to find enough stuff for a pretty decent stew."

Later, Travis carried a bottle of champagne and two glasses to the parlor, then added more logs to the fire. A quiet dinner with little conversation had given Olivia the time she needed to relax and prepare for her rundown on the meeting. She hadn't given Travis any of the important details of her inheritance after Uncle Lionel's visit. Maybe she should have been more open with him—but she hadn't—and now everything would come out at once. Olivia wasn't sure how he would take the news. Hell, after the events of the day, Olivia didn't know herself.

Travis handed her a half-full glass of champagne. "Can we talk about the meeting now?"

After a long swallow, Olivia sat down on the sofa. She eased back on the seat and crossed her legs. That didn't feel right, so she slid forward, stretching her legs out in front of her and crossing them at the ankles. She contemplated her champagne flute and the bubbles dancing in the firelight.

Travis leaned against the mantle, taking a sip of champagne. He nodded for her to begin.

"I've inherited my grandmother's estate which consists of an old plantation on the James River and all of its contents. There's also a town house in Norfolk where my grandfather spent most of his time." Travis's eyebrows shot up, but he didn't say a word, so Olivia continued. "Some artwork and various items passed down from my grandmother's Astor ancestors—and a suite at the Waldorf Astoria."

Travis's expression was somewhere between disbelief and amusement, with one eyebrow up and a quirky grin. "This is a joke . . . right . . . Livy?"

She scooted back on the seat and crossed her legs at the knees. The position somehow made her feel a little more in control. She took another swallow of champagne then sighed. "No. It isn't. Neither are the shares of stock in Uncle Lionel's company—worth somewhere around a hundred million."

Travis moved over to the club chair and plopped down. "How could you not know about this? I can't believe your mother never talked about growing up on a plantation."

Olivia didn't like the harsh, accusatory tone in his voice.

"She said she grew up on a farm in Virginia. I was a *kid*. I didn't ask for details—at least not until it was too late. Even in her diaries she calls it a farm."

Olivia leaned forward and set her glass down on the table a little harder than necessary. "Look, my mother left that life behind, and I don't know why. Growing up, her life with us was all we knew, and as kids, that's all that mattered."

"Honey, I'm sorry. It's just that this is a real shock."

Olivia picked up her glass and went to stand in front of the fireplace. "You think *I'm* not in shock? You should be happy, Travis. You're going to marry a very wealthy woman. You love boats. Boats are your business. Well, you're *really* going to love mine." She took another sip and raised her glass in a toast. "Today is going to change our lives forever."

Travis's puzzled expression said his mind hadn't quite caught up yet. "Are you talking about boats? Your grandfather built boats. Did you inherit a boat as well?"

"I believe you know the name McLeod and Morrison?"

"Shit! Olivia, you don't mean *that* McLeod? That's a giant corporation."

"Yeah, I know."

"You inherited that too? Your mother was *that* McLeod? But, they build *ships!*"

"I only inherited half of the company. The Morrison brothers own the other half."

"Nowhere in my wildest dreams did I consider, even for a moment, that your inheritance would be this monumental. I never connected your mother's maiden name with the giant shipbuilding McLeod." Travis rubbed the back of his neck. "Why would I?"

"I didn't either. But think about it. Everything was right in front of us if we'd only read between the lines. Now, it makes sense why Frank Sinatra was pleased to meet Mom. He knew that it was McLeod and Morrison battleships that were going to help win World War II. Grandfather said that by the end of the war, they'd be richer than the Astor's ever dreamed of—because they were building the Navy's fleet of ships!"

Travis raked his fingers through his hair without saying a word. Then leaning forward, he rested his elbows on his knees, rubbing his hands together.

This wasn't the reaction Olivia hoped for. He didn't look ready to celebrate.

"What's wrong, Travis? I know this whole thing is a shock for you, but what about me? I didn't even know the details until today. It's not like I've kept a big secret from you."

"When you first mentioned that your grandfather built boats, I naturally thought of small, custom wooden boats that you might find plying the waters of the Chesapeake Bay. But, you're talking *ships*."

There was more bothering him than boats versus ships.

"What is it, Travis? What are you really feeling?"

He waited too long to answer. His frown deepened. Olivia's heart plummeted.

"I love you, Olivia, and I love the life I've envisioned for us. I've built a business that's giving me a generous six-figure income. With the various properties I've been snatching up over the last ten years, I'm considered an important man in the community. People look up to me as a leader. I've even thought about politics down the road. We can have a comfortable and happy future with our kids growing up with the same island adventures I had. Now, would any of that be possible?" He hesitated, searching her face. "I'm a small-town guy, Olivia. Can I even cope with the life you're offering?"

Wow. She'd never considered he might feel inadequate. She wasn't asking him to run the company, for heaven's sake—just be her husband.

"I understand how you must feel. This inheritance has taken me by surprise—turned our life upside-down. I wish I had a little time to come to terms with this, but I don't."

Travis frowned with a slight jerk of his head, as if she was about to throw another curve ball at him and he wanted to be ready. "What do you mean?"

"I have to meet with my grandmother's attorney in Virginia. He'll give me the details and explain what happens next."

"When do we have to leave?"

"Not we . . . *me*. Monday. I fly out of Cleveland Hopkins Monday morning."

Travis got out of the chair and stood before her. "We'll deal with this, Livy . . . together."

Olivia nodded, there were no words left to say. Travis's voice held no emotion, he had the blank look of a man who couldn't quite get a grasp on everything—and that worried her. Travis had become her rock. She needed his support. Olivia reached out and took his hands in hers.

Travis attempted a smile, but Olivia could see his heart wasn't in it. "I need time to sort through this. I think I'd better go home for the night."

"Travis, please stay. I need you . . . now. Tonight. Tomorrow."

"I'm sorry, Livy, I really need to go."

"Travis, don't wimp-out on me when I need you the most!"

Travis reached out, putting his hands on her shoulders, and giving a gentle shake. "Look Olivia, this bomb shell didn't just land on you. It's landed on me as well. And I need time to shovel through the fall-out and come to terms with it—and I need to do it alone!"

Olivia followed him to the side door. He was rejecting her when she needed his support. Her life was about to change, and he didn't want to be with her. He wanted to go home—and just what did that mean? She thought they were making a home—together—here. He had become her whole world, and she needed him. She needed him tonight. But she wouldn't beg.

Olivia waited until Travis finished with the last button on his coat. "I love you, Travis."

Travis took her in his arms, pulling her tight against his chest. "We had our life together all planned out. This news has changed everything." He kissed her forehead. "I still love you. I just need time to think."

It wasn't until Olivia heard the click of the deadbolt that she allowed her eyes to well and the tears to stream down her cheeks.

By Sunday afternoon, the last of the few essential items were carefully placed in the one piece of luggage Olivia would take. She took her time choosing the two fashionably-cut suits that shouted designer. The black Chanel and the navy blue with shoulder pads, out-to-there, and a pinched-in waist. She knew from her years under the critical eye of her former mother-in-law that clothes make the woman. Once she understood the battleground, she would find what she needed in the shops of Richmond. Later, a shopping trip to New York for a whole new wardrobe could be arranged. After all, if she was to win this war she needed proper armor.

Travis's raised voice calling her name brought Olivia back from 5th Avenue and to the reality that there were still unfinished issues between them. A knot tightened in the pit of her stomach by the time she reached him in the coatroom. She entered just as he finished hanging his coat on the hook. Olivia knew that determined look and tried to cut him off before whatever was on his mind came flying at her.

"Hi, honey, I'm so glad you . . ."

"I'm going with you."

Olivia noticed the carry-on bag sitting on the floor next to Travis's coat. Whatever she expected it wasn't this. "What are you talking about? Going where?"

"I'm going to Virginia with you," Travis said with impatience. "This trip is not something you can handle on your own. You said you'll have a fight on your hands. So, I'm going."

"Travis, I'm . . ." A million thoughts and feelings raced through her at lightning speed, all of them unexpected. Why wasn't she elated to have him at her side? This was the man she was going to marry. The man who stood by her and the man she loved. Why did she feel this sudden panic? Was she protecting him against the unknown hell she might well be walking into? Did she want to make decisions on her own, without Travis interfering? What she did know was all the little voices in her head were shouting *NO*.

Travis moved toward her. "You're what?"

"Travis . . . no. You can't come with me."

"Are you crazy? Livy, you're my fiancée, and I intend to take care of you. You have no idea what you're getting yourself into."

Maybe that was the problem . . . not knowing. Not knowing who she was, where she came from. Not knowing an entire side of her family. This new part of her life was private and a personal problem only she could solve.

"I need to do this alone, Travis."

"With my help, you can get this whole inheritance over with, so we can move on with our lives. Your share of McLeod and Morrison is worth billions, and the plantation must be in the millions. We sell them off and travel the world, maybe keep the suite at the Waldorf—you love New York. I'll sell my business and devote myself to running our lives. But first, we have a wedding to plan, and my mother is getting anxious for us to set a date."

Olivia's chest tightened. She couldn't breathe. A feeling of overwhelming panic sent chills through her. Her heart pounded. She needed to *breathe*. The future could be no worse than this horrible feeling of being trapped, with the walls of her life closing in. She didn't want to rush through the formalities and come back and move on as though nothing had changed except for a swollen bank account. She needed time to find her mother, her grandmother, and all the ancestors she never knew. She needed room to understand who she really was. With both Win and Brian, she'd assimilated into their lives. She and Win had moved into his parent's guesthouse and his father had given her a job as his assistant in *his* hospital. She'd moved into Brian's mansion and slid into his lifestyle. She'd never believed her needs or wants were important—that *she* was important.

But now, for the first time, Olivia's life was her own. And Travis wanted to take it away from her.

Before her heart had a chance to talk her out of it, Olivia slid the engagement ring from her finger.

Taking his hand in hers, she placed the ring in its palm. She closed his fingers to hold it tight. Olivia brought his hand to her lips.

"What are you doing, Livy?"

"I just can't do this now."

"Does this mean you don't want to marry me now that you're rich? Are you calling off the wedding?" His eyes wide with disbelief and a voice that cracked with pain, was not enough for Olivia to change her mind.

She took a deep breath. "No. I'm not. But try to understand. This has nothing to do with you."

"Then what, Livy?"

"How can I possibly marry you when I have no idea who I am? You are surrounded, within a few miles, by your amazing family and more friends than you can even count. They graciously took me in without question because you love me." Olivia threw up her hands in frustration. "I have no one but a few weird friends."

"It doesn't matter."

He still didn't get it. "Yes it does—at least to me. When I vow to God and the world that I will honor you, I want you to believe it. How can you even consider marriage to someone with an unknown past? You know who your ancestors were. I don't know anyone past my grandmother and grandfather Thompson. Hell, I don't even know my mother."

"I know you in my heart. That's all that matters."

"Please, Travis. Just keep the ring for me."

His shoulders drooped in submission, his lips pursed as he dropped the solitaire into his pocket. "It'll be waiting for you . . . and so will I."

12

The door of the last overhead compartment snapped shut. The stewardess took her place at the front of the first class cabin and prepared for the pre-flight speech. Olivia's gaze shifted to the small round window. She would soon leave the mountain of dirty snow behind. It had all been efficiently cleared from the runways and was now covered in the gray haze of jet fumes.

The seatbelt clicked into place, and Olivia gave the strap across her lap a tug. She massaged her bare ring finger.

Giving Travis the ring back had been an impulsive move. One she should have been regretting, but she wasn't. She still loved him. But when he announced that he was going with her to finalize her inheritance so they could get on with their lives . . . well . . . that just sent her blood to a rolling boil. She wasn't going to let husband number three dictate her future—those days were over. This was her life, her family, and she would come to terms with it in her own way and in her own time. If Travis really loved her, he would wait.

Olivia had met with Nick Tanner Saturday morning to let him know she'd changed her plans about the Captain's house. Rather than having him convert it to a bed and breakfast, she would spare no expense for him to bring it back to its former glory. Her only explanation to his question about the cost was that she had come into a sudden inheritance. She intended to keep the details of her inheritance quiet for now. She suspected that by the end of the day the whole town would know Olivia had inherited something in Virginia and a lot of money went with it.

Her world vibrated with the scream of the engines, then the huge bird was thrust into the blue unknown. Olivia squeezed her eyes tight and whispered under her breath the words that only she could hear. "Mom, Grandmother, please watch over me."

The stewardess approached. "Good morning Mrs. Bentley, can I get you something to drink? Coffee, tea, juice?"

"Tomato juice, and you can make it a Bloody Mary."

Olivia thought about the journal tucked safely in her purse. The flight wasn't long but she would need to use the time wisely. There could be valuable information between its pages. With a tasty drink on her tray table, complete with celery, she opened her purse.

SUNDAY, JULY 1, 1945

I should have realized there was a reason other than William's party for all this money being spent on my appearance. Mother and I arrived at Sheffield Court just before noon. Frances was our maid for the day and took us to the pink and green suite with the walls covered in giant hydrangeas. The rooms were used for visiting royalty and I wondered why all the fuss over Mother and I. A light lunch was served in the sitting room and I ate mine on the small balcony overlooking the formal gardens. Frances unpacked our luggage as we ate tiny sandwiches and fresh fruit. Mother's hairdresser arrived around 3:00 and turned the pink marble bathroom into a makeshift salon. My hair was pulled up and back off my face until it was a vision of black curls that tumbled down the back. It was a coiffure fit for a Roman goddess. Later, Frances tied the enormous crinoline around my waist then gently eased the yards and yards of petal soft silk over my head, careful not to mess my hair. The gown is even more beautiful than Mainbocher's sketches. Mother nodded her head with approval then picked up the black velvet box from the dressing table and took out her pearl choker. She said it was time to pass on the Astor dog-collar to me as it had been presented to her on the day of her Coming Out."

I stood before the mirror looking like a princess. The necklace was cool and heavy against my skin. I counted ten rows of pearls held in place by bars of diamonds and an elaborate diamond clasp at the back. I'm glad I have such a long neck, otherwise it would surely choke me. Mother left to join Father downstairs while I was to wait until summoned. I'd been instructed on how to glide down the marble staircase without tripping and falling on my face. There's a real art to making an entrance. Frances came to say everyone was waiting for me. I hesitated at the top of the stairs as I'd been instructed. There must have been a hundred people, and all eyes were on me. I descended the wide marble treads that seemed to go on forever. I prayed I wouldn't trip. My mind was a blur until I reached the last step and saw William's outstretched hand.

"Well done old girl. You look absolutely regal. Every woman here is green with envy. Nice pearls. Can you swallow?" He could always put a situation in perspective and his humor set me at ease.

After dinner we were taken to the conservatory, which had been cleared for dancing. A stage had been built in a corner for the band. William thanked the guests for their support and good wishes and asked that I join him for the most important moment of his life. I had no idea what he was talking about but went to his side and took his out-stretched hand.

William smiled down at me and squeezed my hand. He told the guests how we had been friends since I had left my cradle, and that he wanted to make sure that I would be waiting for him when he returned at the end of the war. My heart did flip-flops when he got down on one knee. In front of everyone in the room, he asked me to marry him.

No one moved or spoke and I do believe not a breath was taken. I felt the pressure of the choker around my neck. I looked down at his hopeful face. I wondered what had happened to Jennifer. I wanted William to tell me he loved me. This was not the time to ask *questions, duty demanded that I say yes. There were shouts of joy and applause as William slipped the diamond ring onto my finger, then stood and took me in his arms and kissed me. The band began to play and the enchanted evening went on until dawn.*

Olivia paused, remembering her own wedding reception to Winston Montgomery III. "Oh, my God," she whispered. The day was the same—history had repeated itself. She had dressed at Win's house in a pink and green room with a pink marble bathroom. One of her mother's gowns had been carefully lifted over cascading curls. It had been a wonderful silk creation with the delicacy of butterfly wings. Then the pearl choker was placed around her neck. Olivia had worried she'd trip with each step down the grand staircase. The only difference in the two events was Win waited at the bottom to place the large diamond on her finger.

Olivia's gaze shifted to the clouds beyond the window. The enchanting image of her mother in the portrait had been a wonderful part of her life for as long as she could remember. It had been painted by a famous artist of the time, and Olivia had to fight the auction house to keep her treasure. Now she understood where the pearl choker came from, and the beautiful mystery gown. Any question about the painting and the gown had always been avoided by her mother, with promises that one day she would explain everything. But her mother never got the chance. Later, Olivia had found the elegant box from Cartier's containing the choker in a safe deposit box, but she never knew its history. Olivia remembered her mother's sad voice the last time she'd asked about the gown. "Father probably had it burned."

MONDAY, JULY 2, 1945
I'm so happy and so much in love. William came for lunch today and later we played tennis and swam in the pool. We've made our families very happy and today we began making plans for the future. We decided to wait until after the war is over to get married. After all, there doesn't seem to be any place in Europe left intact for

our honeymoon. We talked about how much fun we would have traveling and where we would live, how many children we would have and which schools they would attend. Tomorrow, I will go to Sheffield Court for the day.

TUESDAY, JULY 3, 1945

I'm even more in love. Life with William will be so wonderful. We rode in the morning. He's so dashing on horseback, and almost as good a rider as I am. Lunch was served on the terrace and afterwards we walked hand-in-hand through the gardens. I'm terribly afraid of losing William to this dreadful war. I'm so happy at Sheffield Court, I feel like a princess. I'm going back tomorrow.

WEDNESDAY, JULY 4, 1945

I'm so angry with William I could spit. He just refuses to listen to reason. He told me on our morning ride that his father has secured a position for him at the Pentagon. I was so excited. I told him how wonderful it would be. He could come home often and our lives wouldn't change all that much. It wasn't until later while swimming in the pool that he dropped the bomb. His strong sense of honor and responsibility wouldn't allow him to shirk his duty to his country. He needed to be fighting from the very decks of the ships that were making us richer by the day. This spoils all my plans! It's so unfair!

THURSDAY, JULY 5, 1945

It was too hot to ride this morning. The humidity just hangs in the air ready to take your very breath away. Besides, I'm having one of those horrid female times of the month and could not bear the thought of being bounced around on the back of a sweaty horse.

Wearing my prettiest sundress, William and I spent most of the day in the cool confines of the library at Sheffield Court. I never really studied or appreciated the grandeur of the room before. Growing up, it was always the fun room with secret panels leading to hidden staircases to the bedroom above and the wine cellar in the basement.

Today, William explained how the room was taken apart, piece-by-piece from a sixteenth century castle in England and brought here on one of his father's ships. The carved linen-fold paneling still has the faint smell of wood smoke. It was fun making up stories about how all the various nicks and gouges happened to be. We played chess, and he let me win. We danced to our favorite records and he held me extra close. Later, while sitting on the long leather sofa, he took me in his arms and told me how much he loved me and how happy we would be raising our family within those very walls. I was about to plead my case again for him to reconsider the Pentagon position when his two younger brothers bolted through one of the secret panels and careened past us, laughing all the way to the hall door. That ended William's vows of love and he drove me home soon after. I hate those two brats!

FRIDAY, JULY 6, 1945

I didn't see William today. He called early to say he needed to spend the day with his father. The oddest thing happened just after dinner. My future father-in-law stopped by on his way back to Norfolk. He was very angry. He had tried, once again, to convince William to see things his way, but the more he pushed, the more stubborn William became. I expressed my feelings and told him how I was also trying to change his mind. He smiled and patted my hand and said that it was a shame that a beautiful young lady in my position didn't have a nice new automobile of her own. He winked and said that it could certainly be arranged if William took a liking to Washington. How strange!

SATURDAY, JULY 7, 1945

I stayed home today. William telephoned and spent the entire time complaining in a raised voice about his father and the war. I don't like this. I feel like I've suddenly been thrown in the middle of what should be between father and son.

It's still dreadfully hot. My dress stuck to my damp body and the fans did nothing but push the humid air around the room. I only went outside to swim. I didn't even go to the barn to visit Sinatra. Maybe tomorrow will be cooler.

SUNDAY, JULY 8, 1945
It rained all day. I stayed in my room and listened to records and thought about Sheffield Court. One day it will be mine. It's such a contrast to life here. I've always loved my home. It's one of the largest and grandest of all the old Virginia plantations and quite comfortable. But Sheffield Court is only twenty years old and more than three times our size. William doesn't like the fact that his father's architect raided and pillaged the English countryside to fill a house with ancient rooms that very few would ever see. A museum he calls it, complete with an indoor swimming pool and a bowling alley in the basement. The house is filled with cooled rooms and all the latest conveniences. It takes a staff of twenty to run the house alone, plus the outdoor staff for the grounds, stables, and garages. It must cost a fortune. What puzzles me most, now that I see both households, is where does Father's money go? We get by with only five live-in servants for the house, plus our farm manager and his help, and the chauffeur. Mother is very conservative with the household budget. I must ask Father about this.

MONDAY, JULY 9, 1945
This is the worst day of my life! William is gone! He didn't even come to see me. He just called on the telephone. How could he do this to me? I feel so humiliated and angry. He said a desk job would kill him faster than any enemy fire. He needed to leave now, before his father could do anything to prevent him from joining the Pacific theater. He kept saying, over and over, that I should remember the wonderful days we've had this week together and have faith that he will return.

TUESDAY, JULY 10, 1945
Mr. Morrison blames me for William leaving. He telephoned today to say that I failed in my duty to him. If I had acted like a woman

and not a little girl who follows William around like a puppy, he would be safe and not out there trying to get himself blown-up. Mr. Morrison said that William has an obligation to the family and the business. That is more important than wearing a pretty white uniform and being saluted by idiots. I didn't like his tone when he said I should act like a woman and not a little girl. I remember his comment when he was here last that I deserved a new automobile. I'm certainly old enough to know that some women use sex to get what they want. Could Mr. Morrison have expected me to have sex with William in order to keep him here and follow his father's orders? All this frightens me. I won't tell Mother about this. It could cause bad feelings between our families. It will be my secret.

WEDNESDAY, JULY 11, 1945

Father came home today. After dinner, I found him relaxing in the library with a cigar and brandy. I talked about my visits to Sheffield Court and how much it must cost to operate compared to our farm. Father must be angry about something regarding Mr. Morrison because he was quite free with his opinions. He explained how all of the Morrison's profit from the business goes to support their excessive lifestyle. Father says Sheffield Court was built on a scale to match the great estates of Europe. And there's the lavish entertaining of everyone from Hollywood movie stars to presidents, not to mention a two hundred foot yacht. It all costs money, big money, and the more they spend, the more they need. He warned that they would lose everything if anything ever happens to the business. Father's conscience will not allow him to flaunt his wealth like that, nor should I when I take control of that museum they call home. He said that our money is safe and available if we need it. Whatever disaster may present itself we can survive quite comfortably. It's a greedy and dangerous world and those who dangle their wealth before the masses are the first to be shot down. I wonder if that was meant to be a warning to me. If I'm not careful, I could someday lose everything.

13

"Excuse me, Mrs. Bentley, but we'll be landing soon. May I please take your glass?"

"Oh. Sure." Olivia glanced up at the stewardess. "I guess I lost track of the time."

"You were pretty engrossed in your book. I didn't want to disturb you."

"Thank you." Olivia carefully placed the journal back in her purse.

Olivia's gaze shifted to the window and the approaching city below as they broke through the clouds. The passages she'd just read gave her a glimpse into the Morrisons' lifestyle. She needed information on the history of McLeod and Morrison. There appeared to be a huge contrast between the two families considering the income between the two men must have been about the same. She needed to research Angus McLeod. And what about William Morrison? How did he and Mom suddenly become engaged when there was no mention of any kind of formal courtship, or even casual dating? And what ever happened to Jennifer?

The grinding of the landing gear pulled Olivia's gaze from the small round window. Her pulse quickened with anticipation of what the next few hours would hold.

The plane rolled to a complete stop. Olivia unbuckled her seatbelt. The first-class stewardess approached then stood with her back to Olivia. "If I can have your attention please. I'm sorry for the delay, but I'll need you to remain in your seats for a few more minutes."

Olivia shifted in her seat to get a better view of those sitting in the rows behind. She searched for what or who caused the holdup. Could there be a celebrity amongst them?

The stewardess bent down to speak with her. "Mrs. Bentley, I have your briefcase and coat. Please follow me to the door."

Olivia thought back to the moments when she'd first boarded the plane. She'd been impressed with the attendant who'd offered to take her briefcase and hang her coat in the locker. She'd shrugged out of the mink and handed both items to the attendant. She thought it was normal behavior toward first-class passengers. Perhaps it wasn't.

This was awkward—everyone was staring at her. The door to the cockpit was open, the pilot and co-pilot still flipping switches. Another stewardess stood in the doorway to coach, blocking anyone from leaving. Olivia got out of her seat and followed. Maybe she should apologize to the other first-class passengers for causing their delay . . . nah, just follow, no eye contact.

Once out in the waiting area, the stewardess handed Olivia her coat and briefcase. "If you'll please step into the cart, the driver will take you to the baggage claim area."

How many times had she run from gate to gate on tired feet as transport carts passed her by with never an offer of a lift? "Are you sure this is for me? I'm perfectly capable of walking."

"It's all been arranged, Mrs. Bentley. Please step into the cart."

The seats in the waiting area were all empty. A line of folks were being held back behind a rope barricade—all of them watching her.

The stewardess glanced back toward the gate. "Please, Mrs. Bentley. I need to get back to the other passengers."

Olivia shrugged and climbed on and took a seat, placing the folded coat on her lap. The driver immediately steered the cart away from the gate. Olivia watched the attendant release the rope barrier and everyone rushed into the gate area. Was this special treatment part of her new life or someone's concern over her safety?

She put her hand out to brace herself when the cart came to an abrupt stop under the Baggage Claim sign. Olivia spotted her bag on the carousel. It was the only one . . . where was everyone else's luggage?

The driver turned to face her. "May I please have your claim ticket? I'll be right back with your bag."

Olivia handed him her ticket and stepped out of the cart. A man dressed in the most bizarre suit she'd ever seen strode toward her. His grey hair, parted down the middle, was held in place by a generous amount of hair cream. Olivia noted a rather short build. Wearing a brown plaid suit, white shirt, and bow tie, he could be traveling with Barnum and Bailey.

"Olivia Bentley?"

"Yes?"

"I'm Horatio Dumbarton, your grandmother's attorney." He reached out his hand to shake Olivia's then slipped a tip to the driver.

Olivia set her briefcase on the floor then unfolded her coat.

"Here, let me help you on with that," Horatio took the mink and held it up.

Olivia, impressed with his old world manners, slipped both arms into the coat. "Thank you."

"We'd better hurry. The car is just outside. I promised security I wouldn't be long."

His gravely voice was laced with the expected Southern drawl, while his old fashioned clothes certainly matched his name. He bent down to pick up her bag and briefcase. Olivia got a whiff of Old Spice and a rather sweet smelling pipe tobacco. Then she followed him to the car.

A man wearing an airport uniform stood at the front of the car. He looked her up and down like he'd been expecting Elizabeth

Taylor and got a nobody instead. He opened the rear door and waited while she settled herself in the back seat.

Horatio placed her luggage in the trunk then tipped the security guard. He got behind the wheel and turned the key. Why had he found it necessary to personally pick her up rather than send the limo she'd expected? And why was he parked in the *No Parking* zone with security standing guard?

Once they'd eased into the flow of traffic Olivia leaned forward. "Mr. Dumbarton, is all this special treatment really necessary? I was practically dragged from the plane even before the pilot had a chance to leave his seat, then my bag was already waiting when I got to the carousel. Do you have any idea how long I have waited in airports around the world just to get a glimpse of my luggage?"

"Rushing you through the airport was extreme. But I must get you to the office and the meeting with the Morrison brothers before anyone knows you're here."

"Meeting? I thought I would have a day or two to prepare."

"I'm sorry, Mrs. Bentley, but the element of surprise is paramount. You can freshen up and change in the ladies lounge at the office. Lunch will be waiting for you. You'll have just enough time to eat and relax for a few minutes. Our meeting is in two hours."

Olivia massaged her naked ring finger. If Travis were here he'd be holding her hand and reassuring her that everything would be okay. He'd handle everything. But, this was her life. She needed to make her own decisions. After all, she'd just met Travis last Memorial Day. He'd slipped the ring on her finger at Christmas, and now, less than a month later she was having doubts. Not doubts about her love for Travis, but doubts about herself. Somewhere in this mess she needed to find Olivia Bentley.

"Will there be any time for you to brief me?"

"Now, while we're driving. That's why I thought it best for me to pick you up." His eyes met hers in the rearview mirror. "You may want to take notes. You'll find a legal pad in the pocket of the seat back."

14

Horatio spent thirty minutes with Olivia while they ate a lunch of chicken salad on croissants and fresh fruit. His office took up the entire third floor in the building that had survived since the 1830s. It was the top floor and would have had a commanding view of the city back in its day. Now it was just a speck amongst the high-rises of the twentieth century.

"I'll leave you now to freshen up. The brother's first impression of you is important. Remember, the sacrifices your grandmother made were to insure that you inherited those shares. The Morrison brothers don't know you exist."

The rumpled suit she'd had on since early that morning wouldn't do. They needed to view her as a woman of power.

Her luggage sat on the sofa in the ladies lounge. It took a full half hour to dress but the reflection in the long mirror was worth every minute. Her royal-blue wool suit shouted Yves Saint Laurent. The wide shoulder pads accentuated the severely cut front of the jacket that ended at a nipped-in waist and peplum. A pencil-slim skirt ended just below her knees. The simple white silk blouse's top three buttons were left open showing a single strand of pearls.

Three soft taps at the door—Horatio was ready for her.

"Wow. They're not going to mess with a women who looks like she belongs on Dynasty."

"Thanks . . . I think. Is it show time?"

"The Morrison brothers are in the conference room. It won't hurt to let them cool their heels a bit."

Horatio ushered Olivia to a small room used as a library. He hesitated before a narrow bookcase then pulled out a book along the left edge, midway from the top. Reaching in, he pulled a lever near the back, and a door swung open. "There's a tiny room beyond. It was helpful during times of war and economic unrest to know what your adversaries were about. Gives us an edge in today's world. You mustn't utter a sound."

Olivia poked her head into the dark space. "Is there any light? Will I be able to see?"

"I'm afraid the only light comes from the peephole, and I'll leave this door ajar. You can see and hear everything going on in the conference room. Remember, they can also hear you. The brothers are expecting me to turn over the signed shares in McLeod and Morrison. I want you to wait in there until I'm ready for you."

Olivia followed Horatio into the closet-size room. He turned toward the paneled wall then slid a small disk to the side, revealing a hole about the size of a quarter. He put his index finger to his lips and left the room.

Olivia moved to the hole, placing her hands on either side, and put her eye to the peephole. She wondered about the people who'd stood in this windowless space. According to Horatio, the building had been here long before the Civil War and still had the musty scent of the times and souls long gone. She shivered. The hairs on the back of her neck prickled. Ghosts? At any other time the mere possibility of sharing the tiny space with ghosts would send her racing for the door, but she needed to focus on the present. Through the peephole, Olivia could see the room clearly. Sun streamed in through the wavy old glass in the tall windows. A large cut-glass pitcher of water and several glasses sat on a silver tray in the center of the table.

Olivia's teeth clenched at the sight of the Morrison brothers. Clive and Wilson were just as Horatio had described them. They were both somewhere in their fifties. By the looks of their suits, they'd both put on more than a few pounds—one sneeze and buttons would fly. Both had black hair, too dark to be natural and not a sign of grey at their temples. That, along with their rather ruddy complexions, gave Olivia the impression they probably shared a somewhat excessive lifestyle. They could have been twins, except that Clive was the one with the horn-rimmed glasses and a neck bulging over a well-starched collar. He drummed his fingers on the table—a sure sign of impatience.

Wilson leaned forward so he could see around Clive and focused his attention at the end of the table. "What are you doing sitting way down there big brother? You're gonna miss all the action when we take control of McLeod and Morrison."

Olivia's breath caught. Her attention drifted to William, the man her mother had been in love with. He was a good ten to fifteen years older and seemed to bear little physical resemblance to his brothers. His thick, wavy grey hair emphasized chiseled features. Although seated, Olivia guessed he'd have a rather athletic physique under the expensive Italian suit. Brian always preferred Italian. Her late husband had taken pleasure in her education of the great couture houses around the world. Gold cufflinks caught the afternoon sun streaming in through the windows. This was a man with attention to details. Why would he choose to sit at the end of the table, quite a distance from his brothers?

William showed no emotion at his brother's comment. "I find the air down here much," he paused a beat. "Cleaner."

"You don't want to miss out on the fun." Clive snorted. "After we get our hands on those shares we're gonna celebrate. All afternoon. Aren't we, Wilson?"

"Nothing is going to happen until we get those shares." Wilson growled. "What the hell's keeping him?" He nodded toward the center of the table. "The bastard's not offering us anything but water. I could use a good single malt right about now."

Olivia smiled. The boys were getting antsy. Good.

Horatio entered the conference room and hesitated for just a moment before moving forward to a chair midway down the table, across from Clive and Wilson. "Good afternoon, gentlemen. Thank you for coming on such short notice."

Clive pushed his glasses further up on his nose.

Wilson reached in his pocket and removed a silver cigarette case.

Horatio pulled out the chair, placing a stack of papers on the table, and sat down.

Wilson flipped open the case and removed a cigarette. "Look, can we just get on with this? Just sign over the old lady's estate to us, and we'll be out of here." He snapped the lid shut then tapped the cigarette several times on the case. He carefully placed the case on the table, as if it were a piece of priceless art.

"Yeah, you've put this off long enough. What's the problem?" Clive asked. His voice brimmed with irritation.

Olivia seethed. These two buffoons showed no respect for her grandmother. Clive and Wilson saw the meeting as merely a formality and were anxious to get on with their day of celebration—a day to celebrate the death of Olivia Maureen McLeod.

Well, that was about to change.

Horatio wove his fingers together and placed them on the table in front of him. "There is no problem . . . at least not as far as I'm concerned." His Southern drawl was as smooth as buttermilk. "There are two parts to Olivia McLeod's estate, her personal property and that of McLeod and Morrison. The three of you are not entitled to her personal property."

Wilson pulled a lighter from his pocket. He flipped open the lid. His thumb stroked the flint wheel touching the flame to the cigarette. He took a long drag before speaking.

He's stalling, thought Olivia. Maybe they expect to get every-thing—the whole kit-and-caboodle.

"Okay, fine, we don't care what happens to her personal prop-erty." Wilson's voice was controlled—the voice of a man used to giving orders—not taking them. "Just turn over the papers for her share of the company."

"May I ask, Wilson, why you're in such a hurry? Why is this so important right now?"

Wilson studied the tip of his cigarette.

Olivia held her breath. Wasn't anyone going to answer Horatio?

William cleared his throat and leaned forward, clenching his hands on the table. "I guess I should speak for Wilson since he seems to be having difficulty coming up with a believable story." He paused for a beat. "My brothers wish to expand McLeod and Morrison to include a site on the West Coast and buy out a com-pany that builds planes . . . bombers. They've been planning this for several years now, but Mrs. McLeod and I were against it from the beginning. That kept everything on hold, but now, with her shares of the company going to the three of us, it puts the whole plan in favor of my brothers." He turned his attention from Horatio to Wilson, his glare as deadly as dueling pistols. "They'll have the control they need to go forward. It's two against one."

"Interesting." Horatio stood and walked toward the door.

Olivia stepped away from the peephole. So, it was more than just greed that drove the brothers. They wanted to build airplanes, and she was standing in their way. Well, Horatio was about to drop a bomb, right in the middle of their plans for Western expansion.

Horatio opened the conference room door. "Gentlemen, excuse me for just a moment. There is someone here that I would like you to meet."

Olivia was already out the door and met Horatio in the hall. He took her hand and whispered, "Are you okay? Just relax and leave the talking to me."

"I'm fine. I can't wait to stick a pin in those two blowfish!"

Horatio chuckled before opening the conference room door. "You're about to get your chance."

He opened the door and entered.

Wilson pulled the ashtray closer, snubbing out his cigarette. "What is this, Dumbarton? Quit stalling and get on with the details."

Horatio stood to the side and motioned for Olivia to enter.

Olivia paused just inside the door. She knew how to make an entrance and she'd carefully dressed for the part.

William stood. The color drained from his face. "Maureen," he murmured. His expression was that of a man who'd just seen a ghost. Slowly, a knowing smile appeared then deepened until it reached his eyes. It was the look of a man who's been reunited with a lost love. Once again he murmured "Maureen." Olivia remembered the passages from the diaries and could imagine this man swimming, dancing and riding with her mother during those hot summer days following their engagement.

Clive, craning his neck forward, pushed at the bridge of his glasses.

Wilson balled his hands into fists. "Who is this? And what does she have to do with our business?"

Clive smacked the table with the palm of his hand. "Yeah, what's she doing here?"

William's smile broadened. "Calm down, boys. I believe this lovely lady is going to have a lot to do with our business."

"Are you nuts? We don't know this broad," said Wilson.

"Yeah, never saw her before. And why are you smiling? You don't know her either," Clive shouted.

William sat down without a word.

Horatio guided Olivia to the head of the table and pulled out the chair. "I would like to introduce you to Olivia Thompson Bentley . . . your new partner in McLeod and Morrison."

"Good afternoon, gentlemen," Olivia said in her most confident, business voice.

Clive leaned forward, his cheeks turning an unflattering shade of crimson. "No! We have the old man's will." He slammed his fist on the table. "She has no right to anything!"

"Shut up, Clive!" Wilson's frown deepened. Olivia could almost hear the wheels spinning in his head. "Okay, maybe somehow there's a way she can inherit personal property from the old lady, but I know for a fact she can't touch the company. Angus made sure of that." His Southern drawl was now laced with venom.

For the next hour Horatio read Olivia McLeod's will, line-by-line, explaining the intricate details as he went along. When he finished, he pushed the papers to the side. "Well, gentlemen, that's it. All spelled out in irrefutable language. Mrs. Bentley is your new business partner." Horatio paused with the grin of a Cheshire cat before continuing. "I'll give her a few days to settle in at the farm then I'll bring her around. I'm sure one of you will be happy to give her a tour of the shipyard."

The three brothers remained quiet. What could they say? Horatio had made each item perfectly clear. He'd handled each objection with a confident answer—and she'd let all those blazing-hot daggers their eyes had thrown her way bounce off with the skill of Wonder Woman.

Wilson, growing redder by the minute, a vein bulging in his neck, reached for his cigarette case. His teeth clenched. He dropped the case into his jacket pocket and stood. Clive followed suit. Neither of them seemed to be breathing.

"You'll hear from our attorneys. This isn't over yet, Dumbarton," Wilson growled.

Both men stormed out of the conference room without even a glance at Olivia.

William waited until they were gone, the door slamming behind Clive. He stood then circled the conference table, never taking his eyes off of Olivia. He stopped before her and took her hands in his. "It's a pleasure to meet you, Olivia. I would have known who you were had we met in Fiji. Seeing you walk through that door was like watching Maureen enter the room." He raised her hand to his lips. "Welcome home, Olivia."

His voice resonated with assurance. Maybe he actually cared about her. He was, after all, once engaged to her mother. Perhaps she had at least one friend in the enemy camp. She had a feeling, deep in her gut that she was going to need a friend if she was to survive whatever Clive and Wilson planned. She was sure they were already strategizing for their next move. They came to the meeting thinking it would just be the formality of signing over the shares— they left with a new business partner. They would not give up easily, not with the Western expansion at stake.

With a wink, William released Olivia's hand and headed toward the door. With his hand on the knob, he glanced over his shoulder. "I wouldn't worry too much about those attorneys my brothers threatened you with. They all work for me."

15

Olivia pulled the front of her mink coat around her while she waited for Horatio to open the car door. She might be in the South, but it was still January. She settled onto the leather front seat—it smelled of Old Spice. This time she didn't want to sit in the back. She didn't want to miss a thing. She'd successfully run two hospitals by following her number one rule—*know your opposition and never go into a meeting unprepared.* She left the meeting feeling she hadn't followed her own rule. Now she needed to step up her game and collect information. Olivia needed to know the street names, buildings, and landmarks of Richmond. She wanted to know its history—she needed to know everything.

"I love old buildings, and I noticed many of the architectural details while I waited in your office."

"As I'd mentioned during lunch, the building dates to the 1830s, some thirty years before the war. Richmond was the capital of the Confederate States of America." Olivia could hear the pride in his voice.

"Although I don't know a lot about the Civil War, I do remember the fall of Richmond," Olivia said remembering her history classes and the movie *Gone With The Wind.*

"The Union Army captured Richmond early in April, 1865. President Davis abandoned Richmond and fled south on the last open railroad line. The retreating soldiers were under orders to set fire to bridges, the armory, and warehouses containing supplies as they left. It's known as the Evacuation Fire, and April 3, 1865, is known as Evacuation Sunday."

"Wow! I'm impressed with your knowledge of history."

Horatio glanced toward Olivia. "Those of us who were born and raised here know those dates as well as our own birthdays. As a youngster, I played in the very fields and woods where camps stood and battles were fought. I have a tin box full of everything from ammunition to buttons."

"How did your building survive the fire?"

"The next day, the Mayor went to the Union Troops and surrendered the city. It was the Union troops who put out the fire before it reached this far. Back then the building was a bank with reinforced walls. It's survived pretty well over the years."

"I'll have to find some books and read up on the subject," Olivia said, already thinking she'd need to find a library.

Horatio chuckled. "You won't have to look far. You'll find plenty of books at the house. The *best* way to learn is to visit Shirley Plantation. We'll be passing the entrance in a few minutes. You'll also want to visit the many battlefields and army camps located all around the area." He turned to face her with a smile. "The farm isn't much farther."

They were moving away from the city now. Olivia thought back to the meeting. Her role was not so much as a participant but rather an observer. Horatio had made that clear during the briefing. The dynamics of the Morrison brothers were laid out on the table for all to see. To be picked apart, dissected, and analyzed, with each man playing a different role.

Clive was impulsive and all mouth, Wilson the thinker. Although prone to the dramatic, he appeared to be the controlling factor, with Clive following at his heels. Olivia wasn't sure where William fit. According to the passages in the diaries, her mother had clearly not liked, nor trusted, the young boys, and it appeared for good reason. Today, William had shown his true colors to everyone present and was not ashamed to do so, even at the cost of his brother's future plans. Olivia wasn't sure if she could count him in as a player on her team, but she desperately wanted to.

The brothers clearly never expected any obstacles in taking total control of McLeod and Morrison upon her grandmother's death. Clive and Wilson hadn't accepted the fact that Angus, in his determination to eliminate Maureen from his life, could have left a loophole so big as to let his granddaughter step in. How Clive and Wilson came into possession of the will was not known, but they obviously had not studied it well enough. They were clearly blindsided by today's events, and, according to Horatio, would retaliate . . . and soon.

Olivia turned in the seat to get a better view from the side window. Traveling on State Route 5, they passed mile after mile of dense woodland. She noticed the sign for Shirley Plantation and a minute later Horatio pointed to the road leading to Berkeley Plantation. "The first official Thanksgiving was held here in 1619. The three story, red brick mansion was built in 1726, and is the ancestral home of presidents William Henry Harrison and Benjamin Harrison."

"I can't believe I'll be living on a farm surrounded by so much history. I'm looking forward to exploring it all." What had she just said? Visiting plantations and battlefields takes time. And from what she'd just learned, further exploration could take months—years, even. At best, she had just weeks before she needed to return home.

Horatio slowed the car as they approached an unmarked gravel road. He made the turn and drove through dense woods until it gave way to plowed fields on both sides of the road. A fairly new barn off in the distance gave evidence that the farm, at least, was doing well. But, a house was nowhere to be seen. The fields ended at more woods, heavy with undergrowth. Horatio stopped. A dirt lane branched off to the right. It didn't appear to have been used in years. Before them, on either side of the road, were tall, crumbling, brick posts that still managed to support a large slab of stone with the name FAIRFIELD carved in ornate letters. Her heart sank. If this was any indication of the house's condition, then perhaps Travis was right that she should sell and move on.

"That's original," said Horatio as they passed through.

Olivia scooted forward to get a better look through the windshield. "Is this where my property begins?"

"No, you own everything from State Route 5 to the river and on both sides of the lane for as far as you can see."

The woods gave way to tall, majestic trees lining the road, their graceful branches reaching across in a welcoming arch.

"But, what about the fields we passed?"

"A farmer leases the land for his crops. Mostly corn and soybeans."

The lane came to an abrupt end at a high brick wall and tall ornate gates. Although the bricks appeared ancient, the old gates opened with ease at the touch of the remote Horatio pointed at the small black box on the wall.

The gates closed behind them. Horatio followed the wide drive of crushed brick and stone as it curved through an orchard then straightened. Horatio brought the car to a stop. He nodded toward the view beyond. "Welcome to Fairfield."

A rose-colored brick house, a good city-block wide, sat amongst a stand of ancient trees with a lush lawn sweeping down to the banks of the James River. The large three-story central portion, with dormers across the front, was stately and true to its Georgian heritage. What appeared to be small, two-story houses had been connected to the main house, creating welcoming arms that drew her in. She'd been on edge since landing at the Richmond International Airport. Now, a sense of calm washed over her.

"I was expecting a rundown old farm. How could my mother have kept this from me? She grew up here . . . amongst America's history."

"She had to. You know the wording in Angus's will. There could be no contact or all would be lost."

"What little my mother said about her childhood led me to believe it was spent on an old Virginia farm. It must have been awfully hard for her to walk away from this." Olivia shook her head in disbelief. "What was so horrible that she had to leave?"

Horatio patted her hand in a fatherly gesture. "Maybe you'll find the answers inside."

16

oratio took a moment to grab a large, brown, expandable file from the back seat and tucked it under his arm. The handsome front door, so typical of the Georgian period, opened before Olivia had her foot firmly placed on the wide, worn stone steps. A woman, of African-American descent, stood to the side of the door. There was no welcoming smile, just a stiff posture and slight nod of her head.

Horatio didn't wait for formalities, instead ushered Olivia through the door and into the massive, paneled hall. "Olivia, this is Sarah Harrison, your housekeeper and cook. She was born here and knows the house and grounds as well as anyone."

"Welcome to Fairfield, Mrs. Bentley." Her light brown complexion was sprinkled with freckles. Dark brown eyes raked her new employer from head-to-toe, but gave no indication, one way or the other, of an opinion.

Olivia reached out her hand as she would to anyone she'd just met. "I'm pleased to . . ."

Horatio shoved the large file toward Olivia. "These are the household records, accounts, and bills I've paid for the last few months. I need to get back to the office to prepare for tomorrow."

Olivia took the folder. This was awkward. Horatio had seemingly ignored her attempt at a warm introduction to her housekeeper.

"I'll pick you up at nine o'clock in the morning. We'll swing by the bank in Norfolk so you can be added to the accounts."

This was another change in plans that Horatio sprang on her at the last minute. Was this going to be a pattern with him? If so, she'd quickly go crazy just trying to keep up.

"Tomorrow? You told the Morrison brothers you'd give me a few days to settle in before taking me to the shipyard."

"The element of surprise, my dear." Horatio winked. "We can't give those boys even a day to come up with some devious plan against us."

Horatio nodded at a tall, black man approaching from a side hall. He was dressed for work with a dark-green flannel shirt tucked into jeans. His soft-soled boots made only the slightest sound.

"Olivia, I'd like you to meet Benjamin, Sarah's husband, your chauffer, and manager of the farm."

Wow, he's imposing, thought Olivia. He had to be a good six foot three and built like a brick wall. His long strides quickly closed the gap between them.

The grin and twinkle in his eyes was all Olivia needed to relax. "It's a pleasure to meet you. That's quite a list of responsibilities. I'm impressed."

Benjamin smiled with a slight nod. "Thank you, Miz Olivia. Now if you'll allow, I'll get your bags and take them to your room."

Horatio made the move to follow Benjamin to the car, then turned back. Reaching into his pocket, he pulled out a set of keys and handed them to Olivia. "I almost forgot to give you the keys to your grandmother's office and desk."

Sarah frowned while fingering the ring of keys hanging from her belt loop. She glared at Horatio with pursed lips.

Olivia rolled the two keys around in the palm of her hand. Why did Horatio have the keys? What was so important that Horatio felt it necessary to keep the keys—what was in the office?

Sarah closed the door behind him. She was neatly dressed in khaki-colored slacks with a sharp crease down the center of each leg that had obviously been recently pressed, and a simple white, long-sleeved shirt. The fingers of her right hand adjusted the ring of keys so they hung neatly from a dark brown belt. Sarah appeared to be a no-nonsense woman with an acute attention to detail.

Seconds of silence went by. Olivia needed to say something that would break the ice. She'd already blown the handshake attempt. With a sweeping glance that took in the elaborately paneled walls and ornate staircase, Olivia found the perfect opening. "This is a beautiful entrance hall."

"Hmmph" Sarah rolled her eyes. "This is much more than a mere hallway. Why, in the heat of the summer this was often the most comfortable room in the house. As you can see, the front and back doors line up perfectly to allow cross-ventilation. The heat is drawn up the stairway to the third floor." Sarah adjusted a vase of flowers sitting on a drop-leaf table. "These chairs and tables have lined the walls since 1730. Back then they were ready to be set up for a game of cards with friends and neighbors, or perhaps a light meal."

Olivia did the math in her head. Two hundred and fifty-five years old. She'd best not sit on them. "Very impressive."

"Yes, ma'am. I'll take you up to your room now," said Sarah in a voice that left no doubt that the history lesson was over.

Olivia found the soft squeak of the stairs comforting. Another hall, equally as wide as the one she'd just left, ran the depth of the house on the second floor. Windows at each end provided natural light. Sarah stopped just outside of what appeared to be a corner room on the side of the house facing the river.

"This was your grandmother's room," Sarah said with a new softness in her voice.

Ornate paneled walls washed in an eggshell blue greeted Olivia as she followed Sarah into the room. A huge tester bed, hung with silk draping's the same color as the walls, dominated the room.

"This bed is original to the house. Your grandmother had it refitted for today's queen-size mattress."

Olivia wrapped her arm around the end post, her hand caressing the carved tobacco leaves. It was, after all, the tobacco crops that made Virginia planters rich. She turned, still running her fingers along the edges of the leaves, to get a better look at the opposite side of the room. For the first time she noticed the large painting above the fireplace.

Olivia gasped. With a chill racing through her veins she placed a hand over her pounding heart. She walked to the center of the room to get a better look at the portrait.

"I agree, it is rather creepy looking," said Sarah.

The painting was of a woman, well past her prime, sitting sidesaddle on a dark bay horse. She wore a black cape, the hood resting toward the back of her head revealing a rather angular, determined jaw and sunken cheeks. This was someone who lived a harder life than that of a pampered lady on a plantation. But it was her hand, casually holding her gloves that drew Olivia to the fireplace. Standing on her toes, she could see every brush stroke. The subject in the painting wore the same ring as the woman in black who'd appeared in Olivia's nightmares since that horrible night— the night before the death of her family.

"She's your great-grandmother, Alexandra McLeod. She always wore a black cape. Said she couldn't be bothered by tight fitting coats. All those buttons just slowed her down."

The nightmares had been so real. Olivia clearly saw the ring in her last dream. Could there actually be a connection between the women in her dreams and her great-grandmother? "This is just too weird."

"I know, ma'am. I'll have Benjamin take it down."

Olivia reached up and touched the canvas. She felt love and a sense of contentment emanating from her rather stern-looking great-grandmother. This was the woman who'd tried to warn her of imminent danger, through the nightmares that had plagued her since she was fifteen. She couldn't lose her now. "No, leave it. I rather like it."

"Hmmph." Sarah moved to a door on the opposite side of the bed. "There's a bathroom here and a dressing room. Your great-grandmother added bathrooms to the house after they bought the plantation from the Fairbanks."

Olivia moved to the windows. Huge trees dotted the wide expanse of lawn bordering the river. "The back yard is beautiful."

Sarah let out a heavy sigh of impatience. "That's actually the front of the house. The roads were so bad back then that folks found it easier to travel by the rivers. The big houses were built facing the water."

"Really?" That made sense. She certainly couldn't imagine ladies bumping along that long drive in a carriage. The road from Richmond probably wasn't much better.

"Yes, ma'am. Now I must see to dinner. I'll serve at seven o'clock sharp."

"Sarah, where was my mother's room?"

"Just across the hall. The only room with flowered wallpaper."

Sarah hadn't said where the dining room was. Olivia hurried to the door to catch Sarah before she got to the bottom of the staircase. She reached the hall just as Sarah disappeared through a door opposite the staircase. Olivia had toured many houses built during the 1700s. She would, most likely, find the dining room on one side of the front door, or was it the back door? Olivia wished her meeting with Sarah had gone better. Although Sarah had been polite, Olivia definitely felt prickly vibes from her. With a glance toward her great-grandmother's portrait, Olivia headed back into the hall in search of flowered wallpaper.

Olivia found her mother's room to be considerably smaller than her grandmother's. She was surprised at the flamboyant style of the late 1930s Art Deco. All the furniture matched. It must have been purchased as a suite. The bed of light wood had a high-arched headboard that connected to a pair of oval bedside tables of burl wood. A metal lamp in the shape of a woman holding a frosted glass orb sat on a table in the corner. Olivia moved to an ornate dressing table consisting of two rounded front sets of drawers inlayed with many woods in a fan pattern. The two ends held a round mirror in the center. Olivia imagined her mother's silver-backed brush and comb sitting there along with colorful perfume bottles. Olivia pulled open the drawers . . . all of them empty. She got up and checked the drawers in the dresser. They too were empty. Had everything of her mother been stripped from the house?

The only place left to check was the closet. Olivia opened the door to find an empty space, except for a stack of old records on the shelf. She pulled them down and found Frank Sinatra's on top. Olivia let out a long sigh of relief. Her mother's cherished albums had survived. The portable phonograph waited on a cabinet. Could it still work after all these years? She glanced at her watch. It was five o'clock. No time to listen to old Blue Eyes. If she rushed, she just might be able to unpack her bag and take a quick shower before dinner.

17

Olivia hesitated just inside the doorway of the large, square dining room. A sage-green chair rail divided plastered walls in a soft cream color. Heavy damask drapes in a deep apricot dressed the tall windows overlooking the river. A table that could easily seat a dozen people sat below an exquisite crystal chandelier in the center of the room. Olivia noticed only one place setting at the head of the table. Was she to eat alone? Did she dare ask to eat in the kitchen? Better not. Someone thought to light a fire in the fireplace on this chilly evening—probably Benjamin.

Sarah entered through a swinging door at the far corner of the room carrying a large silver tray just as the tall case clock in the hall finished chiming seven times. She took the tray to the sideboard while Olivia settled herself in the comfortable armchair.

"It's just simple chicken and dumplings. I didn't know how many folks you'd be bringing with you, so I made plenty."

"I wouldn't bring anyone without telling you first," said Olivia. Sarah appeared to be wearing a chip on her shoulder. Why? What had she done to offend a housekeeper she'd just met? The reason would have to wait. Dinner smelled yummy, and she hadn't eaten since the sandwich in Horatio's office at noon.

Sarah poured white wine into a goblet. Then set it in front of Olivia.

Olivia admired the beautiful glass before she picked it up and took a sip. The deep cuts could only be Waterford—an old pattern. Her grandmother had good taste.

Sarah set the silver butter dish next to the basket of corn bread to Olivia's left. "I'll bring coffee later with dessert. Just touch the button next to your right foot, and I'll come for your plates."

"Thank you, Sarah, this looks delicious."

"I hope you enjoy it, ma'am."

Olivia had two helpings, and the corn bread was the best she'd ever eaten. If Sarah considered this a simple meal then Olivia would, at least, eat well. After finishing the last morsel on her plate, Olivia leaned back in her chair. She studied the ornate plaster ceiling. Elaborate raised medallions covered the entire space. The wiring on the chandelier was attached to the outside of the crystal arms. It must have held candles before electricity. She needed to get a closer look. She got up and moved to the center of the table. Placing her hands for support, she leaned over as far as she could and looked up.

Olivia didn't hear the door swing open until Sarah entered carrying a tray. "Waterford. Your great-grandmother brought it back with her on a trip to Europe and had it wired for electricity."

Shit, why was she feeling like a child who's just been caught with her hand in the cookie jar? This was her house and she could look all she wanted. Olivia went back to her chair without saying a word.

"I brought coffee and a piece of my lemon meringue pie." Sarah set the pie in front of Olivia and poured the coffee. "While you finish, I'll go on upstairs and unpack your bags."

"Oh, you don't need to do that, Sarah. I unpacked before I dressed for dinner."

"Taking care of your needs is my job, ma'am." Olivia recognized Sarah's expression as the same one her mother used before scolding the twins.

"I'm sorry, all this is new to me. Just give me time and I'll figure it out."

"Yes, ma'am. I'll be in the kitchen if you need me," Sarah said as she headed for the swinging door.

Olivia continued observing the beautiful details of the room while she ate. She wished Travis were here. Perhaps she wouldn't feel so much like an alien with him at her side. Maybe that was the reason Sarah assumed Olivia would bring folks with her—for conversation and company.

Half an hour later Olivia touched the button on the floor. Within seconds Sarah came through the door.

"Thank you for the lovely dinner. It's been a long day. I think I'll turn in early."

"What time would you like breakfast, ma'am?"

Any more decisions today and Olivia's head was going to explode. Sarah was waiting for an answer, and Olivia needed to get comfortable giving her orders. "How about seven o'clock? That will give me time before Horatio picks me up to explore the house . . . if that's okay with you?"

"It's your house now, ma'am. I took all the dust covers off the furniture and got the bedrooms ready for your guests. You don't have to ask for permission. Just tell me what you want."

That chip just got bigger. Why the attitude? This was much too early in their relationship for a confrontation. "Okay, Sarah. I'll see you in the morning."

Back upstairs, in the large luxurious bathroom and dressing room, Olivia changed into her favorite nightgown. With the generous amount of marble and ornate fixtures, Olivia calculated the space must have been taken from an adjoining room sometime before the 1920s. Exhausted both mentally and physically, Olivia crawled between the sheets. She'd left the bathroom light on and cracked the door just enough to give the room some light. She glanced up at the portrait hanging over the fireplace. "Sorry, Great-grandmother. I don't think I'm ready to sleep in a dark room with you watching me." The words came out as if she were talking to a real person in the room. "Oh, boy. This is weird." She rolled over on her side and pulled the covers up over her head.

Olivia awoke at her usual six o'clock. She'd slept through the night, something that hadn't happened in more years than she cared to remember.

She got out of bed and walked over to the portrait. "I have a weird feeling you had something to do with that. Thanks, I feel ready to take on the world, *and* the Morrison brothers."

Dressed in casual black slacks and a cashmere sweater, Olivia arrived at the dining room door just as Sarah finished arranging the place setting. The glow from the chandelier highlighted her light brown complexion. A healthy spattering of freckles spoke of a biracial heritage. It was an interesting face. Not pretty . . . maybe the word was handsome. A few laugh lines creased the corners of her eyes and mouth. So far there was no indication that she ever laughed.

Sarah hesitated at the door. "I'll bring your breakfast. Would you like coffee or tea?"

Her tone was cold. She was all business.

"Tea sounds good this morning."

Olivia sat down and smoothed her napkin on her lap a second before Sarah came through the door. The plate she set before Olivia could feed two. "This looks delicious. I love ham."

"This is Virginia ham. We smoke it right here on the farm. I'll be right back with your tea. I steeped a pot of Earl Grey."

Olivia moved the grits around with her fork. She'd never acquired a taste for the staple of the South. But unless she wanted to take a chance on offending Sarah she'd better try a little harder. With Olivia's mouth full of what amounted to grainy wallpaper paste, Sarah returned with a silver pot of tea.

"Just ring if you need something."

Olivia nodded. It was all she could manage with a mouth full of goo. Still trying to swallow, Olivia poured tea into the dainty little cup. The tea helped wash the glob down while she cut a piece of ham. It only took one bite of the delicious looking ham for Olivia to grab for the half-empty cup. Salty! How could ham be this salty? She gulped down the tea to cleanse her palate before she turned to the biscuits and gravy. She sighed. They looked good, but if she didn't want to get on Sarah's bad side, she'd better finish the ham and grits. She needed more tea. But the pot was empty and her plate still full.

Olivia tapped the button under the table. In less than a minute Sarah came into the room. "Can I get you something, ma'am?"

"I'd like more tea, please."

Sarah raised an eyebrow and shook the pot. "It'll be just a few minutes, ma'am."

While she waited for the tea, Olivia looked at the salty ham and the bland grits. Maybe if she dipped a piece of ham into the grits it wouldn't taste quite so salty. It turned out to be a palatable combination. Olivia started in on the biscuits and gravy while she waited for the tea.

Sarah arrived with the steaming pot of Earl Grey. "Will that be all ma'am?"

Olivia nodded her thanks with a mouthful of biscuits.

She refilled her cup with tea and placed a dab of grits on a small piece of ham. Olivia took a bite then washed it down with a swallow. A short time later, and after drinking two pots, she was able to sit back in her chair, proud she'd finished. Now, the only problem was how long her bladder could hold out before exploding.

Olivia anticipated the eminent rush to the nearest toilet when Sarah came into the room. "It looks like you enjoyed your breakfast, ma'am." Sarah picked up the silver pot and shook it. "You sure do like your tea, ma'am."

Feeling frustrated, Olivia didn't know if it was proper to broach the subject that'd been bothering her since her arrival, but she had to try. "Sarah, please call me Olivia."

Sarah shook her head. "That was your grandmother's name, ma'am."

"Well, my middle name is Maureen. Would that work?"

"That was your mother's name, ma'am."

This wasn't going well, but Olivia couldn't give up just yet. "There have been a few people in my life I've allowed to call me Livy."

Sarah's large brown eyes focused on Olivia's. Her brow knit as if a battle raged within her. "Yes, ma'am."

"If you must call me ma'am, then what am I supposed to call you?"

"Sarah . . . just plain old Sarah."

This was going nowhere. She didn't know where she stood with Sarah. But she couldn't deal with it now.

Olivia got to her feet. "Where's my grandmother's office?"

"Take the passage to the back of the house . . . turn right through the next room . . . then follow the hallway until it ends. The door to the office is on the left, just before the library."

Sarah definitely had an attitude. "Take the passage?"

"The entrance hall, as you called it. It's commonly known as the passage in these grand old houses."

"And the closest bathroom?"

"Once you get to the hallway to the library, it's the first door on your left."

Olivia found her way without trouble. She expected to find a powder room, but this was a full bath, complete with claw-footed tub and pedestal sink, not unlike the fixtures found in the Captain's house.

After finishing in the bathroom, Olivia turned left and headed down the hall until it ended at a wide arched doorway. The magnificent library ended any further thoughts of finding the office. Olivia could just make out a walled garden through the large Palladian window. Overstuffed sofas and chairs in a mix of patterns created comfortable seating areas in the center of the room. Small tables and lamps were strategically placed for late night reading. A drop-leaf table sat beneath the window on the river's side of the room, waiting for a game of cards or perhaps a picture puzzle. The only wall that didn't contain bookshelves sported a large fireplace and French doors going out onto a screened porch.

According to her mother's journals she'd spent many hours in this cozy room of knowledge. A clock chimed drawing Olivia's attention to the mantle. It was eight o'clock, and she still needed to check out the office. She headed back out into the hall. There were only two doors, fairly close together. She opened the one without a lock. She stepped into a small closet. Two of its walls had large brass hooks at shoulder level. A yellow rain slicker, umbrella and a fleece-lined sheepskin jacket hung on one wall. Olivia stepped out and closed the door. She pulled the keys out of her pocket. The door closest to the library contained a new deadbolt. The key slid easily into the lock.

The room was smaller than she expected, with just one window looking onto the driveway and an unadorned fireplace next to it. An enormous roll-top desk took up nearly one whole wall. The opposite wall, which would be behind the library fireplace, held a long table and two ladder-back chairs. A rather small door in the corner concealed steep stairs leading to the floor above. But further exploration would have to wait for another day.

A brief search of the desk and file cabinets produced nothing more than estate-related information. Engrossed in investigating the desk's many small compartments, Olivia jumped at the ringing phone. Glancing at the multi-line phone sitting next to the desk, she wondered if she should answer. Fear of stepping on Sarah's toes won over and then the ringing mercifully stopped.

It wasn't long before Sarah knocked on the doorframe. "There's someone named Megan on the phone for you, Ma'am." Sarah stood with her hands on her hips.

Olivia reached for the handset. "Thank you."

"You can answer the phone yourself, you know," Sarah said with impatience.

"I'm sorry. I just assumed the call was for you. I didn't think anyone would be calling me yet."

"We have our own line in the kitchen. If you don't answer by the fourth ring, I'll pick-up."

"Thank you. I'll remember next time."

Olivia put the phone to her ear. "Hello, Meg?"

"Olivia, are you okay? I was just about to hang up. Travis gave me your number."

How wonderful it was to hear a friendly voice from home. "I'm fine. My housekeeper told me it's okay if I answer the phone."

"Why wouldn't you be able to answer your own phone?"

"For the same reason I'm not supposed to unpack my own luggage."

"What? I don't understand." Meg sounded confused.

"Never mind. Let's just say that life in the South is like learning a whole new language. I'm beginning to see how a war could have started between the North and the South. At least I haven't been called a Yankee, yet."

"So, I guess you don't want to hear how I'm bored to death with this job. I think they hired me just to please Patsy. Any snot-nose kid out of school could easily handle this routine of filing and some Accounting 101."

"I'm sorry to hear that. I know how you like a challenge. But give it . . ."

"Oops, gotta go. I'm on the hospital's time-clock and I hear the pitter-patter of my bosses heels coming down the hall."

Olivia slowly replaced the handset and looked over the many cubbyholes still waiting to be explored. It was nice talking to Meg, even if it was just for a couple minutes. Their stormy friendship, lasting more than twenty plus years, should have ended the year before when Olivia left East Side General. But she trusted her. Meg had proven to be a good friend, and friends were currently in short supply. It would have been so much nicer if her first call could have been from Travis.

With a heaving sigh, she pulled the roll-top down in place with a thud.

18

Olivia sat on the bench in the dressing room, tugging the zipper up the last inch on her knee-high, black leather boot.

The knock on the doorframe startled Olivia. Sarah stood with her hands folded at her waist. "Mister Dumbarton has arrived, ma'am. He's just now come through the gates."

"Thanks, Sarah. I'll be down in a minute." Olivia expected her to leave and head back downstairs to let Horatio in. But she hesitated for a second, a frown creeping across her brow.

Olivia stood, smoothing the pencil-slim skirt of her black Chanel suit. "Do I look okay?" Sarah's eyes rested on the mink coat draped over the chair in front of the dressing table. "Am I a bit over-dressed? This would be fine up North."

"No, you look good, ma'am. I'll go see to Mr. Dumbarton."

Olivia moved to stand before the full-length mirror.

Mirrors didn't lie. She looked damn good. She could kiss whoever invented shoulder pads. They gave her the power of a Major General and the strength of a linebacker. Olivia felt ready to take on McLeod and Morrison.

Horatio turned right onto Route 5. The car's heater blasted hot air in Olivia's direction. At this rate her face would melt before ever reaching Norfolk.

Horatio pulled down the visor, shielding his eyes from the morning sun. "We'll get to the shipyard around eleven."

"Eleven? It's a two-hour drive?"

"Sometimes more. Sometimes less. All depends. Summer brings the tourists. We'll be passing Williamsburg."

The longest commute Olivia had ever made was half and hour. Granted, during major snowstorms it could reach an hour or more, but that rarely happened. She'd picked up a map of Virginia at the auto club in Sandusky on her way back from the meeting with Uncle Lionel and Stanton. The distance from Charles City to Norfolk hadn't looked that far.

"How often did my grandmother make the trip?"

"A few times a month. Sometimes more if she had a lot of her charity events going on." Horatio patted Olivia's hand. "Benjamin drove her. She used the time well. The backseat in her big Cadillac is outfitted with a phone, a bar, and a desk that folds down from the back of the front seat. She loved her two hours of quiet time."

Now, all those passages Olivia had read in her mother's journals about her father's infrequent visits to Fairfield made sense. There were few references made about her father, especially during the war years. He seemed to travel a great deal and for long periods of time.

"Horatio, where did my grandfather stay? I've been reading my mother's journals and I know he didn't spend much time at Fairfield."

"The house in Norfolk. Been in your family since it was built in 1792. McLeod House belongs to you now."

Olivia vaguely remembered Uncle Lionel mentioning a house in Norfolk when he came to Marblehead to notify her of her inheritance. Horatio had briefly gone over the contents of her grandmother's will in his office before the meeting with the Morrison brothers. Somehow she had forgotten about this house, maybe because her mother had never mentioned it in the journals. Interesting. Olivia realized she knew practically nothing about her grandfather.

"Most of the bridges over the James are relatively new. The trip in your grandfather's day took even longer. He had a couple really fast boats he often used. Docked right in front of Fairfield."

"So I take it you're pretty much screwed in an emergency. No getting to the office in a hurry. No running back for a forgotten briefcase or report."

Horatio chuckled. "There's always the McLeod and Morrison helicopter."

Houses, fast boats, a car with a bar and a desk, and now a helicopter. The enormity of her inheritance suddenly hit. Her chest tightened. She couldn't breathe. Olivia snapped the air vent closed. She wanted to open the window. She needed cold air—almost as good as a splash of cold water.

"Don't you need a pad or something to land those things?" Olivia asked as she unbuttoned her coat.

"There's one outside the wall, near the service gate. You wouldn't have noticed it from the house."

Scooting forward to the edge of the seat, Olivia shrugged out of her coat and tossed the mink onto the back seat.

"Oh, I'm sorry, my dear. I didn't think about the heater being turned up so high." Horatio moved the lever to midway on the dial. "Forty degrees must feel down right balmy to you."

"Thanks. I would have let you know before I passed out."

Horatio patted Olivia's hand again. "I'm glad to see a hint of that sense-of-humor I've heard so much about over the years."

Liver spots. The hand patting reminded Olivia of her grandfather Thompson. His hands had liver spots. Gramps had patted her hands often, usually when Gran was in one of her moods. Her strict nature never understood the needs of a teenager, but Gramps did.

"I'm surprised you know so much about me. You obviously did your homework."

"Olivia, my dear, I've known of you since you were born."

A chill raced down Olivia's spine. "But how is that possible?"

"A deep hatred started brewing within your grandmother toward Angus when he cut off all contact with her only child. Olivia loved her daughter more than anything in this world. In the beginning, your grandmother didn't really believe Angus would follow through with his threat of disinheriting her as well. Maureen was his only child, and your grandmother felt certain he would want to know how she was doing. But just when it seemed he *might* give in, his anger would flare up again. That's when her obsession with revenge took hold."

Olivia clutched her hands. "She hired you as her attorney?"

"Yes. In a fit of rage, Angus threw a copy of his new will at your grandmother to show her he wasn't making idle threats. I was young and ambitious and determined to help this heartbroken woman who was being treated so unfairly. It could only have been the good Lord himself who showed me the passage. I couldn't believe a loophole had been left for us, but there it was."

The direction sign for Williamsburg loomed off in the distance. What could her mother have done to cause such anger in her father? From everything Olivia had read so far, he'd treated her like a princess. Unless the problem was Fred. Angus, and apparently Mr. Morrison, had tried to prevent the marriage between Maureen and Fred. Olivia swallowed the lump in her throat.

"As long as your grandmother had no contact with Maureen or any child of Maureen's, she would inherit her husband's entire estate. There was no mention about who *she* could or could not name as her heir. Having no contact with her daughter and grandchildren just about killed her, but she did it."

The lump crept back up, along with a pain in her chest. Olivia swallowed pushing them back. "I've hated her nearly my entire life because I thought she'd abandoned us. I hope she never realized."

"She was so proud of you. Lionel Montgomery sent me the financial reports for his company in which she owned stock. He used to slip newspaper clippings, photos and letters about you into the pages of those reports. I relayed everything to your grandmother by way of New York, so nothing was ever kept at Fairfield."

"Really?" Shock at what Horatio had divulged crept through her.

"Yep. There's a secret compartment in her desk where she kept everything. She couldn't take the slightest chance that Angus might make an unexpected visit to New York and find them."

Hot, burning, rivers of tears streamed down Olivia's cheeks. Had it been worth all the sacrifices Grandmother had made? For what? A battle over a company? Olivia would rather have had her grandmother. She needed her grandmother twenty years ago—the summer she'd caused the death of her family.

Olivia searched her purse for a tissue. "It's so unfair." Horatio handed her his handkerchief. "There's so much to deal with—and it's all new to me."

"Life here really isn't so different from what you've already experienced. Fairfield is similar in size to the Montgomery estate in Cedar Hill. It's only about two hundred years older. If you could survive the strict protocol laid down by your mother-in-law, then you can surely deal with Sarah and our Southern ways."

"But that was diff . . ."

"No it wasn't. You dealt with servants and entertaining while married to Brian, and don't forget your mansion in Marblehead is also a historic property. You've won more than your fair share of major battles. I have no doubt you'll win this one as well."

He was right. But right or not, this was more than a battle. And like any General, Olivia needed a tactical plan.

Horatio reached over and patted her hand. "You do have friends here." His smooth Southern drawl soothed ragged nerves. "Give us a chance, Olivia. Just open your eyes . . . and your heart."

Warmth from deep inside dried the tears. Yes, she was going to make friends. After all, she'd already found a grandfather. Olivia squeezed Horatio's hand.

They'd made the trip from Fairfield to Norfolk in under two hours. Horatio waved at the guard in the McLeod and Morrison guardhouse. The wide gate slid open with the clank of steel-on-steel.

"You'll like Gertrude." Horatio glanced at the rearview mirror as the gate closed behind them. "She started with the company right out of college—about forty years ago. Your grandfather hired her as his secretary a year later, and then your grandmother kept her on after his death. You can trust her without question."

Horatio pulled up to the McLeod and Morrison administration building and turned off the ignition. The shiny bronze plaque on the wall identified the parking space as belonging to McLeod. "The first McLeod arrived from Scotland and settled in the area in the late 1600's to build some of the finest sailing ships on the Chesapeake. Only later when steel starting replacing wood that the merger with Morrison Steel of Pennsylvania had occurred. Imagine, it could have ended up being McLeod and Carnegie if the deal had been favorable."

Olivia sprang from the car before Horatio had time to grab his briefcase. "I love the Art Deco period," she said as she grabbed her coat from the backseat.

Shifting her purse from one hand to the other while she pulled on the mink, Olivia pointed toward the ornate frieze above the entrance. "This is magnificent. Look, its Poseidon poised above waves."

"This building was erected in 1930, the same year as the Chrysler Building in New York. It was old man Morrison's idea to show the world that nothing but the best would be produced by McLeod and Morrison. And, of course, he placed the building right up front, along one of Norfolk's major roads, where everyone driving by could see it."

Mom mentioned her concern over the Morrison's lavish lifestyle in her journal. She'd even questioned her father about the difference between the families' spending habits. This certainly was an example of that extravagance. "Where's the original building?"

"Out in the middle of the shipyard. Your great-great-grandfather McLeod built a new factory office in 1850 after the previous one burned down. The threat of fires had always been a problem, so he incorporated the latest fire prevention technology and built with brick and stone. It's mostly used for storage now. You'll be able to see it from your office. Clive wants to bulldoze it, but Wilson wants to turn it into a gym. McLeod Shipbuilders moved to this location in 1730. The yard has expanded many times over."

"Oh my God." Her breath caught in her throat. Horatio's words couldn't have shocked Olivia more had he told her that her ancestors were from Mars. "My ancestors were here on this spot struggling to survive since before the United States was even a country. Two hundred and fifty-five years and those ass-hole brothers want to strip me of my heritage."

No way was that going to happen.

Olivia slapped her black leather clutch bag against her leg. "Sounds like the brothers are already making changes to *my* family's business. We'll see about that. There's a new McLeod moving in."

Horatio held open one of the tall, ornate bronze doors. "Chin up, Olivia. We're taking the enemy by surprise."

Olivia's stiletto heels clicked along the marble floor.

Horatio guided her to the office at the far end of the hall on the fourth floor. He entered the room then stopped, setting his briefcase on the desk. "Where's Gertrude?" He asked in a calm, inquiring voice.

From the doorway, the office appeared large enough to have a sitting area. Tastefully decorated with colors of mauve and blue, Olivia got a glimpse of cherry furniture, typical of what might be found in Williamsburg. Horatio blocked her view of the person behind the desk.

Taking a few steps into the room, Olivia abruptly stopped at Horatio's side.

Good God. The young woman, with Farrah Fawcett hair, seated behind the desk wore a suit jacket in hot pink polyester.

This wasn't Gertrude.

"Hi, I'm Candy. Can I help you?"

"Of course you are—like a box of Good & Plenty," mumbled Olivia.

Horatio grabbed his briefcase and headed toward a door on the far side of the room.

Candy jumped out of her chair, planting her hands on the desk. "What are you doing? You can't go in there!" She leaned forward.

Olivia inhaled sharply. One more deep breath and Candy's breasts were gonna bust loose. Even in the North, this much cleavage wasn't appropriate in a business setting. Horatio was getting quite the eye-full.

"I asked you where Gertrude is." The veins in Horatio's neck bulged.

"She doesn't work in this office anymore." Candy reached for her phone. Long, florescent pink nails tapped in a number.

A steno pad and pen were the only objects on the desk. The credenza held nothing but a vase of flowers. The typewriter sitting off to the side was tightly covered, not that those nails could type anything legible. What was Candy's job? Every one of Olivia's secretaries had kept a messy office. Even her office could have been described as organized clutter.

Horatio opened the door. "What the hell?" He took two steps into the room.

That didn't sound good. Olivia followed Horatio to the doorway.

A glass and chrome desk sat in the middle of the office. Brightly-colored abstract oil paintings lined the dark paneled walls. A yellow leather sofa and two zebra print chairs sat on a large red area rug.

"Looks like Candy did the decorating," Olivia whispered as she shuffled past Horatio and moved further into the room.

"What's going on here?" Olivia and Horatio turned toward Wilson's raised voice coming from Candy's office.

"I'm sorry, Wilson, they just barged in. I tried to stop them."

"Sounds like trouble just arrived," Olivia murmured. "Hmm. She called him Wilson. Interesting."

"What are you doing in my office?" Wilson bellowed as he rushed past Olivia and Horatio to stand behind his desk.

His paisley tie hung limply over a bulging belly. Didn't look like he'd made any attempt to button his suit jacket. Yep, the overweight Blowfish still fit. Perhaps turning the old building into a gym wasn't a bad idea.

"I tried to keep them out, Wilson. They want to know where Gertrude is." Candy slumped in the doorway twisting her hands. Hot pink glowed in the late-morning sunlight streaming in through the windows. Her skirt was short—way too short for business. With black stockings and higher-than-high heels, she looked more like a hooker than the secretary of the CFO of a major corporation.

"Never mind. I'll handle this." Wilson spoke to Candy, but his eyes never left Olivia.

He was assessing the opposition. Olivia's lips pulled at the corners ever so slightly. What he saw was a black mink coat, framing an expensive black suit, adorned with the appropriate single stand of pearls. Good thing Olivia chose to pull her hair into the chignon that morning. Every warrior needed a helmet. Was that a twitch of his left eye? Yep, it did it again.

Horatio took a few steps toward the desk. "Well, well, Wilson. I bring Mrs. Bentley to her office and look what I find. Did you even wait until Olivia McLeod was cold in her grave?"

"What does he mean, Wilson?" Candy sounded confused. "This is your office and you got rid of all that ugly old furniture."

Wilson glared at Candy. "Get back to work." He touched the corner of his left eye.

Horatio remained calm—the perfect Southern gentleman. "I'll ask one more time. *Where* is Gertrude?"

Horatio's grip on his briefcase tightened. His knuckles turned white—a tiger—one snarl away from a pounce.

Wilson tucked his hands into his trouser pockets. "She found a job that suited her better, down in Human Resources."

"I want to see Olivia's office returned to the way it was and Gertrude back where she belongs." Horatio spoke in a slow, determined voice that left no option for debate.

The dueling men gave Olivia time to take in her surroundings. This was no more a working office than Fairfield's dining room. Not a single file folder or computer report in sight. Two doors, side-by-side, filled the space along one wall. Both closed. Perhaps a private bathroom? And the other, maybe a closet or some kind of workroom. Paneled walls, reminiscent of the captain's cabin in an old Errol Flynn movie, fought with chrome and glass. She wanted to take a look out of the massive corner windows. Olivia wanted to see what her grandmother had seen—what she had been keeping safe—waiting for the day when Olivia would take over.

Candy strutted further into the room to face Wilson. "You said this was going to be your office as soon as the old lady died."

Wilson took his hands out of his pockets and placed them on either side of him on the desk. "Not now, Candy," he said through clenched teeth.

Candy jammed her hands on her hips. "But you promised I would be your secretary as soon as you took over and got Gertrude out of the way."

Are we having a little tantrum? Candy better watch how far she throws those elbows back. Pink buttons are ready to explode and Wilson's in the direct line of fire. Olivia found the relationship between the two interesting—she's no more a secretary than Betty Boop.

"Enough, Candy! Get back to work." Wilson's eyes narrowed. His hands balled into fists. "Listen, Dumbarton, this is my office. You'd better get this woman out of here until our attorneys say she has a right to be here. At that time I'll find a suitable office for her."

"This has always been the McLeod office. Now it's Olivia's. So I'm giving you forty-eight hours to put this back as it was."

Candy turned and took a few steps toward the door then hesitated. "I thought Olivia was dead. Now you say she's gonna move back. This isn't fair! Wilson, I don't want to move to a different office."

Wilson's ruddy complexion turned bright red. Could he actually be feeling embarrassed by Candy's actions? She's no secretary. He pointed in the direction of Candy's office. "Go! Now!"

Clenching her fists, Candy stomped out of the office with a toss of her blonde mane.

Despite the tantrum, and the whining, she had a pleasant voice. A part of Olivia actually felt sorry for her. Candy was way out of her league. Where *did* he find her?

Leaving Horatio and Wilson to spar over her legal rights, Olivia followed Candy back to her desk.

"Look, I realize this is all quite confusing so let's start at the beginning. I'm Olivia Thompson Bentley. My grandmother was Olivia McLeod and upon her death I inherited her shares in this company, just like she inherited them from her husband, Angus."

"I get it now." Candy sat down in her desk chair, tugging at the low-cut jacket. "Wilson likes me to dress like this."

"I don't imagine you fit in with the other secretaries. It must be hard for you."

"I don't have any friends." Tears welled in her eyes. "So this really isn't going to be Wilson's office?"

"No, Candy. I believe you'll need to plan for another move."

Candy opened a drawer and pulled a tissue from a box. She wiped her eyes then leaned forward resting her folded arms on the desk, covering her breasts. "Yeah. Wilson isn't going to like this. He has a temper, you know."

Olivia glanced toward the open door and the sound of raised voices beyond.

"I noticed."

19

The gate slid to the side as it opened. Olivia waved at the guard from the front seat of Horatio's Cadillac. "Well, that didn't go well."

"I misjudged Wilson. I didn't expect him to move that quickly. I only hope we can retrieve the files that were removed along with the furniture."

"What files are you referring to? They must have been important to Grandmother if they've disappeared."

"Half of the first floor is taken up by a state-of-the-art computer center. However, your grandmother liked keeping all the older reports—especially the financials—in hard copy. All she had to do if she had a question about something was go to one of her file cabinets. She didn't like requisitioning a report from the Data center just to have them run the wrong one."

The answer to her grandmother's death, if she was murdered, could be in those cabinets. "We need to find those files before Wilson makes them disappear," said Olivia.

"Not necessarily. Gertrude took carloads of reports out to Fairfield."

Looked like it was going to be Olivia's job to search those files. She'd been reviewing and analyzing reports since her first job out of college. How hard could this be? "What do we do next?"

"We'll stop for lunch, then I'm dropping you off at the house. I'm calling William. I wonder how much he knows about this."

"How could William not know?" Olivia's heart sank at the thought that he could be in on this. Her mother had loved him—he'd been her fiancé.

"He's not here on a day-to-day basis. His main office is in DC where the majority of his work relative to government contracts is done. He has the corner office across the hall from yours. He rarely uses it. At least it will be yours once Wilson removes himself and that ghastly furniture from the premises."

"Why do you think Wilson moved into Grandmother's office? He or Clive must have taken over their father's office after he died. From everything I've learned, I'm sure the Morrison offices would have been far bigger than the McLeod."

"You're right. Clive and Wilson have the corner offices at the other end of the building. Not only are they larger, but they have a magnificent view of the Elizabeth River."

"So it's Wilson's way of eliminating whatever power the McLeod name may still have." It was going to take more than expensive clothes to intimidate those boys—Olivia needed to be smarter. "What about Candy? I wonder where he found her? She certainly isn't secretary material. I never once heard her refer to Wilson as Mr. Morrison."

"Wilson has a very capable assistant. Candy is little more than a receptionist. He'll tire of her and move on to someone new. I'm betting on sooner, rather than later. Wilson's anger toward her steamed like a pressure cooker—he was ready to explode."

Images from the first meeting in Richmond flashed like an instant replay. "He's got an eye twitch when he's irritated. A bulging vein in his neck gives away his anger. He also clenches his fists. Wilson had the same physical reactions during the meeting in your office."

"Very observant. Your attention to details will come in handy down the road."

What else did Olivia have to do? Her office had disappeared and Horatio did all the talking. Correction, Horatio did all the demanding. Today's events could be added as another obstacle for her to overcome. That stack was getting higher—any higher and she wouldn't be able to knock them down.

Horatio pushed the visor back in place. "You have a pensive look on that lovely face. Something else bothering you? Want to talk about it?"

That's just what her grandfather Thompson would have said. Always quick with his opinion, but never told her what to do. She missed those days. "Sarah and I have gotten off to a rocky start. I'm sure it's my fault. Everything is new, including the food. I hate eating my meals alone in that massive dining room. I'm messing up, big-time. I'm afraid she doesn't like me. Sometimes, I just want to scream. I don't know how to ask her for help."

"Olivia, it's your house. You can have your meals served to you in any room you choose. Your grandmother often ate in the library or her office. She liked watching old black and white movies and often ate in front of the TV."

"Really? I would like that. But I don't want Sarah to feel like I'm being difficult."

"Olivia, she works for you. You pay her very well. Give her time, you'll have no greater ally."

"I don't want her to feel like I'm some upstart ordering her around."

"Sarah's always known about you. After Angus died, your grandmother was free to talk about you—she just couldn't have contact. Has it occurred to you that Sarah might be having a hard time as well?"

The Ice Queen? There hadn't been so much as a tiny bit of warmth from Sarah. Not even a hint that there might be a crack in her icy shield.

Horatio pulled into the parking lot of an old house with a sign in the front yard claiming to have the best Southern food within fifty miles.

"Olivia, I can't help you with that. It's one of those things you and Sarah will have to work out yourselves." Horatio patted her hand. "Right now, I want to make sure you stay alive long enough to solve your differences with Sarah."

A numbing chill coursed through Olivia. Horatio believed someone killed her grandmother. Did he think she was next? Maybe now was the time to get this out in the open.

Horatio got out and walked around the car and opened Olivia's door.

Her heart raced.

He helped her out and they walked toward the porch steps.

"I'm thinking your comment just now was no joke. You really do believe someone murdered Grandmother. Are you thinking one of the Morrison brothers?"

The hostess greeted them, and Horatio asked for the table in the far corner. The Victorian furnishings, floral wallpaper and lace curtains were meant to feel warm and homey. But all Olivia felt was cold.

They both ordered the fish chowder with a side of cornbread.

"Yes. I'm as sure as I can be that either Clive or Wilson was responsible for the death of your grandmother. I don't think they could have done it alone."

No, of course not. Neither one was stupid enough to have actually killed her. Most likely they paid someone else to do the job. But who?

Horatio leaned forward. "About a year ago she began complaining about being tired. I didn't think much of it at the time. Most old people complain about being tired."

"Didn't she see her doctor?"

"Sure. Your grandmother had a heart condition and a history of pneumonia. A complete physical was done. The tests were within normal ranges."

The waitress brought their tea.

"She wanted to attend your husband's funeral, but she said she was just too old and too tired to make the trip. She'd just bought a new Gulfstream so she could travel in comfort and luxury—even has a bedroom in the back. Benjamin or Sarah would have gone with her. Three months before her death, your grandmother complained about being sleepy and feeling physically weak. She needed Benjamin to help her up and down the stairs to her room. Finally she became so weak that Benjamin began carrying her."

Olivia wasn't a doctor but she'd spent enough years in the medical profession to know it certainly sounded like poison—but how? And didn't poisons work quickly? "Horatio, was she still going to the office when the symptoms began?"

"Yes. Your grandmother was not only going to the yard, but her various charities kept her on the go, as well."

Olivia tapped her spoon against the folded napkin. If Grandmother was being poisoned, it most likely started at McLeod and Morrison. But she died months later at Fairfield. "She must have gone back to her doctor. Didn't he, or she, have any answers?"

"She came down with pneumonia again. Not even a few days in the hospital could produce any answers as to why she was so weak, except for the pneumonia. Although, she *was* feeling better when she left and returned home. Her doctor prescribed a higher dose of her medication for her heart and arranged for a nurse to come by every day. A week or two later she was replaced by a nurse that moved in."

That was interesting. What was the nurse doing if the diagnosis was pneumonia? Sarah could have given her a heart pill and medication for pneumonia.

Horatio leaned back. "A hospital bed was brought in and placed in the library. She needed an electric wheelchair to get around, and still the doctor couldn't find a cause. She just kept getting weaker and weaker. And then she died."

How did they kill her if she'd stop going to the shipyard? Olivia needed to find the poison. Maybe it was in with the stuff Wilson removed from the office.

"Did the Morrison brothers come to the house during that time?"

"Just William. He would bring her the reports she asked for. Your grandmother didn't trust Clive and Wilson. In fact, she wouldn't let them in the house once Angus passed. Sarah helped keep them away."

Bowls of steaming fish chowder were placed before them. Next came a plate of cornbread and a saucer of whipped butter.

"I believe the brothers tried to poison your grandmother a year ago when she suddenly felt tired and weak. For whatever reason, maybe because of her infrequent visits, the poison wasn't working fast enough. What I find interesting is that her symptoms escalated once she was confined to Fairfield. The only outsider was the nurse. But she'd already left when your grandmother died."

Olivia spread her napkin across her lap. "Didn't you report your suspicions to the authorities?"

"Sure I did. But she'd had another bout with pneumonia. Her death certificate stated congestive heart failure."

They finished their meals in silence.

The waitress came to remove their plates. She asked if they'd like dessert.

Horatio and Olivia both shook their heads, then the waitress handed the bill to Horatio.

Olivia's stomach twisted. A veil of ice draped over her. "Horatio, are you sure I'm safe at Fairfield?"

He squeezed her hand. "Absolutely. If I didn't think you'd be safe, I'd never let you stay there."

20

As if the morning hadn't been bad enough, Olivia struck out reviewing the financial reports in her grandmother's office. The antique wall clock chimed five times. She'd spent two hours searching page after page, nothing jumped out at her. What could her grandmother have been looking for? The old oak desk chair squeaked ominously as she leaned back in frustration. Olivia envied smokers. It didn't matter what the crisis, whether the meal was good or bad, or they'd just had sex, a cigarette made everything right.

A floorboard squeaked in the hallway drawing Olivia's attention to the door.

"Here's a pot of tea, ma'am. Your grandmother always liked tea at this time." Sarah set the tray on the table. "Will that be all, ma'am?"

"Yes, thank you. Is dinner at seven?"

"Yes, ma'am. I hope you like fish."

Olivia stood and walked to the table. Sarah poured a fragrant blend into the dainty cup then handed it to Olivia.

"Mmm, smells good. I don't believe I recognize this."

"I blend it myself. It was your grandmother's favorite."

With one hand holding the saucer and the other steadying the cup, Olivia took the few steps back to the desk. Sturdy mugs were more in her comfort zone. Drinking from fragile cups was another thing she'd need to work on. Back at the desk, Olivia took a sip. "Delicious. I detect layers of herbs, floral undertones and orange. This may become my favorite afternoon pick-me-up."

Sarah nodded and left the room.

Still cold as ice. There had to be a way to approach Sarah. Somewhere, under that frozen façade, there was a warm, caring person. Horatio seemed to think so, and Horatio hadn't been wrong yet. Olivia wasn't about to give up this battle—hell, compared to Wilson, Sarah was no more than a skirmish.

What Olivia needed now was help—and a friendly voice. She knew Meg would be home from work by now. Megan O'Brien had helped her wade through financial reports in the past. She'd been the one to unravel the mystery of who'd been altering Olivia's reports to make it appear she was embezzling funds from East Side General Hospital. Perhaps Meg could do it again.

Olivia picked up the phone and dialed Meg's number.

Meg answered on the third ring.

"Meg, it's Olivia."

"Hey, I'm sorry about hanging up on you like that yesterday, but my supervisor . . ."

"Never mind. I've got a problem. I think you can steer me in the right direction."

"Sure. Fire away."

"My grandmother left me a rather cryptic note before she died. She felt something was very wrong. I think it may have been with the company finances. I've been reviewing the financial reports I found locked in my grandmother's desk. Everything seems to add up. Yet, she was worried about something."

"Are there multiple types of reports?"

The chair's wheels dragged across the worn rug. The faded oriental was nearly threadbare, but still Olivia needed to give her chair another strong push to reach the long table next to the desk.

Earlier, she'd laid out the various reports in stacks, with like ones together.

"Yes, and they all have notes written in the margins. Some of it makes no sense."

"Tell me," Meg said, a hint of interest creeping into her voice.

"Well, some of the Profit & Loss's go back two years. All the rest go back a year or less."

"What's the most recent date?"

Olivia had the stacks organized in order, with the most recent dates on top. "It looks like a report of customer orders and release dates, dated November 1984. My grandmother died in December." Olivia rubbed her forehead. "She has some arrows and numbered notations between a few of the lines." Olivia scanned the page again then shoved it aside. "I can't figure this out. I'm totally frustrated."

"Don't worry. It will all make sense," said Meg with an encouraging tone in her voice.

"I have one more pile." Olivia pulled a stack of documents forward. "These are supplier lists. It looks like contract dates and question marks have been penciled along the margins." Olivia fanned through them. "All the reports are marked up."

"Okay, now look at the expense section of the P & L, and tell me if there are any notations next to supplier names." Meg sounded excited.

Olivia shuffled through the reports. Maybe she was on the right track after all. "Yes, there are some. They match the ones she had contract notations next to."

"You need to find someone who your grandmother may have confided in. But it sounds to me like she was verifying expenses against orders."

Olivia leaned back feeling a bit more confident. The chair gave another ominous screech. She'd have Benjamin attack it with a squirt of oil. "Well, at least it gives me a starting point."

"All this is giving me a headache."

The line had been silent for too long. "Meg, are you still there?"

"Yeah, just thinking." In the pause, Olivia could hear her breathing. "How about your grandmother's secretary? Can you trust her?"

"I haven't met Gertrude yet. Apparently, Wilson, the CFO, buried her down in Human Resources."

"Sounds a little fishy to me. When will you be going back to your office?"

"I have no idea," Olivia said with a groan. "Grandmother's office was stripped and everything put in storage. Horatio wants me to stay here at the house until after he meets with William. I'm not to venture any further than the immediate area. Not even down to the river or out beyond the gate."

"Wow! Olivia, this sounds bad. Is there something you're not telling me?"

"I'm sorry, Meg, but it's a long story. I'm fine. Just a little tired. This house is amazing. It'll give me time to explore. Thanks for your help. I'll let you know what I find."

"Olivia, do you want me to come there and see what you have?"

Olivia rubbed her neck. "No, thanks. It's been a long, frustrating day. I'll call you. Bye for now."

Feeling too tired to continue with the financials, Olivia poured the last of the tea into her cup and headed to the library. Although large in size, the room felt warm and comfortable. The scent of old books reminded her of the libraries of her youth. The overstuffed sofa looked inviting. Olivia glanced at the mantel clock—there was time for a quick nap before dinner. She sat down and punched the center of a throw pillow to make the perfect dent for her head, then stretched out.

She closed her eyes.

The unfamiliar room could be in an old factory with its brick walls and high ceiling. Only a minimum amount of light found its way through the grimy windows set high up near the ceiling—too high for Olivia to see out. Huge machines, rusting in a pool of oil, sat idle. Why was she here? The soft squeak of rubber-soled shoes on concrete let Olivia know she wasn't alone. Fear turned her blood to ice, her heart raced. She scanned the walls for the door. There wasn't one. How had she gotten in? She ran toward the machinery. There had to be a door on the other side. The footsteps grew louder. Olivia glanced over her shoulder. A man, covered in seaweed, was chasing her. He waved an oar over his head—he had no face. She stumbled. With one giant leap he was on her. Olivia tried to fight off her attacker. "No! Stop! You're hurting me!"

"Ma'am, wake up. You have to wake up now."

It was Sarah's voice. She'd saved Olivia from the attacker.

Olivia struggled to open her eyes. Someone hovered over her—Sarah. "Were you hitting me?"

"I wasn't doing anything but trying to wake you up. It must have been a bad dream. I came to tell you dinner's ready." Sarah helped Olivia into a sitting position.

"I'm sorry Sarah, I must have been more tired than I realized." Olivia closed her eyes and took a deep breath. "I just wanted a quick nap."

"Does this mean you don't want your dinner?"

Olivia opened her eyes to see Sarah's concern. A comforting hand rested on her shoulder. "I'll be fine. Give me a few minutes in the bathroom, and I'll be ready for dinner."

Olivia leaned over the sink and splashed cold water on her face. She grabbed a towel and blotted her face. Where did this nausea come from? Olivia frowned at the ghastly image in the mirror. Concealer would take care of the dark circles. Hopefully, a good night's sleep would take care of her bloodshot eyes.

Sarah had said fish. Olivia's stomach rumbled all the way to the dining room. The Chesapeake Bay area was know for it's many varieties of fish. Olivia's mouth watered. Perhaps, there would be crab cakes waiting for her.

Sarah placed the platter within easy reach of Olivia.

Olivia grabbed the back of her chair. She was hallucinating. She had to be. There was a dead fish lying on the dining room table. Her stomach did a flip-flop.

"Is something wrong, ma'am? You're as white as a Magnolia blossom."

"Sarah, could you skin that or perhaps carve it for me? I have a problem eating something that's watching me."

"Sorry, ma'am. I didn't think." Sarah picked up the platter.

"It's okay. Everything else looks delicious. I'll just go ahead and start."

Sarah retrieved the platter then stopped before going through the swinging door. She glanced over her shoulder. It was the first time Olivia saw her smile. "So I guess this means I should wait a while before serving you greens cooked in bacon fat and pigs feet."

"Yeah. You might want to go easy on my Yankee palate."

Sarah winked before turning back toward the door.

Was the Ice Queen melting?

The tea tray was gone an hour later when Olivia returned to the office. Funny thing, she couldn't remember leaving the office earlier. She remembered talking to Meg, but nothing after that until Sarah woke her from a nightmare.

Evenings were supposed to be spent with Travis, not in a musty office. They'd build a fire and bask in its warmth while enjoying a bottle of wine. The evenings always ended the same—making love before glowing embers. She missed Travis. Olivia needed to hear his voice. She needed to hear that he loved her.

The financials would have to wait. Tomorrow was another day. According to Horatio's last phone call, the soonest she could return to McLeod and Morrison would be on Friday. Olivia locked the office door behind her and headed to the library.

She kicked off her shoes and stretched out on the sofa, tucking pillows at her back. Once settled, she reached for the phone. Travis answered on the second ring.

"Livy?"

That one word—her name warmed her heart. "Travis, I miss you so much."

"I miss *you*, Livy."

"I love you Travis."

"Does that mean I can catch the next plane to Richmond?"

"I wish I could say yes, but truth is I'm more confused than ever. I came here with the expectation of finding my mother's past and finding my heritage. As far as McLeod and Morrison, the legal stuff's in the hands of Horatio and William. I'm not willing to bet on the outcome. Wilson made it very clear that he's running the show."

"Are you at least comfortable at the house?"

Olivia chuckled. "Well, I'm comfortable in the library at least. You should see this room. George Washington would fit right in. I believe all the classics are on the shelves. There's history, the arts, and biographies on anyone worth knowing. Lots of books on every phase of government since we've had a government, and books on every war I've ever heard of and some I haven't. And, of course, you can't be on a plantation and not have books on farming, animal husbandry, and the proper handling of slaves, dated 1837."

"Are you happy there?"

"At least in Marblehead, I saw all of the rooms before I bought the house. I owned this house before I even got here. I still haven't seen the kitchen. There's a wing of the house I haven't explored, not to mention the grounds and outbuildings."

"Well, Livy, it doesn't sound like you need me as much as I need you. I hope you can find yourself, your mother's past, and come home. This is where you belong."

The hurt in Travis's voice ripped at Olivia's heart. She loved him with all her heart. He was the man she wanted to spend the rest of her life with. The problem was that she didn't have a clue where her new life would take her.

"I'm really tired, Travis. I do love you." Olivia yawned. "I'm drained. How about I call you tomorrow?"

"Sure. Good night, Livy."

Olivia grabbed a pillow, cradling it tight against her chest. She wanted, more than anything, to ask Travis to come. She needed him. But she had no idea what was ahead. Olivia turned off the lights and checked the locks on the doors and windows before leaving the library. She'd made checking the locks a nightly ritual at the Captain's house. Fairfield, on the other hand, had an elaborate security system that would announce anyone entering the grounds, let alone try to crawl through a window. She needed to relax. Surely lock checking was something that Sarah and Benjamin had a handle on.

The stairs creaked beneath her feet. Olivia found the sound comforting—just like the stairs in the Captain's house. She was too tired to do more than brush her teeth and slip on a warm nightgown before crawling into bed. Her great-grandmother's face glowed in the soft light from the bathroom.

"Goodnight, Great-Grandmother."

21

Olivia unfolded the napkin and placed it in her lap. She'd had another night of uninterrupted sleep. She wanted to believe her great-grandmother Alexandra had something to do that, but it was probably just mental exhaustion.

Sarah backed through the swinging door and carried the silver tray to the sideboard. "I hope you like scrambled eggs, ma'am. I added bacon instead of ham. I can bring you a slice if you'd like." She brought the plate to the table, placing it in front of Olivia.

"This looks delicious, Sarah. The bacon will be enough. Thank you."

Sarah set a basket of steaming biscuits next to a selection of three different jams.

"I'll just go and get your first pot of tea. A good strong English Breakfast Tea." Sarah disappeared behind the door before Olivia could tell her that one pot would be enough.

Olivia was taking the last bite of a biscuit when Sarah came back with the tea. "This is the most fabulous jam I've ever tasted. The Paterson family, back in Marblehead, makes jam for a living and I have to say that your jams are better. Not so sweet."

"Thank you, ma'am. I made all three myself. I can't take credit for the butter though . . . that came from Kroger."

Once upon a time Olivia and Brian had a beautiful dining room and fine, French china. She never ate there when home alone. It was a room filled with laughter and conversation with friends. Olivia glanced up at the ceiling. She didn't need to sit beneath a Waterford chandelier to enjoy her breakfast. It would have been delicious had it been served on everyday dishes and eaten in the kitchen.

Sarah poked her head around the door. "If you're finished ma'am, I'll clear the table."

"You're an excellent cook, Sarah. I'll just head to the library and get out of your way."

Olivia stood and turned to leave then stopped. "Oh, I forgot to tell you. Horatio wants me to stay here for the remainder of the week. But don't go to any trouble, a sandwich for lunch is fine."

"Yes, ma'am."

For more than an hour Olivia searched the desk and the file boxes stacked in the corner. The boxes Gertrude brought from McLeod and Morrison. The problem was she didn't know what she was looking for. Frustrating as it was, Olivia could go no further with the financial reports without help. She locked the desk and put the key in the pocket of her slacks.

"Excuse me, ma'am, but you have a caller. I put him in the gentlemen's parlor."

Olivia jumped, placing her hand over her heart. "Sorry, Sarah, I didn't hear you." Olivia guessed there weren't many floorboards in the whole house that didn't creek, so how did Sarah get around without a sound? "I have a caller?"

"Yes, ma'am," Sarah said then walked back down the hall.

Where would one put gentlemen callers? Olivia could chase after Sarah and ask—and appear stupid—or figure it out for herself. There couldn't be too many options. Parlors would be in the oldest part of the house.

When Olivia reached the main hall she found the very masculine room. The ornate paneling covered all four walls with built-in cabinetry in the corners. Dark green damask drapes framed the windows. But it was the tall man who stood casually against an intricately carved billiard table that filled the room with his presence. William Morrison.

Olivia had been right in her assessment of him in Horatio's conference room. He was tall, trim, and incredibly handsome—and wearing Armani.

He took a step forward. "It would appear this is your first time in this room. You look rather amazed." William reached out his hand.

Yes, Olivia *was* amazed—at both the room and the man. She took a few steps forward to take his outstretched hand. "Mr. Morrison, it's nice to see you again."

"Forget the formalities. It's William. I see confusion written all over your face. Horatio didn't tell you I was coming, and now you're wondering what role I play in this. Whose side am I on and why am I here?" His smile was warm and friendly. "You're so much like your mother. She wouldn't demand answers and throw me out either. She would listen first."

Olivia gave a warm chuckle. "I've been wondering what role you play in this drama. Actually, my confused look stems from the fact that you're a dead-ringer for Mom's favorite actor. She saw every Cary Grant movie he ever made and most several times. She kept a scrapbook of photos and articles she'd cut out from movie magazines."

"Interesting. I thought she was in love with Frank Sinatra."

Olivia motioned for William to sit in one of the two dark green leather chairs flanking the window. "You are correct in your assumption that this is the first time I've been in this room. I haven't had time to explore." Olivia moved to the opposite chair and sat down. "I thought Horatio was meeting with you today."

William leaned forward. "I'm meeting with Horatio this afternoon. He doesn't know I'm here. I was shocked to hear what Wilson did. I'm truly sorry. I'll make it right and put back the McLeod office as it was. I've contacted Gertrude and asked that she take anything she needs and work with you here. She was loyal to your grandmother, and she'll be loyal to you, as well. She'll arrive Monday at nine. When everything is in place, you'll both move into your offices at the yard."

William spoke with confidence and instantly she trusted his message. "Does this mean you believe I have a legal right to my grandmother's shares in the company?"

"Olivia Maureen McLeod was a smart and determined woman. If she and Horatio found a way to get even with Angus, then bully for her." William smiled. "I'll know for sure this afternoon. If it's true—and I can't imagine Horatio putting you through this if it isn't—then I'll support you."

"Thank you, William. I do trust you. My mother loved you, but she didn't marry you. I have to wonder why."

William leaned forward and took both of Olivia's hands in his. "I loved your mother . . . I still do. I carry her in my heart."

Olivia's heart wrenched at the sadness she saw in William's eyes. "Then what happened?"

"We were both being manipulated—your mother from the day she was born. I went along with it from the moment she captivated me with those mesmerizing violet eyes and her trusting soul. Helping her escape was the only honorable thing to do."

The chiming of the tall clock in the hall brought Olivia back to the present. "I'm sorry, William, I haven't offered you anything to drink. But, then again, I don't know what we have. Maybe I should find my way to the kitchen and check out the fridge and pantry. I'm sure a house this size has a pantry. Or maybe it would be better just to ask Sarah."

William stood and chuckled as he pulled Olivia to her feet. "You poor thing. Is it really that bad?"

Olivia shook her head. "You have no idea! I don't know the front of the house from the back. I just learned that I'm allowed to answer the phone, but I'm not permitted to unpack my bags. I shudder to think about how I'm going to handle dirty laundry."

"Perhaps Gertrude will be able to help." William took a few steps toward the door. "I must leave. I have stops to make before meeting with Horatio."

They walked side-by-side until William reached the hall closet. He pulled his overcoat from the hook and shrugged it on. Funny, mused Olivia. William appeared more comfortable in her house than she did.

"I left my card on the billiard table. Call me if you need anything."

They moved outside without another word. Olivia watched from the stoop as William got behind the wheel of a black Mercedes and started the engine.

The big sedan wound its way through the orchard toward the gates. Sadness filled Olivia's heart. William was the only link to her mother. She didn't want him to leave. She wanted to trust him. She wanted this man who still loved her mother to turn around and come back. But most of all, she wanted him to tell her that everything would be okay.

22

The swing creaked ominously under Olivia's weight. She'd needed a walk outside to clear her head after William's visit. With no particular destination in mind, she'd found an old wooden swing in the orchard. Questions about her mother's past and what led her grandfather to disown his only daughter swirled around in her head. She needed to know where or if she had a place in McLeod and Morrison. But, at the moment, she needed fresh air, even if it was cold. She pulled her coat collar further up around her neck and pushed off with her feet.

The crunch of leaves caused a moments unease.

It was just Benjamin.

"Mornin', Miz Olivia."

"Good morning."

"I see you found the swing. There's been a swing hangin' in this orchard since your momma's first one, maybe even before."

"Mom always liked swings. Dad put one up in the back yard for us kids, but I think she used it more than we did."

"The orchard was a safe place for her to play. There was always folks 'round to keep an eye on her."

Olivia stopped swinging. "Were you here when my mother was little?"

"Oh, no ma'am. I grew up in Richmond. But everyone knew the stories 'bout the little girl who was a prisoner here. And when she grew up—she ran away."

Was that how the neighborhood saw her? A prisoner? Olivia shivered at the thought and pulled her coat tighter.

"It's too cold for you out here. You should go ahead to the house."

Olivia laughed. "This isn't cold to me. Not when I'm used to snow up to my knees. I was just admiring the house and figuring points of reference. My room is the back corner of the center section and the office down to the far left. I see now why it takes me so long to go back to my room for the office keys when I forget to put them in my pocket."

"Do you know anything about Fairfield?" Benjamin asked with pride in his voice.

Olivia leaned forward, still holding the ropes. "No, I don't. Please tell me."

"The center part was built in 1730. After your people bought it sometime in the 1890s, they built a new kitchen for one of those big new wood stoves with ovens. Came all the way from New York. Without fear from fires with those stoves, the new kitchen was built closer to the house. Later, your great-grandma connected the overseer's house and the kitchen to the big house."

"Yeah, I can see that now. The bricks are different, but they still look old."

"The big house was over a hundred and fifty years old when the dependencies were attached."

How could her mother have kept this place a secret? Fairfield was older than the United States. Uncle Lionel had said that our forefathers met here to plan the Revolutionary War. She should have been bursting with pride to fill her children with wonderful stories. What had happened? Her mother was becoming more of a mystery by the hour.

"How 'bout I show you some of the outbuildin's?"

Olivia got to her feet. "Sure. Lead the way."

They walked back toward the house with Benjamin pointing out the various fruit trees.

"I see now how the separate kitchen had been attached to the main house, with a two-story addition between."

The curtains moved in one of the kitchen windows. How long had Sarah been watching? Why? Surely she has more important things to do.

Benjamin came to a halt at a brick building with large chimneys at each end. "When the new kitchen was built your great-grandma used this as a school room."

"Huh. There were enough children here to have a school?"

"Yep. Kids came from the neighborin' farms."

They walked side-by-side down the drive, to the end of the house. A high brick wall enclosed a large area. A delicate iron gate drew Olivia for a closer look.

"Alexandra's rose garden. She loved her roses. Built the wall to keep the deer out."

"It must be beautiful in the summer."

"Yep. The pool takes up a lot of the space now."

"Grandmother Thompson had a rose garden."

It definitely warranted a closer look—maybe in the spring—if she was still here.

"Come on. There's a lot to see," said Benjamin as he moved off in the direction of the barns. Olivia followed, the stones crunching beneath their boots.

Benjamin pointed to what appeared to be a quaint little house set high off the ground. "The necessary house."

He climbed the narrow brick steps then ducked as he entered through the open door.

Olivia followed him up the steps and into the room with windows on two sides. "It's a five-holer, complete with a fireplace." Did five people actually feel comfortable using the facility at the same time? Hopefully, they were of the same gender. "I suppose there was a fireplace tender who's job it was to keep the privy warm." Olivia asked with a chuckle.

"Yep. 'Course, your great-grandma put bathrooms in the house when she built the new kitchen.

Olivia followed Benjamin back outside and continued toward the barns in the distance.

Various brick structures lined both sides of the driveway. Benjamin pointed out the icehouse, the well house, the smokehouse, the laundry, and the dairy.

Olivia peeked her head into the icehouse. It appeared to be a very deep pit lined with brick. A ladder attached to the side went to the bottom.

"Blocks of ice were stacked in layers with straw between. The big house had ice all summer." Benjamin pulled the door shut and lowered the wooden bar. "The icehouse and the well house are original to the farm. The smokehouse, laundry and dairy were hit by cannon balls and destroyed. Was our soldiers done it—firing at the Yankees from camps across the river. Sometime after the war they were re-built.

"If this was a plantation, where are the slave cabins?"

"Oh, they're long gone. Before the war, a whole village of slave cabins sat out near the fields. Nearly two hundred slaves lived there." Benjamin pointed to the North. "After the tobacco crops ruined the land, most of the slaves were sold to cotton plantations down South."

"What happened to the village?"

"Union soldiers camped up and down the river. The soldiers tore down the empty slave cabins—used 'em for firewood."

Olivia's imagination stepped back in time to the scent of wood smoke and gunpowder. History settled over Fairfield like morning dew.

"What happened to the rest of the cabins?"

"The ones out beyond the wall were for slaves tendin' the house and grounds. Your great-grandma had them torn down and built those nice houses just outside the gates.

Continuing down the drive, past what looked like a four-car garage, Olivia saw the barn and a newer stable beyond.

Benjamin pointed to the gates just beyond the stable where Olivia saw the metal roofs of several bungalows. "Sarah and I have a house out there. For some time now, we've been livin' in the cook's apartment over the kitchen."

Olivia pointed toward the barns. "Is that the stable where my mother kept Sinatra?"

"Yep, your great-grandma had it built for her expensive Thoroughbreds she brought down from Boston. Your grandma kept her Arabians there."

"I know all about Sinatra. Can I explore the stable on my own?"

Benjamin scratched his head then nodded. "That should be okay. But be careful." He turned his back to the barn. "I expect we'd better get back to the house. Sarah will have your lunch ready soon."

Olivia's desire to explore the stable would have to wait. Thoughts of William's visit gnawed away at her during lunch. It wasn't so much why he felt it necessary to see her in person, when a phone call would have sufficed. But it was her feelings toward him. He was one of the Morrisons—the enemy. Yet, for some irrational reason, she trusted him. He had the answers to all her questions about her mother's past. She'd bet her life on it. All she had to do was ask. But she also knew there were two sides to every story. She needed to hear her mother's side first.

Olivia headed upstairs to her room and the journal she'd left in the drawer next to the bed.

After crossing the hall, she stood just inside her mother's room. Beautifully furnished in the Art Deco style, so popular in the '30s and '40s, but lacking any personality or indication that a young girl once slept there.

Some of her mother's things were packed in a box in the attic of the Captain's house in Marblehead. They belonged here.

Olivia glanced around the room. A beautiful pink satin chaise-lounge, with its back shaped like a shell, sat in a corner next to the desk. Olivia settled in with her mother's journal, opening to where she'd left off on the plane.

WEDNESDAY, AUGUST 1, 1945

It's been several weeks since I've written. William is stationed on the battleship Missouri. I miss him terribly. I think about our carefree times together. Ever since he left Mother and I talk about nothing but the war. It's so depressing. When will it end? Will our lives ever be the same? The hot summer days drag by. I swam in the pool for hours, then helped Mother with the monthly budget and paid the help. I feel very important now that I'm learning how to run the household. It's a huge responsibility. I should write Daisy. I miss her.

FRIDAY, AUGUST 3, 1945

This was a wonderful day! Father drove home today in a sporty 1941 Packard convertible and presented me with the keys. It's tan with a black top and gorgeous red leather interior. He told Mother she has to stop being so protective of me. I'm a grown woman and need a life outside of Fairfield's walls. He sat next to me while I drove up and down the lane and around the farm until he was comfortable I could handle it. He'll have our chauffeur teach me about changing tires and how the engine works. Father said the war will be over soon. I wonder how he knows the war's going to end? That means William will be coming home. I pray every day for his safety. I'll write and tell him all about my new car. I miss him terribly.

Olivia closed the journal over her finger to keep her place. McLeod and Morrison battleships were in the Pacific. Grandfather obviously knew the bomb would be dropped, ending the war. Mom never talked about the war much. Based on what she'd written, it sounds like her father kept his role with the war department a secret from his daughter. Interesting.

Olivia opened the book.

SATURDAY, AUGUST 4, 1945

It's after midnight and I'm sitting on my bed too excited to sleep. I drove my car to the USO social. I parked up front near the door so everyone would walk by and admire it. I think it got more attention than I did! I will have to ask Mother for gas coupons before the tank gets low. I never had to think about coupons before since there was always someone on the household staff to worry about those things. Mother didn't go because she and Father had something important to discuss. I wonder what it is?

Mother never misses a chance to attend a party. Father told us that he knows a man, Lynn Sherman, who's invented a portable air conditioner that fits in a window. Father will have enough delivered so we'll have one for every room. I hope it's soon. I think I'll wash and wax my car tomorrow.

SATURDAY, AUGUST 18, 1945

The Japanese government surrendered on the 14th. Everyone is still celebrating. Horns can be heard in the distance even though the end of the war is not official yet. President Truman has ordered full restoration of all consumer products. Rationing will end and we can buy anything we want! Mother is leaving in the morning for New York to meet with ER. I'll ask her to buy me dozens of silk stockings. I hope Daisy will be coming home soon. We deserve a shopping trip. It's been ages since I've gotten new clothes. I'll write her tomorrow.

I'm worried. Still no letter from William. Maybe my letters to him have been lost or delayed.

Who was ER? Olivia absentmindedly tapped the journal on the arm of the lounge. She'd never considered her mother to be self-centered, but this young Maureen seemed to be more upset because the war curtailed her shopping than the horrors happening beyond our shores. And only a passing concern about William. "Mother. Mother. Mother," said Olivia and opened the journal.

SATURDAY, SEPTEMBER 1, 1945

So much is happening and I'm completely confused. I drove myself to the USO social. Mother said we will continue to make life as happy as we can for our servicemen and the socials will continue. I met someone new today. His name is Fred Thompson and he is from a small town in Ohio. He caught my eye because he was such a wonderful dancer. He seemed rather shy about talking to me so I asked him to dance. I can't believe I've become so bold. We danced and talked and it was as if I had known him all my life. We are the same age. As different as our lives are, we are so much the same. We both are engaged to people we have known all our lives. His fiancée is the daughter of his parents' best friends. They became engaged just before he left for the Navy. It was always assumed that they would one day marry, just like me and William. I hope William comes home soon.

MONDAY, SEPTEMBER 3, 1945

Mother and I couldn't leave the house all day. We gave the staff the day off so they could be with us and listen to the news on the radio. It was all about the official surrender yesterday of the Japanese aboard the battleship Missouri. We nibbled on leftovers off-and-on all day. It was like a big festive picnic. Just think, William is there and is a part of history. I'm so proud of him. I'll write him tomorrow and tell him how much I love him and can't wait for him to come home. I'm going to marry a real war hero.

The ringing phone startled Olivia. She glanced at the old style rotary-dial phone on the table. Sarah had told her to answer the phone or she'd pick up on the fourth ring. Olivia grabbed the handset.

"Hello?"

"Livy, is that you?" Travis sounded surprised to hear her voice.

"Yep, first call I answered on my own."

"I miss you. How's it going?"

"I'm in Mom's room reading her diaries. Dad finally came on the scene. She met him at a USO dance. The war just ended and William is stationed on the *Missouri*. I'll have to ask him for the details the next time I see him. Can you imagine? He was actually there when the Japanese surrendered."

"The *next* time you see him? You mean the next time since your meeting in Horatio's office."

"No. He stopped by yesterday to apologize for his brother's behavior at the shipyard. William promised that Wilson would put my office back the way it was when it belonged to my grandmother. I can't imagine my mother giving him up. My father was handsome, but William is like Cary Grant minus the dimple in his chin." Olivia smiled remembering their meeting. "I like him. I don't know why, but my gut tells me I can trust him."

"Sounds like you're settling in and liking it there. You won't be coming home any time soon. Will you?"

Olivia could almost hear him grinding his teeth in impatience. "I'm sorry, Travis. This isn't just about finding out who my mother was and collecting some shares in McLeod and Morrison anymore. Something major happened here back in '45 and '46. It changed lives. It stole my grandmother from me. This is like a huge jigsaw puzzle with key pieces missing—I have to find those missing pieces."

"I understand, Livy. Actually, the reason for my call was to let you know that I'm staying at the house. Nick's crew is back at work, and this way I can take care of Spooky. Stay as long as you want. We're fine, except that it sure is quiet around here without you."

Olivia clenched her teeth. Her pulse quickened. He'd moved into *her* house? Just like that? And to take care of a cat that needed virtually no care. Nick could easily handle that job. He couldn't have asked her first? Wasn't their engagement put on hold? He was making another stab at controlling her life.

"Livy? Are you still there?"

"Yeah. You took me by surprise. We hadn't talked about you moving in."

"You're upset aren't you? I can hear it in your voice. Okay. I'll move out. I was just trying to help."

Olivia took a deep breath then let it out slowly. "Travis, it's okay. You can stay. I have enough to deal with here."

"I love you, Livy. I'll call tomorrow."

"Love you, too." The words came out, but they were just words—an automatic response. Olivia's mind wasn't on love—it had switched to William.

Olivia set the handset on the cradle. No, she wasn't ready to go home and she wasn't ready to argue with Travis about his living arrangements. In fact, it might be a while before she'd be ready to leave Fairfield. Something horrible happened in this house. Something that made her mother leave and never return. The journals held the story.

23

Putting Travis's call out of her mind, Olivia's finger slid along the bookmark in the journal.

SATURDAY, SEPTEMBER 8, 1945

I'm shaking with excitement. Tonight I attended a formal dinner in Richmond celebrating the end of the war. I accepted the invitation because it was my duty, and, more than anything, I hoped Fred would be there. I was late and feeling rushed as I hurried through the garden gate. I wanted a minute to compose myself before entering the ballroom where dozens of tables decorated in red, white, and blue stood waiting for the onslaught of merrymakers. My heart stopped when I saw him standing alone against the rail smoking a pipe. I know I behaved like a schoolgirl as I stumbled over my words, but he didn't seem to notice. We were seated at different tables for dinner. Every time I looked his way he was watching me. After the meal was finished and speeches were made, the band began to play. This time it wasn't the frenzied jitterbug, but a romantic waltz. I melted in his arms. Tingles ran up and down my spine. My heart raced, and time stood still. I wanted the dance to go on forever. The evening ended far too quickly. I must see him again. I know it is wrong, but I must see him again.

MONDAY, SEPTEMBER 24, 1945

What's wrong with me? I seem to have no control over my thoughts or emotions. I think about Fred all the time. I need to feel his arms around me. It is all so exciting and I can't wait to see him again. The ring on my finger reminds me that I should be thinking about William and our future together now that this horrid war has ended. I've sat with Mother and Miranda listening to all the broadcasts. I've loved William all my life. We're going to have a wonderful life together. If I love William, then what am I feeling for Fred? I must write Daisy. She will understand.

"Gee, Mom. It's called lust." Olivia laughed out loud. "And who is Miranda?"

SUNDAY, SEPTEMBER 30, 1945

Mother mentioned we should begin planning for the wedding. William and I need to set a date. I asked Mother how love felt and how did she know she loved Father before she married him. She said love is only found in fairytales and novels. She had great respect for Angus and with time, she grew to love the man that he is. She said I should focus on my duty to the family and not meaningless words. I know she's correct and I should be thinking about which designer should make my wedding gown and the color of the bridesmaid's dresses. I must focus on my duty to William and my family. But my body wants Fred.

MONDAY, OCTOBER 1, 1945

I can't believe Daisy's letter! She's engaged! Michael asked her to marry him after she told him of her plans to return home by Thanksgiving. How is she going to survive in that wilderness? I can't imagine how horrible it will be living on a cattle ranch. She can't do this! I need her here. I'll write to her tomorrow.

SUNDAY, NOVEMBER 4, 1945

It's been a month since I've written and I asked God for forgiveness in church today. This is difficult for I can't write about what I don't understand myself. I'm in love with Fred. I realize that I have been since the beginning and I've been trying my best to ignore my feelings. But I can't ignore the way my body melts when he holds me. His kisses ignite a flame that smolders, heating me to an inferno. I fall asleep at night with thoughts of Fred making love to me. I don't want to be a virgin any longer. There has to be a first time for sex and I want it to be with Fred. I've started smoking and taken quite a liking to Manhattans and Highballs. It takes the edge off my problems. I write now only because I must say what is in my heart. Yet I fear the consequences should Mother or Father find out. I don't know what to do. I'm afraid of my feelings for Fred and ashamed of my betrayal to William. God help me.

THURSDAY, NOVEMBER 22, 1945

It was truly a day of thanksgiving. The war is over and life is slowly getting back to normal. The Morrisons were here for dinner, less William who is still aboard the Missouri. Wedding plans became the lively topic and were being discussed by our mothers in the ladies parlor as if William and I didn't matter. I sought what I thought to be the neutral ground of the library and our fathers. Instead, I stepped into a heated discussion of William's future role in the company upon his return home. It's obvious that neither William nor I have any say in our futures. I excused myself from any further socializing by saying that too much rich food wasn't agreeing with me and I needed some fresh air. My leisurely walk ended when the horses began screaming in alarm. I ran as fast as I could to the stable. The horses reared and kicked at their doors. I found Clive and Wilson sitting in an empty stall setting fire to a pile of manure pies. Fearing the small fire could spread, I immediately stomped it out. I yelled for the boys to get a bucket of water to throw on the floor. With the danger over, I grabbed the boys by an arm and marched them back to the house. The Morrison family left after Mr. Morrison gave the boys a mild scolding for nearly setting our barn on fire. I hate to think what they'll be like by the time they're adults. I spent the rest of the afternoon grooming

Sinatra and the other horses while one of the grooms scrubbed the stall floor. I hate those brats. They're nothing but trouble.

SATURDAY, DECEMBER 1, 1945

I received a disturbing letter from William today. He states his father has arranged for him to be home for Christmas. However, he has notified his father that his duty to his country comes before family. His ship and its crew depend on him and that's where he'll spend Christmas. He hopes I'll understand and promises that next year we'll be together. Perhaps he'll consider the Washington post and we can find a house in Georgetown. This news should be making me very happy, since it is exactly what I've dreamed of. Yet I feel that my world is closing in on me. I don't know what I want anymore. Can I really be in love with two men?

MONDAY, DECEMBER 3, 1945

I'm doomed! I feel like running away! Mother just told me that the Morrisons are having a big holiday celebration for the service men and women stationed in Norfolk. They've rented buses to transport everyone and I'm sure that Fred will be there. She said the high ranking officers and their wives will spend the night and we'll do so as well. Fred thinks I'm an ordinary girl from an ordinary family. What am I going to do?

SUNDAY, DECEMBER 16, 1945

I couldn't write until we returned home. I'm worried. It all started so wonderfully in our suite, the same one Mother and I always use. Father said that I looked like a princess and I wore the silver Norman Norell gown with the exquisite design in sequins. It's wonderful to be able to wear heels over two inches high again, and I wore my sexy satin high heels. I'm so glad the restrictions were quickly lifted. I hated having to look frumpy.

Everything was going along so well and Mr. Morrison said that I was the most beautiful girl there. William would be proud. Then the last bus arrived and Fred walked through the door. He saw me right away. He walked over to me with the biggest, most heart-melting smile. I panicked. I was afraid someone might notice. I put my hand out and said how nice it was to see him again and then introduced him to Mr. Morrison. I quickly moved over to another group and motioned him to stay away. He looked completely confused and walked around like a lost puppy. After determining that the library was unoccupied, I motioned for Fred to join me. I hurried him over to the secret panel and led him down to the wine cellar. He took me in his arms to tell me how much he loved me. He couldn't hide his confusion when he looked around and asked how I knew about the secret panel. I pushed him away and told him that this is who I am. Sheffield Court will one day be my home. William Morrison is my fiancé. I also told him that Angus McLeod is my father and that's why I've refused to talk about myself. Fred was visibly shocked. He said it felt like I'd just driven a dagger into his heart. It was at that moment that we both heard what sounded like a shuffling and a scraping sound. I motioned for Fred to stay quiet while I searched the rows of wine. I prayed that it was rats and not someone to whom I would have to explain why I, the daughter of Angus McLeod, had brought a sailor down to the wine cellar. The room was empty and I returned to tell him that we must leave before I was missed. I told him that I was not the girl he thought I was and our relationship needed to end. He looked angry. He said that indeed I was not the woman he'd fallen in love with. He would not have thought me capable of playing so cruelly with a man's heart. The library was empty as I looked through the peephole. I ushered him out into the hall to return to the others. I collapsed into the nearest chair shaking with emotions I didn't have time to identify. It was only a few minutes later that Mother found me and scolded me for not paying enough attention to their guests. If she only knew!

I didn't talk to Fred again and later I saw he'd left with the first group to return to the base. I'm glad he left early. I no longer had to worry about how I acted around him or keeping my love for him locked tightly behind polite expressions. I managed to get through the evening in a manner that made Mother and Father proud. Mother said I've become a social asset to the family.

A social asset? That's what her mother was? A mere McLeod asset? Her mother must have been torn apart with guilt. In love with two very different men and knowing she could only chose one—William, Mr. Right, and Fred, Mr. Wrong. Then there was the sound of something or someone in wine cellar. Olivia hoped it was rats and not Clive and Wilson—was there a difference?

MONDAY, DECEMBER 24, 1945

What a strange day this has been. I spent most of the day thinking about Fred. I just know that I hurt him terribly, but what else could I do? I didn't mean for him to fall in love with me and I must not think about my feelings for him. We went to Sheffield Court for the annual Christmas Eve dinner. Mother and Mrs. Morrison set the wedding date for Saturday, June 1st, and hoped the weather wouldn't be unbearably hot. William is still on the Missouri and his father kept talking about the many sacrifices William has made in order to honor his duty to his country and family. Mr. Morrison kept looking at me like he was lecturing a wayward child. Clive and Wilson kept snickering. Could they know about Fred? I felt very uncomfortable the whole evening and was glad to get back home.

Olivia got to her feet and set the journal on the bed, then walked to the window. Moonlight glistened on the James River. Had her mother stood in this very spot trying to sort out fragile emotions? Had she weighed duty against happiness, hoping for some sign that would lead her in the right direction?

Images crept into her mind of how her mother had been so intent on helping those less fortunate in Cedar Hill. If a family lost their home to a fire, Maureen was the one to set up a fund at the Montgomery Savings and Loan. Each year she organized clothing drives in September for the children at the orphanage on the edge of town. During the Christmas holiday, Olivia was expected to arrange for a donation box in the school's principal's office for toys that would be wrapped and delivered on Christmas Eve for the orphans. Olivia always assumed her mother just liked helping others. She understood now—it was her duty.

"Oh Mom, I can't imagine how you dealt with the turmoil that must have boiled within you. The guilt for those you left behind," Olivia sighed.

Something didn't feel right. A major piece of the puzzle had to be missing. Olivia walked back to the bed. She sat cross-legged with elbows resting on her knees and her chin resting on her hands. Her mother had been molded from the time she was born to honor family, country, and McLeod and Morrison. She had organized the scrap drives and sold war bonds to help with the war effort. Falling for a serviceman at USO socials didn't seem so bad considering the circumstances. After all, they were both engaged to others. Her mother revealing who she was at the party should have ended the relationship with Fred. So how did she end up marrying him anyway? What had William done to her? Olivia needed to know the answer to that before her next encounter, whether it was social or business. She couldn't look William in the eyes without knowing what had happened. Her gut said she could trust him—was he actually the enemy, out to destroy her like he'd done with her mother?

"Excuse me ma'am. It's after seven. Did you forget about dinner?"

"Oh, no. I mean yes. I completely lost track of the time." Olivia followed Sarah to the hallway. "I'm so sorry."

Damn. This was no way to get on Sarah's good side. Three days at Fairfield and already forgetting meals. And Sarah went to so such trouble preparing exquisite meals. This couldn't happen again—not even for what might happen next in the journal.

24

Lengthy phone calls from Horatio and Gertrude took up most of Thursday morning. Horatio filled Olivia in on his progress with her inheritance and Gertrude needed information that Olivia was able to find in the office.

She'd no more than finished her last call from Gertrude when Sarah brought a lunch tray.

"Thank you, Sarah. I think I'll go upstairs and continue reading after I finish my lunch. There's just one more of my mother's journals left."

"Yes, ma'am. I'll check on you later."

How can one live in the same house with someone who is all business? She barely cracks a smile.

Back in her mother's room, Olivia picked up the book on 1945 and set it on top of the others. Even after reading the last entry there were no clues as to why her mother hadn't married William. Her parents had gotten married on May 6th, 1946. This last book would hold the final chapters. Why had Maureen McLeod walked away from a life that most girls could only experience in their fantasies? Did she have any idea what life as a housewife in small town USA would be like? Olivia's childhood memories had been of a mother who'd been an okay cook. Not the great cook that her grandmother

Thompson had been. And after being ridiculed for years by her mother-in-law about Maureen's poor housekeeping skills, Maureen had hired a cleaning lady who came in once a week. Why were there magnificent gowns in a middle-class closet? Her mother had aristocratic manners and speech in a town where few had more than a high school education. Her mother was like a princess turned into a pauper. Why hadn't she noticed?

Olivia, more eager than ever, grabbed the book inscribed with 1946 in gold letters.

She opened the cover.

WEDNESDAY, JANUARY 2, 1946

Mother and I both suffered from hangovers, the result of too much merrymaking last night. I guess one's body gets used to massive amounts of alcohol as you get older. Mother just complained of a headache and was quite grumpy, while I spent most of the morning in the bathroom hugging the toilet. Neither of us could imagine leaving the suite. We spent the day in our robes and slippers talking about everything from life after the war to my marriage. Mother talked most of the day about the wedding and which designer will make my gown. The reception must be here at the Waldorf. June 1ˢᵗ seems awfully soon, not that my feelings about anything matter. It's all just another big party for Mother and Cousin Carrie to orchestrate. Mother called down to Clarence, ordering him to reserve the ballroom. I wish I could talk to William. He makes everything seem better.

THURSDAY, JANUARY 3, 1946

This was a horrible day. My feelings are in a jumble and I just want to put the brakes on life. Mother and I had lunch with Cousin Carrie and all she talked about was my marriage to the most eligible bachelor in the country. Cousin Carrie emphasized the grand lifestyle I'll have and how I'm making my Astor ancestors proud. We discussed possible menu choices, colors and flowers, and, of course, the guest list. I think it's up to 400 poor souls who must sit through a dozen boring toasts that no one will remember, and who are only there for the drinking, dancing, and the business deals that will be made along the way. I just wanted to scream for them to stop, but good manners dictated that I smile and agree. Will I ever be in control of my life? I tried taking charge this afternoon by going ice-skating in CP. I told Mother I was going with friends from the building, but I went alone. I talked to total strangers and laughed until my sides hurt. I felt alive and free. For a moment I thought I saw Clarence standing by a group of men. But then he was gone. I do hope it was my imagination. He'd tell mother for sure. I wish I could talk to William.

Olivia glanced up.

Hmm. Mom is getting a bit defiant. She's sneaking off on her own to skate in Central Park. Not the smartest thing to do, unless Central Park didn't have muggers in 1946. It appears the seed for wanting control of her life has already been planted.

SATURDAY, JANUARY 5, 1946
We're on the train heading for home. Mother isn't talking to me so I've moved to the club car to write. I can't take a chance that she might grab this and begin reading.

Yesterday was horrible and I'm more confused than ever. All this talk about the wedding has made me more aware of my feelings toward William and Fred. I know that I love William and have since I was a little girl, but it isn't the passionate feelings I have for Fred. I made a big mistake when I told Mother about Fred. She got really angry. She told me I must remember my place in society, and feelings aren't important enough to ruin one's life. Love doesn't pay the bills and it takes a lot of money to keep me in the lifestyle into which I was born. She said the love I have for William is enough to keep me happy for the rest of my years, and if lust must be a part of my life, then do it discreetly and out of the public's eye. She said Fred

*is poor. Living a deprived life may be an adventure in the begin-
ning, but it would get old fast. I was not raised to be the servant of
a middle class family with a needy husband and dirty little whining
brats. She forbade me to ever mention Fred's name again. How does
she know Fred is poor? How does she know what his family is like? I
don't know if he is poor or not. It isn't important to me.*

*I love Mother, but I must keep my feelings to myself. I have no
one that I can talk to.*

I'll order another Manhattan and write to Daisy.

TUESDAY, JANUARY 8, 1946

*It was a wonderful day. I met Fred at the cinema in Richmond as
we had arranged. He's forgiven me for my deception and says it
wouldn't matter if I were the future Queen of England. He loves me
for myself and will always love me. I don't even remember the movie,
we held hands and kissed and vowed that our love will survive
the monumental obstacles before us. I was free to love and could
forget duty, responsibilities, and family. There was only one uneasy
moment when I thought I heard the familiar snickering of Clive and
Wilson, but when I turned around there was only a neatly dressed
man behind us. I checked the few people milling around the lobby
after the matinee and on the street outside, but there were no familiar
faces. I do worry about those two. They thrive on trouble.*

*I received a letter from Daisy. Her wedding will be held at their
church in Richmond on Saturday, April 27ᵗʰ and she wants me to be
her maid-of-honor. She's coming home next week and we can begin
planning her wedding. I'm so excited for her. At last I'll be able to
talk about Fred. I must find a new hiding place for my diary. I feel
eyes everywhere.*

WEDNESDAY, JANUARY 9, 1946

*Father came home for my birthday and we had a lovely dinner. The
Morrisons were to join us, but something came up at the last minute and they couldn't come. I'm glad because my feelings for Fred*

continue to trouble me and I would have found it very difficult to talk about the wedding. Mother and Father presented me with a beautiful box from Tiffany's, and when I opened it my heart stopped. The most beautiful diamond and pearl tiara I had ever seen lay before me. Father boasted that it had been designed for a European princess. The war nearly bankrupted the small country and Father was able to purchase it for me. Mother said a copy would be given to Charles James to help with the design of my wedding gown. I know this should be making me excited for my marriage and future with William. Instead, I feel a huge weight resting on my chest. My whole life has been arranged for this moment and all I want to do is run far away.

THURSDAY, FEBRUARY 21, 1946

I'm worried. Fred hasn't contacted Daisy for the location of our meeting. Ever since I told Daisy of my relationship with Fred she's helped us by taking his telephone calls and then getting the messages to me. We usually go to a movie or sometimes a park and we're always very careful not to draw attention to ourselves. Daisy thinks it's romantic. I think it's dangerous, but I can't stop. I love Fred with all my heart. What am I to do?

FRIDAY, FEBRUARY 22, 1946

Mother and Father had a terrible argument on the telephone today. I'm sure it was about me. Mother slammed the phone down and announced that we would leave tomorrow for New York to order my trousseau. Daisy will come along. I'm sure Mother asked her in order to keep me focused on my wedding.

SUNDAY, MARCH 10, 1946

We've returned home. Daisy and I had a truly wonderful time in New York and I hardly ever thought about Fred. We fell into our beds exhausted each night and woke excited about the events of a new day. We were treated like royalty as we chose designs from Mainbocher,

Norman Norell and Charles James, my three favorite American designers. Charles James has designed a wedding gown that any princess would be proud to wear and the tiara will be my crowning glory. Daisy kept saying over and over how lucky I am as she helped choose armloads of clothes without a concern for cost. It was two weeks of living a fairytale with my best friend. I didn't want it to end.

"Here you are. It's nearly four o'clock, would you like a pot of my special tea?"

Olivia jumped. She hadn't heard Sarah come into the bedroom. That woman can sneak around without making a sound. Olivia peeked down at Sarah's shoes, black serviceable-looking things with rubber soles. Maybe that's how she does it. No leather to echo one's steps on wooden floors.

"Yes. Thank you. I love your tea."

After Sarah left the room Olivia went to stand before the empty closet. It was small. There'd been so many references to her mother's vast wardrobe and what she would wear to each event mentioned. Surely there had to be an additional closet somewhere. The only other door in the room led to a bathroom.

Sarah returned with the tea several minutes later. "I won't bother you again, ma'am. Dinner will be at seven."

"Sarah, my mother's closet is rather small to hold all of her clothes. Do you know where she put the rest of them?"

"There's a room at the top of the stairs she used as her closet."

"Thank you. I'll check it out." Olivia moved to the chaise lounge. She took a sip of the fragrant tea and picked up the journal. The closet upstairs would have to wait. Her mother and father would be married in less than two months. Something important was about to happen.

SUNDAY, MARCH 17, 1946

We've been back a week and I've not heard from Fred. There have been no telephone calls at the designated times, nor has Daisy been able to reach him. It seems strange after everything we shared. Maybe he doesn't love me anymore. He was feeling guilty knowing his family was busy planning for his wedding. At least Mother and Father are no longer quarrelling. I wonder what changed? Mother has been on the telephone all day with Cousin Carrie working on wedding details. I've got a bad feeling in the pit of my stomach.

WEDNESDAY, MARCH 20, 1946

I'm really worried now. Daisy got the brilliant idea of driving to the naval base. She told the guard she was Fred Thompson's fiancée from Ohio and hopefully she would have the chance to talk to him. Although Daisy swore she was very convincing, she was told there was no Fred Thompson registered on the base. She must be mistaken as to his location. I remember the names of two of Fred's friends and Daisy is going to contact them and find out what is going on. I realize it could be as simple as he doesn't want to see me anymore. But surely his name would still be on the roster of enlisted men. I'm sure now that he doesn't love me. Perhaps he doesn't know how to tell me. I have to believe what we had is over. I need to move on with my life. William and I will be happy, although the love I feel for Fred will last forever.

Olivia set the journal aside and refilled her cup. Her father disappeared without a trace, and any record of him being at the base disappeared along with him. How bizarre.

What had Sarah said about her mother's closet upstairs? Olivia swallowed the last of the tea and set the cup back in its saucer. She swung her legs to the side of the lounge and stood. Sarah had said the top of the stairs. How hard could that be?

The staircase continued up another flight. Olivia took the stairs two at a time. A hallway ran the length of the central portion of the house with a window at each end. She turned the knob on the first door on her right.

Olivia stepped into a room containing the same floral wallpaper as her mother's bedroom. Two walls were lined with etched glass paneled closet doors. The design was of a peacock, it's tail trailing to the bottom of the glass. A black lacquered Chinese screen stood in a corner next to a matching dressing table. She walked over to a seat fitted into a dormer window. The James River glistened in the setting sun. Wow. This was every woman's dream. A dressing room fit for a Hollywood starlet—and something else her mother had kept a secret. What wonderful stories her mother could have told of this magical room. How many more surprises did this house hold? She hurried over to the closet and pulled opened the doors—empty. She checked the drawers. All were empty, just like the bedroom.

With a long sigh of frustration, Olivia left the room, pulling the door closed behind her.

25

She hadn't been upstairs long enough for the waning afternoon sun to have brought on this gloomy feeling. Not even the cheerful floral wallpaper and soft pinks could dispel the melancholy hovering over her mother's bedroom. After reading the diaries, it appeared that every trip to New York brought new clothes. One would think her mother had lived for shopping. Yet, that wasn't the mother she'd known growing up. Her wardrobe had been stylish, but not excessive.

A long, drawn-out sigh of defeat escaped from Olivia's lips. The window into her mother's past wasn't at Fairfield. No remnants of Maureen McLeod could be found within these timeworn walls.

She touched the switch filling the room with a soft glow. After filling her cup with tea Olivia returned to the journal. The closet upstairs had been a dead end. Nothing new had surfaced except that her mother had a dressing room fit for a princess. After settling into the comfy lounge, Olivia opened the journal to where she'd left off.

SUNDAY, APRIL 7, 1946

I should have known this was no ordinary Sunday dinner at the Morrison's when Mother insisted she choose my dress and helped me with my hair. After our usual greetings, Mr. Morrison said a wedding gift had arrived. It was in the library and there was plenty of time for me to unwrap it before dinner. I really wasn't interested in anything having to do with the wedding. I'd had about enough of being told what I must wear and when I'm to open presents. What I wanted to do was stomp my foot and say no. What I did was to head down the hall to the library. I wish I hadn't been in such a foul mood when I walked into the room and saw William leaning against the desk. I ran to his outstretched arms. It was a wonderful evening for everyone, although William seemed different somehow. Troubled. It was as if his thoughts were far off in another world. I wish I felt the same flames raging inside me when William took me in his arms and kissed me. I wish my body melted into his when he says he loves me. I wish I could find the passion I feel with Fred. I do love William. How can I love two men?

MONDAY, APRIL 15, 1946
William came by for lunch. He apologized for not calling. He'd been in a lot of meetings with his father at the shipyard. Something just seems wrong. He kept looking at me like he was seeing me for the first time. He kept asking me odd questions about my friends and how I've been spending my time. What friends? He knows my only friend is Daisy. Could he somehow know about Fred? He barely mentioned our wedding plans or where we'll go on our honeymoon. When I thought he would leave without even a kiss, he asked me to spend tomorrow with him on his father's yacht. I have this bad feeling in the pit of my stomach. It's like I'm stuck in the middle of everyone else's secret. I have to look at this positively. I haven't been on a cruise since before the war. This will be wonderful. It's the perfect way to spend a lovely spring day being pampered in luxury. I wonder what I should wear? Something absolutely smashing!

TUESDAY, APRIL 16, 1946
Today started out wonderful and exciting. It ended with me being confused and frightened. I don't know where to begin. I wore one of

the new playsuits that Daisy convinced me to buy during our shopping spree in New York. William picked me up in his new Cadillac convertible and whistled as I came down the steps. Mother looked very pleased with herself, as if this was all her idea. My long navy blue and white striped skirt concealed the matching shorts underneath. William's gaze settled on the low square neck of the matching top while he held the car door open. We drove along the James River where the Americana II is docked. The 200-foot yacht is so impressive and I felt a sense of power knowing this floating palace would soon be at my disposal.

William gave orders to the captain while I headed to the bow. It had always been William's and my favorite place to watch the world go by. William soon joined me, but it wasn't the same. We weren't children anymore. He put his arm around my waist and pulled me close. I rested my head on his chest as the yacht slowly pulled away from the dock. Later, after a delicious lunch, we lounged on deck chairs. William talked about his time on the Missouri. It was our love and knowing he was coming home to me that made war bearable for him. He'd kept my picture in his shirt pocket. I felt guilty when I thought about my betrayal of this heroic man who had endured so much for duty. I couldn't listen anymore and got up and headed to the stern. The wind pressed my long skirt against my legs as I walked unsteadily to the rail. Perhaps it was the two bottles of wine we polished off during our meal, or maybe it was the Manhattans that always seemed to be at hand. Feeling free and a bit tipsy, I reached for the long zipper on the front of my skirt and pulled it up to my waist. William quickly caught up and smiled. He looked down at the navy blue shorts now framed by the long flowing skirt. His smile melted my heart. He told me I'd grown up since he'd left. Then he bent down and kissed me. I wanted to feel the fire and the passion so I kissed him as I'd done with Fred. William pulled back as if he were surprised by my boldness. Taking my hand he guided me across the deck and through the double sliding doors to the main salon, then down the stairs to his father's stateroom.

He said we were only getting away from the envious eyes of the crew. The room was luxurious. It was a man's room. William took me in his arms and told me how much he loved me. His kisses found every inch of my face and neck while his hands explored, removing first my skirt then gently lifting my bodice over my head. His hands caressed my breasts, sending a thrill of shivers through me. He inched my shorts to the floor, leaving me standing naked before him. My heart pounded, my head spun. I reached out to him. William caught me in his arms and carried me to the large bed. He slowly removed his clothes. I couldn't take my eyes from his beautiful body as he climbed in bed next to me. His caresses and kisses became demanding. I rode a wave of desire that blocked out all conscious thoughts. I wanted him. I wanted William to make love to me.

I still don't know what I did wrong. I don't know what suddenly made him say, "I can't do this" and then he got off the bed. He kept apologizing as he tossed me my clothes and told me to get dressed. My offer to make the bed only made him angry. He clenched his jaw and threw the comforter on the floor. He yanked at the sheets and messed up the bed. He refused to tell me what he was doing. I begged him to tell me what I'd done. He telephoned up to the captain, telling him to return to the dock. William tried to make idle conversation for the rest of the trip, but the look of anger never left his face. He said it had nothing to do with me. Then who? I'm so confused. Fred has mysteriously dropped off the face of the earth, and my fiancé finds me sexually repulsive.

Olivia poured the last of the now lukewarm tea into her cup. Sarah's special blend tasted as good as it smelled. Afternoon tea was going to become a pleasant ritual.

The latest passages in the diary were certainly a strange set of events—a royal set-up in today's world. Maureen's parents and future in-laws are angry—at each other and at her. Fred disappears into thin air. William magically appears. Then everyone is happy again. Maureen is swept off on a fairytale cruise that ends with William mad. He messes up the bed and then it's all over. That whole sex-in-the-cabin thing was obviously planned by William. But why stop? The rather inebriated Maureen was certainly ready to make love to her fiancé. Olivia couldn't imagine how difficult it must have been for her mother to be in love with two different men. William was a love that had always been comfortable and easy. Fred, a magical love that was exciting and spontaneous. It sounded like Mom had to be drunk to feel passion with William.

What the hell was going on?

Olivia needed to keep reading.

MONDAY, APRIL 29, 1946

Daisy's wedding is over and the happy couple is on their honeymoon. It's taken me two weeks to write. I'm confused. I keep thinking about the boat trip. It was wonderful until I got drunk. I'm so ashamed of my behavior. I acted like a cat in heat. Mr. Morrison announced at Sunday dinner yesterday that William and I will spend our honeymoon on his yacht. We'll cruise the Caribbean for a month since the rest of the world is in a state of chaos following the war. Watching Daisy these past few weeks has only emphasized how unhappy I am, and how different our weddings are. Hers was truly a happy, wonderful event cradled in love. Mine is a theatrical production with William and I merely the actors. The only people happy are our parents. Even William is looking at me with concern. I just want to scream and make everything stop. I'm not sure that I want to marry William. What if Fred returns after I'm married? I just want everything to go away. But the wheels are in motion and the wedding must go on. It's my duty.

TUESDAY, APRIL 30, 1946

William picked me up and we went to his favorite restaurant in Richmond for dinner. He'd reserved the private room where we could talk without being overheard. He's sensed my change since his arrival and doesn't want a loveless marriage any more than I do. We both agreed that the wedding, if it takes place at all, should be postponed. The problem is that we have little say in the matter. William explained that our marriage was planned shortly after I was born and will cement the future of McLeod & Morrison. A shipbuilding dynasty is at stake and the game must be played out. Unfortunately, William and I will be the losers. I've trusted William all my life. I know he'll figure out a way for us to deal with our parents and be happy. I do love William and if we must marry, I'll make our marriage work. But I still think about Fred and the wonderful life we could have had together. I wish I knew where he was, and if he ever thinks about me. Life is hard.

What happened to her father? Obviously he'll show up and marry her mother. She needed to keep reading. Olivia's hand shook as she swallowed the last of her tea. She rubbed her brow with one hand as the other replaced the cup in its saucer. Her fingers had gone numb. She shook her hands to bring the circulation back then tucked the book alongside the arm of the lounge. She felt weak. Maybe she needed to close her eyes for just a few minutes.

"Wake up ma'am. You just gotta wake up!"

Was that Sarah yelling at her? Olivia was sure she'd just closed her eyes to rest them for a minute. Why did Sarah feel it necessary to scream? Couldn't she have just knocked on the door like any normal person?

Olivia opened her eyes. Sarah's blurry face was inches away.

"You okay, ma'am?"

Olivia blinked several times. The fog began to clear. "Yeah, I guess I just fell asleep. How long before dinner is ready?"

"Ma'am, it's *been* ready. I got worried when you didn't come down. Do you always nap like this in the afternoon?"

"No. I never take naps. This is very unusual." Olivia massaged the back of her neck. "I'll be right down after I throw some cold water on my face."

Sarah moved to the door, shaking her head. "Maybe you should see a doctor."

Fifteen minutes later Olivia sat down to dinner as the hall clock chimed for the eighth time. She finished spreading butter on a warm biscuit when Sarah came through the door with a plate of roast beef and vegetables.

"This looks delicious. I'm starving. It's just what I need to get over this weak feeling I've had all day."

Sarah frowned. "Your Grandma got . . ." She stopped short of finishing the sentence, then shook her head and turned toward the door.

"What were you going to say about my grandmother?"

"It was nothing important. Enjoy your meal."

Forcing down the last forkful of green beans, Olivia set her napkin on the table and leaned back in her chair. Offending Sarah at mealtimes was not an option. She needed to stay on Sarah's good side—and so far that wasn't easy to achieve. Finishing each meal with a clean plate produced a rare smile from Sarah. She was obviously proud of her culinary skills. So, Olivia would continue to finish what Sarah put before her. Eating *this* meal had been a mindless task.

She couldn't get the diaries out of her head. Her parents' anniversary was May 6th, yet on April 30th, her father was still missing. Something huge had to happen in the next few pages.

"How are you feeling, ma'am? I see you finished your dinner," Sarah asked as she moved the dirty dishes to a tray.

"I'm fine. Whatever it was, your cooking took care of it. The meal was delicious."

"Thank you, ma'am."

Olivia pushed back her chair and stood. "I'll be upstairs." She headed toward the door. There were no sounds behind her. Sarah wasn't clearing the dishes. Olivia glanced over her shoulder.

Sarah had plates in each hand, but her eyes were on Olivia. A deep frown etched her brow. She'd been about to say something about Grandmother. What was it? What is she hiding?

26

She hesitated at the threshold of her mother's room. What little moonlight found its way in hung by thin threads, casting everything in eerie shadows. There was a sense of sadness, too. Olivia pressed the light switch. The shadows disappeared. She moved to the chaise lounge and the journal of 1946.

WEDNESDAY, MAY 1, 1946

This is the most wonderful day of my life! William called to say that he's accepted the position at the Pentagon. He's driving to Washington and would like me to join him. At first I said no. I didn't want to spend hours cooped up in a car talking about whether we should or should not postpone our wedding. But William convinced me that getting away from Fairfield and Mother was just what I needed. I can always trust William to know what is best for me. Neither of us had anything to talk about as we drove through Richmond, then headed north to Washington. William kept telling me to relax. Everything would work out fine. I wasn't so sure when he turned into a motel parking lot in Fredericksburg. He looked at me with the sad eyes of a man defeated in battle. We pulled in front of cottage number five. After helping me from the car, he motioned for me to go in alone. Even now, I can't believe what happened. I entered the dimly lit room and saw Fred standing with outstretched arms. We didn't stop kissing and declaring our love until we heard the knock on the door. William entered and pulled a pack of cigarettes from his jacket pocket, lighting one as he settled into a chair. Fred and I sat on the bed holding hands while William proceeded to tell us the most remarkable story.

Clive and Wilson had been playing in the wine cellar, the night of the servicemen's holiday party. They saw Fred and me when we entered from the library's secret panel. They listened for a while and then snuck out through the service door, taking the tunnel to the garages. The next day the boys told their father what they had seen. Mr. Morrison hired a private investigator to follow us. Mr. Morrison arranged for Fred to be transferred to Pearl Harbor where he was to stay until after the wedding. At the same time Mr. Morrison arranged for William to return home. William was told to woo me back and hopefully I would forget about Fred. That's what the boat trip was about and why William messed up the bed, to make it look like we'd had sex. But William loves me too much to be a part of their traitorous schemes. He used his connections at the Pentagon to have Fred discharged. William then arranged for Fred to arrive in D.C. where he caught the next train to Fredericksburg.

William gave us the rest of the day to be alone while he drove on to Washington to finalize his new position. Fred and I spent a glorious day together, and we agreed never to be apart again. William picked me up at nine. I told him how much I loved Fred, and he offered to help us. I think he's enjoying putting one over on his father and beating him at his own game. Mother was already in bed when I got home, so our confrontation must wait until morning. I'm scared, but I truly love Fred with all my heart.

THURSDAY, MAY 2, 1946

My stomach is churning. I feel sick. This morning, I told Mother I was in love with Fred. I want to cancel the wedding with William. She yelled, stomped her foot and threw her favorite Wedgewood bowl across the room. I've never seen her so angry. She called Father. He's coming home tomorrow. I thought she would understand my feelings and protect me. But I see that I was wrong. Mother spent the rest of the day trying to convince me that love is not as important as family and responsibilities. She insists I honor my commitment to William. I feel terrible. I feel cheap and dishonest. I'm letting my family down. What will Mother do about the wedding plans and the hundreds of people who expect to attend the Wedding of the Year? I know Fred is waiting for my call. I don't know what to tell him. How can this be happening to me?

FRIDAY, MAY 3, 1946

I want to die! Mother woke me early to say Father and Mr. Morrison were waiting for me in the library. I dressed in my most conservative brown suit, as if I was going to my execution, but nothing prepared me for what happened. Mother was told to remain in the room. At first I thought Father would go easy on me, but Mr. Morrison spoke first. He accused me of betraying William and my family and acting like a common slut. He demanded the wedding go on as planned. My indiscretions would be overlooked. My future behavior as William's wife was to be spotless. William was destined for greatness, and I had been groomed to be at his side. I would not shirk my duty or I would suffer the consequences. I said I didn't want to enter into a loveless marriage. William and I deserved better. Mr. Morrison shouted that marriage had nothing to do with love, and I was to fulfill my obligations to the families and the future of McLeod and Morrison. I wanted to break down and cry. My knees shook, but I forced myself to stand straight and proud. I declared that I cared nothing about McLeod and Morrison. I loved William as a brother and always would, but I was going to marry Fred. Father's face turned red. He slammed his fist on the desk and said I would obey him, or I would be disinherited. Mother tried to protest, but both men shouted for her to be quiet. Father promised that if I married Fred, I would never see my parents again and would never see a dime of McLeod money. Mother broke down in sobs and left the room. I stood firm and told them both that I would make my own decision. I walked out of the room as William's father shouted that he'd take care of the situation, as he should have from the very beginning. I promised myself that I would never bow down to the evils of power again.

I collapsed within the cool sheets of my bed, feeling my world crumble around me. The tears came quickly and didn't stop until Mother sat down beside me an hour later. She took me in her arms, resting her head on mine. Mother asked if this was truly what I wanted. Did I understand fully what I was giving up? She explained that Father and Mr. Morrison had left the house. She overheard Father tell Mr. Morrison that he'd meet him at Sheffield Court. They'd take care of business there. Father would return early tomorrow morning. If I was going to leave it had to be tonight. I asked why she suddenly wanted to help me. She said her love for me was greater than her duty to her husband. Mother called William and explained what had happened. He called back a few minutes later with a plan.

William will pick me up at the old brick posts along the drive at midnight, out of sight of the house and prying eyes, and drive me to Fredericksburg. He will then drive on to Washington and his new job with the Navy like nothing has happened. Fred and I will catch the first train to New York and go straight to the Waldorf. I'm to pack the clothes I keep there including my trousseau that's been arriving from the various stores and couture houses. Mother will call Clarence and let him know the situation. She'll have Cousin Carrie arrange for our marriage. I write while I wait in my room for the moment when I'll leave this house forever. I pray Father never finds out how Mother has helped me, or the consequences could ruin her life. I don't want him to punish her for what I've done. I'm more afraid than I've ever been in my life. I must be very careful. There's no time to say goodbye to Miranda. No time for a last ride on Sinatra or even grooming and a carrot. No time for a last walk around my beloved farm. I'll carry the memories of Fairfield in my heart forever. I wish I didn't have to leave Mother. How will I go on without her?

"Oh my God!" The words exploded. Her heart pounded. Olivia read the last entry again.

Her blood boiled. Olivia threw the journal to the floor. This couldn't have happened. Not to her mother. How could her father have turned on his only child? Mom had always seemed so normal. How could anyone live through such treachery and be normal? She'd always avoided questions about her past like it was nothing.

This wasn't *nothing*!

"Travis. I have to tell Travis," Olivia said as she reached for the phone and dialed.

Travis picked up on the forth ring.

"Livy?"

"I know it's late, but I had to call." Olivia took a deep calming breath. "I can't keep this to myself a minute longer. "

"No. It isn't late. Spooky and I were just enjoying the last dying embers in the fireplace. Were you running? You sound out of breath."

"I have the answers!" Olivia swung her legs over the side of the lounge. "I know what happened!"

"Calm down. You have the answers to which of your many questions?"

"Why my mother married my father and not William. And what made her walk away from her family. And why she was disinherited."

"Wow, Livy. I'm all-ears."

"It was ugly—like a conspiracy. You're not going to believe what happened. I think I would have killed old man Morrison! It all started when . . ."

Twenty minutes later Travis had the whole story.

"Sounds to me like Mr. Morrison was going to have your father eliminated. Pearl Harbor wasn't exactly a safe place at the end of the war. Fatal accidents could happen."

"No wonder my mother said that she'd tell us about her life when we were old enough to understand. Looking back, I don't think I was ready at fifteen for the whole story."

"Hmm. I'm thinking there was more to your grandmother's paranoia about kidnappers—like a way for her to control your mother's life. Her school activities were controlled by the head mistress—and guess who controlled her? Your mother only mentioned one friend by name—Daisy, who just happened to live next door. She went to a private all-girls school. There were to be no guys in her life except for William," Travis paused. "Getting my drift?"

"You may have a point. I know how she got away, but not how they got married. More reading for me tomorrow." Olivia stifled a yawn. "But right now, I'm heading to bed. I've felt weak and a bit nauseas all evening. My fingers are even getting numb from holding the journals for so many hours."

"I hope you feel better. Maybe, take it easy tomorrow."

"All I've been doing is sitting and reading."

"If you're not feeling well, maybe you should see a . . ."

Olivia cut him off. "I've been under a lot of stress. Nothing to worry about."

"Are you sure? I'm only worried 'cause I love you."

"I love you, too," Olivia yawned. "Good night. Talk to you tomorrow."

Olivia turned out the lights and headed across the hall to her room. The hallway lights were on. Should she turn them out or wait and let Sarah turn them out? Her arm tingled. She'd figure out the lights tomorrow.

Fifteen minutes later Olivia finished in the bathroom and climbed into bed. She pulled the sheet and comforter up, tucking it under her chin. The moon's rays brushed across the portrait over the fireplace. "Well, Great-Grandmother, I sure could use another good night's sleep. By the way, I'm beginning to like it here. But not what happened to my mother."

27

Olivia leaned over to get a closer look at the clock sitting on the bedside table. Five forty-five. For the fourth day in a row she'd made it through the night free of disturbing thoughts and nightmares. She couldn't remember a time since the death of her family, twenty years before, when she'd awaked free of guilt, anxiety, or just the troubling times around her. But here she was, happy, refreshed, and ready for a new day. She didn't know how it could be possible, but she was sure that the peaceful night had been a gift from her Great-Grandmother Alexandra. Tossing the blankets aside, Olivia jumped out of bed and headed for the shower.

Olivia grabbed the last clean pair of underwear from the drawer. She couldn't put off the discussion with Sarah about who was responsible for dirty laundry any longer. Nor could she go too much longer without a shopping trip. Assuming her days would be spent in meetings, Olivia had brought more business attire and fewer casual clothes. The black wool slacks and matching cashmere turtleneck would have to do for another day.

"See you later, Great-Grandmother." Olivia gave a quick wave in the direction of the portrait as she headed into the hallway. Did she actually just wave? This should feel creepy—but it didn't.

A hint of dawn danced across the James as Olivia pressed the call-button on the floor with her toe. Sarah entered the room as Olivia took the last sip of tea.

"Breakfast was delicious. I love blueberry pancakes."

"Thank you, ma'am." One corner of Sarah's mouth tipped up. "Today being Friday, the temporary staff will be coming in. They'll handle the cleaning and laundry."

The laundry. How Olivia handled her dirty clothes was still an unanswered question—she was wearing her last pair of clean underwear.

Sarah seemed to read her thoughts. "Put your dirty clothes in the hamper in your dressing room. The laundry is taken to the basement and returned to your room by the end of the day. Sheets are changed once a week. Let me know if you want it done more often. Five people will be working on the first and second floors. They'll try to stay out of your way."

"Not a problem, Sarah. I'll spend the day reading in my mother's room."

Leaving Sarah to clear the table, Olivia headed upstairs.

She'd just reached the top step in the second floor hall when she heard the crunch of tires on the driveway. Must be the cleaning people. Olivia hurried over to the hall window overlooking the driveway. The sunrise illuminated an ominous line of indigo clouds lurking to the north. Living on the Marblehead Peninsula, Olivia knew all too well that snow would be arriving soon.

The hood of a white van peaked from the corner of the house. She craned her neck to get a better view of the drive. She needed to get to a window overlooking that part of the property. Olivia glanced to her left. The door to a bedroom stood ajar. From there she should be able to see the drive and kitchen wing.

Olivia noted sage-green paneled walls and graceful Queen Anne furniture on her way to a window to the right of a fireplace.

Two doors on the side of a minivan opened and four women got out. Their ages appeared to be somewhere between early twenties and mid forties. A man exited from the driver's seat. The brim of his hat obscured his face as he followed the ladies to the cellar steps.

Olivia hadn't paid much attention to the cellar door with the short peeked roof above on her walk with Benjamin. He hadn't pointed it out as being an historic feature of the house. So the entrance hadn't interested her at the time—but now it did.

The kitchen wing appeared huge. There must be three or more rooms on the second floor of the part that connected the main house to the kitchen. There was some serious exploring to be done—but first she needed to follow the workers.

Olivia didn't encounter anyone on her trip back downstairs and out the back door to the driveway then around the corner to the steps.

Why had the help entered the cellar? Surely a house of this size would have the laundry in the kitchen wing, along with the various cleaning supplies. Could a two hundred and fifty-five year old basement be anything more than a dark, damp hole in ground?

Olivia hesitated. The well-built steps were fairly new. The brick and mortar couldn't be more than fifteen or twenty years old. Interesting. So far she hadn't seen anything that was less than a hundred years old. Why had the steps been replaced? What did the basement contain that was important enough to keep the steps in good condition?

The cellar door opened on well-oiled hinges. Olivia found herself in some sort of anteroom. Empty tables lined two walls. The floor and walls were made of bricks that continued into an arched ceiling. A tall man would have to duck.

Voices came from the next room. She moved to the side of a wide arched opening, but didn't enter.

"I wonder what she's like?" It was a young woman's voice—soft-spoken with a slight Southern accent. "Can you imagine inheriting all this when you didn't even know your granny?"

"She knew all right. Had to. You don't come into money like this without knowin' 'bout it 'aforhand." The raspy voice sounded older. Perhaps someone who'd smoked for many years.

"Poor old Mrs. McLeod. She was so nice. Always remembering us with a gift at Christmas," the young woman said.

"Now you watch," said the smoker. "This upstart Yankee's gonna sell the place and head back North. You watch."

This would be the perfect time to waltz in there and introduce herself. Pour on the charm and show them she was no upstart Yankee. But she'd been eavesdropping. Not the best first impression.

"Stop this talk and get to work!" The voice was deep and male. "Ginny and Violet, take the second floor."

Someone turned on a faucet. A bucket was being filled drowning out the voices.

Several vacuum cleaners and a couple large canvas bags resting against a wall was all Olivia could see without moving closer to the doorway.

One woman came into view, either Ginny or Violet, and grabbed a vacuum. The other woman reached for a bag and moved away. They both carried buckets filled with spray bottles and rags.

The cold brick wall pressed against Olivia's back. She could open and slam the outside door and pretend she'd just happened upon the cleaning staff—awkward, better not. One or more of them would surely tell Sarah they'd met her in the basement, which she hadn't been shown yet. She'd have to explain to Sarah why she was snooping around and not upstairs reading, or she could continue to cower against the wall. Cowering felt better—unless she got caught.

"Laurie and Jeanette take the first floor," said the man. "I'll bring the mops and buckets."

The other two women took their vacuum and bag and moved back into the room.

"Move it. All four of you . . . upstairs! And no more gossip unless you want to deal with Sarah's wrath." The male voice shouted over the clanking of mops and buckets. "I'm right behind you."

A door closed above. Olivia let out the breath she'd been holding and moved into the next room. Whatever she expected it wasn't the large brightly lit laundry room. Olivia walked over to a large machine. Her grandmother Thompson had a mangle in her basement to press sheets and curtains. Fairfield had two.

Newer wooden steps led upstairs. Based on the location in relation to the outside door, they should come out somewhere in the kitchen wing. Massive hand-hewn beams supported the floor above. Olivia moved to another arched opening and a room beyond. Sun streamed in through a small window. The walls, covered in stucco, helped make what looked like a kitchen and dining room clean and cheerful. Paper lunch bags sat on top of an old trestle table with a bowl of fresh fruit in the center. Another archway led to what amounted to a wide hallway with several doors on both sides, each of them with heavy locks. But it was the massive steel door at the end that drew Olivia for a closer look. She tried to move the handle. It wouldn't budge. Between the layers of rust and the heaving brick floor, it was obvious the door hadn't been used for decades. What could be on the other side? Olivia ran her hand over the surface. It was cold.

Heavy footsteps and a thudding sound came from the direction of the laundry. One of the women had come down whistling.

Olivia pressed herself into the corner. Chances were the whistler wouldn't enter the hallway leading to nowhere. What could be stored behind three locked doors? A wine cellar perhaps? That would make sense, but what about the other two? It was too soon in her relationship with Sarah and Benjamin to bring up the subject of locks and the mysterious steel door.

The unmistakable sound of a washing machine filling with water drowned out her thoughts. The whistling stopped, followed by a female voice doing a very poor rendition of Madonna's, *Like A Virgin*. The lid dropped on the washer. Whoever had been in the basement was now heading back up the stairs.

Further exploration of the basement would have to wait. This was her opportunity to get to her mother's room before anyone else came downstairs. Dashing back the way she'd come, Olivia noticed one of the white canvas bags sitting on the floor near the washer. Laundry bags. There had been two. Someone else would surely be down soon.

A thin layer of snow dusted the driveway. Olivia wrapped her arms around herself and dashed for the main door. Shit. What if the door had automatically locked behind her on the way out? She needed to be more careful about such things. Explaining to Sarah how she'd been locked out of the house when she was supposed to be in Maureen's room was something else she didn't want to deal with.

Olivia thanked God and Great-Grandmother Alexandra for the door being unlocked, and she dashed upstairs to her mother's room unnoticed.

The journal lay squarely in the center of the desk. Olivia's skin prickled. She picked up the book and moved to the lounge. She had tossed the diary on the floor the night before. Who had been in the room?

"Excuse, me ma'am. I don't mean to interrupt. I thought you might like to have your lunch up here. The dining room is getting a good cleaning this morning."

"Oh, no. This will be fine."

"I've made you a chicken salad sandwich and a piece of the pecan pie from last night. How about if I just put the tray on the desk?"

"Yum. That was the best pecan pie I've ever had. I think you've got a secret ingredient."

Sarah set the tray down and turned to leave. At the door she hesitated and looked over her shoulder. "Bourbon."

After finishing her lunch, Olivia went back to the chaise lounge and picked up the journal.

TUESDAY, MAY 7, 1946

At last Fred and I are comfortable in the Pullman, and on our way home. Where that is exactly, I'm not quite sure. I'm also not sure of the reception that's awaiting us. But I'm sure our love is strong enough to weather whatever is ahead. There is, for the moment, time to write as the miles clatter beneath our wheels. This will most likely be the last time I experience the power and luxury of my Astor ancestors. It's that very power, and knowing how to use it, that has brought Fred and me safely to this exciting point in our lives together. I must start at the beginning of our amazing journey when I left Fairfield forever.

The long trek along the lane with several layers of clothes under a raincoat was exhausting. I'd been careful and stayed to the side beyond the trees in case Father came home during the night. He did that sometimes. I saw the headlights slowly approach then go out. It only took William a minute to toss the suitcase in the back seat. He helped me get into the car with all my bulky clothes and we headed back down the lane with the lights still off until we reached the road and were safely on our way. As the miles flew by without a sign of anyone following, I began peeling off the layers of skirts, blouses, and dresses that Mother had helped stuff me into so they wouldn't take up valuable space in the suitcase. I couldn't risk leaving my journals behind for someone other than me to read. Besides, they're the story of my life and all that will remain when I'm dead. Mother put them in a satchel that I slung over my shoulder. It broke my heart to think I might never see Mother again. But she promised that she would see me as soon as she could arrange something. William dropped me off at Fred's cabin in Fredericksburg. Before leaving, he gave me a hug and told me to have a wonderful life. I could always count on him if I got in trouble. I'll write to him when I get safely to Ohio.

Fred and I made the first train to New York City that morning. I couldn't risk anyone seeing us enter the Waldorf. I telephoned Clarence from Grand Central Station and told him we'd find our way to Track 61 under the hotel. He could meet us there. But he said no, that civilians on the little used track would draw attention. Instead we met him at the delivery entrance. The three of us took the service elevator to the suite. Mother had already given Clarence orders to put all the boxes that arrived from the stores in crates. My new Louis Vuitton luggage had also arrived. I packed while Fred and Clarence planned a way to get us away safely before Father realized I was gone. With the luggage placed carefully in the last crate, Clarence hammered the nails securing the lid. I felt as though the life I knew had just been nailed shut. It was gone forever. Clarence wheeled the crate to the service elevator. I took a few precious minutes to write Mother a short letter telling her how much I love her. I placed it in the secret compartment in the desk. Fred and I arrived at the loading dock to find a Macy's delivery truck. Clarence helped with the last of our crates and motioned for us to climb in the back of the truck. He assured us we'd be safe for the short ride. The truck would drive back to Macy's. If the driver was sure no one was watching, he would double back to Cousin Carrie's. Saying goodbye to Clarence and the Waldorf was hard. They had both been a part of my life for as long as I can remember. I wonder if I'll ever see them again. I hope so.

Fred and I clung together, wedged between the crates, as the truck rattled down the streets. After coming to an abrupt stop, the doors flew open and Cousin Carrie was there to greet us. She never liked Father, and seemed to be taking enormous pleasure in thwarting his plans for me. Clarence called to say that Father's men were watching the hotel. But as far as he knew, all of the employees could truthfully say they had not seen us.

Yesterday evening Cousin Carrie surprised us with a wedding ceremony, complete with flowers and the minister. We had no more than finished our vows when Clarence called to say that Father was in town asking questions. He and his men would no doubt be calling on his wife's cousin.

An hour later we boarded the Astor's Pullman car, which sat on a siding in the railroad yard, under the cover of darkness. Fred was amazed that a train car could be so luxurious and even more amazed that it was available for us to use. Our departure was not scheduled for another day, so we had to wait until our luggage arrived and the provisions for the trip stowed. Fred and I sat all night dozing and listening for any signs that Father may have remembered the seldom-used Pullman and come to investigate. The screeching wheels and the jolt of the coupling to the train nearly knocked me to the floor. The forward movement announced that we were finally on our way. Fred and I went out to the car's rear railing. Holding hands, we watched the New York skyline disappear against the magnificent sunrise. I have nothing now but Fred.

Seven hours later, I watched my husband's face and listened to his gentle snores. Apparently the rhythmic rocking of the Pullman had lulled him to sleep. He looks like a man without a care. We've safely escaped Father and his men. Fred is happy to return home to the loving arms of his parents. It was such a great adventure in the beginning. Now, I'm not so sure. The clattering wheels take me closer to the unknown. Jackson cares for our every need, efficiently moving around the tiny compartments. Jackson has been taking care of the Astors and their guests aboard the Pullman rail car for more than a decade. He prepares exquisite meals in the tiny galley. Throughout the day he freshens our berths and tidies the lounge area and somehow magically appears to refill glasses of lemonade or empty ashtrays. Thank God and Cousin Carrie for Jackson. I couldn't do this.

I still worry that Father has somehow found out where I am. Jackson lowers the shades at the windows whenever we pull into a station to prevent anyone from looking inside. We'll spend the night in the Collinwood yard, east of Cleveland, until the Pullman can be hooked to a southbound train going to Mansfield, Ohio. Cedar Hill is too small to have its own rail line. I've never lived in a small town. To hear Fred describe Cedar Hill, it sounds like one big family. I've never been part of a big family. I think it'll be wonderful.

WEDNESDAY, MAY 8, 1946

We're once again rolling along rails of steel. I keep remembering Mother's warnings that being a housewife without servants will be difficult. I admitted my fears to Fred last night. He assured me that being a housewife is easy, and his mother will be there to help. There wasn't much time for the exact details of being a housewife since Fred began unbuttoning my blouse and skirt as he talked. I was totally distracted. I guess you could say we've been on the run since Fredericksburg. At last the Pullman was stationary on the siding, and not about to roll one of us onto the floor from our narrow berth. For the first time we could relax and feel safe in each other's arms.

After last night, there's no longer any doubt in my mind that I married the right man. It was as though we sailed away together on a sea of passion. Time and place disappeared. My whole body ached for his touch, his mouth, and the fire that exploded as he entered me. Later, Fred's strong arms cradled me as I drifted into dreams of contentment. His passion was there to wake me. We made love until the morning sun signaled a new day.

The jolt and clatter of the coupling announced that I was once again rolling into the unknown. The smell of coffee brewing reminded me that I must get on with the day. We're due to arrive in Mansfield mid afternoon. I think I'll change into my periwinkle suit before we arrive. First impressions are so important, and I'll be quite a shock to Fred's parents.

Olivia rifled back through the pages to check the dates. It was almost a week before her mother's next entry. The pages were filled with the frustration of being a housewife.

Resting the open book on the side table, Olivia's gaze went to the bed. She could almost see her mother wrapped in loving arms. Maureen and her mother were both making sacrifices that would change their lives forever, and all in the name of love. Olivia could imagine her grandmother's heart being ripped apart as she helped her daughter pack.

She'd wanted answers about her mother's life. Even after reading the details, Olivia found it hard to believe. It took great courage for her mother to leave her life behind and walk into a life she knew nothing about. She had no idea what being a housewife meant. It appeared the only thing Mom ever worried about was what she was going to wear.

Olivia wished she could hear her grandmother's side of the story.

Olivia got to her feet. She paced back and forth across the room. She could understand her mother keeping the drama leading up to her leaving a secret from her young children. But didn't it ever occur to her that one of her children might have to deal with her past? Knowing about her family . . . *my* family would have helped prepare me for life at Fairfield.

The week before she died, Mom had mentioned she'd been engaged to William. But she left out the details. What if the journals had been lost or destroyed over the last twenty years? Dealing with this inheritance without knowing the facts would be so much harder. She saw William differently than she had in Horatio's office. If she hadn't read the real story, would William have told her what happened? Not the best way to start off a relationship with a man who may just be my only ally here.

Sarah appeared in the doorway. "Ma'am, are you okay? I've heard you walking back-and-forth for some time now."

"You heard me walking?"

"This part of the house is over two hundred years old. The floors have a voice all their own."

Olivia chuckled. "Thanks for checking on me."

"The help have all gone. I usually do a simple meal on Friday's. Would you mind spaghetti tonight?"

"No, that sounds fine. I'll just freshen up and be down at seven."

Interesting. Had Sarah actually been concerned or had the sound of squeaking floors irritated her?

Sarah pushed open the door within seconds of Olivia pressing the call button with her foot. "That was no simple spaghetti dinner, Sarah. I'd be willing to bet your sauce simmered on the stove all afternoon."

"Thank you, ma'am. I'm glad you liked it. There's one last piece of pecan pie left."

Olivia patted her stomach. "As much as I hate to, I'm afraid I'll have to pass on the pie. There isn't room for another bite."

Olivia pushed her chair back and stood. "I'll be in the library making a phone call."

"Yes, ma'am."

The faint odor of furniture polish and ammonia now mixed with the sent of old books. Olivia settled into the corner of the sofa for her nightly call to Travis.

He answered quickly, as if he'd been waiting.

"Hi, Livy. Spooky and I miss you."

"I miss you too." The words came out automatically in response. "How was your day?"

"Okay. Nick and his crew were here all day. The house smells like a lumber mill."

"Speaking of Nick, I explored the basement this morning . . . at least part of the basement. I can't wait to get him here to see this. It makes the one in the Captain's house look like a root cellar."

Travis didn't respond. Maybe the connection went bad.

"Didn't you hear? It's amazing. Thick, brick walls and floor and massive beams. It's built like a fort. He's going to love this place."

Travis waited a beat. "What I heard is that you can't wait to show the house to Nick. But I don't remember you asking *me* to come."

What was his problem? He sounded pissed. "Travis. You don't understand."

"I think I do. Look, I'm tired."

"Travis. Listen, I'm . . ."

"I have a busy day tomorrow. I'll talk to you tomorrow night."

"Travis. Don't hang up."

He didn't hear—the line had already gone dead.

The decorative pillow at Olivia's side took a direct hit. After giving it another good punch she tossed it to the far end of the sofa.

Travis hadn't given her a chance to tell him what she'd found in the diary. The reason she'd been in such a hurry to call him was to tell him that she'd finally learned the whole story of why her mother had married Fred and not William.

Should she call him back and apologize? For what? He was the one who got all pissy. No. She'd let him stew overnight and call him tomorrow.

28

Olivia picked at the grits on her plate. She still didn't like them, but at least the ham wasn't quite so salty—or maybe she was just acquiring a new taste.

Sarah appeared at the doorway without a sound. How *did* she do that? Had she found a way to levitate above the floors?

"Are you still feeling poorly, ma'am? Didn't breakfast agree with you?" She crossed the room to Olivia's side. "Or maybe you just don't like grits."

Sarah's knitted brows showed genuine concern.

Olivia desperately wanted to confide in someone. Maybe that someone could be Sarah. She couldn't worry about hurting her feelings or second-guessing her any longer.

"I miss my mother. I was fifteen when she died. I've been reading her diaries. When I'd ask about where she grew up, my mother would just say 'an old farm in Virginia.' And here I am, and this is not just an old farm." Olivia's voice caught as she swallowed her sorrow. "I haven't found a single thing of my mother's. It's like she was never here. *Nothing.*"

Olivia wiped a tear with the corner of her napkin.

Sarah nodded. Was that a slight smile of compassion?

"Her diaries tell me a lot about her life and feelings after the age of sixteen, but I know nothing of the little girl. I inherited Fairfield, the house in Norfolk, a suite at the Waldorf, and the McLeod shares in a company that builds *ships*, for heaven's sake. And I only found out about them a few weeks ago. I'm *trying* to find my mother in all of this."

"I understand." Without another word Sarah picked up the plate and left the room.

Olivia let out a long sigh in defeat. So much for compassion. She added heartless to Sarah's list of qualities.

Olivia folded her napkin and placed it on the table. She pushed back her chair. What could she do on a Saturday morning? Perhaps she'd find solace in the library.

The swinging door opened with the sound of a whirr. Sarah held the door for an ancient woman in a motorized wheelchair. Her snow-white hair, cut short, surrounded a face that sparkled with life. Wrinkles covered a round face and although her skin was darker than Sarah's, they shared the same eyes and mouth.

The old woman's glazed dark-brown eyes held Olivia's. With the slight movement of her hand on a switch, she moved the wheelchair forward.

Olivia glanced up in time to see the love in Sarah's eyes as she let the door swing closed behind her. "I'd like you to meet my mother, Miranda."

Miranda. Olivia had run across the name several times in the journal. Could this woman be Maureen's Miranda?

"Come here child, let me see you." The raspy voice was unsteady, but clear.

Olivia bent down so Miranda could get a closer look. Her shriveled hand reached out to stroke Olivia's cheek. Taking Olivia's hand, a wide-eyed Miranda turned toward her daughter. "This is my Maureen. She's come home and all growed up."

"No, mamma, this is Mrs. Bentley, Maureen's daughter."

Olivia got down on her knees next to the wheelchair. She reached out to grab the gnarled hand in hers. "My name is Olivia."

Miranda frowned and shook her head. "No. Olivia died. She said I could have her chair when she passed."

"That was my grandmother. I'm glad she gave you this lovely chair."

"I'm happy you came home." Miranda frowned. "Things are different now." She shook her head. "You were gone a long time."

Sarah patted her mother's shoulder. "I'm sorry ma'am. She just turned ninety-five and she gets confused."

"*No,* I don't!" Miranda wrung her hands. "I know *everything.*"

"Maureen was my mother. I know that I look like her," soothed Olivia.

Miranda pursed her lips and shook her head.

"It's okay." Olivia patted her hand. "I have a nickname that only very special people can use. They call me Livy."

"That's a pretty name. It sounds like a flower. Now get up, and we'll go to your playroom."

Olivia followed the whirr of the chair to the room down the hall. For all the times she'd walked up and down the hall on her way to the library and office, she hadn't paid much attention to the informal sitting room.

Olivia moved to stand in front of the heavily carved fireplace—so typical of the Georgian period. A landscape hung above of a beautiful rose garden. "This was the playroom?"

"All yer toys was here and later the television. Yer mamma listened to the radio and knit while she watched you play. We could all watch you in here so nothing bad would happen to you. This was yer mamma's favorite room when Mister Angus was alive. Did you forget? I forget things sometimes."

Was it in this fireplace that Angus burned the last letter from her mother—the letter that ignited the hatred in her grandmother's heart?

"I see you like the library better now." Miranda waved an arm directing Olivia to follow.

The chair whirred to life. Olivia followed it to the library at the end of the hall.

Miranda stopped before going into the library.

"What's wrong, Miranda?"

"Miz Olivia died over there." She pointed to the Palladian window. "Her bed was in front of the winda so she could see the garden where you played. She knowed how you used to sneak down in the middle of the night and swim in the pool, as naked as the day you was born. My bed was over there."

"What do you mean, Miranda? You slept here too? With my grandmother or when Maureen was alive?"

"I was worried, you see. Miz Olivia was always strong and healthy as a body can be. Oh, her ticker was off a might. But it didn't slow her down none, until she got sick all of a sudden like. Somethin' just didn't sit right. I got it in my head to watch over her."

"Thank you, Miranda. I'm sure she appreciated your concern."

"Miz Olivia gave me this chair. She said I could have it when she passed."

"I know, Miranda. And you drive it very well."

Olivia followed Miranda to a corner of the library. The old woman pointed to the lower shelves. "See. All yer books are still here."

Well-worn copies of *Robinson Crusoe* and *Heidi* were there along with some of Olivia's other childhood favorites. She sat on the floor and crossed her legs. After scanning the row, she pulled *Grimms' Fairy Tales* from the shelf.

"That's just the way you'd sit when you was little."

The image of her mother came to mind. Olivia and the twins would all be sitting cross-legged on the floor listening to every word.

A chill jolted Olivia back to the present. A strong whiff of rose. Where had that come from?

Maybe she'd find a rose pressed between the pages. Olivia turned the book on end and shook. An old photograph fell into Olivia's lap. The photo was of a young girl sitting on the lap of a woman who was reading to the child.

Olivia handed the picture to Miranda. "Do you know who they are?"

Miranda smiled. "Acourse I do. Yer mamma's readin' you a story. Don't you remember?" She handed the photo back to Olivia.

The girl was perhaps five or six. Even in black-and-white Olivia could tell it was her mother. With a lump in her throat, she held the photo to her heart.

For the next several hours Olivia listened to wonderful stories of her mother's childhood. A new energy flowed through Olivia's veins. Fairfield had been her mother's home—a wonderful home. Olivia would make it her home too.

Miranda's mind had an exhausting way of jumping from the present to the past, sometimes in the same sentence. So far the seemingly unrelated scraps of information didn't provide Olivia with any new insights on how her grandmother spent her last hours or why Miranda felt the need to watch over her.

Sarah knocked on the doorframe. "Excuse me for interrupting. It's time for lunch. Ma'am, give me fifteen minutes to get Mamma ready then I'll bring yours to the dining room."

Miranda's mouth turned down at the corners in a pout. Like a child that's just been scolded.

"Sarah, would it be okay if I ate with Miranda?"

Sarah frowned. "Benjamin joins us at the family table for lunch."

"I would like to join you, too. Besides, I haven't seen the kitchen yet."

"Yes. I want Lily to eat with us." Miranda's voice filled with enthusiasm.

Olivia squeezed Miranda's hand. "It's Livy," she said in a raised voice.

Miranda jerked back her hand. "I'm old—not deaf," came a raspy shout.

The chair came alive with a whirr. "Now come along Lily. Time for your lunch."

29

Miranda's stories about growing up at Fairfield flowed across the kitchen table for the next two hours. Steamboats—from ferries to cargo ships—docked at the Landing, and later, Mr. Angus arriving in one of his fast speedboats. The industrial revolution changed life in Norfolk and Richmond. Motorcars replaced carriages and the new fancy garages were built at Fairfield for a new generation of McLeods.

The intercom buzzed, announcing someone at the front gates. Olivia jumped at the raucous sound. Everyone looked toward the monitor.

Sarah pushed her chair back and stood. "It's Mister William, ma'am. I'll bring him to the ladies' parlor."

Miranda clapped her hands and winked at Olivia. "'Bout time he's come a callin'."

Olivia got up from the table and headed toward the parlor. What was spinning in that jumbled old head? Whatever it was, life at Fairfield had taken an amusing turn.

She glanced around the parlor. Should she be seated, or standing when he arrives? Hmm, standing always gave her more confidence and she still wasn't a hundred percent sure of William.

He entered the room and walked over to where Olivia stood with her back to the window. "I wonder if I'll ever be able to look at you without seeing Maureen? You even have her violet eyes." Taking her hand, he guided her to the sofa and sat beside her. Still holding Olivia's hand, he looked up at the painting of her grandmother that hung above the fireplace. "I always liked your grandmother. I have a much greater respect for her now that I realize what she was able to pull off."

Olivia found the slight pressure of William's hand reassuring. Her father had held her hand when she'd fallen off her bike, or when she'd needed an emotional boost. This felt good, too.

"I've studied Angus's will and your grandmother's. There's no question that you are the legal heir to her share in the company. You have my support, and I'll due my best to make everything right with my brothers."

"Thank you. And thank you for everything you did for my mother. I've been reading her journals over the past few weeks. Last night I read about how you found my father and brought them back together. Then you helped her escape. You're pretty amazing."

"I loved your mother. I didn't realize how much until she was gone. But I owed her that. I owed her a chance at happiness."

This man, who looked like Cary Grant without the dimple in his chin, had sacrificed a lot for her mother. A hint of sorrow lingered in his voice.

"Did *you* ever find happiness?"

His gaze shifted from her to the window. She got the sense that he was staring into the past. "Yes, I did find happiness with Marguerite, a woman my father approved of. He'd convinced me from an early age that love isn't as important as duty. Now, I'm not so sure."

Olivia leaned her head on his shoulder. What was she doing? You don't just rest your head on a stranger's shoulder. But he wasn't a stranger—he could have been her father.

William lowered his head, resting it on Olivia's. She inhaled. The soft scent of some expensive aftershave soothed her fragile nerves. She felt his pain and the lost years.

William straightened, turning his head toward the door. Olivia recognized the whirr coming from the hallway.

The top of a head adorned in white curls poked around the corner.

"Hello, Miranda, it's nice to see you again," said William.

Miranda's chair stopped just inside the doorway. "I'm glad you two is gettin' back together. It hasn't been the same 'round here. Maureen likes to be called Lily now."

"Oh. Really? I don't under—"Miranda interrupted William mid-sentence.

"Miz Olivia gave me her chair before she—"

Sarah nearly ran into her mother's wheelchair as she came to an abrupt stop. "Mamma, what are you doing here? I thought you were taking your afternoon nap. Now back to your room."

Sarah ushered Miranda into the hall and watched her departure from the doorway. "I'm sorry, ma'am, this won't happen again. She's just used to having the run of the house—at least the first floor." Sarah shook her head. "And she can get outside with that thing too."

"Don't worry about it. She certainly will keep me on my toes," laughed Olivia. "I've never had to think of myself as two people before."

Sarah followed after her mother.

William stood and moved to a chair. "I take it from Miranda's comment that she thinks you're Maureen. Although she doesn't seem to realize that I'm now old enough to be your father." A frown creased his brow. "Why do you want to be called Lily?"

"I don't. When Miranda and I were introduced she got confused by me having the same name as my grandmother. I told her she could call me Livy, which she heard as Lily. She associates it with the flower." Olivia shrugged. "I guess I'm stuck with it."

William nodded.

"Miranda seems to have had a very strong attachment to my grandmother. Do you know in the last months of her life Miranda slept in the library with her? Apparently she felt the need to protect my grandmother from something or someone. Who knows if she'll ever remember what that was?"

Miranda's stories were so vivid. She could be extremely clear about the past. If only there was a way to trick her mind into thinking about the night Grandmother died.

"Miranda took it upon herself to watch over your mother from the time she was born. There may have been an incident that I'm not aware of, but all of a sudden there was this fear of your mother being kidnapped. Your grandmother built the walls around the portion of the property closest to the house. That made a big impression on Miranda—she was the one who kept this place going."

"She was the housekeeper?"

"Yes—for most of her adult life." William's brow furrowed. "I don't remember when Sarah took over—she and Benjamin were already married."

This was interesting news. Miranda had played a huge part in life at Fairfield and yet there had been only a couple references to her in the journals. Maureen only wrote about herself and William. It was up to Olivia now to fill in the rest.

"I thought Sarah was born here at Fairfield, yet there was no mention of her in the journals. Where was she during all of this?"

"Your grandmother wanted to help Miranda's daughter make something of herself other than a house maid. So Sarah was sent to live with a family in New York. Your grandmother even paid for her college education. It was after Angus died that Sarah came back to help her mother."

"I'm glad you told me this. I have a better understanding of the relationships now. And why Sarah doesn't have much of a Southern accent."

"Maybe having this time here at the house will be good for you. You may come to see a different side to your mother—and your grandmother."

"Horatio told me not to leave the property. I'm supposed to send Benjamin for anything I need until I hear from him."

"That's a good idea."

"William, Horatio believes someone killed my grandmother."

"I know. He told me. It's why he's being so protective of you. The only reason Horatio and I are comfortable leaving you here is because Benjamin and Sarah are watching over you."

So they knew, too. Did everyone know her life could be in danger? Maybe this wasn't the time to mention that Horatio and Uncle Lionel put Clive and Wilson at the top of their suspect lists.

William smiled—a sly smile—like he could read her mind.

"You think it was my brothers, for the obvious reason of getting your grandmother's shares of the company. I don't believe either one of them is that stupid—they have too much to lose. However, I tend to believe that *someone* killed her, or at least helped her over the edge. It was very convenient timing."

Olivia nodded. "The answer is here—I'm sure of it."

William stood and moved toward the door. "I should leave."

Olivia followed him across the room.

"Be careful, Olivia, I don't want to lose you, too."

The important question was why did he lose her mother? What happened? Maybe William wouldn't answer—but she had to try.

"You loved my mother. Why did you let her go?" Olivia took a breath. "Actually, from what I read in her journal, you *pushed* her away. Why?"

William halted mid-stride. He spun around, his expression grim.

"I want the *real* story. Not the sugarcoated version," demanded Olivia

William sat in the sturdiest chair in the room, as if he needed the extra support. He wove his fingers together in a tight fist.

Olivia nestled into the corner of the sofa and waited while he gathered his thoughts.

"I loved Maureen. I would have made her happy. If it was passion she wanted—well, I could have given her that, too." William inhaled deeply then blew it out. "God. She was all I ever wanted."

"You sent her away."

William slapped the arm of the chair. "I saved her life!"

Olivia's heart plummeted.

"It started with Fred. Clive and Wilson saw the two of them in the wine cellar and told our father."

"Okay, I know about that—and the private detective he hired."

"I'd been in meetings at the shipyard. I overheard my father talking to Angus about getting Fred relocated to Pearl Harbor. Your grandfather was adamant that Fred not be hurt. He just wanted him out of the way. Father emphasized how dangerous Pearl Harbor was and said he'd try to get Fred an office job until the end of the year."

William shifted in his seat.

"After Angus left the office my father made a phone call arranging for Fred to have a fatal accident. I couldn't let that happen."

"Oh my, God!" Olivia jumped up and moved to the fireplace. "Did your father really have that kind of power?"

"I'm afraid so. I arranged for Fred's discharge—my father and I have the same name, so it wasn't hard to do. Watching Maureen and Fred together at the motel was a test. I saw, firsthand, how much she loved him. Of course, being the Naval hero that I was in her eyes, I figured that I could still win her back. And I intended to—until I got the frantic call from your grandmother."

Olivia stroked her brow. "You lost me at the motel."

"Unfortunately, Maureen chose that time in her life to begin standing up for herself. And worse yet, she threw fuel into the fire, by telling my father she cared nothing for McLeod and Morrison. Up until then, she'd pretty much done what she was told. She'd lived the life that was put before her without question. I believe the Maureen McLeod that our fathers saw that day scared the hell out of them."

"According to the journal, the men abruptly left together. Do you know where they went?"

"Sheffield Court. I don't know the details."

Surely her grandfather wouldn't have let any harm come to his daughter. Maybe he *was* angry with her—angry enough to cut her out of his will—but nothing more. There was more to this story than her mother could have known . . . maybe more than William knew.

"So you stepped in. Why?"

"Even if I won Maureen back, she would have lived under a microscope. She would just need to make one wrong move. Look at a diplomat the wrong way. Get drunk at a cocktail party. I'd already heard my father arrange to have Fred killed." William took a deep breath. "I loved her enough to keep her safe. I knew my father—he could have had her killed."

Olivia could no longer choke back the tears. "Why?"

"To protect the reputation of McLeod and Morrison and its future leader . . . me."

William stood and pulled a handkerchief from his pocket. He handed it to Olivia as he headed for the door. He turned at the hallway. "Now you know."

Olivia wiped her tears. There was nothing left to say.

"Like I said, Olivia, be careful."

She sat down on the sofa and let the tears flow. She cried for the pain her mother could never share, for the love of the grandmother she never knew, for the utter tragedy of it all.

Olivia leaned against the corner of the sofa tucking her legs under her, resting her head on her folded arms. The soft scent of roses drifted around her pushing away the tears.

Fortunately, Sarah didn't look up when Olivia entered the kitchen. She wasn't ready to explain her red eyes.

"I see Mister William left. I made a fresh pot of coffee, just in case the two of you wanted some." She continued rolling out dough on the table. "Everything okay? He was here a long time."

William's story was one she needed to keep to herself—at least for now.

"He told me how much he loved my mother." Olivia picked up the coffeepot. "Where will I find the cups? And don't come over, your hands are covered in flour."

"In the cupboard next to the sink."

Olivia reached up and grabbed a mug. She glanced over her shoulder toward Sarah. "Can I make you a cup?"

"No. Maybe when I'm done. But thank you for asking."

Olivia filled her mug and set the pot back on its warming plate. A buzzer went off. She jumped at the unexpected sound. The monitor next to the intercom came on showing Benjamin's truck passing through the front gates.

Hmm. A remote. So you don't need someone in the house to release the gates like with William earlier. Maybe it *is* possible to get onto the property undetected.

"Sarah, how many people have the remotes that open the gates?"

Sarah frowned. "Besides Benjamin? I have one in my car. Horatio has one, and your grandmother's Cadillac has one. There may be an extra one in the garage. Why?"

Olivia took a sip of coffee. If Grandmother's car wasn't being used since she was ill, could someone have taken her remote? She'd have to check out the car and also look for the spare. Maybe tomorrow she could explore the garage.

Olivia kept her back toward Sarah. "I was just wondering."

"That's only for convenience. The camera still shows the gates and who is coming or going. And if the camera failed, the buzzer would still let me know someone had passed through the electronic eye."

It didn't appear an intruder could have gotten in undetected by way of the gates, even with a remote. Maybe that was a dead-end. She'd find time to further explore the grounds. There had to be another entrance down by the barns.

Olivia took another sip of coffee. "What about the lawn along the James? Couldn't someone enter the property from the river? What about during a power failure?"

"Motion detectors. Alarms sound and the cameras cover the lawn. We turn them off if we're outside. And we have generators that come on if the power goes out."

"Interesting. I think I'll top off my cup and go to the library. I have some phone calls to make." Olivia hesitated, holding the kitchen door open. "By the way, I really like that rose-scented room freshener you're using in the parlor."

Sarah looked back over her shoulder. "What freshener?"

Olivia let the door swing close behind her.

The library was definitely her favorite room. Warm and comfy . . . a room you could kick back and put your feet up. Olivia made her little nest in the corner of the sofa, plopped down and reached for the phone to call Travis. It rang before she had a chance to dial.

"Hello?"

"Olivia, it's Emily."

"What a surprise. I'm happy you called."

"Well, you've been on my mind . . . I mean . . . a lot. So I had to call."

"Emily, it's amazing here. Not at all like the Captain's house."

"Oh my, God, Olivia. There's death all around you! Don't you feel it?"

Emily Elfin was the realtor who'd sold the old Captain's house to Olivia. They'd immediately become close friends, even if Emily was a little quirky. Olivia knew how easy it was for Emily to go off on a psychic tangent.

"Emily, people have been dying in this house for more than two hundred and fifty years. I guess it's something your extrasensory perception would pick up on, but truthfully . . . no, I don't feel it."

"I've been right about you being in danger before. You nearly died."

"Emily, you know I don't believe in all this ESP stuff."

"I'm feeling anger. Real strong anger close to you."

Olivia sighed. Emily was about to go psycho again. "I'm in the library where my grandmother died. It appears someone might have helped that along." She moved a pillow aside and sat up straighter. "I don't feel anything creepy."

She needed to change the subject.

"Is everything okay in Marblehead? I know Travis is staying at the house while I'm gone.

"Everything is fine. I stop by every day to check on him. Nick and his crew are there during the day. The renovations are coming along nicely. You don't have to worry about a thing."

"Thank you. You're a good friend. How about I call you in a few days?"

"Sounds good. Take care. And the next time you call, do it from a different room. That one is just full of anger—and not just from your grandmother."

Maybe there *was* something to Emily's psychic gift. Grandmother would certainly have been angry. Grandfather used the library as an office when he was at Fairfield, and from Mom's diaries, he could get angry, and before it was a library it was the overseer's house. His job was to deal with the slaves. A cloud of anger was understandable.

How she'd found the photo of her mother and grandmother came to mind. Maybe there were others tucked away in her mother's favorite books. Olivia pushed herself up and out of the sofa and wandered to the corner where her mother's books sat on the lowest shelves. Sitting cross-legged on the floor, she pulled each book out and turned them upside-down to shake out any photos.

An hour later and there were still no photos. "Damn. Nothing, not even a scrap of paper," Olivia muttered as the phone rang.

Jumping up, Olivia rushed to table next to the sofa where she'd left the phone. She answered on the second ring.

"Hello?"

"Wow. I see you have the phone answering figured out. How's it going?"

"Travis. It's wonderful to hear your voice. So much has happened since we talked last."

Olivia plopped down on the sofa, tucking her legs under her.

"You sound excited. It must all be good."

Hmm. Not all good, but the bad stuff needed to wait. His protective instincts might kick in and he'd jump on the next plane to Richmond. Travis still needed to be kept at a distance—at least for a while longer.

"I found Miranda! You remember—the name in the journal. She was the housekeeper here when Mom was growing up. Well, she's still here, and she's Sarah's mother. Well, her mind isn't always here—she has dementia. She thinks I'm Maureen. But I'm learning a lot about Mom when she was a child. I even found a photo of her sitting on her mother's lap during story time. It fell out of *Grimms' Fairy Tales* and is the only photo I've found in the whole house."

"Speaking of Sarah, how are the two of you getting along?"

"We seemed to turn a corner today after she introduced me to her mother. I even had lunch with them in the kitchen. It's been snowing. Not a lot, but enough to cover the ground."

"I called to say—"

"Oh, yeah. William stopped by again. He, too, believes someone murdered my grandmother. He doesn't think it was his brothers. But someone got into this house and I have to figure out how."

She left out the part about a contract going out on Fred and William sending her mother off to the boonies to save her from his father. Travis wasn't ready for this bit of news. She wasn't so sure what to make of it either.

"Livy, please be careful."

"Don't be silly. I'm always careful," said Olivia absentmindedly.

"Yeah. Right," Travis snorted.

"How much trouble can I get into? I'm stuck here. I'm not allowed to leave."

"Listen, Livy. My plans have changed. The Mid-America boat show is this week at the Cleveland Convention Center. My cousin, Michael, and our service manager set up our booth. I intended to be there on Monday and stay until the show closes. Attendance is up this year, and they need me—now."

"Don't worry about a thing. The house will still be standing when you get back."

"Emily comes by every day to check on me. I called her and she'll get the mail and feed Spooky. Nick and his crew are scheduled to be here all next week, so we're covered."

"When do you leave?"

"I'm packed and ready to go. I'll call each night when I get back to my apartment. You can also leave messages on my machine."

Travis Tanner owned Cleveland Yacht Sales, Port Clinton Yacht Sales, and Toledo Yacht Sales. Three years earlier, Travis purchased a small four-unit apartment building near the boat yard where he kept a unit for himself when he was in Cleveland. His cousin Michael managed both.

"Be careful, Travis. And don't worry about me. I really am fine."

"Love you," said Travis, then the line went dead.

"Love you, too," she muttered putting the phone back on the table.

She loved Travis but she wasn't ready to deal with his help. When she'd left Marblehead, Travis was telling her how he'd deal with the Morrisons, and help her sell the farm so they could get back home and plan their wedding. Well, Fairfield was beginning to feel more like home every day, and her head was spinning with people telling her what to do.

She sighed. At least the boat show was going to keep him busy for the next week.

Olivia got up, put the pillows back in place, turned out the lights and headed upstairs.

Half an hour later, she crawled into bed.

Alexandra's face glowed in the stream of light from the bathroom.

"It's been an exhausting day. Good night, Great-Grandmother."

30

Olivia poked at the mound of grits on her plate. She liked having Sunday breakfast in the kitchen with Sarah, Benjamin, and Miranda instead of the elegant dining room. She hated grits.

Sarah stood and grabbed Benjamin's empty plate and took it, along with her own, to the sink. "You seem a bit down-in-the-dumps this morning. Didn't you sleep well last night?" Sarah looked back over her shoulder at Olivia. "Are you sure you don't want Benjamin to remove that creepy painting of your great-grandmother from your room? I sure wouldn't want her staring down on me all night."

Olivia washed down a forkful of grits with coffee. She would acquire a taste for this Southern dish that seemed to be served with everything if it killed her—just to please Sarah.

"No! She's been trying to warn me of impending danger since I was fifteen. I just never knew who she was."

Miranda and Benjamin's eyes widened. Like she'd just told them there were ghosts dancing in the library. But then, they didn't know about her bizarre dreams. Olivia couldn't imagine telling them her story after just one week—but as unexpected as it was— they were looking like her new family.

Olivia finished the last bite of scrambled eggs as Sarah returned to the table. She glanced around the table studying each face in turn. Any sign of disinterest and she'd change the subject. But everyone, including Miranda, seemed eager for her to continue— there was no turning back now.

"The first dream came when I was fifteen—I was being chased along an ocean-side cliff by someone in a long, black-hooded cape. Then I'm falling through the air and land on the rocks below. That's when I woke up—with a sore back."

Olivia took another sip of coffee. The memory of that dream returned along with the horror that followed.

"I had the dream twice that week. On Sunday, a police officer came to my grandparent's cottage. He told us Mom, Dad, and the twins had been killed in an automobile accident."

Sarah pushed her chair back and stood. "We heard about that. Your grandmother was devastated." Sarah walked over to the counter and brought back the coffee pot. "Mr. Lionel arranged for her to be there for the funeral. She was never the same after that. Like she'd given up on life. I think it was you that kept her going."

Olivia raised her cup toward Sarah to be refilled. "The dream came again just before my husband nearly killed me when his car ran off a bridge." Her throat tightened, her eyes burned with unshed tears. "It was the night our baby died."

Benjamin reached over and patted Olivia's hand. "I drove your grandmother all the way to Ohio. She wouldn't let me stop for anything but gas and food. She went to the hospital as often as she could—and only when she knew you'd be sleeping. Mr. Lionel took her through a side door so her name would never show up on hospital records."

"She had her own plane. Why didn't she fly?"

"The pilot would have had to file a flight plan and there would have been records of her landing in the Cleveland area. The trip had to be a secret."

Olivia nodded. "I understand."

Benjamin and Grandmother had been to Cedar Hill. Olivia thought back to her time in ICU. She'd felt so alone and unhappy—like she had nothing to live for, wanting to join her baby girl. And now, all these years later, she realizes she had a family who cared about her—who loved her. If only she could go back or turn back time. She'd gladly give up her inheritance just to be wrapped in her grandmother's arms.

Olivia wiped a tear with her napkin. "I know from Uncle Lionel, that if it had been known that Grandmother had contact with Maureen's daughter, then I couldn't inherit her shares of the company. I remember a woman dressed in black standing at my window in ICU. Uncle Lionel said I must have been dreaming." A sharp pain pierced Olivia's heart—Uncle Lionel had lied to her.

Sarah put the pot back on its warming plate and returned to the table. "Did you ever have the dream again?"

"Once. It was during a horrible nor'easter, last year. By this time I'd figured out that the dream was a premonition, a warning that something bad was going to happen to me. I locked myself in the house with windows rattling and steam pipes banging. But this time the dream was different. As I turned to look behind me, I saw the blue-veined hand of an old woman wearing a gold signet ring. She was reaching out, trying to pull me back from the edge." Olivia inhaled deeply then continued. "I didn't connect the woman in my dreams to a real person until I walked into the bedroom upstairs and saw the painting. There she was, sitting on that big horse, wearing the same cape and ring. It's such an unusual design. I would know it anywhere."

Benjamin's mouth hung open, Sarah's eyebrows couldn't go any higher, and Miranda glowed with a sly smile. But, no one said a word.

"I feel calm and safe with great-grandmother watching over me. The painting needs to stay right where it is."

Miranda wagged her finger at Olivia. "I knowed Missus Alexandra, and that's just what she did. She took care of everybody 'round these parts."

"Are you sure, Miranda?"

"She was there with my mamma when I was born in 1890. She was there to help with near all the babes here on the farm—and the neighbors, too."

Sarah frowned. "You never told me this."

Miranda pursed her lips. With a flick of her finger on the wheelchair's switch, she moved back from the table. "Wasn't never a reason to. Fairfield was a terrible mess after the war, and the freed men were a-leavin' for jobs up north. When Missus Alexandra and her man bought the place, it was a real wreck. She bought my mamma a new cook stove. Built her a big new house with bedrooms and a bathroom. She made the old cookhouse into a schoolroom. All us young'ns had to learn to read and write. After years of teachin' us herself, she got a real teacher to come three days a week."

"Did you ever tell Maureen this part of Fairfield's history?" Oops. She'd just let her mother's name slip out. She needed to be more careful.

"Don't remember. How come *you* don't remember?" Miranda's finger moved the lever on her wheelchair, backed up then moved to Olivia's side. "Do you remember the stories 'bout Sargent?"

Olivia shook her head. "No."

"That big stallion sure did love her. Why, he knowed every time she had to go tend to someone in these parts. He was knowed to jump his pasture fence and head back to the barn fer his saddle. If he started kickin' his stall door, the grooms knowed to get him ready 'cause the missus would come flyin' in to get him. He'd just stand and wait fer her to come out of the house or barn or wherever she was even if it was hours. It wasn't safe 'round these parts after the war, specially fer a lady out alone."

"Wow! That's some story. What happened to Sargent?" Olivia asked.

"He died of old age. Near broke the Missus Alexandra's heart. She buried him up in the corner of his pasture. Has a real fine stone marker. Miz Olivia buried Sinatra next to him."

Olivia hadn't seen the stable yet. She added the pasture to the growing list of places to explore. "Benjamin, do you think you could show me the stable later today?"

"Sure, and the garages and dairy barn. How 'bout later this afternoon?"

Sarah stood and moved around the table to Miranda. "As interesting as this has been, we need to change for church. Will you be okay here by yourself, ma'am? We won't be gone long, the church is just down the road."

Olivia hadn't connected the fact that it was Sunday and church. It had been over twenty years since she'd attended regular church services. Maybe this would be a good time for her to search the garage for the extra remote. If it's not there then perhaps someone used it to get onto the property—maybe they're still using it.

Benjamin pushed his chair back. "Don't you worry none. I'll set the alarms when we leave. Just remember not to go out outside."

"No problem," Olivia said. That eliminated searching the garage, but there was still half of the second floor she hadn't seen, and most of the kitchen wing. She'd been at Fairfield for a week now, yet Sarah hadn't taken her on a tour of the whole house. Why not? Surely she would be proud to show-off such a magnificent place—unless there was something Olivia wasn't supposed to see. It was the perfect time for house snooping.

Olivia watched the kitchen monitor as the ornate gates closed after a white sedan passed through. She wasn't sure how long a church service lasted—maybe an hour? And talking with friends after, and then the drive home . . . she calculated an hour and a half would be her maximum time to explore. She'd better keep to the second floor.

She took the stairs two-at-a-time then hesitated when she reached the hall. Three doors stood open, her room, her mother's old room, and the sage-green room with the beautiful Queen Anne décor. Three doors had remained closed for the entire week.

Olivia moved to the door opposite the green room. The shinny brass knob turned with ease. She entered a room fit for royalty. Paneled walls painted a creamy yellow were the perfect background for the elegant Chippendale furniture. Luxurious gold brocade dressed the windows and bedding, including the canopy over the bed. Olivia thought about her friends who might come for a visit. Who could she possibly put in this room—no one. Then Uncle Lionel came to mind—he'd probably love it.

A door to the right of the bed stood slightly ajar. The room beyond was brightly lit. Olivia walked in and gasped. She'd just gone from eighteenth-century elegance to European opulence. Golden hued onyx covered the walls and floor of a bathroom. The graceful tub and pedestal sink were adorned with gold-plated fixtures, as was the shower in the corner.

Olivia blinked. "Jeez, Grandmother, what were you thinking?" muttered Olivia as she backed out. She took a few minutes to open drawers and check out the wardrobe—all were empty. She quickly ran to the green room and checked those drawers and wardrobe—those, too, were empty. They were simply guest rooms, nothing more. Just what was it she expected to find? Maybe the reason her grandmother died, or something of her mother's that showed she actually grew up here? What was she not supposed to see?

Besides her mother's room and the sage-green room, there were two other doors on that side of the hallway. She opened the door closest to her mother's and walked into her mother's bathroom. She'd only been in the room once and hadn't noticed the second door leading to the hall.

Only one closed door left in the hall. She'd once seen Sarah go through that door. After a quick calculation, Olivia decided there wasn't enough space left on that side of the house for another bedroom. She hurried down the hall and turned the knob.

She entered a hallway with shelves along one wall ending at another door. Stacks of pillows, linens and supplies filled the rows. She felt the soft, luxurious towels as she made her way to the other door. Olivia's neck prickled, a shiver raced up her spine as she turned the knob. Warning sirens went off in her head. Maybe she should stop—go back—back to the safety of her room—and Great-Grandmother Alexandra.

Olivia clenched her teeth. What was wrong with her? This was her house and she had every right to open the door. A short set of steps led down to another hallway. Three sets of doors lined both sides—all were open. The ceiling was lower than the rest of the house and the plastered walls were trimmed in simple moldings. These must be the servant's rooms. She had to be above the kitchen wing. She passed two bedrooms that were comfortably furnished, then a bathroom. All appeared to have been redecorated in the last ten years.

Only one door left. Olivia stepped into a living room complete with sofa, recliner and a rocking chair. She remembered Benjamin telling her that they lived in the cook's apartment above the kitchen. She headed for what looked like a bedroom and bathroom when a sound startled her from behind. She turned around.

"What the hell?" she exclaimed. The far end of the room could have been in a James Bond movie. She moved toward shelves lined with ten monitors labeled, RIVER, MAIN GATE, SERVICE GATE, BARN, GARAGE, CEMETARY, LANE, STREET, HOUSE FRONT, HOUSE BACK. A spider web of cables connected the monitors to control panels with switches and lights—all blinking red. A desk area in the center contained a multi-line phone and sitting in its own holder—a microphone. "Shit, you could track spaceships from here. No one could get onto this property undetected. The killer had to be someone who had access to Grandmother beyond the property—or inside," Olivia murmured.

A light flashed yellow. A monitor came on showing the white car driving down the lane toward the front gates. Then a second monitor showed the gates as they slowly opened.

Olivia's heart raced. They were back. She couldn't let them find her in the 007 room. They'd chosen not to show her this, even though she knew about the monitor in the kitchen. Why? She couldn't risk destroying their relationship by having them find her snooping in their apartment. She had to get back downstairs.

Olivia rushed out of the room. She saw the stairs and hoped they led to the kitchen. They did. She leaned against the doorframe to catch her breath. She needed to look busy . . . or something. There was still coffee in the pot. Out of breath and with her heart racing, she poured herself a cup. She took the still hot coffee to the table and sat in the same chair she'd used earlier. She willed her breathing back to normal and took a sip of coffee—it tasted like tar. She plastered a welcoming smile on her face as the churchgoers entered from the mudroom.

Sarah set her purse on the table. "I hope you haven't been sitting here the whole time," she said in an apologetic voice.

"Nope, just making myself at home. I couldn't resist the smell of your pot roast any longer."

"Hey, Miz Olivia, it's a beautiful day. How 'bout I show you the barns and stable after dinner."

"Wonderful. I'll just run upstairs and get my coat so I'll be ready when you are."

"That fur thing you wear?" Benjamin shook his head in disapproval. "I don't know when the last time you was in a barn, but they're dirty. And those high-heel boots won't even get you that far."

"Sorry, Benjamin, but this is as casual as I have at the moment. I didn't know how long I'd be here so I didn't bring clothes suitable for traipsing around the farm. I figured I'd have time for shopping to pick up whatever I needed." Olivia gestured to encompass the room and gave an amused laugh. "I never considered I'd be on house-arrest."

Benjamin looked at his watch. "How 'bout we go in an hour— right after dinner? I think we can find everything you need at Thalhimer's in Richmond."

"As much as I need different clothes, I'm not supposed to leave the property."

"I promise not to let you out of my sight. You'll be okay."

"Works for me."

Olivia stood before the long mirror in the dressing room feeling comfortable in her Gloria Vanderbilt jeans and blue and white-stripped shirt, complete with shoulder pads. She cinched a wide yellow belt and twirled around with a smile. Her shopping trip had been a success.

"Excuse me, ma'am." Sarah stood in the doorway.

"I'm glad you're here, Sarah. I moved my grandmother's clothes to one end of the closet to make more room for mine. Thank you for emptying the drawers for me, they're perfect."

"You're welcome. We can go through your grandmother's things when you have time. I've left everything as it was when she passed."

"There's no rush, Sarah. I have a lot of other things to worry about first."

"I understand. Supper is ready."

Olivia followed Sarah into the kitchen. "Meatloaf and mashed potatoes? Really?"

Sarah chuckled. "I've watched you pushing around those grits."

"But I'm trying. Maybe a little at a time instead of a huge mound?"

Miranda's eyebrows shot up. "Even all growed up, you still don't like grits?"

Olivia remembered her mother's very basic culinary skills. It was nice to know her aversion to grits came naturally.

An hour later, with a stomach ready to burst, Olivia stood and excused herself from the table. "That was a wonderful meal, Sarah. I think I'll spend the rest of the evening in my room."

"Sleep well. See you in the morning."

Ever since Miranda appeared Sarah had become a new person—friendly, even. And spending the afternoon shopping with Benjamin had been a real treat. The only thing that would make the day perfect would be to have her grandmother at her side.

She must find out what happened. There had to be something from the days leading up to her grandmother's death. Maybe she should start with her clothes.

Olivia opened the closet doors. She checked every pocket hoping to find something that would lead her in the right direction. Nothing. She stood back studying the array of garments hanging before her. Interesting. There were a few obviously couture gowns, a few expensive business suits, and day dresses. Then there were all the threadbare slacks and shirts. Olivia fingered the once expensive trousers. They appeared to have spent considerable time in the garden. A stranger looking at this closet would assume it was for two women . . . a socialite and a farmer.

Olivia propped pillows against the headboard then crawled into bed. She'd had another exciting day—too exciting to keep to herself.

Travis was busy in Cleveland . . . she'd call Uncle Lionel.

She grabbed the baby-blue Princess phone from the bedside table and dialed. He picked up on the second ring.

"Hello?"

"Uncle Lionel, I'm sorry to be calling you on a Sunday night, but I couldn't wait a minute longer. I found my family. I found my mother."

"You sound happier than I've heard you in a long time."

"Thank you for pushing me to come here. My Great-Grandmother Alexandra's portrait watches over me at night. Uncle Lionel you're not going to believe this, but she's the woman in those nightmares I told you about."

"Yes, I remember the painting. Rather gloomy."

"Oh, Uncle Lionel. I'm so ashamed of the anger I felt growing up toward my grandmother. I wish I could have known her."

"She loved you very much, Olivia."

"I know that now. Benjamin, Sarah and even Miranda spent the weekend making the past come to life for me. I'm determined to find out how and why my grandmother died. I'm proud to be named after her."

"You can trust Sarah and Benjamin to watch over you—believe me on this, Olivia." He paused a beat. "Miranda's still alive? She has to be a hundred by now."

"Close to it," Olivia chuckled. "Her mind wonders. She thinks I'm Maureen and calls me Lily. Never a dull moment."

"Sounds interesting. Please keep in touch."

"I'll call you next week. Gertrude will be working from here until William feels it's safe for us to go back to the shipyard."

"Remember my warning, Olivia. You must be careful."

Olivia swung her legs over the side of the bed. She needed to ask Uncle Lionel one important question.

"One more thing. Do you know anything about some high-tech security equipment? Real high-tech—like CIA level."

"I should. I arranged to have it installed."

Olivia jumped down from the bed. She paced back and forth within the limits of the phone cord. "I don't understand. *You* did this? Why?"

"About two years ago, your grandmother began complaining that someone was stealing files from her office, that reports were being altered. She thought her signature was being forged on documents. I talked to Gertrude who thought your grandmother was just imagining it, suffering from old age, becoming forgetful."

"Why wasn't Gertrude taking her seriously?"

"Because in each instance Gertrude found the reports. A year or so ago, your grandmother began complaining that someone was playing tricks on her at the office and even stealing valuable items. She said someone was trying to drive her crazy and have her committed so they could take her money."

Olivia's heart tightened. "Oh my, God. Grandmother must have been so frightened." And it was awfully convenient that Gertrude was the one to find the missing items.

"Six months before she died, her paranoia escalated—off the charts. She insisted that someone was trying to kill her. She had me upgrade her security system to the latest state-of-the-art equipment."

"Wow. Did she feel safe after that?"

"I suppose so. She became a recluse—never left Fairfield except for her hospital stays."

"Uncle Lionel, despite everything you did, all the precautions— you still believe someone poisoned her?"

"Yes, I do."

Olivia ended the call and slammed the phone down on the bedside table. "Damn-it. Just how involved was he in Grandmother's life? What else hasn't he told me?" Olivia asked her great-grandmother's portrait.

Her chest heaved in anger. Her fist landed squarely on the mantle. "What else don't I know about this place?"

Olivia pleaded through a blur of tears. "Please watch over me, Great-Grandmother."

31

No grits this morning—French toast and strawberries. Olivia stabbed a berry. Last night, Uncle Lionel said Benjamin and Sarah could be trusted to watch over her. *Could* they be trusted? How does Uncle Lionel know for sure? How does he know what's going on here? They'd had plenty of time to show her the equipment upstairs. Why hadn't they? Maybe they think she doesn't care. Maybe they think she plans to collect her money, sell the farm, and head back home. Or, maybe, they were waiting to see if they could trust *her*.

"You okay, ma'am? You haven't said a word since you sat down."

Olivia glanced around the table. Benjamin shoveled syrupy toast into his mouth like coal into a boiler. Miranda had nodded off.

Should she tell them about the conversation she'd had with Uncle Lionel last night? See what kind of reaction she'd get from Sarah and Benjamin when they find out she knew about the updated security equipment. Her gut said no—best to keep the call to herself.

"I guess my mind is on what Gertrude and I can accomplish today."

"I understand. I imagine this is a new world for you." Sarah said as she gathered up Miranda's plate and moved to the sink.

"If you only knew," Olivia murmured under her breath, her words drowned out by the running water.

The security buzzer sounded. Miranda's head jerked up. "What? What happened?" Her hand reached out to grab the edge of the table.

Sarah rushed to her mother's side. "It's just Miz Gertrude comin' through the gates."

Olivia glanced at her watch. Nine o'clock, right on time. She got up from the table and headed toward the door. "Sarah, bring Gertrude to the office. I'll go and get everything ready for her."

Gertrude was not only punctual, but efficient, as well. After Sarah made the introductions Gertrude went right to work. Olivia guessed her age at late fifties, early sixties. Her relatively wrinkle-free complexion was in sharp contrast to her nearly white hair pulled back in a bun. Gertrude sharpened the last pencil and placed it with the others in the highball glass—the one with the McLeod coat of arms etched on the outside. Gertrude turned the table into a makeshift desk, checked the file cabinets, and made sure the copy and fax machines were still in working order. The reports that meant nothing to Olivia were stacked neatly and sorted by date.

Gertrude licked the tip of her index finger then flipped through the reports for the second time. "Mrs. Bentley, I don't see the equipment list. It's the only one that your grandmother checked regularly. Are you sure this is all of them?"

"Yes. She had all of the reports together. Can you tell from her notes in the margins what she was looking for?"

"I was her secretary, ma'am. She didn't confide in me. I know what she asked me to bring to her here and what her routine was at the yard."

"How often did you come here?"

"The last year she was alive, I came once or twice a week. I took dictation and typed her correspondence, both for the yard and her various charities. She stopped attending functions that year, but she kept up with everything else."

"Gertrude, I thought I'd gone through all the file cabinets last week. I don't remember seeing any charities labeled."

"You wouldn't unless you knew what to look for—your grandmother coded them."

"Coded?"

"Mrs. McLeod had codes for everything she didn't want folks snooping around in. She figured if someone did get ahold of her files she'd make it hard for them to understand."

"Interesting. I didn't know that about her."

This was all so frustrating. It was looking like Grandmother was paranoid about everything. First the concerns about Mom being kidnapped and needing guards at Fairfield to watch over her, then the last few years when she thought someone was stealing from her office. And now it looks like she was even concerned about her charities. And she couldn't forget the fact that Grandmother thought someone was trying to poison her.

"Gertrude, can you look over those reports while I study the charity files? My grandmother was looking for something, and we need to find out what that was."

"I'll type out a list of the various charitable organizations and their codes. That should make it a lot easier for you."

The morning slipped away with only the sound of shuffling papers until Sarah knocked on the doorframe. "I think it's about time you ladies took a break. Lunch is ready in the dining room. I made your favorite chicken salad, Miz Gertrude."

"With grapes and pineapple?"

"Of course. And plenty of almonds," Sarah said as she turned and headed back down the hall.

Olivia put down the folder and got to her feet. "Wow! How come she makes you your favorite food on your first day?"

Gertrude stood. "You haven't been here long enough to have favorites."

Even though she wasn't sure if she could trust her, Olivia found Gertrude's appearance impressive. Her tall, trim frame carried the conservative tan tweed suit with an air of confidence. They marched down the hall together with Olivia taking two steps for every one of Gertrude's.

"I sure do like Sarah's biscuits," Olivia said. "I bet you know your way around this house better than I do."

Gertrude slowed and turned her head toward Olivia. Her eyes bore deeply into Olivia's, as if to read her thoughts. "I've been coming here for a long time."

It was after three o'clock when Gertrude placed the pencil in the glass and pushed the reports aside. "I'm sorry, Mrs. Bentley. I'm not going to be any help to you. I'm a secretary—and a good one at that. But I'm not an accountant. I haven't a clue what I should be looking for. I figured something would jump out at me . . . but nothing."

Olivia turned toward her with a sigh of defeat. "It's okay. I'll think of something. What we need is a financial detective."

"Is there such a thing?"

Olivia gave Gertrude a sly smile as she picked up the phone and dialed. "I know of one."

She didn't have long to wait before the call was answered. "Hi, Meg. It's Olivia. How would you like to take a break from that exciting job of yours?"

"Well . . . sure, what do you have in mind?" Meg sounded surprised to hear from her.

"We have a stack of financial reports that look harmless, but I think my grandmother died looking for something."

Gertrude's eyebrows shot up.

She'd looked genuinely surprised at the comment. Or maybe Gertrude was surprised that Olivia knew her grandmother hadn't died of old age.

"Meg, I need you here. Do you have any vacation time you can take?"

"Well, no, but I do believe I feel the flu coming on."

Olivia chuckled. "You poor thing. I'm putting Gertrude on the line. She'll make your airline reservations for you."

Half an hour later, Gertrude announced that Meg would arrive the next afternoon.

Olivia felt a ray of hope. If anyone could untangle this mess, it was Megan O'Brien.

An hour later Olivia and Sarah watched the kitchen monitor as Gertrude drove through the gates. "It was nice to see her again," Sarah said. "Was she able to help you?"

"Yeah, sort of."

Thoughts of Gertrude being the possible killer pushed every other thought to the back of Olivia's mind. She was the one person who had access to her grandmother at the shipyard and the house. She knew her schedule and probably arranged her schedule much of the time. She wrapped her arms tightly around herself, willing away the bubbling fear rising from the pit of her stomach.

Olivia grabbed the back of a chair. She wished she could confide in Sarah—but she couldn't. "I'll be upstairs in my room."

Five minutes later Olivia huddled amongst the pillows on her bed, holding the Princess phone to her ear. She pressed the buttons for the one person who would understand.

"Uncle Lionel, I'm so glad you answered. I'm really afraid."

"Olivia, what happened?"

"It's Gertrude. I think she's the killer." A shiver racked Olivia's body. "You told me I'd be safe here. You and Horatio told me not to leave—but Grandmother was killed in this house."

"Correction. Your grandmother *died* there. Now calm down. Tell me what happened?"

"If Grandmother was poisoned, then Gertrude had access to her, both at the yard and Fairfield. She was here a lot and knows the house . . . she told me." Olivia glanced at the closed bedroom door. "What about Sarah and Benjamin? They could have done it . . . or helped Gertrude." Olivia whispered. "I could be locked in a house with the killer."

"You're safe, Livy"

Olivia's hand trembled. "Get me out of here!"

"Listen to me, Olivia. There is no place on earth where you'd be more safe than you are right now," he paused a beat. "You have to trust me on this."

Olivia inhaled the fresh, calming scent of rose petals.

"Okay. You're right and nothing *really* happened. I don't know what came over me except an overactive imagination. Meg's coming tomorrow to help sort out the reports. That should be fun," Olivia said with a cross between forced humor and sarcasm.

"You're safe, Livy. I won't let anything happen to you."

"Thanks, Uncle Lionel. Talk to you soon," Olivia said and hung up.

She rolled over and tucked the pillow under her head and closed her eyes. She'd forgotten how much she loved the scent of roses.

Olivia drummed her fingers on the kitchen table.

"Staring at the screen isn't gonna get your friend here any sooner." Sara said as she set a fresh cup of coffee in front of Olivia. "I can bring her to the ladies parlor when she arrives."

"Thanks, but I want to greet her when she steps out of the car."

"I understand. Having your first guest must be exciting for you."

"Meg and I met when we were twelve. Our families had cottages next door to each other in Marblehead. We only saw each other during the summers." Olivia took a sip of steaming coffee. "Then . . . when we were fifteen Meg played a horrible trick on me. That was the summer my family were killed. We didn't see each other again until the year I stayed at the cottage to recover from the accident."

"So, the two of you made up and have been friends ever since?"

"Far from it. The next morning Gran and I closed up the cottage and went back to Cedar Hill."

"So how come you're friends now?"

"As fate would have it, Meg was working in the accounting department of East Side General Hospital when I took over as Vice President. It remained a tenuous relationship until last year."

Fortunately, the buzzer ended Olivia's journey into her past with Meg. She couldn't go there again. So much of her pain had its roots firmly buried in Meg. In the end it was Meg who unraveled the plot that would have sent Olivia to prison.

The black Cadillac pulled up to the steps as Olivia stepped out onto the stoop.

Meg opened her door and jumped out before Benjamin, in his chauffer's uniform, had even gotten his door open. Olivia shook her head. Meg never was one to stand on protocol.

Meg spread her arms out to her sides. "Wow. *This* is your mother's *farm?*"

Olivia laughed at Meg's exhilaration. "Come on up and get out of the cold."

Meg raced up the stairs and embraced Olivia in a huge hug. "This isn't cold—I left Cleveland in a blizzard."

The two walked arm-in-arm into the house where Sarah was waiting just inside the door. Olivia glanced back over her shoulder to see Benjamin pulling a suitcase from the trunk of the car.

"Meg, I'd like you to meet Sarah, Fairfield's housekeeper . . . and the most fabulous cook."

Olivia turned her head in Sarah's direction so Meg couldn't see, as she rolled her eyes and winked.

"Welcome to Fairfield, Miz Megan. We're having a bit of a problem with the grits."

Benjamin entered the hall. "Which room would you like me to put Miz Megan's luggage?"

Meg twirled around. "Wow. The last time I was in a house like this was when I went to President Garfield's house on a school fieldtrip."

"Really?" Olivia chuckled. "This one's a little older." She let Meg take in the grandeur surrounding her.

"You can put her bag at the top of the stairs, Benjamin. I'll let Meg choose her room."

Olivia hooked her arm through her friend's and headed toward the staircase. She inhaled and felt a warm sense of pride settle over her. She glanced back at Sarah. "Hmm. I really like the rose scented air freshener."

"Freshener? Smells like old wood and beeswax to me," Sarah said with a frown, then shook her head and walked toward the kitchen.

Olivia stopped first at the green Queen Anne room. "I thought you might like this room."

Meg stepped inside. "Hmm. Nice. Looks old. I'd be afraid to touch anything."

The gold Chippendale was next. "Jesus, no! I don't have the pedigree for this one." Meg backed out of the room. "Don't you have anything in this century? With a bed I can plop down on?"

"Yep, I think I have just what you're looking for." Olivia said as she marched down the hall to her mother's room.

She grabbed Meg's suitcase on the way and set it on the bed. "Mom's room."

"I love it," Meg screeched.

Olivia gestured to her right. "The bathroom is through that door. Make yourself comfortable and I'll be right across the hall— then we'll go down to the office."

"Meg, you've been hunched over those reports for the last three hours. Don't you have anything to say?"

The first thing Meg did upon arriving in the office was to familiarize herself with the reports Gertrude had left in three piles. "I can't see anything wrong with them. These equipment lists Gertrude sent over don't set off any alarms. I have no idea what your grandmother was looking for."

Olivia frowned, her lips pursed in frustration. "What about the notations in the margins?"

She'd been sure Meg could unravel the puzzle and come up with whatever it was that Grandmother was looking for.

"Well, Livy . . . I know I'm letting you down, but they don't mean anything to me." Meg took a deep breath. "Perhaps it's some kind of code your grandmother used. If that's the case you need to find the key."

"Code. Yeah, Gertrude said Grandmother used codes for every-thing. She was totally paranoid." Olivia threw down the folder she'd been reading on a women's shelter her grandmother funded. "Great. Now we have to look for a key."

"I'm sorry, Livy."

"You're my only hope. I'm sure my grandmother was murdered for something in those reports. What I haven't figured out yet is what or why." Olivia picked up the folder she'd tossed. "Maybe tomorrow you can help me with the charities. At least I have the key for those."

Footsteps in the hallway caused both Olivia and Meg to look up. Sarah stopped at the open door. "I don't know how much longer I can keep dinner before it isn't fit to eat."

"Oh my, God. I'm sorry, Sarah. The time got away from me. We're finished for the day. Give us a couple minutes to lock up."

"Miz Megan, what would you like to drink?" Sarah asked.

"Well, do you have Diet Dr Pepper?"

"No, but we have Diet Coke. I'll have Dr Pepper for you tomorrow."

"Coke will be fine. Just bring me the can. I don't need a glass."

Sarah raised her eyebrows and nodded, then walked back down the hall.

Meg swallowed another forkful of Beef Wellington. "I could get used to this real fast." She stabbed a piece of potato. "I don't know what kind of sauce this is, but I could eat the whole bowl full." Meg popped the potato into her mouth and continued to talk. "I can't believe you live like this. It's like a different world."

Olivia couldn't believe Meg talked with her mouth full. "Sometimes I eat in the kitchen. And this world has a language all its own—and I'm still learning."

"Well, I'd move here in a heartbeat," Meg said, still chewing.

"You've only been here three days. I think it might be a little premature to think about moving. This is your first trip to Virginia."

"First trip to the South." Meg gulped down the last of her drink. "I don't think a trip to Disney World counts."

Olivia took a sip of Merlot then set her glass down. "I enjoyed showing you around the farm, at least the parts I know. I still haven't been to the stables or cemetery."

"Miranda's a hoot. Did you say cemetery? You even have your own cemetery? I'm telling you . . . I'd never leave."

Olivia couldn't help but smile at the image of Meg eating like it was her last meal. The can of Diet Dr Pepper sat on the two hundred year old Chippendale table, under an eighteenth century Waterford chandelier, as out-of-place as a homeless man squatting in the middle of Tiffany's.

Thursday evening, Meg and Olivia sat cross-legged on her mother's bed discussing the events of the past three days.

"I wish I could stay longer and help you, but I can't push this flu episode much further. Besides there isn't anything in those reports to die for. Unless you can figure out what those notations in the margins are, there isn't anything else I can do. I would love to hang-out here and be waited on, but the fact is, unlike you, I'm not independently wealthy and need to work for a living."

"At least you helped with the mountain of charity files. I'll ask Horatio how I should proceed with them."

"And I helped you sort all those archive boxes upstairs. Who would have thought there were rooms above the office? This is the coolest place ever. But I *do* need to leave."

"I know, Meg. I'll have Gertrude make your reservations first thing in the morning."

Analyzing the reports was a long shot but she had to try. If any-one could figure this out it would be Meg. Perhaps she had this all wrong. Maybe they we're just dealing with the meaningless doo-dling of an old woman. Perhaps the reports had nothing to do with her grandmother's death. Could it be something at the shipyard? Was that why Wilson eliminated her office?

No . . . her gut said the answer was in the reports. Grandmother found something that got her killed. It couldn't all have been over the Western expansion. McLeod and Morrison didn't need to build planes—they were doing just fine with ships.

32

Sarah set a fresh pot of coffee on the hotplate on the sideboard and cleared the breakfast dishes. She brushed crumbs from the table and set a clean ashtray in front of Meg. "It being Friday, ma'am, the cleaning crew will be arriving around nine."

"Thanks, I think we'll head to the office and stay out of their way."

Meg pulled a pack of Salem Menthols out of a bright orange leather case and went through the ritual of tapping the cigarette on the box before lighting it. She took a long drag while frowning at Olivia. "Do we have to? I've spent way too much time in that office. Can't we spend my last day doing something fun?"

"I have an idea," said Sarah as she backed up against the swinging door with the tray of dirty dishes. "There are albums of old pictures of Fairfield dating back to the Civil War in the library. You'll find them in the glass fronted bookcase."

"Thanks, Sarah. That sounds like a great way to spend the morning." Olivia said while refilling her cup with the steaming coffee.

The girls were sitting cross-legged on the library floor when the phone rang. Olivia glanced at the mantle clock as she answered—9:30. "Hello?"

"Olivia, I have some news."

"Gertrude . . . Good morning. What have you got?"

"I have Megan on a two o'clock flight to Cleveland. The furniture has been put back in your office. Wilson tried his best to make the transition difficult for me but William intervened. I plan to work at the yard and to make sure everything is in place and ready for you."

"That was fast. When should I return?" Olivia asked.

"Although the furniture is here the files are scattered everywhere. It could take me several weeks to locate all of them and put them back in order. No use you coming until I'm finished."

Olivia wanted to jump in and help. Maybe find out how her grandmother was being poisoned. She wanted to see what Gertrude brought back into the office.

"Gertrude. Let me help you."

"It would be better if you didn't. I'll look for any notations that might help decipher the strange markings on the reports you have at the house."

It was clear she wasn't needed . . . or wanted at the yard. Was there something Gertrude didn't want her to see? She could use her authority and demand to be there when the files arrived. But she also couldn't afford to alienate Gertrude. Best not to make waves.

"Thanks, Gertrude. Let me know if you find anything."

Meg and Olivia spent the next hour putting together a pictorial history of Fairfield until Meg needed to head upstairs to pack.

Benjamin drove Meg to the airport after an early lunch. She'd only been at Fairfield a few days but she had filled the house with a new energy. On their walk around the property, Meg opened up in a way she'd never done before. Olivia hadn't realized Meg's marriage had been such a disaster, or the divorce so ugly. She knew her husband had custody of the kids, but she never guessed he'd bad-mouthed her to the point where her children seldom spoke to her. Olivia felt a new admiration toward her friend who could remain so outgoing despite her hardships.

There had to be something she could do to help Meg—but what?

Olivia settled into one of the comfy sofas in the library. There'd been so much going on at the farm the last few days she'd forgotten to call Emily for an update.

Olivia picked up the phone and dialed Emily's office number. "Hello?"

"Emily, it's Olivia."

"Hi, Livy. Look, I'm late for an appointment to show a house in Port Clinton. Everything is fine here, and Travis will be back from Cleveland on Monday. Don't worry about a thing."

"Okay, but I . . . just . . . wanted . . ."

Emily interrupted. "I really do have to go. I'll call you. Bye"

Everyone back in Marblehead was carrying on very well without her—even Travis. Right now, she had a job to do and she needed to stay focused. Going to her office at the shipyard was out of the question until William gave her the go-ahead, which allowed her plenty of time to work on how Grandmother died.

The first place to start was the facts. Olivia stood before the Palladian window. Her grandmother had died in a hospital bed placed in this spot. Olivia glanced across the room where Miranda's cot had been placed in front of the door leading to the porch. That eliminated anyone from entering from the outside, even if they somehow bypassed the alarms. The security system monitored everyone entering and leaving, and all the gates had been locked.

If her grandmother had been poisoned, did she just happen to die on that day, at that moment—or did someone help her along? Uncle Lionel said it was impossible for someone to get in undetected. Olivia thought back to the diaries. Her mother never mentioned *how* she was able to get in and out undetected. Perhaps the answer was in the old photos.

Olivia took the albums from the 1930s and '40s over to the table in front of the window. She opened the cover of the oldest one and began studying the photos.

A thumping sound out near the old barn drew her attention. Benjamin, wearing his fleece-lined jacket, was chopping wood. It seemed odd that he didn't have some younger man handle the strenuous outdoor chores. Maybe he liked the physical labor—he did appear to be in excellent shape for a man in his mid-sixties.

Olivia turned page after page to the rhythmic chopping sounds. There were quite a few pictures of a light-haired young girl on a pony—obviously not her mother. Picnics on the lawn along the riverbank, badminton nets and croquet courses in the summer. Every page had blank spots where photos had been removed. Whoever was responsible for removing any trace of her mother's existence at Fairfield had done a very good job of it. So far all she'd found was a photo stuck in a book and a stack of old records. Half an hour later the chopping stopped. Olivia looked up to see Benjamin, with ax in hand, walk through the barn door.

It couldn't have been more than five minutes later when Olivia heard a door close in the hallway. She looked up to see Benjamin standing at the door wearing the same red flannel shirt he'd been wearing at breakfast.

"I see you found the old photo albums. You'll learn a lot about the old days."

Olivia glanced out the window. Surely if he'd walked back toward the house, she would have noticed. And when did he have time to take off his jacket?

"See you at dinner, Miz Olivia."

"Benjamin, how did you . . ." He'd already gone before Olivia realized she was talking to thin air. She jumped to her feet and raced for the doorway in time to see Benjamin getting a royal chewing-out by Sarah. This wasn't the moment to interrupt for a simple question that could wait.

Olivia leaned against the archway. How had Benjamin done that? He was chopping wood, then she saw him go into the barn and not five minutes later he's in the house. Surely it would take him longer than five minutes to walk along the drive to the house.

Where was his coat—the closet?

Olivia crossed the hall to the small closet she'd seen on her first day, and opened the door.

Yep, his jacket was hanging on a hook.

"What the hell?" Olivia murmured. Wet boot prints led from the closet to the library, but only in one direction—out. There were none facing into the closet. So how did he hang up his jacket, unless he was already *in* the closet?

Olivia stepped into the small space, placing her feet on the wet footprints. She faced the wall where Benjamin's coat hung from a hook. Where had he come from? Olivia looked over her shoulder at the paneled wall behind her. It was the only wall free of hooks. She turned around placing her hands against the wall—it was cold. Why would an inside wall be that cold? She took a step back and studied the paneling. One section didn't meet evenly at the corners. Olivia ran her fingers along the corner. Cold air seeped out—it was a secret door.

She pushed on the wall—nothing happened. She remembered a horror film where the bad guy hid in a secret room. He'd twisted a hook to get in.

Olivia tried twisting the first two empty hooks—nothing.

She removed Benjamin's jacket and tried that hook—nothing happened.

"Damn," she mumbled and gave the wall two heavy jabs in frustration.

A section of the wall opened a couple of inches without a sound. There was enough space for her to reach in with her fingers and pull the panel open.

"Holy shit," she mumbled.

Olivia poked her head out the door and checked to see if Benjamin or Sarah were in sight—the hall was empty.

Olivia's heart pounded like a jackhammer. "Oh, well. It's *my* house."

Olivia reached inside the opening and found a switch, flooding the space in light. She pulled the hall door closed, took a deep breath then headed down the steps. She shivered as she studied the space. She was in a brick-lined tunnel going in two directions. It was too cold and damp to explore without a jacket. She headed back up the narrow brick stairs to the closet and grabbed Benjamin's coat.

Back down in the tunnel, Olivia needed to make a decision. Should she go right or left? She glanced back up the stairs—left would take her to the center of the house, right would lead where? The rounded ceiling was barely high enough for Olivia to stand without her hair touching the slimy bricks. She took a deep breath. Her lungs filled with the damp, stale scent of a place locked in time. Crude electric lights, attached to the wall on her right, dripped in cobwebs dimly lighting the way.

She went to the right. Within the tight space, the walls felt as though they were closing in on her. Olivia forced herself to concentrate on the hint of fresh air wafting through the passage.

She had no way of knowing how far she'd gone, passing a small boarded-up opening in the wall, before coming to a fork in the passage. The ceiling height here was much higher—high enough for Benjamin to stand. She paused long enough to decide which direction to take first.

Far off in the distance to her left she could barely make out another set of brick steps. The source of the fresh air definitely came from her right. But she had no idea how long this tunnel might be due to a bend about fifty feet ahead. She chose the right. Rounding the bend a large metal door loomed ahead. It was different than the one she'd seen in the basement. This one had crisscrossed bracing containing large round studs. It looked more like a door you'd see on a ship. She'd been so focused on the door that she hadn't noticed that the floor slanted downward until her foot shot out from under her. "Nooooo," she bellowed with arms flailing in all directions as she righted herself. "That was close," Olivia said as she took a step back.

She caught her breath and looked at the floor—it was covered in green slime. Between the slime and the door was approximately six feet of muddy water. There was no way to go any further without rubber boots. The bottom couple of inches of the door had rusted through allowing a stream of light and fresh air into the tunnel. The door obviously led outside—but where? A lever handle, bigger than anything she'd ever seen, kept the door securely in place.

"This is a dead end . . . for now." Olivia turned and went back to the intersection. She continued on until coming to another set of brick steps. At the top, the door opened into a small storage room. One window provided light. Various cans lined the shelves, from motor oil to rat poison. A bag of fertilizer sat in the corner. Olivia opened the door and walked into the old barn.

"Interesting. So that's how Benjamin did it." There was no time to explore the ancient structure. She could come back anytime. Right now, she needed to get back to the house.

Olivia headed back down the steps, closing the secret shelf unit behind her. She'd made so much progress in her relationship with Sarah and Benjamin, that she didn't want to ruin it by having them find her snooping—although, you really couldn't snoop in your own house. Never the less, she hurried back along the tunnel until she reached the stairs she'd originally come down.

She hesitated. The tunnel continued. Surely she had enough time to go a little further. She hadn't gone far when the tunnel made a slight turn to the left. In front of her was another steel door. This one was simple in design, just a single smooth panel. The rusty hinges didn't look like they'd moved in decades. Could it be the same door she'd seen in the basement? Another set of steps, along the tunnel, led up. Olivia went to the top and grasped a handle. Her hand froze. Sarah and Benjamin were arguing. Whatever was going on between them, she didn't want to find herself in the middle of it. She ran back down and along the tunnel until she came to the steps that would lead back to the closet outside the library.

Olivia turned the iron handle and the wall opened silently. She slipped off Benjamin's coat and pushed the wall back in place. After being careful to hang the jacket on the same hook, Olivia left the closet and hurried back to the table in the library.

Olivia's hand pressed against her chest. Her heart raced like a freight train. How many other secrets did Fairfield hold?

With Meg gone, Olivia once again joined Benjamin, Sarah, and Miranda for dinner in the kitchen. She debated whether she should mention that she'd found the tunnels and see what their reactions would be. Yet, she wanted one of them to tell her. Then she wouldn't feel so much like they were keeping secrets from her. What should she do?

Benjamin patted her arm. "You okay, Miz Olivia? You lookin' like you have a might heavy weight on those shoulders a yours."

This was her chance to see if one of them would talk about the tunnels or choose to keep them from her. "No, just thinking. I saw you chopping wood out near the barn earlier. The next minute you were standing outside the library door. How did you get in the house so fast?"

He grinned from ear to ear—like a Cheshire cat. "I went through the tunnel."

Best to act stupid and see how much they tell her. "What tunnel?"

"I guess no one told you about them."

Olivia turned toward Benjamin. "Why don't *you* tell me about them."

"Two houses on this land got burned down during Indian raids. A lot of folks died. So when they built this house they dug tunnels to hide in and escape. One goes to the river and the other to the old barn."

"Wow. That's amazing. My house in Marblehead has a tunnel that goes out to Lake Erie. It was used for bootlegging."

Benjamin nodded. "When you saw me, I was comin' from the closet in the hall. Back in the old days it was a way fer the overseer to escape slave revolts."

"Where does the tunnel go now?" Olivia asked as she looked at both Sarah and Miranda. Sarah nodded her agreement.

Miranda rubbed her hands together. "You was always a sneekin' down there. Remember?"

Olivia gave Benjamin a beseeching look to continue.

"To the store room in the old barn and out to the river. Course the river tunnel is all cut off now. Years ago, before my time, the entrance caved in. Just a rusty old door to hold back the riverbank." Benjamin stretched his legs out in front of him and clasped his hands on his stomach. "Another steel door leads to the basement, but you can't open it anymore. And the closet under the front stairs has steps, too."

Olivia leaned forward. "Who knows about the tunnels?"

Benjamin pushed back his chair. "Huh?"

"How many people know about the tunnels?"

"Oh. Well . . . don't you worry none. I'm the only one uses um to get around, especially in bad weather."

"Who else knows?"

Miranda clapped her hands. "I knows."

"Just Sarah and Miranda." He scratched his head as if it would help him remember. "Everyone else is dead."

Back in the library, an uneasy feeling nagged at the back of Olivia's mind. She searched through cabinets and drawers until she found old drawings of the property and buildings. She spread them on the table and compared the drawings of the house and property to the photos she'd looked at earlier. No reference to tunnels was indicated on any of the documents from 1730 to the present. The barn and the boat dock were both located inside the high brick walls, and the entrance at the river was well hidden. But that entrance didn't exist anymore. She needed to ask Miranda if she remembers when it caved in.

Security was tight, not even a power failure could put the sophisticated system out of commission. Her grandmother had been safe from intruders at Fairfield, and so was Olivia. So why was that sick feeling resting in the pit of her stomach?

The following week flew by. With Miranda always close at hand, telling stories from the past, Olivia felt her mother's history come alive. She eagerly awaited the next memory to surface from a mind locked in time.

The fine brown stone crunched beneath the narrow tires of Miranda's wheelchair as she and Olivia passed the old necessary house. "I'm glad Sarah suggested we take advantage of this warm, sunny morning for a walk. The snow has all but melted." Olivia reached down and tucked the blanket around Miranda's lap so it wouldn't slip.

"Remember, Lily, how you'd throw yer old toys down the holes? You sure was angry when yer goldfish died. Why, you throwed yer fish and the bowl down the hole. Was 'bout the time you reckoned it was a good hidin' place. Yer mamma ordered it padlocked."

Olivia knew by now to stay in character as Lily. Any reference to herself only confused Miranda with her mind fixed in the past. "It was a wonderful place to grow up. I've forgotten most of it."

Miranda stopped on a rise next to the stable. "You had yer pony."

"Munchkin."

Miranda looked up with a huge grin. "See, you *do* remember."

From here they could look out over the many acres of lush lawns, the orchards and the stately house flanked by once important out-buildings. "Yer mamma never wanted you a-feelin' like you lived behind prison walls. Miz Olivia tried her best to give you every-thin' to make a little girl happy." Miranda clutched the arms of the wheelchair. Her brow furrowed signaling troubled thoughts. "The rest of us worked to keep you safe."

What had it been like—living in a gilded cage? Miranda had spent her whole life at Fairfield. She'd lived through the happy times and the sad times. She was the only person alive who knew the real story of Maureen McLeod. Olivia *must* stay in character.

"Where did I ride Munchkin?"

"Don't you remember?"

Olivia shook her head in response.

"The grooms took you round the farm. Mostly you'd ride with Daisy when she'd come a-callin' on her pony."

"Miranda, how did she get in?"

Miranda waved a hand toward the far side of the barn. "The farm gates a-course. She just whistled. You raced around here with little notice of what was in front of ya. Why that pony of yers had yer mamma's flowers flying in all directions."

"Who let her in? Who heard her whistle?"

Miranda threw her arms up. "The guards, a-course! And Sarah thinks *my* mind is gone bad!"

Miranda's gloved hand reached for the controls. Her chair whirred to life. She turned back toward the house.

"I thought we were going to the stable to see Sinatra's stall," Olivia said.

"I'm cold. We need to go back to the house . . . now."

"But, Miranda, I thought we were . . ."

"Don't argue, Lily!"

Olivia followed the slow-moving chair back to the house. What had she said to piss Miranda off?

Sarah met them at the ramp leading up to the kitchen door.

Olivia hopped onto the ramp preventing Miranda from going any further. She bent down removing Miranda's hand from the controls. "What's wrong? Why are you suddenly so angry with me? What did I do?"

Tears filled Miranda's eyes. "Miz Olivia had guards to protect *you*!" Miranda screeched. "There were no guards to protect *her*! Just *me*!" The pain in her eyes seared Olivia's heart. "Just *me*!"

Olivia moved to the side to let Miranda pass.

Miranda's fingers moved to the controls and the chair moved forward.

Sarah's hands rested firmly on her hips, waiting for an explanation.

"I'm sorry, Sarah, I don't know what happened. Miranda was telling me about Daisy and my mother riding their ponies across the property. Then she mentioned something about guards, and the next thing I know she was angry."

"Your grandmother hired guards to watch over Maureen and the grounds. She took one of the old store houses near the barn gate and turned it into quarters for the men."

"I didn't know. It wasn't mentioned in Mother's journals." There was still so much Olivia didn't know. What was it about guards that caused such anger in Miranda?

Sarah remained quiet as she watched her mother negotiate the chair through the kitchen doorway. Her gaze shifted to the far side of the property, as if she could see through boxwood hedge and the trees beyond.

"Daisy's back. Her mother passed just after Christmas. She's been staying at the Landing."

33

Benjamin slid the large stable door to the side. "You ride, Miz Olivia?"

Olivia took a deep breath. The scent of manure and hay still lingered, clinging tenaciously to the massive old wood beams. The elegant row of stalls could have housed prized horses in Saratoga or Lexington, but it had been many years since these walls echoed with the nickering of contented Thoroughbreds and Arabians.

"Not for a long time." Olivia's eyes met Benjamin's. "Not since the car accident."

Olivia felt a warm sense of pride as she gently ran her fingers across the brass plate, mounted to the stall, with the name Sinatra engraved in script. Above it was Sargent's much older, more ornate plaque.

Benjamin nodded his understanding. "It was your grand-mother who brought the first Arabian to Fairfield. Before that it was Thoroughbreds. The planters loved horse racing, and Missus Alexandra was proud to bring Sargent down here from her father's stable in New York. She's the one who designed and had this built. It's one of the finest in all of Virginia."

"So, Sargent was a Thoroughbred?"

"Yep, and if you get a hankerin' to get back in the saddle, I can get this old place ready in no time flat."

Sunlight streamed in through the high windows giving brilliance to the brass Victorian-era fixtures running the length of the building. Olivia studied the row of elegant stalls with the ornate ironwork above as she walked back toward the large, tall-ceilinged carriage room. She didn't know a lot about woods, but the wood that lined this magnificent space looked a lot like her grandmother Thompson's mahogany piecrust table. She looked forward to showing this architectural masterpiece to Travis.

"Thanks, Benjamin, but I have quite a lot on my plate." She stopped at a golf cart. It appeared to have been recently used. She noticed slush residue along the sides. "It looks like this may be the local means of transportation."

"It comes in handy. You're welcome to it any time."

"Could this go as far as Daisy's house?"

"Sure. Just follow the old service road down to the wharf and you'll see the house off in the distance . . . big thing with a porch and columns across the front. You can't miss it. Called Fiddlers Landing."

"That's an odd name."

Benjamin raised his foot, resting it on the fender. "Back when Fairfield was a working plantation, the landing was the wharf where the sailing ships and barges came in for the tobacco and to drop off supplies. A big warehouse stood next to it, but it ain't there now. The Yankees used it for a hospital during the war and burned it down when they left."

"But where did the fiddler come from?"

"Well, the tale goes that the fella who watched over the wharf found a fiddle in a crate. Spent the next years learnin' to play the darn thing. Captains didn't need to know where the wharf was, just followed the sound of the fiddle."

She could listen to the rich history of Fairfield all day, but right now she needed to focus on how someone could get access to the house. Grandmother had hired guards to protect the grounds, yet she'd read in the journals how Maureen would sneak in and out undetected. She was missing something—but what? Perhaps Daisy had the answers.

"Benjamin, how do I get out through the service road gate?"

"There's a keypad. I change the numbers every week. A couple of the smaller gates have the same code." Benjamin pulled a notepad and pen from his jacket pocket and scribbled down the code. "I'll give you the new code when I change it."

"I'm not supposed to leave the property. Will it be safe for me to visit Daisy?"

"You'll be fine. Stay on the lane runnin' along the river. Tell me or Sarah before you go."

The little-used lane connecting Fairfield to Fiddlers Landing was, indeed, easy to follow and away from the public's eye, including any river traffic. Olivia slowed at the wharf, the first time she'd been out in the open since leaving the gate. The large, Southern style home sat on a rise overlooking the James. Olivia felt a sense of belonging. This was the same path her mother had traveled many times—at first on Munchkin, then on Sinatra, and finally in her Packard convertible. She couldn't miss the woman standing on the front porch, with arms waiving over her head. Sarah wasn't exaggerating when she'd said Daisy was excited about having Maureen's daughter over for a visit. Hopefully, Daisy would have a few pieces to the Fairfield puzzle.

Olivia followed the lane up to the house.

"Welcome, Olivia. Just leave the cart there in the drive. If you aren't the spitting image of your mother."

Olivia barely had both feet planted on the porch when Daisy had her locked in a hug strong enough to break a rib. "I've been waiting for the right time to call you, and here you are. We have so much to talk about."

Olivia lifted the tote bag she'd taken with her from the front seat of the golf cart. "I come bearing gifts." She reached in the bag and pulled out a decorative tin box. "This is from Sarah. She said you'd know what it was."

"Her special blend of tea. It's been my favorite ever since she began making it. Please thank her for me."

Olivia presented Daisy with a bottle of wine. "Sarah also sent this."

Daisy held the bottle as if it were a priceless art object. "Oh my. This is from your private collection. The 1959 Chateau Lafite Rothschild was your grandmother's favorite. Its a lovely Bordeaux, still young and will only get better over the next twenty years or so. We'll enjoy this together. You also have several cases of the 1934 which are magnificent."

"Ah . . . I have a private collection? I have a wine cellar?"

Daisy chuckled. "A very nice one. You'll have to ask Sarah to show it to you."

Olivia thought back to her exploration of the basement. She'd found two locked doors. One of them must be the wine cellar. What could the other room hold that would be as valuable as expensive cases of wine? One more thing to ask Sarah about.

Daisy hooked her arm through Olivia's and guided her to the open door. "Let's get you out of those boots and jacket. I do believe we're going to have an early spring. Although even a late spring on the James is a whole lot better than an early spring in Montana."

Daisy's medium-length grey hair was brushed back from a round face with far too many wrinkles framing large brown eyes and a generous mouth. It was a face that had seen many years in a harsh climate and perhaps dealt with more than her fair share of life's challenges. But still, it radiated happiness with a glow from within. Her straight, narrow frame fit elegantly in a sleek black wool pantsuit, adorned with a large silver and turquoise squash necklace. Olivia felt certain she would look just as elegant in jeans and a Stetson.

"I love your turquoise necklace. Although I've always admired American Indian jewelry, I don't own any," Olivia said.

"We'll have to fix that. Montana has a large Indian population. I have some magnificent pieces. I'd love for you to have one of them.

I wasn't sure if you'd had lunch so I had my housekeeper make some sandwiches and those little pecan tarts your mother loved."

Olivia followed Daisy to the cheerful dining room overlooking the river.

Daisy waved one arm toward the walls. "My mother loved floral prints. There's barely a room in the house that isn't covered in flowers. Please sit down. It's wonderful to have you here."

"Hmm, reminds me of Grans house in Cedar Hill. That generation must have been into overstuffed furniture and flowers."

"I like the change from the heavy log timbers and masculine furniture at home. This brings out the little girl in me," Daisy said wistfully.

Olivia scooted her chair up to the table. She placed her napkin in her lap then reached for an egg salad sandwich. "I've been reading my mother's journals, but there are huge gaps. I learned this morning about how you used to ride your pony through my grandmother's flowerbeds. I know you were my mother's best friend. I've seen many photos of you in the albums . . . unfortunately . . . none of Mom."

"We were only a year apart in age, so we became friends right from the start. You see, our mother's were friends, so we played together while they visited."

This was something else her mother hadn't told her. Olivia's friends, CeCe and Vanessa had always been hanging around, so she understood the importance of good friends—friends who'd become her family after her parents and brother's car accident. It would have been nice to know that her mother also had a good friend. The list of what she didn't know was growing longer.

"Your mother and I talked often after her marriage. I visited Cedar Hill several times. She'd asked me to be your godmother."

Olivia choked on the sip of tea she'd taken. Godmother? Daisy had been to Cedar Hill. This was unexpected news. Surely she would remember a strange new face visiting her mother.

"What? I don't understand."

"We decided my being a part of your life would only bring questions which couldn't be answered. It would bring unwanted attention to your mother's life here and put your grandmother in a very difficult position. So Lionel Montgomery was chosen as your godfather."

Olivia searched her memory for anything related to Daisy. "Mom did get letters from an old friend and they'd talk on the phone sometimes. But I don't remember you coming to Cedar Hill."

"You were about five on my last visit. You followed me around like a puppy, all the while asking questions. You loved my stories of Indians and life in Montana. You'd wear my jewelry and gallop around the house on your imaginary Indian pony. I gave you a child's silver bracelet with small turquois."

A vague memory of pretending to be an Indian princess percolated in Olivia's mind. She'd worn a complete costume, complete with headdress, for Halloween one year.

"I remember the bracelet. I wore it until my growing wrists nearly flattened it out. I still have it."

"Your mother and I decided it was best if I didn't come again, instead I'd call late at night after you'd gone to bed."

It was too bad Mom and Daisy couldn't have come up with a plausible story for their friendship. Having someone to call Auntie would have made the tragic times so much easier. She would have had a family and trips to Montana. How different her life might have been.

"I was at the funeral." Daisy reached over and squeezed Olivia's hand. "I stayed with Lionel and his family in Shaker Heights."

Olivia's chest tightened. She blinked back tears. How had she missed this? Grandmother *and* Daisy were there at the funeral. These women who'd loved Mom so much just walked away when the young Olivia needed them most. All for McLeod and Morrison? What a waste of precious lives.

"My grandmother Thompson was strict. She'd never liked Mom. You have no idea how much I wanted a family. I would have given anything to have you and Grandmother in my life. I wouldn't have cared about the company or the money."

"I'm sorry, Olivia. You've been thrust into a world you know nothing about. I'm sure you don't even know whom you can trust. And you're desperately trying to find out just who your mother really was. You're the lonely little girl who grew into a beautiful young woman controlled by manipulation and power—just like your mother."

Olivia finished the last pecan tart. She placed her napkin on the table.

"Olivia, can you stay for a few more minutes? There's something I think you should know." Daisy pushed her chair back and stood. "We'll be more comfortable in the living room."

How much more could there be? And now there was a serious note in Daisy's voice. Olivia stood and followed her to another flower filled room in shades of green and mauve.

Daisy motioned for Olivia to sit on the sofa. She sat down beside Olivia turning sideways and taking her hands in hers.

"Your grandmother called me after Lionel told her about Brian's suicide. She was devastated. I took the next plane and stayed with her at Fairfield. Her health had been declining and she was too weak to attend the funeral. Lionel kept us informed. Then we got the news about your financial situation and loosing your job."

Olivia's gut wrenched. She knew the story. It was in her grandmother's note. The one Uncle Lionel gave her when he told her of her inheritance.

"Your grandmother couldn't bear to leave you again. You needed her—and she needed you. We talked it over and she called Lionel to say she was selling her shares of the company to the Morrison brothers. She was done fighting them. Your welfare was more important to her. She'd bought the new Gulfstream with the latest technology. If Lionel or your grandmother got wind that the brothers had discovered you and that you could inherit or that you were in any kind of danger, then her pilot could have you here in a matter of hours.

Unfortunately, by this time, Lionel didn't know where you'd gone. We later learned you'd been living on your boat until you bought the old Captain's house. Your grandmother got really sick and went into the hospital before she contacted the Morrisons. I had to fly home for a family emergency and wasn't here when she died."

Her grandmother *had* loved her enough to give up McLeod and Morrison. She was too late. Someone was already planning her death.

Olivia's chest heaved. She wrapped her arms around Daisy and let twenty years of tears and sorrow flow.

Daisy rested her head on Olivia's. She rubbed Olivia's back and shared her pain.

"You're going to be okay, Livy."

She'd called her Livy. She sounded just like the mother she'd lost so many years before.

Olivia pushed away. She wiped her eyes, "I want my mother. I want to find the mom I never knew."

Daisy stood. "I understand," she said, then reached down and pulled Olivia to her feet.

Olivia moved toward the door. "I think I should leave. I'm not usually this emotional."

At the front door, Daisy handed Olivia her jacket. "Have you ever been to New York?"

Olivia pulled on her boots. "Yes. My husband, Brian, and I often went there for shopping and the theater."

"What are you going to do with the suite at the Waldorf?"

New York was the least of her problems. First, she needed to figure out how someone could gain access to Fairfield undetected. She needed to figure out what was so important in the financial reports. Then there was the Morrison brothers—was one of them responsible for her grandmother's death? Or Gertrude—she was now at the top of the list. And she needed to find a way to live with Miranda while pretending to be Maureen.

"I really don't know, Daisy. Maybe I should give it up." Olivia opened the door and stepped onto the porch.

"I would like to show you your mother's New York before you make that decision."

Back at Fairfield, Olivia found Sarah and Benjamin in the kitchen. Thankfully, Miranda hadn't gotten up from her afternoon nap. What had transpired over the past two hours still raced around in Olivia's head. She certainly wasn't ready to deal with yet another mind buried in the past.

Sarah looked up from kneading dough. "How did it go? Was Daisy happy to meet you?"

"She's taking me to New York."

"Wow! When?" asked Benjamin as he poured coffee into his mug. "Can I make you one, Miz Olivia?"

"No thanks, I just had lunch. We leave tomorrow."

"Benjamin, you'll need to bring Olivia's bag down from the trunk room." Sarah wiped her hands on her apron. "What did she tell you to pack?"

"Just my toothbrush . . . and my money."

"I'll call Clarence," said Sarah as she headed for the phone. "And your pilot."

34

"Close your mouth, Clarence," Daisy said with a chuckle. They stood near the clock in the lobby of the Waldorf Astoria with Clarence holding Olivia's hand.

"I know . . . it's like looking at a ghost. You'll get used to it."

Clarence turned toward Daisy. "Oh, I'm sorry. What happened to my manners? It's good to have you back."

Daisy motioned toward Clarence with a flourish. "To everyone who live in the upper floors of the Towers, Clarence *is* the Waldorf. He's much more than our Concierge, he's a friend and confidante."

Clarence's six foot plus trim frame stood erect, defying the fact he must be in his mid to late sixties. Thick grey hair, generously peppered with red, rested above a high forehead. Well-defined, rather thick arched eyebrows set off clear blue eyes. He would have been extremely handsome in his younger years.

"It's so nice to finally meet the man who apparently had been taking care of my grandmother for a very long time."

"And your mother. Now, would you like to go up and see your suite?"

Clarence led the way, holding the door open that would take them into the lobby of The Towers, and the elevator ride to the forty-second floor.

Clarence inserted a key into a slot marked 42. "You'll need a special key for the forty-second floor. I'll show you where your grandmother kept the spare set of keys."

Olivia pulled a white leather key case with the Waldorf's logo embossed in gold from her handbag. "Sarah gave me these before I left Fairfield."

Clarence glanced at the case as he held the elevator door open. "Yes, those are your grandmother's keys."

The three walked to a door with a polished brass plate labeled 42H. Olivia's mind flashed back to the diaries. Her mother mentioned the bedroom that she shared with Daisy on her visits, and her mother's room. There were vague mentions of a living room and kitchen. Olivia assumed she'd find a comfortably furnished hotel-type suite similar to those she and Brian had shared on their travels.

Clarence O'Connor turned the key in the lock.

Olivia took a deep breath as the door swung in. She stepped into a small foyer with one door on the right and a large archway leading to a round gallery beyond.

Clarence pointed to the door. "This is the staff entrance. It leads to the kitchen, butler's pantry, and workroom."

The sound of Olivia's heels resonated across the black and white marble floor. A round, gilded, table sat in the middle of the gallery. A large crystal chandelier hung above. The table was bare now, but Olivia could imagine a beautiful floral arrangement sitting in the middle. Dozens of photographs of famous people lined the walls.

Clarence pointed to one of the photos. "Here's your grandmother and Eleanor Roosevelt, they were good friends. They worked on many projects together."

Olivia now had a name for the mysterious ER initials she'd read in the journals. She followed Daisy through to the salon beyond.

Daisy twirled around with her arms outstretched. "Isn't this grand?"

The huge room appeared locked in a bygone time. The original Art Deco furniture looked as it must have been when the hotel opened in 1931. A grand piano sat in a corner to the left of a marble fireplace—a Steinway. The large, heavily carved desk drew her to the opposite corner. Horatio had said there's a secret compartment in the desk. Olivia wondered if she could find it?

"I saw a similar piece in a museum in France." Olivia ran her hand over the ornate panels in the upper doors. "French Gothic, dating around the 1850s. The one in France had a secret compartment hidden behind the fretwork above the doors. It seems out of place in a room of Art Deco."

"I know the story," exclaimed Daisy. "It belonged to Caroline Astor who gave it to her daughter, Carrie. Cousin Carrie didn't really like it and gave it to your grandmother when she moved in here."

"Wow! Caroline Astor!" If the rest of the suite was anything like this room, Olivia was going to need a lot of time to explore. "Grandmother could have entertained royalty here."

"She did," boasted Clarence.

Olivia turned to face Clarence and Daisy. "I feel like I'm in a time-warp."

"Your grandmother always said you can't improve on perfection, so why change something for the sake of change? It's been painted a few times and the drapes changed, but these are the same colors. The rug was replaced awhile back, but it's an exact copy of the original."

Olivia moved to the window. The sun glistened off the Chrysler Building. What a wonderful view this would be at night.

With a twinkle in his eye Clarence guided Olivia toward a door that stood ajar. Pushing it open, he let her walk past him into her grandmother's boudoir. On one wall was an ornate black lacquer dressing table with gilt trim and a bench of petal pink silk with long fringe and tassels. The opposite wall held a floor-to-ceiling mirror with a heavy frame. It looked French—and old. A door with beveled glass drew Olivia for a closer look. She found a small terrace beyond. "The view from here must be magnificent at night," Olivia said.

"It is," said Clarence as he opened the door to the bedroom.

Olivia entered a room furnished in the Art Deco style with touches of European elegance. The damask drapes and matching bedspread soothed the senses in the same grey palate as the rest of the apartment. Olivia's attention immediately went to a large painting hung opposite the bed. A lump caught in her throat as she gazed upon mother and daughter in evening gowns seated together in the salon. The artist beautifully captured her grandmother's love and pride for her daughter, while Maureen gazes off into the distance. Perhaps she sees her future with William. Olivia had found her beautiful mother at last. She wiped a tear from her cheek.

Clarence cleared his throat as he looked up at the portrait. "It was painted the year your mother turned sixteen. They often went to the opera together. Your grandfather was seldom here."

"I'm surprised he didn't have this destroyed when my mother left."

Clarence moved closer. "He nearly did. Shortly after Maureen left, your grandmother came here for an extended visit. I think she needed to get away from Virginia and her husband. Well, old Angus showed up unexpectedly one Saturday, and all hell broke loose. I was summoned to the suite and heard the shouting before I ever got to the door. Angus ordered me to take down the portrait and dispose of it. Your grandmother was hysterical and begged him to leave it alone. She promised to have it put in storage so he wouldn't have to look at it, but that only made him angrier. For a minute I thought he was going to hit her, he was that mad. 'Dispose of it! Now!' I had no choice but to climb onto a chair and take down the painting. As I walked thru the door, he shouted to me, 'I want it off the premises within the hour.' I was secretly in love with Maureen. I couldn't bare the thought of destroying her portrait. I ended up taking it down to the laundry, wrapped it in sheets and took it home that night.

This was taking holding a grudge to the extreme. Olivia was glad she'd never met her grandfather. She couldn't imagine their relationship being anything but explosive. It was a good thing that her mother had gotten away from him. How could her grandmother have stayed with him? Why didn't she walk away? How different life would have been.

"But how did the painting get back here?"

"The day after I heard your grandfather passed away, I brought the painting back and had it re-hung."

"I bet my grandmother was thrilled to see it again."

Clarence nodded. "We'd been notified by her pilot that she was on her way to the hotel. I met her at the door and escorted her to the suite. She broke down in tears. She asked over and over 'How is this possible? How can this be?' I told her the story. When I was finished, she wrapped her arms around me and kissed my cheek. 'You are the most loyal friend I have ever had' she said, and from then on we became real friends. Within these walls, that is. Outside I was still concierge and her servant. We shared stories, feelings, and fears. I miss her."

Olivia's chest tightened. So much love within these walls, and so much heartache.

"I hope you'll be my friend as well, Clarence."

Clarence patted her shoulder. "I'll leave you now to get to know your grandmother. Please feel free to call me should you need anything. I'll leave my card with my personal phone number on the table in the gallery." He moved to the bedroom door, and began pulling it shut. Before it closed, Clarence poked his head back in. "Welcome home, Miss Olivia."

Olivia sat on the end of the bed. She gazed up at the painting with Clarence's parting words still echoing in her mind. Yes, this did feel like home—Mom's here.

Leaving the room with a new sense of belonging, Olivia found Daisy sitting in the salon with a magazine.

"Do you know the last time I looked at this Life magazine was after the three of us spent a long day shopping for your mother's trousseau? Can you believe this place? Nothing has changed. I found this in the bedroom drawer where I put it last. It's rather creepy."

"Are you sure? Forty years is a long time."

"Well, Maureen's room seems smaller somehow. But then everything seems smaller than what I remember. I swear even the hotel lobby seems to have shrunk."

Olivia's gaze swept the room. "I feel like I've stepped onto an old Hollywood movie set. I expect Greta Garbo, wearing a long, slinky satin gown, with a cigarette holder poised in her hand to appear at the Steinway in the corner."

"She may have. Cole Porter ran his fingers across those ivory keys on many occasions. Your mother knew him."

Cole Porter? Eleanor Roosevelt? What other famous faces was she going to find on the walls of the gallery? Like Alice in Wonderland, she had fallen into an unknown world.

Daisy jumped up from the chair, tossing the magazine on the seat. "Come on. There's still time for a trip to Saks and Bergdorf."

Heads turned at the sight of the two elegantly dressed women being seated in the Empire Room at the Waldorf that evening. Olivia wore a dramatic short cocktail dress she'd found at Bergdorf's. Its black satin skirt rounded at the hips with a one-shouldered bodice of white satin. A crisp pleated fan in the same black satin fabric adorned the wide strap. Daisy had chosen a sleek, grey silk cocktail dress with an overdress of grey lace studded with tiny seed pearls.

The waiter left after taking their dinner order. He wasn't gone a minute when the wine steward arrived at the table with a bottle of Champagne. "Compliments of the house, ladies."

Olivia and Daisy looked at each other. "Clarence," they said in unison.

The steward left the table after filling each elegant flute. Daisy raised her glass. "To our first successful day of shopping."

Olivia raised her glass. "To shopping." She set her glass on the table. "Speaking of shopping. My mother went on in great detail about the many shopping trips to New York. She mentioned you joining them on several occasions over the years. Her journal was full of the many items purchased, especially on the last trip for her trousseau. But I must say she didn't do your exuberance justice. You make an ordinary outing into an event."

"She had some truly beautiful couture clothes. My favorite was a silver gown made by Mainbocher."

"I know the one. It was as delicate as butterfly wings. I wore it for my wedding reception along with the Astor Choker."

"Really? You still have it?"

"Actually, I have just about all of Mother's clothes. I couldn't part with them. My favorite is one I've never seen, except in a painting. It hangs over the fireplace in my parlor in Marblehead."

"Maureen looked like a princess. Your grandfather could have funded a small army for what he paid for that white gown. Yards and yards of precious silk just after the war ended. I can't imagine where Mainbocher ever found that much silk."

"Do you know what happened to it? Mother said that her father had it burned."

"I wouldn't put it past him. He was stubborn and ruthless. Your grandmother sent that painting to your mom in Cedar Hill before Angus could destroy it."

Olivia finished her meal with only the occasional question or comment while Daisy recounted the many happy visits to the Waldorf.

Daisy set her napkin on the table and let out a long sigh. "It's late, Olivia, and we need our beauty sleep for a fresh round tomorrow. It'll be a magical day of couture houses. You're going to have a new, wonderful experience."

Olivia could have taken the opportunity to tell Daisy that she was well versed in the magic of couture. But why spoil the moment? Daisy was having too much fun playing fairy godmother.

The next morning after a long shower, Olivia walked thru the boudoir door wearing the thick white bathrobe with the Waldorf's monogram she'd found on the bed when they'd gotten back from their shopping trip the day before. She liked the word boudoir so much better than dressing room. Wrapping a fluffy white towel around her wet hair, she followed the aroma of fresh coffee through the living room to the dining room.

"Good morning, sleepy-head. I ordered breakfast," said Daisy. "I don't know what you like so I ordered a little bit of everything. The French toast here is wonderful."

Clarence pulled out her chair as she approached the table. Sensing another presence in the room, Olivia glanced toward another doorway. A pretty red-haired girl holding a coffee pot stood at the entrance to what must be the kitchen.

"This is Colleen," said Clarence. "She'll be your maid while you're with us. She'll come in twice a day to clean and straighten the suite and to serve your meals. Call down to the desk if you need her at other times. Will you be bringing your own maid when you visit in the future?"

Olivia looked toward Daisy. "I don't know. Will I?"

Daisy shrugged. "Probably not for a while, Clarence."

The French toast *was* delicious, but so far she'd only taken a few bites. Her life was becoming overwhelming. Housekeeper, maids, drivers, pilots, how many other people would she be responsible for? Back in Ohio, she'd been the maid, the cook, and the driver. Sure, when she was growing up, Mom had a woman come in once a week to clean. Brian and she had his housekeeper, Consuelo, but nothing like this. How was she going to cope? How does one learn to manage a personal staff, and how much staff does one woman need?

"Colleen is my niece's youngest. She's very loyal and dependable. I'll see that she is available for your future visits. Once she learns your needs, she'll have everything ready for you on your arrival."

Olivia didn't yet know if there would be future visits. But this wasn't the time to broach the subject of giving up the suite.

Half an hour later, Olivia pushed back her chair. "I think I'll go and get dressed. Thank you for being here, Clarence . . . to introduce Coleen . . . but we can manage tomorrow."

She remembered something just before she reached the boudoir door. "Clarence, I smell lavender in the bedroom and bath."

Clarence grinned, as if he were about to divulge a secret. "It's in the linens, Mrs. Bentley. Your grandmother had the laundry wash her towels and sheets in lavender-scented water. She found it soothing."

Olivia shook her head in amazement and continued to the bathroom to dry her hair. Lavender-scented water? Really? What if she decided she'd prefer rose-scented water? Would her sheets suddenly smell like roses? She'd better not get used to these luxuries. Washing in scented water might be a little too much to ask of Sarah.

By noon, Daisy had given Olivia a tour of the large, elegantly furnished apartment, including the guest suite with its separate entrance. Olivia examined the contents of the closets and dressers in both bedrooms. A box on the shelf of her mother's closet contained old record albums from the 1930s and 1940s and what seemed to be all of Frank Sinatra's.

"I recognize many of the items in my mother's room from the descriptions in her journals. It's remarkable the room has been preserved as if she would come back one day, even though she has been dead for twenty years."

Daisy stood before the framed, autographed photo of Frank with the ticket to the Paramount Theatre for October 12, 1944, proudly displayed in the lower corner. "I have this same photo and my ticket hanging on my den wall back home. I'll never forget that night." Daisy straightened the frame. "It would have been like Ed Sullivan taking you backstage and introducing you to the Beatles."

35

Snowflakes glistened on tips of mink. The two fashionably dressed women waited while the Waldorf's doorman hailed the next cab. The admiring looks from passersby confirmed Olivia's feeling that she was a bit overdressed for a mere shopping trip. What was wrong with her down-filled jacket and slacks? "I wish I hadn't let you talk me into this fox-trimmed mink jacket."

"Don't be silly. It's fabulous on you," Daisy said. "Very chic."

"But Brian bought me a full-length mink in Paris. And I have a mink stole and another mink coat in my grandmother's closet back at Fairfield. Do I really need this?"

"Yes, you do! It'll go with everything from a gown to jeans."

The doorman opened the cab door and Olivia slid in.

"Trust me, Olivia. Your mother did."

"Chanel," said the doorman to the driver.

Traffic crawled along with the taxi locked somewhere in the middle of the pack, going nowhere fast. Olivia played with the clasp on her handbag. "We could have walked the few blocks and been there by now."

Daisy turned toward Olivia. Taking the handbag, she stuffed it between them on the seat. "And appear on the threshold of the House of Chanel red-faced and gasping for breath? Where is your *class*, Olivia?"

Olivia focused on the scene outside the window. Pedestrians with their heads down scurried along the sidewalk. The snow was coming down heavier now and she was glad to be warm and dry.

"Where you ladies from?" Asked the cab driver. His accent could have been Australian, or perhaps South African.

"Big sky country . . . Montana," Daisy said with a slight Western drawl.

Olivia's glance moved from the side window to the front seat. Wisps of sandy-colored hair peeked out from under the driver's cap. "Ohio."

"Well, for now. But she's also from Virginia, and maybe right here in the big apple."

"Just one more block," said the cabbie.

The cab came to a stop alongside the curb. Daisy rummaged in her purse for her wallet and paid the fare. The cab pulled away leaving Olivia and Daisy on the sidewalk in front of the impressive façade of Chanel.

Daisy patted Olivia's hand. "Now, you just leave everything to me. I know this is rather intimidating but just relax and have fun. I'm a good customer, and we'll be treated well."

Olivia brushed the snow from her jacket then glanced around the shop, spotting a single customer in the back.

Daisy slipped out of her long black coat. "Ah, there's Henrí. I do believe he's noticed me. Just follow my lead, and you'll be fine. He's just going to adore you."

Daisy took a couple steps forward as Henrí approached with arms streatched out and a broad smile. Olivia smiled in anticipation of what was sure to happen next.

Henrí shook his head as if he couldn't believe his eyes. "Mrs. Bentley! How wonderful to see you again!" He took both of Olivia's hands in his and leaned forward to kiss her on both cheeks. "It's been too long—and poor Brian, what a tragedy. But now you are back, and all is well."

"Thank you Henrí, you are too kind." Olivia motioned toward Daisy. "I believe you know Daisy Winslow. She was a good friend of my mother's."

Henrí hesitated a moment, as if searching his mind. "Yes, I do remember. Winslow, Texas, I believe."

Daisy gave a forced smile. "Winslow, Montana."

"I'm so sorry Madame, it's been awhile." Henrí took a step back, clasping his hands in front of him. "Now, ladies. How may I be of service?"

Daisy responded without giving Olivia a chance to speak. "Olivia is in need of new business attire. Something that will show the world she is competent and in control. The latest styles, but not ostentatious or flamboyant. And perhaps a cocktail dress and a ball gown."

"Show the *world*?" Henrí asked in a bewildered tone.

"Olivia's inherited her grandmother's entire estate."

Henrí switched his gaze to Olivia. "And did I know your grandmother?"

"I believe Olivia McLeod was one of your clients," Olivia said in a soft but firm voice.

Henrí's arms flew up. "Olivia McLeod was a legend in this town! What a surprise! But you never mentioned her. I'm sure I would have remembered seeing you together."

Olivia hated admitting to everyone she met that she never knew her grandmother. How could a woman who'd turned thirty-six just a few months before not know that she was the granddaughter of one of the wealthiest women in the world? You didn't hide these kinds of things in 1985. It wasn't as if her mother had never mentioned that her maiden name was McLeod. Why hadn't the name McLeod ever triggered a question in Olivia's mind? It's not a common name—not like Smith or Jones.

He appeared to be waiting for an answer. "I just recently found out. It was a surprise to me as well."

Henrí took on the posture of Napoleon. "Leave everything to me. I assume you're staying in the suite. I'll send everything to Clarence.

Four hours later, Olivia and Daisy left Chanel. The gray, snow-filled sky had turned to blinding sunlight. Steam coiled upward over wet sidewalks. Olivia inhaled deeply, giving her lungs a jolt of cold air. She studied the façade of the building next door. "I know you wanted to hit Dior next, but would you mind if we just went back to the Waldorf? I can't imagine enduring another person with a tape measure. I'm mentally drained and couldn't possibly make another expensive decision."

Daisy hesitated at the impressive door at 21 East 57th Street. She turned toward Olivia with raised eyebrows. "Will we get the same treatment here as we did at Chanel?"

"Possibly. They're my two favorite designers."

"In that case, I think we should leave Dior for tomorrow. Since we have the time, would you mind walking?"

Olivia pulled her collar high up on her neck. The silky softness of mink soothed a weary mind. "Walking sounds good."

It was obvious from her long stride that Daisy was well accustomed to walking. And from the way her coat gaped open, flapping in the breeze, it didn't look as if the cold temperature bothered her a bit.

Daisy slowed her pace to allow Olivia to keep up. "This morning I told you that you'd be treated well in my company, but I never expected to be treated like royalty being in yours. And I've *never* been served a champagne lunch!"

"I think it was Grandmother that got us the lunch. It was a first for me as well."

They waited with the tourists at 57th and Park Avenue for the light to change. Cameras hung around strained necks, heads all turned to the tops of ornate buildings. A group of Chinese, speaking in their native tongue stood with a camera in one hand and a map in the other. "Is this the way it was when you and my mom stayed here?"

Daisy stared off in the distance, a frown creeping across her forehead. "No. It was the war years. A black cloud hung over the city reminding us that death was just around the corner. It was a time of rationing. Women did men's jobs, and children worked to keep food on the family table. Clarence's uncle was the hotel's manager and got him a job working in the laundry to help his mother make ends meet. I don't believe he's ever worked anywhere else. But New York will always be New York. Even during those troubled years, I thought it was the most exciting city in the world. We still had the theater, the arts, and the shopping—although you couldn't be caught wearing silk stockings even if you had them."

The light changed. Olivia followed Daisy down Park Avenue toward the Waldorf. "So what do you think, Olivia? Do we begin tomorrow with Dior? We haven't been to Saks yet."

"I think we can hold off on any more shopping. I'm still leaning toward giving up the suite. At the moment I'm feeling really overwhelmed about my life and everything that's been thrown at me in the last month. New York feels like more problems that I don't really need. After all, the Waldorf wasn't important enough to my mother to mention it to us—so why should it be important to me?"

36

Tired from their walk from Chanel, Olivia and Daisy waited outside the elevator in The Towers private lobby. When the door opened, Clarence exited. "Good afternoon, Miss Olivia, you look stunning. And so much like Maureen that I have to keep mentally pinching myself. I hope you're not tired of me telling you that?"

"No, of course not. It makes me happy to know I look like her. It keeps a part of her alive for me."

"Before you leave, I need to show you how to open the secret compartment in the desk."

Finding hidden stuff was far more interesting than shopping or the theater. "Clarence, would you have some free time this evening to show me and talk about the past?"

"Certainly, can I buy you dinner in the Empire Room?"

"Would you mind if we have dinner sent upstairs? I'd prefer an evening without tons of people."

Daisy slipped out of her coat and folded it around her arm. "I have an idea. Clarence, do you have menus for Chinese take out?"

"Of course." Clarence's long strides reached the doorman's stand in just a few steps. He returned with three menus. "These are the favorites. Just call in your order and they'll deliver."

Clarence followed Olivia and Daisy into the elevator and inserted his key for the forty-second floor.

"I'll be free around seven o'clock if that's okay with you."

Olivia held the door while Clarence exited the elevator. "Wonderful, we'll see you then."

The crystal clock on the dressing table read 6:00. Olivia took one last glance in the full-length mirror. Between the elegance of the suite and spending most of the day at Chanel, Olivia felt the need to dress for the evening. The silver-grey jumpsuit she'd purchased at Bergdorf's with its plunging v-neckline and puff sleeves that ended above her elbows was both elegant and sexy. She cinched the wide matching belt and straightened the shoulder pads.

Voices came from the direction of the kitchen. Olivia slipped into a pair of grey heels and headed toward the gallery as the outside door closed with a loud click.

"Wow! You look fabulous. And here I am in jeans and a mohair sweater," Daisy said as she came through the service door. "That was the doorman. Dinner has arrived."

Together they carried the many boxes of Chinese to the dining room table. "Are you sure we can just put these boxes down on the table like this? Shouldn't we put something down first?" Olivia asked holding her boxes above the glossy finish.

"We're good. This is some special hard-as-nails kind of finish. Maureen and I spent many hours playing on this table. Besides . . . who's going to yell at us? It's *your* table!"

"You're right. Let's eat, I'm famished."

Both women grabbed containers and opened lids. With chopsticks in hand each took a container.

After sampling everything Olivia picked up an eggroll. "You know, Daisy, I just can't see Mom living here. Oh sure, her photos are everywhere and the clothes she left behind when she ran away with Dad are still in her closet, but it's not *her*. I certainly understand now why Fairfield was called a farm."

Olivia greeted Clarence at precisely seven o'clock. He stopped when they entered the gallery, gesturing toward the walls. "Have you had a chance to look at these?"

Olivia moved to a section next to Clarence. "No, not yet."

"During the 1950s and early 1960s, former president Herbert Hoover and General Douglas MacArthur had suites here."

"I didn't know that," Olivia muttered thinking she should have paid more attention in her American history classes.

"They both became friends of your grandmother. Cole Porter and Linda Lee Thomas also had a suite. The Steinway was purchased so he could play when attending the parties she often gave. Everyone loved and respected your grandmother."

"Here's one of your mom and the Duke and Duchess of Windsor taken in the salon. They had a suite here, so there are several photos of them."

"Clarence, here's one of you. Boy, were you handsome in a tux."

"No, that's Peter O'Toole. He attended one or two of your grandmother's parties. Came with someone . . . don't remember who."

"Here's several of Frank Sinatra!" Olivia squealed with excitement. "Grandmother knew him?"

"Very well. He and his friends often joined in the festivities."

"I wonder if Grandmother told him that Mother's horse was named after him?"

"I told him. And I showed him the signed photo and ticket hanging on the bedroom wall. He remembered the concert and meeting your mom and Daisy backstage. He and Barbara picked up Cole Porter's lease, so they lived here in the '60s."

Wow. Frank Sinatra right here in the suite her mother had called home. It must have been after her death, otherwise Grandmother would have found a way to tell her if she were still alive.

Daisy entered the room and pointed to a color photo of a woman. "Know who this is?"

Olivia moved over for a closer look. "Jackie? Really?" Olivia glanced over her shoulder at Clarence. "So how many other president's wives did my grandmother know?"

Clarence scratched his head. "Hmm. I believe just Eleanor Roosevelt."

She had to be the ER from the journals. "Clarence, were they good friends?"

"Oh, they sure were. Mrs. Roosevelt worked hard on the projects she believed in. She needed money to make them happen and your grandmother had plenty. They were best friends right up until the end."

"Mom mentioned an ER in her journals."

"Yes. I believe your mother met her on a few visits. If memory serves me, Mrs. Roosevelt stayed at Fairfield on occasion."

"Hmmm. I think I know which room." Maybe the Duke and Duchess spent a night in that room of gold as well. "Let's go into the salon. I think I need more time to take this all in. It's rather overwhelming."

Clarence immediately moved to a tall ornate desk in the salon. He pulled several photo albums and scrapbooks from the desk drawers and laid them on a side table.

Then he went back to the desk and pulled out a drawer. "There's a little lever in the back. If you twist and pull it releases the top."

Olivia watched as the whole top section of the desk raised revealing a large compartment. Clarence removed several large envelopes and put them on a sofa. "Why don't you have a seat and take a look."

Olivia pulled the contents from the first envelope and studied them one by one. "Clarence? How can this be? My mother's whole life sits before me! Every photo ever taken of her is here, and her room is a goddamn shrine! Here are pictures of her and dad after they moved to Cedar Hill! Pictures of my brothers and me swimming in our pool, riding our bikes, even opening Christmas presents! Here's Mom and I playing tennis at the country club, and several of her beautifully dressed at cocktail parties and formal events. Then there are the ones of me at proms, graduation, my marriage to Win and our home at the lodge. I can't believe she even had pictures of Brian and me at our house in Shaker Heights during formal dinners and various parties. Who took these? And how did they get here?"

"What I have to tell you is going to take awhile. Would you mind if I fix myself a drink?" Clarence asked as he moved toward an antique cart with beautiful cut glass decanters and glassware.

Daisy stood and headed toward the kitchen. "I'll grab a bottle of wine."

Clarence glanced back over his shoulder. "Can I fix you something, Olivia?"

"No thanks. I'll share the bottle of wine with Daisy. I'm afraid anything stronger will go straight to my head."

Clarence returned with a Scotch—neat and sat down across from Olivia. "The Waldorf was always your grandmother's place. Being an Astor, she was given the opportunity to obtain one of the prime suites at the time the hotel was finished in 1931. In the beginning Angus came for the theatre and social events. But as time went on his visits became infrequent, leaving his wife to enjoy the New York social scene alone. She preferred it that way. Angus could be rather stuffy and opinionated. Maureen seemed to enjoy it as much as her mother. She always said there was more Astor blood in her veins than McLeod. The painting in the bedroom depicts their close relationship. Maureen was following in her mother's footsteps and loving it."

Clarence took a sip then smacked his lips. "Your grandmother sure knew how to stock a liquor cabinet."

Daisy returned with a bottle of Bordeaux and two glasses. She handed one to Olivia and set the bottle on a table.

Clarence rested his glass on his knee and continued. "After the war, Maureen surprised everyone when she chose love over duty. Even her father's threats couldn't change her mind. He became an angry bitter man, and this suite became a refuge for your grand-mother, a place where she could acknowledge Maureen still existed. That almost ended the day when Angus tried to destroy the paint-ing. He threatened your grandmother, saying it may have been her Astor blood that obtained the suite, but it was his money that paid for it, and it could very quickly be taken away."

Her grandmother had been a truly amazing woman. Olivia couldn't believe the lengths she had gone to in order to protect the memories of her daughter. "How was all of this kept from her husband? There is virtually nothing of my mother in the house in Virginia."

Clarence took another sip and glanced in the direction of the bedroom. "The day Angus ordered me to get rid of the painting and stormed out, your grandmother called me back up here. She needed to return to Virginia to make sure that Angus didn't destroy anything important. She asked that I have the small trunk room, off the servant's hall, walled up and Maureen's things stored there. I arranged to have the ornate rococo paneling put up to hide the door. I put everything from Maureen's room on shelves and hung her clothes in garment bags and put them on racks that I brought up from the laundry."

Olivia finished off the last swallow of wine in her glass and held it out for Daisy to refill. "I don't understand who took the pictures of us? How did Grandmother get all this information after Mother left?"

"Lionel Montgomery. Your grandmother offered to invest in his company if he would be her eyes and ears. He met her here four or five times a year. After Angus' death she asked me to put Maureen's room back as it was. She then felt comfortable putting many of the pictures in frames and setting them around the suite, especially on the Steinway."

Clarence swallowed the last of his Scotch.

"I mentioned that your grandmother and I had become close friends. Lionel and I were the only people she trusted. After Angus's death, your grandmother started taking more interest in the company. She had been reviewing the financials and board reports for Lionel's company for years and wasn't as naïve as old Mr. Morrison believed. Then about a year later, McLeod and Morrison expenses increased and her share of the profits decreased. She wasn't concerned for herself. She was wealthy in her own right and planned for her personal wealth to go to you. But she felt strongly that the two younger sons were mismanaging the company. She once told me she thought the Morrisons were making decisions as if there were no McLeods left on the planet.

It got worse after old man Morrison turned up his toes. Clive and Wilson treated her like a senile old woman. They said her opinion didn't matter. They knew all about Angus's will and thought the game was over since she had no heirs. But that old lady had spunk. She'd spent too many years outsmarting her husband in order to preserve your heritage. She wasn't going to let those two idiots spoil her plans. She let them keep thinking she had no heirs, but everything was in place for your takeover. The last time I saw her she told me she was sorry that she wouldn't be around to see it.

"So what you're saying is that my mother and I didn't exist in Virginia so the Morrisons would forget about Mother and me."

Clarence got up and walked back to the decanter and poured himself another drink. "Yep, that was the plan."

Olivia set her glass on the table. "You've just given me the greatest gift in the world, Clarence—the love of my grandmother. Thank you."

Clarence motioned for Olivia and Daisy to follow him. "Come on, I'll show you the hidden door."

They followed him to the servant's hall then stopped beside a gilded panel and pressed it twice. The door opened and all three walked into the tiny room as the light came on. The shelves were empty.

"Clarence, its obvious Grandmother didn't keep anything of value in here. Is there a safe somewhere?"

"Sure." He ushered the girls out and closed the door. They followed him to the boudoir where he pulled back the tall mirror to reveal a large safe. "I have the combination. Your grandmother gave me the number on her last visit. It's almost like she knew she wouldn't be back. Are you looking for something in particular?"

"Yes," Olivia said as she eyed the tall black leather box containing six drawers. She began pulling out the drawers. Each one was divided for its specific contents. There were enough diamonds and precious gems to fill a high-end jewelry store. "It's not here Clarence. I can't find the gold signet ring that Great-Grandmother is wearing in the Sargent painting, the same one Grandmother is wearing in this painting. Do you know the one?"

"Of course, she always wore it. It was the McLeod wedding ring. It contained the McLeod coat of arms. It's probably at the farm."

"No it isn't. And I've asked Sarah."

"Perhaps she requested that she be buried with it?"

"She was cremated."

Clarence gulped the last of his Scotch and walked toward the boudoir door.

"Sorry. I can't help you with that. It's late. I should be going."

He stopped before entering the salon. "I loved her like family. I never told her. Your grandmother was active and perfectly healthy for her age. I expected her to be around for many more years. Then a few months later she was dead." He took a handkerchief from his pocket and dabbed his eye. "I never told her."

37

Olivia woke to the now familiar scent of lavender. It had soothed her the night before after she fell into bed, exhausted by the day's events. She had taken a last look at the photos before putting them back in the box and returning them to the desk drawer. Troubling dreams caused Olivia to have a restless night. The clock on the bedside table read ten after five. She couldn't stay in bed a minute longer. She followed the glow from the nightlight she'd left on in the boudoir to the bathroom. She gasped at her reflection in the mirror over the sink. Dark circles embracing bloodshot eyes were nestled in a major case of bed hair. She turned on the shower then leaned against the wall. Overwhelming feelings that something wasn't right had invaded her dreams. Maybe it was a case of being stressed out. Who wouldn't be stressed with everything she'd learned in the past twenty-four hours? Maybe she should take the box of pictures that she had returned to the lower desk drawer, along with the scrapbook, and store them in the secret room. She didn't want to appear paranoid, but she felt better knowing that they were away from prying eyes. Her image was just a shadow behind the steam-drenched mirror when she stepped into the shower.

An hour later Olivia sat on the floor in front of the Steinway. Her knees drawn up and tucked under her chin, her arms wrapped tightly around them as if they might take off running on their own if she didn't hold them in place. She felt trapped. Trapped within the elegant walls that belonged to her mother and grandmother—a world her mother had wanted to keep a secret.

"I guess I'm not the only one who had difficulty sleeping." Daisy stood in the hallway, still in her nightgown. "Want to talk about it?" she said as she moved to the sofa.

"I don't belong here. This apartment obviously wasn't important to my mother or she would have told me about it. Do you know that she kept all those clothes you helped her pick out for her trousseau? I used to play dress-up in beautiful gowns, pretending I was a princess living in a castle. Mom could have hinted that she actually had lived the life of a princess, once upon a time. But no, her past was a big secret."

"It wasn't her intention to keep this from you. Her death was just bad timing."

Olivia rested her head against her knees. She took several deep breaths then looked up at Daisy. "I think I'm ready to leave. I've had enough of New York . . . and this place."

Daisy clasped her hands and leaned forward. "The story Clarence told last night haunted my dreams until I gave up trying to sleep. Before you decide this is just a piece of frivolous, expensive Mid-Manhattan real estate you can do without, I need you to listen to one more story. Something I probably should have told you earlier, but it was easier to just put it off until the right moment presented itself."

Olivia got to her feet. "It's okay, Daisy, another time will be fine. Let's pack-up and get back to Virginia."

Daisy patted the sofa cushion next to her. "The time is now, Livy."

Slowly she sat, dreading what was surely to come. Her stomach churned.

"One Sunday evening Maureen called me. She was worried about the questions you had asked about her past. The time she had dreaded since she married your father had finally arrived. It was time to deal with her past, to explain her actions and why her family had disowned her. The next day Maureen called again with more excitement in her voice than I had heard in years. You would be turning sixteen in just a few months and it was time you were told."

Daisy shifted her position to better face Olivia. "Maureen and Fred had formed a plan but they needed my help to pull it off. Maureen had seen an article about the Queen Mary and was excited that it was still making transatlantic voyages. She planned to book passage for the following June, after school was finished for the summer, hopefully getting the same luxurious stateroom that she and her mother had used on their trips to England. I had kept in touch with your grandmother over the years, just calling a few times a year to see how she was doing or inviting her for lunch when I was staying at Fiddlers Landing. Communication between mother and daughter could be channeled through me."

Daisy leaned over and rested her hand on Olivia's knee. "It was a wonderful plan, developed over a week's worth of phone calls. Your grandmother was thrilled and had as many ideas to make the outcome a success as did your mother. First, Maureen was to fly with you and your brothers here, to New York, where Clarence would have the suite ready for your visit. Your grandmother was to leave letters for each of you in the desk along with money for a shopping trip and to cover expenses in London. The following week you would leave on the Queen Mary for England. Your grandmother arranged for you to stay with relatives in some of the country's most famous residences. In August, you would return to the suite where your father would be waiting and spend another week as tourists. Clarence would make sure that any souvenirs and photos that you wished to leave for your grandmother would be left in the secret room."

Olivia was stunned to hear the intricate plans. She pushed Daisy's hand away. "Mom never said a word about this."

"Of course she didn't, she never had the chance. The plan was to tell you on Saturday after you got back from your vacation at the cottage. But then she remembered that you wanted to go to your friend's party and they decided to pick you up on Sunday instead. We talked for an hour Saturday afternoon, then I called your grandmother giving her last minute details. Your mother and I talked again that night. We hadn't been that giddy since our last visit here to shop for Maureen's trousseau."

Hurt twisted Olivia's heart. More secrets. "So now, after all this time, you decide to tell me my mother *did* want me to know her story. Oh, if you had only known how angry and hurt I've been since I read Mom's diaries. Did it ever occur to you or my grandmother over the last twenty years that I had a right to know this?"

"I'm sorry, we thought it might be better for everyone if the story was buried along with your mother, at least until you were older. Perhaps by then your grandmother could find a way to bring you into her life."

"I understand why my grandmother couldn't have any contact with me, but you. . . *You* could have contacted me, let me know that someone out there cared about me. *You* had the answers to my mother's past and could have given me a heads-up as to what my future might hold!"

Daisy stood wagging her finger at Olivia. "Listen here. Don't you try to put all the blame on my doorstep. I did what I thought best for my best friend's daughter." Her voice raised an octave. "It was *you* who locked away your mother's journals for *twenty years*. The day after the funeral, you could have started reading. The questions had already been asked and you had a trunk-full of answers. It was just easier for you to ignore the truth."

Ouch. Daisy's words hurt. Truth often did. Olivia's eyes burned. She fought back the tears. Her world had just been turned upside down.

Daisy sat back down and took Olivia's hand. "Your mother didn't just want to tell you her story. She wanted to *show* you. She wanted you to experience her world, right down to the ship she sailed on. She loved you so much, Livy, that nothing less would do. And she spent the last week of her life happier than she had been in years just planning this for you."

Olivia let the tears fall. "So that's why you brought me here." She sniffled. "To show me what my mother couldn't."

"I guess so. But I didn't think of it that way. I just wanted to get to know you, and it seemed the most logical way. I've really enjoyed our time together, Livy. Maureen would be proud of you."

Two hours later their bags sat neatly by the door. Daisy had ordered French toast, bacon and grapefruit for their breakfast. The aroma from a freshly brewed pot of coffee permeated the apartment.

Olivia chewed the last piece of bacon. The Waldorf did make the best French toast. She was going to miss the place. Her grandmother had created an oasis of timeless elegance in a sea of tranquility. It was her grandmother's place. It had been her mother's place. Olivia wasn't sure if it could ever feel like her place.

Olivia pushed her chair back and stood. She glanced around the room at the ornate furnishings before moving to the salon. She picked up the phone and dialed the number for Clarence.

"So, I guess this is it, huh? At least I got one last visit to this treasure. Do you mind if I take the Life magazine?" Daisy asked. "I can't believe it was still in the drawer, right where I left it forty years ago."

Olivia held the phone to her ear and placed her hand over the mouth piece. "Sure, take whatever you want. Clarence is on his way up."

The photos sitting on the Steinway spoke to Olivia in their own silent way. Family she never knew, friends laughing and singing around the piano. Then there were the ones of her. Olivia fingered the frames. Her life spread out for all to see and for her grandmother to cherish. Her grandmother's love was so strong that she sacrificed her own happiness for her granddaughter's future.

Daisy sat with a box of old photos in her lap, pulling the ones she wanted to take back to Montana.

The doorbell rang.

"That will be Clarence. I'll get the door," Olivia said as she hurried through the gallery.

Olivia pulled open the door. "Thanks for coming so quickly. I have a few things that I need you to do."

Clarence eyed the bags with a frown. "Surely, you're not leaving? I expected you would stay at least a week or so."

"We need to get back to Virginia."

"Certainly, Miss Olivia. Would you like me to call Philips for you?"

"I called him already. He'll have the plane ready when we get there. I can't believe I just called my pilot as easily as I'd call for a taxi."

"I'll have the car ready to pick you up out front. Will an hour be too soon?"

"That will be fine. Henrí, at Chanel, will be sending some things during the next few weeks. Please put them in the closet for me. You can reach me at Fairfield or my number in Ohio."

"Don't worry. I'll take care of everything, just as I did for your grandmother."

His tight-lipped smile didn't reach his sad eyes. He had the look of a boy about to say goodbye to his best friend. Olivia had to put him out of his misery. She spoke before she even considered the consequences.

"And one other thing, Clarence. . . I'll be keeping the suite."

38

"Oh, Travis. It's been a week since I returned from New York." Olivia squirmed into the corner of the library sofa. "I feel trapped in this huge vortex, just going around and around while being sucked down into some horrible abyss. I don't know how to get out, and it's making me dizzy."

"Dizzy, Olivia? You're not serious? You're joking. Right?" Travis asked with concern in his voice.

"Yeah. Yeah. It's just that I feel a little lightheaded at times. My arms and legs feel a little tingly —stress—I guess. I've learned so much about Mom, and Grandmother was an amazing woman—a woman who in the end was ready to give up everything just to have me with her. It's a good thing old man Morrison is dead because I think I'd have to kill him for what he did to my mother."

"What about your grandfather?"

"I'd have to kill him too."

"So why are you stressed? You should be elated. Jumping up and down, for heavens sake."

Olivia let out a long sigh. "I don't know. I have the energy level of a snail. All I want to do is sleep."

"Have you told Sarah? Maybe she can recommend a doctor for you to see. Maybe you need some kind of iron shot or B12 or something."

Travis paused a beat. "Emily Elfin gets tired and feels weird and her doctor gives her shots. We all know Emily isn't quite right."

Olivia swung her legs up onto the sofa. She rested her head on a throw pillow. "No, I don't want to bother her. I'm sure I'll feel better once I'm more active again, I felt fine in New York. William called today and said all the legal issues regarding my inheriting the shares in McLeod and Morrison have been cleared. Gertrude will have my office ready for me on Monday. Benjamin will drive me."

"Are you ready? Have you figured out what all those numbers and letters your grandmother put in the margins of the reports mean?"

"No, I'm no closer to an answer. And at the rate I'm going I may never know. William is going to get the press releases ready for *Fortune* and *Newsweek* and I need to be familiar with my routine at the yard before those hit the newsstands. I have a lot to learn in a short amount of time."

"My offer to come and help still stands. I've hired a new sales-man, and my cousin can run the two locations until business picks up at the end of May."

"You really wouldn't mind coming? I know I'd feel a whole lot better having you at my side."

"I love you, Livy. I'll catch the next available flight."

"Travis, I need you to understand how I feel. I know you'd like to help me sell my shares in McLeod and Morrison, give up Fairfield and move back to Marblehead." Olivia paused a beat. "That isn't going to happen. My life is never going to be what it was before I came here. I'm not the same woman you were engaged to. And what's more—I like the new me."

"Okay. We'll discuss all this when I get there. Maybe I can help you with some of the things at the yard. I do, after all, know boats and how they're built. I know. I know. You build ships. But the prin-cipal must be similar. Let me help you."

"I love you. And I do want you here. Don't worry about airline reservations. I'll make the arrangements. It may be a day or two. I'll let you know the details when I have them." She'd also need to let Sarah know there would be houseguests. "Oh, one more thing. Can you bring those photos of my family that are sitting on the shelves in the library? It's time they took their rightful place here at Fairfield. Also, my mother's silver brush set and bottle of Chanel No. 5 that's sitting on the dresser. They belong here in Mom's old room."

"Sure. Just let me know if you think of anything else. See you soon, Livy." The line went dead.

Olivia was ready to bounce around the room with joy. She hadn't felt this good about herself since . . . since, well . . . since last fall when she and Travis had first made love on the *Lovely Lady*. She needed just one more person to make life complete. She needed Meg at her side.

She dialed Meg's number. She picked up after the third ring. "Hello, Meg?"

"Olivia, I'm sorry I haven't called for a while. I did get your messages, but I just haven't felt like talking. I dread going to work. It's just boring as hell, and my kids still aren't talking to me. I can only imagine the lies that their father is pumping into their heads."

"Well, perhaps I can help. How would you feel about moving to Virginia?"

"What? Are you serious? You mean permanently?"

"Yep. I need an assistant I can trust. Have my back, so-to-speak. And I can't think of a better person for the job."

"Wow! What about Gertrude? I thought she was your assistant."

"Gertrude is my secretary at McLeod and Morrison. You would help me with everything else including sorting out all those charities. I have a feeling there's a whole lot to do in New York as well." Olivia crossed her fingers that Meg didn't have something or someone keeping her in Port Clinton. "So, what do you say?"

"Are you kidding? When do I start?"

"Wonderful. I'm so happy. Travis will be coming as well. I'll let you both know when I've made the arrangements. It may be a day or two. Can you be ready by then?"

"I'll turn in my resignation tomorrow. I can have everything I own boxed up in a few hours."

"Boxes? As in several?"

"Yeah, maybe three or four."

"What about furniture and stuff? Gertrude can arrange to have it shipped."

"Don't have any. I rent a furnished apartment on a month-to-month basis. There's nothing keeping me here."

"Pack all the boxes you want, the Gulfstream has plenty of room. You'll get instructions from Phillips when he lands. I assume he can fly into Port Clinton."

"Who's Phillips?"

"My pilot." Olivia noticed Sarah standing in the doorway of the library. "Gotta go, Meg. I'll call you tomorrow morning and let you know what I've arranged," she said then placed the phone on the table.

"Sorry to interrupt, ma'am, but dinner's ready."

"I'll be there in a minute. We're going to have houseguests, Sarah. I've hired Meg as my assistant. I also talked to Travis, and he can come as well."

"That's wonderful news. I'm looking forward to meeting this special man of yours. We can talk about the arrangements after dinner."

"I'll give Phillips a call so he can begin working on the details from his end," Olivia said as she stood and headed toward Sarah. "How do you think Miranda is going to handle this? She is so happy to see William back in my life. I mean back in my mother's life. I'd hate to break her heart again by bringing Travis into the picture."

Sarah turned and began walking down the hall toward the kitchen. "I wouldn't worry about it. Every day is a new day with my mother."

"It's more like every hour!" Olivia said with a chuckle.

Two weeks later, Olivia, Travis, and Meg settled into the comfortable sofas in the library. They had left the shipyard earlier than usual feeling frustrated with the lack of progress each had made. Now that they were using the Cadillac and driving themselves to the yard each day they felt comfortable coming and going as they pleased. Although Benjamin never seemed put out by the long drive he'd been making twice a day, Olivia knew there were a hundred other things he could be doing.

Sarah entered the room carrying a try of refreshments and set it on the table in front of the windows.

"Mr. Travis, are you sure you wouldn't like to try my special tea?"

"Sorry, Sarah, I never touch the stuff. I'll have coffee, but only if it's already made. Don't go to any trouble on my account."

"No trouble, I figured you'd say that. I'll be right back."

Meg took a sip of tea while turning up her nose is disgust. "I just can't get used to this. It really tastes weird. I guess I just need a little tag that reads Lipton hanging from a string for me to like it. But I don't want to hurt Sarah's feelings."

"Don't worry about it. Except for her biscuits and pies, I didn't like half of what Sarah served me for the first few days I was here. It won't bother her."

Sarah brought Travis a large mug of steaming coffee and handed Meg a can of diet Dr Pepper.

"Sorry, Miss Megan, I should have remembered to put it on the tray for you."

Several minutes went by without a word being said until Travis put his mug down with enough force to rattle the tiny round table beside him.

"I've been here for two weeks studying reports, and I haven't come close to being of any help to you, Livy. I thought my knowledge of boatbuilding and restoring yachts would be an asset to you. But building ships is not even in the same ballpark as selling or building yachts. Maybe I should go back home and let you and Meg get on with sorting out your roles here."

Olivia rested her hand on her stomach and closed her eyes for a second. "Don't be silly. I need you here. Look, William will be back tomorrow. Maybe he can take you on a tour of the yard and give you more insight on how the whole operation ties into the reports." Olivia paused to let the nauseous feeling pass. "As for Meg and I . . . well, we are still trying to sort out what we're doing. I wish Gertrude were a little more helpful."

"Okay, I'll give it another week. I'll take that stack of reports with the mysterious notations with me tomorrow. Maybe those letters and numbers your grandmother noted in the margins match with something in the older reports I found in the file cabinets in your office."

Olivia rested her head back on the sofa cushion. "That sounds like a wonderful idea. Now, I think I'll just take a nap until dinner."

Travis got up and crouched down in front of Olivia. He took her hands in his. "It's a beautiful afternoon. How about a walk down by the river? Maybe we could go as far as the old cemetery and you can introduce me to your ancestors."

Meg scooted forward in her chair. "That sounds like a great plan. I need quiet time to study these pages and pages of duties you'll be performing for McLeod and Morrison. And then there's all the charities that want your name or your money or both. I'll see you both at dinner. Now scram!"

Twenty minutes later, an ornate iron bench and tombstones behind it came into view surrounded by an iron fence. Two sailboats silently cut through the calm water as they headed upriver.

Travis held open the gate to let Olivia pass through.

She looped her arm through his. "Do you mind if we sit for a moment?"

"You're not okay, unless being as pale as a corpse is normal." Putting an arm around her shoulders, he guided her to the stone bench overlooking more than a dozen markers of varying sizes and shapes. Some were so old that the names and dates were hardly legible. "What's wrong?"

"It's nothing to worry about. I just got a little dizzy—low blood sugar or something. I should have eaten something with the tea."

"Livy, I'm going to run back to the barn and get the golf cart. We need to get you back to the house as quickly as possible."

"No. Please, just let me sit here for a while longer. I'll be fine in a few minutes."

"Nick's father kept having dizzy spells. Do your hands and feet go numb?"

"Sometimes. Why?" Olivia said as she flexed her fingers.

"Diabetes. Nick's dad has diabetes. We need to get you to a doctor."

"I'm not diabetic. I'm feeling much better. Why don't you wander around. Some of these headstones are really interesting. Then we can take a leisurely walk back."

Travis took his time studying the various markers dating all the way back to 1740. Olivia wondered how long she could fluff off her symptoms as lack of sleep and lack of food. Then there were the cramps that no one knew about. Not often. Not bad. But still they were pretty regular. The walk from the house to the cemetery had taken twice as long. Her legs felt like jelly. She didn't want Travis making a big deal of this on their return to the house. And she didn't want him running off for the golf cart. Somehow she needed to find the strength to pick up the pace on the walk back to the house.

"This place is amazing, Livy. I can't wait to tell everyone back home that you have your own cemetery that's older than the United States. Are you still okay?"

"Yep. Take your time. I'm just sitting here enjoying the view of the river." She needed a few more minutes to gather her strength.

She had felt fine while in New York with Daisy, but after being back at Fairfield for only a week the fatigue and queasy spells began and now she seemed short of breath. These were the same symptoms that her grandmother had before her death. Olivia was certain that someone was trying to poison her as well—but how and why? It had to be someone at the yard.

39

"Look here young man! I was watchin' when you and Lily was walkin' back from the cemetery. I saw the way you had your arm around her, and I've seen the way you look at her. No good is gonna come of this. Mr. William is back in her life where he should be, and I won't have you stirrin' up trouble!"

Travis opened his mouth to say something, anything that would calm Miranda. But she raised her arm as if to swing at him and continued to shout.

"Leave her be, I tell you. Get outta this house and don't come back."

Relief swept through Travis when Sarah rounded the corner of the door leading to the men's parlor.

She stopped short when she saw the scene before her. "Mamma, what are you doing? Mr. Travis is a guest in this house and is to be treated with respect!"

"He's a troublemaker, and I won't have him hurting my Lily."

Sarah took hold of the wheelchair's handles and proceeded to pull Miranda back through the doorway. "I'm terribly sorry about this. She isn't in her right mind. I'll just take her to her room and be right back."

Olivia hesitated at the parlor door while Sarah turned her mother's wheelchair around in the hall. "What's happened? I heard Miranda shouting at someone all the way upstairs."

"I'll explain when I get back. I need to get her settled in her room first."

Wearing a black velour pantsuit with a string of pearls, Olivia entered the parlor.

Travis looked up. He felt like he'd just come to after the knock-out punch in a boxing match. "Can *you* tell me what just happened? Because, I don't have a clue. That's one feisty little old lady!"

"From what little I heard upstairs, it had something to do with me."

Travis came around the side of the pool table taking both of Olivia's hands in his. "I hope you're feeling as good as you look. You have a rather aristocratic air about you this evening."

The doorbell chimed. "I can't imagine who that might be," said Olivia.

"I thought no one can get onto the property unannounced."

"Precisely, unless Benjamin has locked himself out. I now know that isn't possible." Olivia said as she headed toward the door.

Travis stood protectively behind Olivia as she opened the door to find Horatio on the stoop. "Please come in. I forgot about you having a remote for the gates. We were in the parlor so I answered the door rather than wait for Sarah."

After introducing Travis to Horatio, Olivia guided the men back to the parlor. "Did I forget that you were coming? I've been rather preoccupied lately."

Horatio glanced around the room. "No. Actually, I'm here to see Sarah about a piece of old business."

"She should just be a minute. There was a bit of a situation with her mother a few minutes ago and Sarah took her to her room."

"I hope Miranda's okay."

"Her health is fine, but she's having trouble accepting Travis in the house."

Horatio appeared confused. "I don't understand."

"Miranda thinks I'm my mother and have suddenly returned home. William has been here several times, and she believes that we have gotten back together. She doesn't seem to see the age difference between he and I. Right before you got here she verbally attacked Travis for paying too much attention to me. Had there been anything sharp within her reach it might have gotten ugly."

"Have you tried explaining that you aren't Maureen?"

Sarah breezed through the doorway. "Hello, Horatio. I'm glad you're here. My mother is more locked in the past than ever since Olivia arrived. I just don't know how I'm going to deal with this. She's becoming violent toward Travis."

Travis took Olivia's hand. "I think it would be better if I move to a hotel. Maybe in Norfolk."

"No! I need you. We'll figure something out—leaving is not an option!"

Horatio frowned and glanced at Sarah. "Well, if it's just a place for Travis to live and be near the yard, how about the house on Freemason Street?"

Sarah smiled. "Great idea! Nathaniel still lives there and manages the place. William occasionally has VIPs stay there. It's perfect."

Olivia fingered her pearls. "Is that the house I inherited?"

"Yes. The house was built in 1795 by the first McLeod who came here from Scotland. He made his fortune building ships. Your grandfather lived there most of the time because it was so close to the shipyard. He would usually come here, to Fairfield, on weekends. It's been completely remodeled for twentieth century comfort while keeping the eighteenth century charm." Sarah turned toward Horatio. "Can you make the arrangements tomorrow? I'll have Benjamin move Travis's things."

Horatio hesitated. "What do you think, Olivia? Travis will be two hours away."

"As much as I would like Travis close by, they're right. He should be near the shipyard. Meg may want to move as well since she is spending so much time with Gertrude sorting through the various charities."

"Okay, if you're sure. But I came here to help you." Travis glanced at Sarah. "I'm not afraid of a little old lady in a wheelchair."

"I know you're not Travis, but I need you at the shipyard," Olivia said as she wrapped her arms around him.

She didn't need him obsessing about her health and demanding that she see a doctor. Olivia already knew what was wrong with her—she was being poisoned. And that little bit of information she wanted to keep to herself—at least for the moment.

Sarah moved into the hall. "Then it's settled, Travis will move to the house on Freemason Street tomorrow. Horatio, I'll walk you to the door."

A minute later there were just the two of them left in the room. Travis pulled Olivia tighter against his chest. "I love you, Livy. All I want is to be at your side. But maybe this is for the best. Perhaps the answer to your grandmother's death lies in the past with your grandfather."

Olivia stepped back. "Come on, let's go upstairs until dinner is ready."

As they entered the hall they saw Sarah hand Horatio a colorful metal box. It was the tin that contained her special blend of tea.

40

Not one inch of mahogany could be seen through the collection of reports covering the conference table in Olivia's McLeod and Morrison office. Travis looked pleased with himself as he shuffled the last of the pages into their various piles. There seemed to be some semblance of organization to what Olivia and Meg viewed as a hopeless mess.

"Are you ready, Livy? I think I've at least got a few of the pieces to this puzzle." He pointed to a stack. "These are the contracts for specific ships to be built." He then pointed to a row of reports labeled supply orders. "These supplies are for each ship as it's being built, but they don't always match the final manifest."

Olivia shook her head. "I don't understand."

"Me, either," chimed in Meg.

"I think your grandmother was concerned about the overall cost of the ships being built against what was being paid for them."

"I still don't understand."

"I guess the simplest explanation is that the cost of the materials used in the construction was much higher than what was contracted."

Olivia rested her hands on her hips. "So what you're saying is a lot of money is being channeled somewhere else."

Travis nodded. "Yep."

Olivia walked over to her desk, picked up the receiver, and pressed a button. "Gertrude, get Horatio on the phone."

"Why do you need to talk to Horatio?" Meg asked.

"During one of our first conversations he mentioned that my grandmother was concerned about the financial reports. There were more ships being built but the profits were down. When she confronted the Morrison brothers their answer was that supply costs had risen and the profits on each unit were down. Meanwhile, Clive and Wilson were actively buying properties on the west coast for expansion."

Meg's gaze shifted from Olivia to Travis then back to Olivia. Her brow furrowed. "That doesn't make sense. There is no indication anywhere in these reports that this company is financially strapped."

Olivia waited for the dial tone then punched in the number. "That's why I want to talk to Horatio."

William entered the office. "Why do you need to talk to Horatio?"

Everyone glanced toward the door leading into the outer office.

Olivia put down the phone. "William, Gertrude said you'd be dropping by today. Travis has been helping us sort through these reports. I'm hoping he'll find some clue as to what my grandmother was searching for."

William leaned over the piles. "What have you found?"

"Nothing, yet." Olivia picked up a report and handed it to William. "We can't figure out what these notations in the margins mean. My grandmother made these same groups of letters and numbers on different reports."

William scanned the page. "They're slip references."

Travis pulled a sheet off the top of one of the piles. "I have the list of identification numbers for the slips, and it doesn't match."

"These penciled in numbers and letters in the margins are the old identification numbers that were used prior to World War II. Angus continued using the old system that his grandfather developed even though you won't find them listed on any of the computer generated reports."

Travis handed Olivia the page he'd been holding. She glanced at it then looked at William. "So Angus and my grandmother added their own notations to the current reports because it was more familiar to them. It wasn't a special code, just an easier way of tracking for them."

William nodded. "Exactly."

"So, Grandmother was watching the progress of the various ships as they were being built."

William walked over to the windows and pointed to the view beyond. "I assume so. From this corner office you can see almost everything that goes on in the yard. That's why Wilson wanted it so badly."

"It's beginning to make sense now." Travis waved his hand over the stacks of reports. "Livy, give me another couple of days, and I'll have an answer for you."

William turned back to face everyone. "Travis, if it will help you any, you can use my office across the hall. I'll be going back to DC tomorrow."

"Are you sure you have to leave?" Olivia set the pages back on the table. "You've been here less than an hour, and you solved a mystery that I've been working on for more than a month."

"Sorry, but yes. I have a meeting at noon that I can't miss."

"Then can I invite you for dinner this evening? Travis and Meg are living in the house on Freemason Street, and I would love your company."

"You mean you don't like eating huge dinners all alone in that big house."

Olivia chuckled. "That, too."

Olivia slipped her hand through the crook of William's arm and walked toward the ladies parlor.

William glanced down. "Are you okay? You look funny."

She dare not tell him she was having another dizzy spell and she couldn't feel her toes. "Just a little lightheaded. It happens sometimes."

"Are you diabetic?" William's voice held more than a little concern.

"No. I think its just stress."

"My mother has diabetes. It's nothing to ignore."

Her gut said she could trust him, even though he was a Morrison. But could she trust him with her life? Not yet. She wasn't ready to confide in him that she too was being poisoned.

William patted his stomach with his free hand. "Sarah outdid herself on that meal. I should come around more often, although I feel like I should do two laps around the house."

"I really do enjoy your company. I think I would have loved having you as a father, although we both know that isn't possible. I can see why my mother loved you."

"I fell in love with her the first time she looked up at me with those bewitching violet eyes. Your eyes."

Olivia gestured toward two chairs facing each other in front of the parlor fireplace. William settled back in his chair. "Do you mind if I smoke? I've tried to cut back but I still enjoy a cigarette after a meal."

"Of course not." Olivia retrieved an ashtray from across the room and set it on the side table. She sat down and smoothed her skirt over her crossed knees. She was still wearing the suit she'd put on early that morning—it was wrinkled. Sarah would take care of getting it to the cleaners. William pulled a silver case and lighter from his inside jacket pocket. Maybe this was a good time to ask about something that was still nibbling in the back of her brain.

"William, are you aware of a valley somewhere on the property?"

"No, why do you ask?"

"My grandmother left me a note. One that I believe she wrote just before she died. She mentioned that she was very ill and things weren't right here."

"That's odd. Did she say anything else?"

"Just that I need to look to her for the answers that are hidden in the valley."

William wore a puzzled expression while shaking his head from side to side.

"Sorry, I can't help you with that one. She never mentioned anything, but then I only saw her at the yard."

"It dawned on me one day that maybe there was some clue hidden behind her portrait. I had Benjamin take it down, but that turned out to be a dead end."

William stood. "I'd love to stay and help you, but I really have to leave. I have an early flight back to DC in the morning."

Olivia followed him into the hall where he stopped in front of a handsome oil painting of a landscape. It seemed a bit small for being placed at the foot of the staircase.

A deep frown creased William's brow. "I must say I think this work is much more suited to the parlor than here."

"What do you mean?"

"This landscape was over the parlor fireplace. Your grandmother's portrait always hung here at the foot of the stairs."

Olivia walked William to the door as if in a trance. Her blood turned to ice. She closed the door and hurried back to the painting. She must have said goodbye but she couldn't remember. Her heart raced. Who had moved the painting? Why? Maybe William hadn't been able to tell her where the valley was, but she was willing to bet he'd still given her important information.

Olivia glanced over at the staircase as another dizzy spell threatened her balance. She slid down onto the third step from the bottom resting her head in her hands. She slipped off her pumps and flexed her toes to bring some feeling back to her feet.

"Ma'am, are you okay?"

Olivia straitened at the unexpected voice. She hadn't heard Sarah's approach.

"I'm just tired. It's been a long day."

"Why are you sitting on the steps? You look a little pale."

"William and I were looking at this landscape and then he had to leave. He said it used to be in the parlor."

"He's correct. If you're sure you're okay then I'll just go back to the kitchen."

"Yeah, I'm fine. I think I'll go upstairs and turn in. Five o'clock comes around awfully early. Would you mind if I just had toast and your fabulous jam for breakfast? My stomach's been a little weird lately."

Sarah nodded her agreement. "Sure. I'm happy to make anything you like." Then she headed back down the hall and disappeared around the corner.

Olivia stood and grabbed the banister. Her legs felt as strong as string cheese. She took the stairs slowly and, once in her room, fell exhausted into bed. She scooted back against the headboard and inhaled the soothing scent of rose petals. Her heart pounded in her chest. Her eyes drifted up to the steady gaze of her great-grandmother. Alexandra would have faced these problems and calmly sorted through them.

"I need to relax and think logically, Great-Grandmother," she said in a soft voice, just above a whisper. "This fatigue and dizzy spells only started after I came here and stopped while Daisy and I were in New York. And from what I've learned, although not as bad, they are some of the same symptoms that my grandmother had. Who's trying to kill me, too? And how?"

Olivia's gaze shifted to her hand as she absently twisted the blanket into a knot. "Surely Sarah and Benjamin have nothing to gain by my death. I pay them very well. Both received an inheritance large enough to never have to worry about finances for the rest of their lives. I know Sarah and I got off to a rocky start, but we've been working into quite a comfortable relationship." Olivia took a deep breath. "But what was all that business about Horatio coming here to see Sarah and leaving with her special tea tin?"

Olivia crawled under the covers. "I think it's time to see a doctor."

She reached for the bedside lamp and pulled the chain. The moonlight streamed in through the window giving Alexandra an ethereal glow.

"Please help me, Great-Grandmother."

The office was buzzing with activity when Olivia arrived the next morning at nine. Travis was bent over the conference table shuffling reports.

Meg picked a donut from a box on the desk. "Travis and I got here early and brought breakfast."

"Sounds wonderful, I'm hungry."

"I didn't think it was possible for anyone to walk away from Sarah's breakfasts and still be hungry," Meg said while dusting powdered sugar from her blouse.

"I just took enough time for coffee and toast. That was two hours ago, and now I'm hungry."

After choosing a large raspberry Danish, Olivia headed over to Travis.

He held up two reports side by side. "It's all here. She was tracking the costs for each ship under construction and comparing them to the final numbers in the printouts. Now I just need to figure out why."

Olivia took another bite. "What else is happening?"

"The house on Freemason Street is amazing! Everything is as Angus left it. I don't think your grandmother ever went there after his death. At least Nathaniel doesn't remember her being there. Do you mind if I rummage around a little? It's just full of local shipping history."

"Be my guest. Grandfather wasn't someone I particularly want to get to know. Who's Nathaniel?"

"Oh, great guy. He takes care of the place. You'd like him."

"I wonder where Grandmother stayed if she didn't stay there? I can't imagine her making that two hour drive twice a day."

Meg set her donut down on the desk. "I know the answer to that," she exclaimed. "She had a room. Well, it was actually an apartment in the Vivian Dumbarton House for battered women."

Olivia's mouth fell open. "Grandmother was beaten?"

"No. No." Meg took a bite of her donut, keeping everyone in suspense while she chewed and swallowed. "It's kind of a long story, but Horatio's daughter was married to a wife beater. They had a little girl. Of course Horatio didn't know about it until his daughter, Vivian, landed in the hospital in Richmond. Horatio was afraid for their safety and asked for your grandmother's help. She signed them out of the hospital and took them to Fairfield where they lived for the next six months. During that time your grandmother convinced Vivian to file for divorce. Her husband went ballistic and tried to break into Fairfield and get them out, but of course he couldn't get past all the security. He finally tried to come ashore in a small boat at night. I don't know the details, but the next morning the authorities found the capsized boat and his body." Meg took another bite and continued talking. "Your grandmother knew about an old monster of a Victorian mansion a couple streets over from Freemason Street that was about to be torn down by the city. She bought it in the eleventh hour and turned it into the Vivian Dumbarton House. A safe place for battered women and their children. Vivian runs it and her daughter still lives there." Meg paused a beat. "Is that cool, or what?"

Olivia closed her mouth. "Yeah, really cool. I had no idea," she paused a beat. "I wonder what Grandfather thought about that? Grandmother having her own apartment so close to him."

"It's a great house. You really have to see it." Meg brushed more powered sugar from the front of her blouse. "I know better than to pick jelly donuts. I end up wearing the sugar."

Travis moved to Olivia's side. "I know. Why don't you move in with us? There's plenty of room and Nathaniel takes care of everything. You and Benjamin wouldn't have to make that two hour trip back and forth."

"I don't know." Maybe if she weren't living at Fairfield she would start to feel better. She'd find out real soon if that's where she was being poisoned. Uncle Lionel said she could trust Sarah and Benjamin with her life. But how did he know that? Her gut said they wouldn't do anything to harm her . . . but she'd been very wrong in the past. It was certainly worth a try. After all, it was her house. She'd have to see it sooner or later.

Travis took Olivia in his arms. "Best of all . . . we'd be together. I love you, Livy. I hate this living arrangement." He bent down and kissed her lips. "Please."

Olivia wrapped her arms around his neck. "I think I should see the house before making that decision."

41

The following morning, at eleven o'clock, Travis pulled the Ford Taurus he'd rented into a parking space in front of the house on East Freemason Street. The red brick house looked old. One hundred and ninety-five years old to be exact. It looked like all the other houses of that era. Just a few stone steps separated the front door from the sidewalk. This wasn't what she expected. It wasn't the gloomy house well protected behind an iron fence with the shades drawn and NO TRESPASSING signs. It didn't look like the house of a hateful old man. She expected her grandfather to have lived a somewhat reclusive life. This was so out-in-the-open, so vulnerable. She got out of the car and gently closed the door. She wasn't ready to enter that world just yet.

A tiny garden adjacent to the property drew her attention. An ancient black iron fence and a delicate gate held a sign that simply said WELCOME.

Olivia waited until Travis came around the front of the car. "Do I own the garden?"

Meg interrupted. "Yep. It's so cute. Come on, have a look."

A path of crushed shells wound around bushes that would be spectacular come spring. Stone benches sat beneath huge trees that would provide shade during the hot summer months. It was a spot of enchantment in an otherwise busy neighborhood. She followed a narrower path to the right and found herself at the back wall of a single-story brick building with a wooden roof. The path ended, but she could see a break in the thick privet hedge that grew right up to the building. Still, there were no signs forbidding her to enter the yard beyond. Olivia peeked in a window. "It's a potting shed. At least that's what it looks like now. It's not as old as the house, but still old. Its former life could have been almost anything, maybe even a cottage."

Meg took Olivia's hand and pulled her toward the back of the house. "Come on. You gotta see the old well. It's even got a cute little roof over it."

This was the yard of her grandfather, of her ancestors, and now it was her yard. She followed another shell path toward the back of the property to a small gazebo. This would be the perfect place to relax with a glass of wine and a book. Did her grandfather ever sit here and think about the family he'd driven away? The house looked much larger from this side, almost as if it had doubled in size by a later addition. There were several doors and a wide set of stairs leading down to the basement, covered by tiny peaked roofs. The area between the house and the garden was totally covered in brick, right up to the well structure and around the house to other small out-buildings, including what appeared to be a carriage house at the furthest corner of the property.

Meg twirled around with her arms out. "Nathaniel says this huge, old tree is a magnolia. Can you just imagine what it's going to be like back here in the summer? You can have garden parties, and I'll be here to help."

Travis guided Olivia and Meg back toward the end of the house facing the garden. "Yeah. Summer. If she's still here," said Travis. All emotion had drained from his voice.

The back door opened and a tall, red-haired man, perhaps in his later forties, stepped out onto the covered stoop. "Welcome to McLeod House, Mrs. Bentley." Although his expression was serious, the wrinkles at the corners of his eyes and mouth were evidence that there was an easy laugh just waiting for the opportunity to spring forth.

"Livy, I would like you meet Nathaniel. He's amazing and runs this place with the efficiency of a five-star hotel," said Travis.

"I wouldn't go that far, but I do try my best, ma'am."

Olivia reached out her hand to shake Nathaniel's. "It's a pleasure to meet you."

Once inside, Travis showed Olivia where to hang her coat and then followed Nathaniel into the entrance hall. Rich green walls and soft cream woodwork created an inviting room. The walls were lined with an assortment of chairs and tables. A round table in the center held an enormous floral arrangement. But the focal point of the room was definitely the staircase that rose a full two stories.

"Excuse me, Nathaniel. Why are there three doors leading to the outdoors?" asked Olivia.

"Back when this house was built, those coming on foot came in through the front door that opens directly onto the sidewalk. The side entrance had steps for carriages and those coming on horseback. The door that you used was preferred by the family. There are other less formal doors that were, and are still, used by the help."

Olivia nodded. "I love history. I'm sure I'll have a million questions."

"Mr. Tanner, if you'll just give me your keys, I'll bring the luggage and move the car around back to the garage. I've prepared a simple lunch which will be ready in about half-an-hour."

Travis handed him the keys.

Meg leaned against the doorframe leading into the next room. "A simple meal to me is a chili-dog. Believe me, I'm sure Nathaniel doesn't even know how to make chili-dogs or anything that I would call simple. Isn't that right, Travis?"

"Yep. I'll tell you his story later. How about a quick tour before lunch?"

Half an hour later, after viewing the rooms on the second and third floors, Travis and Meg stopped before a door on the second floor. Travis turned the ancient brass doorknob, and Meg motioned for Olivia to enter.

"We've saved the best for last."

Light streamed in from the back patio and garden, washing the ornately paneled walls with an amber glow.

"This is lovely, very masculine. I assume it was my grandfather's."

The furniture contained the exotic woods of the Art Deco period and clearly stated that Angus was a man of his day and not a slave to history. The fireplace was in the same Adam style as the rest of the house, with slate-blue painted detailing. The same blue was embroidered into the bed linens and drapes.

Olivia was standing in the middle of her grandfather's bedroom. The man who'd disowned his only daughter and broke his wife's heart. She never forgave him and Olivia wasn't ready to either. She glanced at her watch. "I think we should head downstairs for lunch."

Travis held up a hand. "Not so fast, Livy. I had a lot of time on my hands when we first arrived. Norfolk is just full of old house museums, many within walking distance of here. I discovered one interesting architectural detail. Most of the homes with paneled walls had cupboards concealed within the ornate panels."

"Okay, Travis. Let me guess . . . you found one in here."

"You're taking all the fun out of this."

He walked over to a square panel next to the fireplace and pressed against its corner. It opened to reveal a sizeable space with several shelves.

"There's another one on the other side. But this one contained a stack of letters and notebooks, which turned out to be journals. Angus had been keeping pretty extensive records of the management of this house, which we found in his desk in the library. But these journals contain his personal thoughts of events that happened both at the yard and here."

Olivia turned and headed back toward the door. "Great, I'm sure he gave all the details of how much he hated my mother. Now can we go down to lunch, before you spoil my appetite?"

Travis threw up his hands in a frustrated gesture.

Meg moved between them. "I think this can wait till later, Travis. We have a lot to go over with Livy. Besides, I'm hungry. We don't want to keep Nathaniel's meal waiting."

The three were just entering the dining room when Nathaniel came through the swinging door with lunch.

Olivia waited as Travis pulled her chair out. "Wow. This room is larger than the one at Fairfield."

Nathaniel placed the three plates at one end of the long table. "Back in the late 1790s, when this wing was added, it had many uses, including a ball room."

"I look forward to hearing the history of the house," said Olivia.

Nathaniel did a quick bow of his head and turned toward the kitchen. "Just ring if you need anything."

Travis pulled out Olivia's chair. She slid in and took the folded napkin, placing it in her lap. "My goodness, is this supposed to be simple?"

A generous portion of a seafood salad rested in the center of the plate surrounded by fresh fruit and French bread sliced on the diagonal and smothered with garlic butter. A sprig of mint dressed a tall frosty glass of iced tea.

Meg took her napkin with a flourish. "Wait till you see dinner tonight."

"You mean you eat like this all the time?"

Travis nodded. "Yep."

"Isn't it wonderful?" Meg said before she took a bite of garlic bread.

Olivia was still raving about lunch when Travis and Meg ushered her into the library that Angus had long ago turned into his office.

The only things sitting on the desk were several file folders stacked neatly in a corner.

"Now for the serious part. What Meg and I have to tell you is going to be hard to believe, but you have to trust us." Travis helped Meg pull up two wingback chairs. He motioned for Olivia and Meg to sit, then moved around to the desk and sat down. "You said we could make ourselves at home. And, quite frankly I wasn't sure if you would ever come here."

Meg turned to face Olivia. "Travis and I started on the file cabinet one evening shortly after we got here. What we found was extraordinary."

Travis folded his arms on the desk. "There was an orphanage here in town. Dated back well before the Civil War. The building was falling down around the kids and ready to be condemned when your grandfather stepped in and built a new one. State-of-the-art facility with everything the kids could want. Not only did he build the children's center, he funded the entire operation. He also made sure that the kids had a good education, and he provided a trust for educational grants."

Meg leaned forward. "Nathaniel graduated from culinary school in New York and studied in France."

"You're not going to tell me Nathaniel was an orphan?" Olivia thought back to the man who had just served the most amazing meal ever. His neat appearance had initially impressed her, from the sharp creases down the legs of his black slacks to his starched white shirt under an argyle sweater vest. His rubber-soled shoes that allowed him to quietly move through the house without disturbing the guests were highly polished. Nothing about him said orphan.

"Yep. Nathaniel had accepted a high profile position in California. Before he left New York he contacted your grandfather to thank him for everything that he had done for him. Said without Angus's help he could have ended up digging ditches for the state. Then a year later your grandfather called Nathaniel and offered him this job at twice what he was earning as a chef. The rest is history, as they say."

Did Grandfather think he could wipe his conscience clean by supporting an orphanage? Sounded like he bought Nathaniel's loyalty—not so magnanimous. He had plenty of money to throw around. It would have been a drop in the bucket for him.

Olivia glanced from Meg to Travis. "I'm not impressed. He had money to burn." She paused a beat. "What else?"

"Angus also financed the construction of a little league park, a pediatric wing at a local hospital, a park complete with swimming pool, and day-care centers around the city." Travis pulled the stack of folders closer and fanned them out in front of him. "The interesting thing is that although he provided the funding, his name is not connected with any of them. It's all here in these files."

Olivia shook her head. A deep frown creased her brow. "Do you know when he started all of this? I've found no mention of this in any of Grandmother's files or notes." She turned to Meg. "Did you find any reference to this in the files you've gone through either at Fairfield or the yard?"

"No. Just here."

"As close as we can figure, it was about two years after your mother left," said Travis as he re-stacked the folders and placed them neatly in front of him.

"Did my grandmother know about this?"

"I don't think she did." Meg stood up and grabbed the top file folder and handed it to Olivia. "Most of the money came from a trust with a generic name. Angus was never mentioned, except on the educational grants, which is how Nathaniel knew who to call and thank."

"Is everything for children?" Olivia asked.

Meg returned to her chair. "As far as we've been able to gather, it appears that way."

"So am I to believe my grandfather suddenly had feelings of remorse and became the benevolent benefactor to the city's children? What about my *mother*? How about saying something like 'Hey, Maureen honey, I'm sorry I acted like an angry fool. I love you. I'll make everything right.' What about helping *her* children?"

Olivia jumped out of her chair and stormed over to the door. "Sorry, but I just don't buy it!"

Travis stood. "Wait, Livy. Please sit back down—there's more."

Meg got up and went over to Olivia. "He's right. There's a lot more. And you need to hear it."

Olivia followed Meg back to their chairs. "Okay, Travis, I'll play along. What else did you find?"

"The letters and journals that I found in the bedroom cupboard contain mostly notes about the shipyard and meetings with the government during World War II. There were a few personal letters on White House stationary, but there were also two letters addressed to your mother in Cedar Hill that were never mailed." Travis pushed two yellowed envelopes to the edge of the desk in front of Olivia. "In these letters Angus begged her forgiveness and the promise to change his will. The first was dated about six months after your mother left, the second about a year later."

Olivia reached for the letters. "But why didn't he mail them? What could have stopped him?"

"It appears that he told old man Morrison of his change of heart. It was Morrison that convinced him that he needed to hold firm and not cave in to weakness. The same thing happened with the second letter a year later."

Olivia glanced from Travis to Meg. "Are you both sure about this?"

"It's all written down in black and white. Morrison had Angus convinced that the company would be compromised if he allowed her back. After all, she dumped William for a man she barely knew."

"But Morrison was going to have my father killed. How could Grandfather trust a man like that?"

"Yes, but Angus didn't know that. Remember, at the time, Morrison was manipulating both Maureen and your grandfather."

"Yeah. It's in the diaries."

Travis continued. "As his only heir, she would own fifty percent of the company and who knows what she would do with it. Besides, how could William ever work with her after what she had done to him? She had walked out on both families and the company. Old man Morrison convinced Angus that Maureen couldn't be trusted."

Olivia stroked her brow. Her thoughts were all running into each other and none making any sense. There was all the information she'd gotten from the diaries, which made Angus look like a dictator. There were the stories from Clarence and Daisy while in New York that her mother no longer existed at Fairfield. She tried to sort them out but didn't know where to start.

"Livy, are you having another headache? Can I get you an aspirin or something?"

"No thanks, Travis. I think I just need some fresh air and time alone."

Olivia stood alone at the old well searching her pockets for a coin. She found a dime and tossed it down the brick-lined hole. "I wish I had all the pieces to this puzzle. I wish I were closer to finding who poisoned Grandmother and I wish I could believe that Grandfather really did love Mom and want her back. I wish I knew what to do next."

Olivia looked up to see Nathaniel step from the potting shed. He glanced from side to side. "Did you say something? I'm sorry, but I couldn't hear what you were saying."

"Oh, hello. No, I was just talking to the well. I'm not sure how many wishes you can get for a dime."

Nathaniel chuckled. "I would think that a woman in your position would have all your wishes granted."

"I wish it were that easy." Olivia leaned against the latticework that surrounded the well. "I'm curious. Why are you still here taking care of an empty house when you are obviously a very talented chef?"

"I made a promise to your grandfather to keep this house and land in order for future generations of McLeods. He wanted everything to remain the same."

"But I thought McLeod & Morrison used this for out-of-town VIPs."

"They do, but it's all arranged through Gertrude or William."

"You're sure he said future generations?"

"Yes, ma'am."

"I'm not so sure he meant my mother. He did a pretty good job of eliminating her from his life."

Nathaniel reached in his pocket for a ring of keys. He pulled one off and handed it to Olivia. "Follow the path until it ends at the old carriage house. There's something in there you should see. Now I must get back to the kitchen."

Olivia watched Nathaniel's back as he disappeared through the kitchen door. She fingered the key. It didn't look all that old. She wasn't convinced she'd find anything of importance, but it was better than going back in the house and listen to Travis and Meg extol the virtuous Angus McLeod. She turned and wandered down the path leading to the carriage house.

It didn't take long to walk the length of the property that extended to the next street. The old red brick of the two-story building had weathered to a soft rose. Tall arched doors opened onto North Bank Street, but on closer inspection it was clear that the key she held wouldn't fit the locks. She followed the path around to the back where she found another door. She inserted the key and twisted. The door opened on well-oiled hinges. The space was well lit from windows high on the walls at each end. Every kind of equipment that might be needed in the maintenance of such a large piece of city property seemed to be housed within the lofty space. What was it that Nathaniel wanted her to see? Maybe it was whatever she saw sitting over in the far corner under canvas. After weaving her way back through the maize, she tugged at the tarp sending it into a pile on the floor. Dust flew everywhere, sparkling in the sunlight streaming in through the overhead windows. Olivia gasped.

"Mom's Packard."

Olivia ran her hand along the enormous fender. She melted into a heap, leaning her head against the amazingly wide white-wall tire. "Oh, Grandfather. I don't know whether to continue hating you, or to love you." Her heart hurt. "You kept Mom's car . . . for her return? You never stopped loving her." Olivia pulled her knees up under her chin. "So you must have known about the loophole in your will. You knew that I would inherit despite the efforts of the Morrisons. Why didn't you tell your wife? Grandmother hated you for all those years for nothing."

The side door opened and closed. Olivia glanced up as Travis wound his way past the tractor. "Nathaniel sent me." He held out his hand and helped Olivia to her feet. "Wow! It's a Packard."

"Mom's."

Travis glanced around. "Who were you talking to?"

"Grandfather."

"I don't understand."

Olivia moved toward the door. "I don't either. Let's get out of here."

Olivia closed and locked the door of the carriage house. She and Travis walked hand in hand back to the house.

Travis closed the bedroom door and moved to where Olivia stood looking out the window. "Are you feeling okay? I know it's been a long day with a lot of unexpected stuff thrown at you. I'd understand if you want to be alone tonight. I don't mind moving to another room."

Olivia continued looking at the garden below bathed in the glow of a full moon. "So much anger of the past could have been avoided if pride had been replaced with humility. All my grandparents had to do was open their hearts and find the path to happiness. They were each fighting for the same outcome, yet neither understood what the other was doing."

"I don't understand. What are you saying, Livy?"

"I've been a fool. I wanted so much to find the answers about the past that I've shut out the present. I've listened to everyone else, and done everything except listen to my heart."

Olivia turned toward Travis. She reached up, wrapping her arms around his neck. "I love you, and whatever my future holds I want to share it with you."

The kiss was long and passionate and then Travis picked her up and carried her to the bed.

42

"Good morning, Olivia, you've become quite the woman about town. I had to bribe Gertrude to schedule a day in the office so Horatio and I could have some time with you."

"I'm sorry, William, but the last two weeks have been non-stop meetings and tours of various non-profit organizations in the area since I learned some rather interesting information about my grandfather."

Horatio pulled an envelope from his briefcase and set it on Olivia's desk. "We have some interesting information, as well, but you go first."

Olivia motioned for them to sit. "Did you know that Angus was quite the philanthropist?"

William and Horatio both exchanged surprised looks and shook their heads in denial. "No, you must be mistaken. Philanthropist is the last word that I would associate with Angus McLeod. Not in a million years," stated William.

"Well, you're wrong. That's what has kept me so busy. I've been visiting the various organizations receiving funding through his trust."

Horatio finally found his voice. "No! Surely, he would have told his wife about something like this."

"Another bit of information about Grandfather. He kept Mom's '41 Packard convertible."

"That's not possible." Horatio slapped the edge of the desk. "Angus ordered everything of your mother's destroyed. He eliminated her from his life."

"Well, he kept her car. It's sitting in the carriage house. Nathaniel says it runs as well as the day it came off the assembly line."

"I never knew him personally, but this isn't the man your grandmother portrayed."

"Apparently the only people he trusted were Gertrude and Nathaniel, and they are both on the Board."

William sat forward in his seat. "What trust?"

"The Hampton Roads Charitable Children's Trust. Its mission is to help in all aspects of children's lives."

"I know of it. It's one of the few trusts that hasn't asked me to be on its Board. Now I know why."

Horatio's fingers tapped the wooden arm of his chair. "Your grandmother was terribly concerned about the amount of cash she inherited. With your grandfather's miserly ways, she thought there should be a great deal more money than what appeared in his numerous bank accounts."

Olivia got up and moved to the corner of her desk. "The trust was setup a few years after my mother left. Money was added in large amounts at first then tapered off each year so as not to bring attention to what he was doing. At the time of his death, the principal was so large that it continued to grow on its own and his involvement remained hidden."

"Your grandmother had a good head for finances. She realized there was money missing and when she couldn't find the source, she blamed it on the Morrison's." Horatio paused a beat. "It sounds like she might have been wrong about that."

Olivia scooted up to perch on the corner of her desk. "I want to start a day care center for our employees here at the yard. I understand that Clive and Wilson are turning part of the old power plant into a gym. I think that's a wonderful idea. There should be room for a day care as well."

William snickered. "Good luck with that idea! The gym is for their use only, not the employees. They won't approve expenditures for anything that doesn't benefit them."

Over the course of the last two weeks, Olivia had found within her the strength and determination of her ancestors. Her love for Travis was growing stronger by the day, and he was once again sharing her bed. She had given numerous interviews with the press and was scheduled to do TV appearances over the next few months. Olivia felt confident in her new role.

"We'll just see about that. Are you with me on this, William?"

"You bet! I love fireworks."

Horatio pulled at his collar and cleared his throat.

"What's the problem, Horatio?" asked Olivia. "You don't like my idea?"

"It's not that." Horatio rubbed his hands on his pant legs and glanced over at William. "Maybe we should talk about this privately."

"Nonsense. There are no secrets here. Lack of communication is what got my grandparents in trouble." Olivia glanced around the room. Everyone nodded in agreement. "Out with it."

"Remember the day that I came to the house and Sarah gave me her tea tin?"

"Of course, and I've been meaning to ask you about that."

"Sarah called me in a panic saying that she thought she might be the one who poisoned your grandmother."

Every inch of Olivia's body went numb, but she said nothing.

"She didn't make the connection until you started showing some of the same symptoms. After you came back from New York, you were fine. The dizzy spells and fatigue started again, but Travis and Meg were okay, and you were all eating and drinking together. *Except* that *you* were drinking Sarah's own blend of tea."

"I love her tea, and so did my grandmother who had been drinking it for years."

"But that batch seemed to correlate with your grandmother's illness. Remember she came home from the hospital feeling fine, then it all started again. Sarah gave me the tea that night so I could have it tested. The results just came back. The tea was loaded with potassium."

"Potassium? Since when is potassium a poison? I take it everyday in my vitamins."

"Excessive amounts of potassium causes the heart to dilate and become flaccid and slows the heart rate. This can cause symptoms of muscle weakness, numbness of the hands, feet, tongue and face." Horatio scooted back in his chair. "Large amounts weaken the heart, causing an abnormal rhythm, and cardiac arrest occurs."

"Okay, I had some of those symptoms, but not enough to kill me. If we were getting it in the same tea, how come it killed Grandmother?"

"Your grandmother had a heart condition where her heart rate was elevated. She was taking medication that had the same properties as potassium. And she was a health nut. I suspect she took extra supplements."

"I get it, Horatio. So when she complained to her doctor that she was being poisoned, her blood work never showed anything other than what she was prescribed."

"That's correct."

"But who would have had access to the tea? Sarah keeps it in the pantry, but no one else ever goes in there."

William stood and walked over to the window. "That's why I'm here—to tell you that I was often with your grandmother before and during her illness. Her doctor suggested a private live-in nurse. I made the arrangement."

"Who knew about the nurse that you hired?" asked Olivia.

"I didn't see a need for secrecy, so the paperwork was on my desk. Anyone going into my office could have read it."

Olivia hopped down from her desk. "How long was this nurse at the house?"

"A few weeks. Then the doctor arranged for a nurse to come in twice a day and check on her because by that time she was feeling better. Then her symptoms got a lot worse, but the doctor still couldn't relate it to anything but a failing heart. That's when Miranda became obsessed with watching over her, and Benjamin brought a cot down from the attic so she could sleep near your grandmother in the library."

Olivia moved to William's side. "So the nurse had full run of the house?"

"I don't really know. I assume she would need access to the kitchen. But she seemed very professional and came with wonderful recommendations and references. I interviewed her myself."

"Do you still have her contact information? I would like to speak with her."

"I'm afraid she's no longer with the agency I used. She left shortly after your grandmother's death and there is no forwarding address."

"I made some calls and was told that her passport was renewed during that time," added Horatio.

"I guess I don't need to state the obvious that it took someone with *very* deep pockets to convince a highly respected nurse to murder her patient. It's time to call in the police."

"And tell them what?" William threw his arms up in the air. "That one, or maybe two, of the wealthiest men in the country murdered your ninety-some-year-old grandmother who had a heart condition? We need *proof*, Olivia!"

"What kind of proof?"

William moved back to his chair. "I don't know."

"Horatio, any ideas of where to go from here?" Olivia asked.

"Not off the top of my head, but I'll work with William."

Olivia slowly returned to her desk. "So this is a dead end until we get proof. I think it's time for me to return to Fairfield. If I haven't been drinking Sarah's tea lately and yet I'm still having the symptoms, then I'm being poisoned here . . . so was Grandmother."

Later that same day, Olivia closed her office door and punched in Uncle Lionel's number on her private line. She still wasn't a hundred percent certain she could trust Gertrude. And this was one phone call she didn't want overheard. She waited an eternity for him to pick up.

"Hello?"

"Uncle Lionel, I'm so glad you answered. I need your help to sort through this financial mess. It's like a maze with twists and turns that go nowhere. Travis has been digging but he's gotten nowhere. Poor Megan gave up a long time ago so I have her handling all the charities. I have no one else that I trust to look into this."

"Olivia, you can afford to buy the best financial minds in the world."

"I need one that I can trust."

"What is it you want me to find?"

"Where are millions of McLeod and Morrison dollars going? And who is moving it?"

"Is that all?" He asked sarcastically. "Have you thought this through? I'd be stepping on the toes of your CFO, your CEO and God knows who else."

"I've given this a lot of thought. And I would suggest very strongly that you bring Jefferson . . . and your car."

"Jefferson?"

"Yeah. Your chauffer that's as big as a bear and as strong as a tank."

"Come on, Olivia, aren't you being a bit melodramatic?"

"I'm *very* serious!"

"The situation can't be so bad that you need Jefferson and a bullet-proof car."

Up until now Olivia had managed to remain calm, but Uncle Lionel just wasn't reading between the lines. So with the assurance that no one was listening she'd have to spell it out.

"Okay, here's what I know. You were right. Grandmother *was* murdered. Probably by her nurse, although we have no actual proof, and we don't know who paid her off, and now she's left the country. I thought maybe Sarah was trying to poison me as well, so I left and moved to the house on Freemason Street with Travis and Meg."

"Olivia, how many times have I told you that Sarah and Benjamin can be trusted? You were safe with them."

"I know. I know. It was Sarah who figured out that it was her tea that contained the potassium that poisoned Grandmother."

"Potassium? Potassium doesn't kill."

"Yes it can. So now I'm moving back to Fairfield." Olivia paused a beat. "There's been so much money-laundering going on over the years that I'm not sure we'll ever figure it out. And my CFO may be a murderer—or maybe my CEO—or both."

"Why isn't Travis staying with you?"

"Because Miranda thinks William has come back into my life after all these years to marry me, and it's made her so happy."

"You're going to marry William? Your mother's fiancé? Why he's old enough to be your father. You can't be serious, Olivia!"

"Of course I'm not going to marry William. He's already married. But Miranda had a meltdown and tried to fight Travis off when she thought he was trying to take me away from William. She went through that heartache once already with my father, and she isn't going to let it happen again. She's like a little Rottweiler protecting me, even from her wheelchair."

"Okay, okay. I've heard enough. I'll need time to put things in order, but I'll be there as soon as I can. Jefferson should be able to leave tomorrow. It'll take him the better part of the day to get there."

"Let me know when you can leave, and I'll send Phillips."

43

"It's so nice being back in the kitchen with you, Sarah. Feels like home."

"This *is* your home now."

"Jefferson called from the car to say he's approaching Richmond. I'm really looking forward to his arrival. I think you're going to like him."

"I know there's a lot troubling you, and I'd like the company. Let me get the last of these dishes in the washer, and I'll get us some coffee."

"I'm glad you didn't say tea! I imagine it's going to be some time before I can look at a cup of tea and not feel a dizzy spell coming on."

Sarah glanced over at Olivia while she filled the coffee pot. "I'm real sorry about the tea. It breaks my heart to think that it was my tea that made you so sick and killed your grandmother."

"No one blames you. Hopefully, we'll find out who's behind this before anyone else is poisoned. I know that someone wants me out of the way. I'm sure glad Jefferson will be here."

"There's a guest suite upstairs in this wing for the hired help that house guests bring with them. I got it ready for Jefferson."

"I know he'll appreciate being near the room at the top of the stairs." Olivia nodded toward the ceiling with a smirk. "I saw the room. I went snooping one day while you were at church. Those are some very impressive security monitors. I also heard the story about how you kept Vivian Dumbarton safe for six months."

"I'll have Benjamin show you and Jefferson the basement."

"Hmm, I'm looking forward to it."

Sarah filled the paper filter with coffee grounds and hit the power switch. "Will Mr. Montgomery be staying here, or in town?"

"I don't know. I'll leave that up to him."

Olivia studied Sarah as she pulled two mugs from the cupboard and set them on the counter. "All this coming and going of people can't be easy for you when you were just used to my grandmother being here. You can hire additional staff if it would help you, and there are those unused cottages on the property for anyone who would need to be here fulltime."

"Thank you, ma'am. The cleaning crew that come every Friday are very thorough. And I love cooking. Let's wait and see how it goes over the next few months. I can always hire someone to help me if the need arises."

"Are you thinking I might just give up on all this drama and head back up North?"

Sarah grinned. "You know, I had you all wrong. Here was this young Yankee waltzing in here with a chip on her shoulder, taking over when you'd never been more than a name to me."

That wasn't how Olivia saw it, but better not to debate the matter. She let Sarah continue.

"It was clear right from the start that you didn't like my Southern cooking, didn't like your grandmother or anything that she stood for, and didn't like me, either."

"That's not entirely true, Sarah."

The coffee maker stopped dripping. Sarah filled the two mugs and handed one to Olivia. "I know that now. We were both thrown into this pot without one knowing of the other, and then life just stirred it up until it was ready to boil over."

"I've learned a lot since I came here—about myself and who I am. About both of my grandparents and how precious life is and how easy it is to waste. And I'm learning about a mother that I only thought I knew."

The buzzer went off and the monitor came on. Sarah glanced up. "I guess that would be your Jefferson. I'll greet him at the door."

"I'll come too," said Olivia.

Benjamin was already waiting on the steps when Sarah opened the door. The three watched as the limo came to a stop, and the driver's door opened. Jefferson got out and glanced across the long façade of the house. He opened the rear door and reached in for a black leather jacket that he slung over his right shoulder.

"Hello, Mrs. Bentley. Nice place you've got here. I was beginning to think I was on the wrong road. Must be two miles long."

"I believe it is."

Washington Jefferson White was the biggest black man that Olivia had ever seen. His uniforms had to be custom made, although there wasn't an ounce of fat on his huge muscular frame. He could have played pro football if he had gone to college, but he would have had to finish high school first. Uncle Lionel had taken notice of the young janitor who could be found practicing martial arts when he thought no one was watching. Lionel took him out of the basement, sent him to driving school and put him under the tutelage of Randolph, his chauffeur for twenty years. Randolph was from the old school, where proper English, impeccable manners, and a good knowledge of automobile mechanics were the primary requirements. But times were changing and driving the rich and powerful could be dangerous if not deadly. Thanks to investment tips and generous bonuses from Lionel, Randolph could retire quite comfortably in south Florida, and leave the world of gangs and gangsters to the very capable Washington Jefferson White.

Sarah leaned toward Olivia. "Very impressive. He can watch over me anytime."

Olivia reached out her hand as Jefferson approached. "Welcome to Fairfield. I'm so happy to have you here."

"It's a pleasure to see you again, Mrs. Bentley. Mr. Montgomery didn't have time to give me the details. He said you would fill me in."

"And I will, but first I would like to introduce you to Sarah, my housekeeper, and her husband Benjamin, who is my estate manager."

Jefferson shook their hands then turned back toward the car. "I'll just get my things. Where would you like me to put the car?"

"You can just leave it there. We'll be leaving first thing in the morning," said Olivia.

Sarah put out a hand and shook Jefferson's. "Not until you've both had a proper breakfast."

"And I should give you a tour of the grounds in the morning. We have an extensive security system that I would like to show you."

"Thank you, Benjamin. I would appreciate that."

Olivia let out a sigh. "Then I guess we'll be heading into town around noon."

Sarah took hold of Jefferson's very muscular arm and ushered him toward the kitchen wing. "I'll show you to your room while Benjamin gets your things from the car. I just made a fresh pot of coffee."

The next morning Olivia watched from the library window, with arms crossed under her breasts. Benjamin and Jefferson appeared to be in what could only be called an animated discussion while standing on the boat dock. Even from this distance she knew it wasn't a happy discussion. Having Jefferson there with her should have been comforting but it only reinforced the fact that someone out there wanted her dead.

"I thought you could use some coffee."

Olivia jumped at Sarah's silent approach. Would she never get used to the woman sneaking up on her?

"Benjamin and Jefferson should be back soon. It's been almost two hours." Sarah said as she handed Olivia the mug.

"I should have gone with them. He needs to know about the tunnels."

"I'm sure Benjamin has already shown him . . . or will. We're all concerned about your safety."

Several minutes passed in silence as both women watched the men walk the property along the James.

"I'm glad you're here, Olivia. Your grandmother would be proud of you."

"I'm glad to be here. I feel good here." Olivia glanced around the room. "I feel at home."

"Pardon my prying, but what are you going to do about Mr. Travis? You can't just leave him hidden away in town. Anyone can see you still love him."

"I know, it's just one more of my problems that needs to be dealt with. I do love him, and I know he's just waiting for me to ask for my ring back. But I can't do it, yet. As my fiancé, Travis's life is in danger. Someone could use him as a target to get at me. I couldn't live with myself if he got hurt because of me. And let's face it, Miranda's heart will break when she learns I'm not marrying William. I need some more time."

"Well, maybe I'm overstepping the bounds of my position, but I think you should get your man back here as soon as you can. Love doesn't come knocking every day, and you sure could use a bit of happiness in your life."

Olivia closed her eyes and took a deep breath. Everything Sarah said was true. There was no arguing any of it. Living apart again was killing her. More than anything, she wanted Travis at her side.

Sarah turned and headed back toward the hall. She stopped and glanced over her shoulder. "And stop worrying about my mother! Just leave that to me."

44

The following day Olivia and Jefferson joined Sarah and Benjamin in the kitchen at Fairfield to discuss Jefferson's take on both properties and how they should proceed.

"Everyone needs to be in one place. Here," stated Jefferson.

"But the house on Freemason Street is so convenient to the yard. No long commute times and there's plenty of room for everyone."

"That house is as close to a sitting duck in a shooting gallery as it gets." Jefferson's booming voice bounced off the walls. "Half the windows in the house sit next to the sidewalk. And that's only about six feet from the street." He threw his arms up. "Oh, and let's not forget that nearly every room on the first floor has a door leading outside, plus the two going into the basement!"

Olivia glanced from one to the other. Jefferson's pursed lips said he wasn't backing down. She really wanted to be in town with Travis. Plus, she and Meg were working on consolidating both sets of charities, her grandmother's and her grandfather's. It was just easier at McLeod House. But Jefferson was right.

"Mr. Montgomery didn't send me here with a bullet-proof car to drive back-and-forth like a damn valet service."

Benjamin and Sarah didn't utter a word as they slid onto their chairs.

"Mrs. Bentley, how can I protect everyone, including myself, in that fishbowl?"

Benjamin cleared his throat. "Miz Olivia, Jefferson and I have looked at the situation and I have to agree. It would be better if all of you were here and he would drive you all together."

"I've seen nearly every square foot of this property and examined the security system. I bet the CIA doesn't have anything better. We need to move Travis and Megan back here."

Sarah turned to Benjamin. "It's time they saw the basement."

"It's a Goddamn arsenal," shouted Jefferson when the bright overhead lights came on.

Never in a million years would Olivia have guessed a room full of guns lived behind the heavy steel door in her basement. Ordinary people don't have military grade weapons—and lots of them. But then, as she was finding out, her grandmother had been far from ordinary.

"How in the hell . . .?" Jefferson muttered.

Sarah turned to Olivia. "As you have learned, your grandmother was big on security. When your mother was just a child she hired guards to live on the property. Later, she installed what was then the best system money could buy. But that all changed the day Vivian Dumbarton's ex-husband got on the property from the river."

"I thought his boat capsized and he drowned. I think the authorities claimed he was drunk."

Benjamin nodded. "Yep. That was the official report."

Official report. Olivia could imagine that night when the ex-husband came ashore. He'd tried unsuccessfully several times to gain access from land so as a last resort he got a boat. He must have gotten at least as far as the lawn when Benjamin was alerted by the cameras. Perhaps he knocked him out. Olivia knew the man hadn't been shot. They filled him full of Grandmother's whiskey and took him and the boat out into the middle of the river.

Olivia nodded her head. Yep, that's the way she would have done it.

"Miz Olivia. Did you say something?" asked Benjamin?

"No. Please continue, Sarah."

"Your grandmother was convinced someone was trying to kill her. She asked William for names of security companies that the government used. Didn't tell him why. After all, he was a Morrison. Once she had the name she called Mr. Montgomery. He arranged for the installation, and got us more guns."

Jefferson whistled. "This is a lot of firepower in the wrong hands. And do you really need a rocket launcher?"

"We've been trained," said Benjamin and Sarah in unison.

Oh crap. Was James Bond going to arrive next? No wonder Uncle Lionel said she was safe at Fairfield. The bigger question was, what else didn't she know about him?

"Okay." Olivia slapped her hand against the large table in the center of the room. She could only imagine how many guns were cleaned and kept in working order on this table. "We follow Jefferson's recommendations and move everyone here. Uncle Lionel should be arriving in the next day or two, and I'll get him started on that rats nest of financial reports. Travis can help where needed. Meg will continue to focus on the charities. Sarah, hire more help if you need it. Have the groceries delivered so you aren't driving around town alone." Olivia paused a beat. "And I'm going to find out who killed my grandmother."

Sarah was grinning from ear to ear.

"What?" Olivia asked.

"Your grandmother would be proud of you. What a team you'd have been."

Benjamin ushered them out and closed the door. It locked automatically.

Sarah stopped before the other steel door that Olivia had seen on her earlier exploration of the basement. "Would you like to see your wine cellar?"

Olivia threw her hands up in a negative gesture. "No." She then headed toward the stairs.

It took two days to sort out the files at McLeod House, as they were
now calling the house on Freemason Street, and to get Meg and
Travis relocated to Fairfield. Angus's personal files and letters were
taken to Fairfield, and all of the files on his charities were boxed up
and taken to Olivia's office at the yard.

Olivia and Meg were in her office putting files away when
she got the call from Phillips that they were an hour out of the
Richmond airport. Jefferson changed into his chauffer's uniform
while Travis and Benjamin removed the last of the boxes from the
trunk. Everyone was officially moved back to Fairfield, and McLeod
House was left in the capable hands of Nathaniel.

Two weeks later, Jefferson was following a daily schedule that
he could live with. After a light breakfast, everyone piled into the
limo for the two-hour ride to the yard. At noon he drove everyone
to McLeod House for lunch and then back to the yard. In between,
he drove Olivia and Megan to meetings with the various charitable
institutions. Then, between four and five, they made the two-hour
drive back to Fairfield. Jefferson changed up the drive times and
routes taken so as not to have a specific routine that an outsider
could plan on. Miranda seemed less hostile toward Travis. But he
left the house before she got up, and she was often in bed by the
time everyone finished dinner. The weekends were another story,
but they were managing. William was staying at his apartment in
Sheffield Court instead of his home in Georgetown. He acted as a
buffer between his two brothers and Uncle Lionel while at the shipyard, and between Travis and Miranda at Fairfield. Uncle Lionel
was working night and day trying to unravel the elaborate web
of money with threads going in all directions, including a Swiss
account. William had moved him into his office across the hall
from Olivia's and was sharing it with Travis. William had also, after
much protest from Clive and Wilson, given Uncle Lionel access to
the company's computer department. Uncle Lionel had brought his
own IBM PC and printer, and with Benjamin's help, turned a corner
of the gold bedroom into a temporary office. If he couldn't unravel

the mess, then perhaps her grandmother was mistaken about the missing money.

Saturday breakfasts were something that everyone looked forward to and no one missed. Sarah outdid herself providing scrambled eggs, French toast smothered in powdered sugar and sliced strawberries, her special biscuits and gravy, ham, bacon, sausage—and, of course, grits. Uncle Lionel and Meg liked the grits.

Olivia placed her napkin on the table. "I can't eat another bite. I'm afraid to step on the scale. My skirts are getting a bit tight. But I sure love Sarah's cooking."

Travis chomped on another piece of bacon. "Maybe we should do a couple laps around the house. I'm liking that gym idea at the yard more-and-more."

"Going outside sounds like a plan. It looks like we're in for another warm day. I'm not so sure about the running part," said Olivia. "Spring has arrived with a burst of color. Have you noticed the magnolias are just beginning to bloom? They grow as tall as the Maples back home."

Meg got up and went to the sideboard. "Anyone else want more coffee?" She filled her cup and returned to her chair. "Outside sounds like too much work. I think I'll head to the library and read. Maybe, check out what's on TV. Do you know I haven't watched TV since I got here?"

"What are you going to do, Uncle Lionel?"

"I'm heading upstairs. I'm working on a new angle—a hunch, really. But I want to keep at it while it's fresh in my head."

"Uncle Lionel, can't you take even one day off to enjoy this fabulous weather? I hear it's snowing up North."

"Not until something begins to make sense. I've gone over these reports five ways to Sunday, and it always comes up the same. On the surface everything is in order, yet my gut tells me there's something rotten just out of sight."

"Maybe you should enjoy the weekend, take a walk along the river; explore the old outbuildings. There's a ton of history here, and you can tackle the reports on Monday with a fresh set of eyes."

Uncle Lionel scooted his chair back and stood. "I'll keep that in mind. See you at lunch."

Olivia watched as he left the room. She knew he'd spend the weekend in front of his computer. She was surprised that Gertrude was still using a typewriter when most of the other secretaries had changed over to the new word processors. Maybe she should look into getting a computer for Fairfield.

Travis took Olivia's hand. "How about a game of pool?"

"Okay." Olivia tapped the button on the floor with her foot. "I'll just let Sarah know we're finished."

Meg got up and headed toward the hall. "See you later."

Olivia and Travis were the only ones left in the dining room when Sarah entered, followed by the whirr of Miranda's wheel chair.

"Breakfast was delicious as usual, Sarah." Olivia watched Miranda as she came to a stop in front of Travis.

"Where's William?" Miranda asked in a chiding tone. She glanced at Travis then focused on Olivia.

"He'll be here for dinner this evening."

"Good." She scowled at Travis then headed out the door and turned in the direction of the library.

"That wasn't too bad. There's hope for us, yet." Travis took Olivia's hand as they left the dining room. "Now, how about that game of pool?"

Travis racked up the balls, in the men's parlor, while Olivia stood at the window. There was a haze of green now on the trees, and spring bulbs filled the yard with color. Her people were safe now and that was all that mattered at the moment.

"Meg seems so content here. She hasn't mentioned the kids in days or reminded us of how bad her life had been. She's doing a fantastic job as my assistant."

Travis pushed on the long rectangular panel in the wall. The door opened to the cubby where the cue sticks stood waiting for the next player. "But you have to be realistic. She can't stay here forever. She's going to need her own place."

"I know. As much as I enjoy having her around she needs to work on creating her own life in her own space. Maybe one of the cottages on the property, or she can move back to McLeod House. She seemed to like it there."

Travis handed Olivia a cue stick. "Ready?"

Everyone had fallen into their own little groove. They were on track and making progress. Her only job now was finding her grandmother's killer. She felt like a hamster frantically racing on its wheel and going nowhere.

"I'm sorry, but I'm just not in the mood for pool. Do you mind if we take that walk now?"

"Fine with me, I'd rather be outside."

Olivia took Travis's hand as they stepped into the passage. "Let's go out the door facing the river." She stopped before the portrait of her grandmother, now hanging on the wall at the foot of the stairs. "William was right, it does look better here."

"What do you mean?"

"According to Benjamin, my grandmother had this portrait of her switched with the painting in the parlor a few months before she died. I thought the painting looked rather strange hanging over the fireplace because she was looking at a blank wall. I'm glad I had him switch them back."

Travis took a closer look. "She doesn't look very happy."

"Portraits rarely showed people smiling. However, Grandmother's expression in the one that's hanging in her bedroom in New York is full of love and happiness. It just oozes from her. By the amount of gray in her hair, I would guess that this was painted sometime after Mom left."

Travis stepped back. "Interesting. Didn't your grandmother's note to you say something about looking to her for answers? Maybe there's something hidden behind the canvas."

Olivia let out a long sigh of frustration. "Well, if she did hide something, it isn't there now. When Benjamin took it off the wall, he noticed that the paper on the back had been sliced open. He says it wasn't like that when he hung it up over the fireplace."

"That's strange," said Travis. "Who would have had the opportunity? Whoever it was felt confident that no one would walk in and catch them in the act."

"Maybe it was the nurse. We'll never know, now let's go outside."

Travis's gaze turned toward the stairs. "Hanging in this spot, she's now looking up toward the landing."

Olivia followed his gaze. "So in her note, she's telling us to look . . . out the window?"

Travis took the stairs two at a time. "No, she wants us to go upstairs."

Olivia followed, but at a slower pace. "I've looked in each bedroom on the second floor. I don't think you'll find anything. But, maybe if we look out the window, we'll see a valley on the other side of the river."

"You're right. She wouldn't hide anything where it could easily be found." Travis then raced up the second flight to the attic above.

"We need to find a valley," Olivia said impatiently. "Any valley around here would have to be outside, wouldn't it?" She gestured toward the window. "So why don't we go outside and look?"

Travis didn't respond. Olivia caught up with him as he closed the first door after poking his head in. Without hesitation he moved to the room across the hall. "Travis, it's too nice a day to spend it exploring the attic."

"Haven't you been up here?" Travis asked as he moved along the hallway.

"No. Just Mom's dressing room. The first room you peeked in."

He opened the next door then closed it without going into the room. Then he went on down the long hall in the same manner. When he got to the last door he entered and stopped.

"This is it."

Olivia spotted the old treadle sewing machine, an over-stuffed chair, a long wooden table, and a dress form. "It's the sewing room."

Travis pointed to the ceiling where it met the outside wall. "And it should have a valley, but it doesn't!"

"What are you talking about?"

"When two roof pitches come together, they form a valley." He demonstrated with his hands. "On the underside they create a V. The room across the hall has it, but this room doesn't. Both rows of rooms have been identical."

"So just what does that mean?"

"It means, my darling, that the valley is missing!"

Travis walked over to the wall and began knocking. "This hollow sound means there's something on the other side. Look at this. The plaster on this wall looks different than the other three walls. I saw some tools two rooms back. See if you can find a hammer."

Half an hour later Travis had made an opening large enough to squeeze through. "I can see a reflection of something on the ceiling." Travis ducked down and crawled inside. "Got it!"

Olivia heard a click. Suddenly the small space was flooded with light. She crouched at the opening. "I can't believe what I'm seeing. It's like finding hidden treasure."

Olivia crawled inside. The stale, musty scent of time surrounded her. "Wow! It's my mother's toys. I've only seen dolls like these in museums and a dollhouse, and look at that darling doll carriage."

Travis scooted over to the trunks. "These all have locks. Run downstairs and get the keys your grandmother left you. She was right. Your mother's possessions were well hidden in the valley."

Olivia hurried down to retrieve the keys, then raced back up the stairs. She paused at the opening in the wall, breathing heavily. "Here, Travis, the keys."

The smallest key fit the lock on the smaller of the trunks. Olivia slowly lifted the lid. She removed an armload of tiny clothes and cradled them to her chest. "Oh my, God, Travis. My mother's baby clothes." Travis unlocked the next trunk. He pulled the items out one by one while Olivia rubbed her cheek against a little dress. They were the items every mother would keep of her beloved child.

There were watercolor pictures drawn by a very young hand, crafts done in clay, baby teeth in a tiny box, a curl perhaps from her first haircut, and lots of photos taken over the course of eighteen years or more.

Olivia set the clothes aside and picked up the teeth. "Can you believe it?" She reached for the curl of jet-black hair. "Her hair was always this color." Tears drifted down her cheek as Olivia gently pulled the hair through her fingertips.

Travis inched his way to the last trunk.

Olivia picked up one of the watercolors. The subject could have been a horse, or maybe a dog, or any brown animal with four legs. "This room contains my mother's life from the time she was born until she left, never to return. Can you just imagine what it must have been like for my grandmother to collect all of this and hide it here? It must have torn her heart apart to seal everything in here. Knowing she probably would never see it again."

Travis unlocked the largest and most ornate of the three trunks. Intricately tooled leather and fancy brass strapping surrounded the top and sides. Olivia had difficulty lifting the heavy lid. "Look, Livy. There's a compartment under the lid."

Olivia slid back a little door. She reached in and pulled out handfuls of photos and letters. "Look at the dates. These are my mother's letters and photos after she married my dad. The first two are postmarked from New York the week she ran away."

Olivia put the letters and photos down. She searched through books stacked in the top tray, "These must be Grandmother's journals. The oldest one dates from the year before my mother was born. It looks like the last is the year she left." Olivia glanced at Travis through a blur of tears. "Here are the answers to all of my questions about my mother that I've been searching for. And I got an added bonus. Grandmother's life is here too."

"Livy, help me lift this tray. Let's see what other treasurers are hidden inside."

Travis looked inside after setting the tray off to the side. "It's filled with tissue paper?"

Olivia removed the top layers of paper. "Oh my God." She reached for her heart. Her blood turned to ice. "I don't believe it. It can't be."

"What's wrong, Livy? You look like you're going to faint."

Olivia gently stroked the luminous fabric. She reached down to the bottom of the trunk and gently lifted the contents in one armload. "Travis, can you take this while I crawl back out, then hand it to me?"

"Sure. Do you want me to hand you anything else?" He asked while trying to take what looked like a dress from her arms.

She ducked down and moved through the opening. "No. Just that."

Once they were both back in the sewing room, Olivia cradled the gown in her arms, burying her face in the soft folds of silk. She laughed and cried then held it out in front of her.

"I can't believe it. I never thought . . . even in my dreams . . ."

"It looks like a wedding dress." Travis stated matter-of-factly. "Is it your mother's wedding dress?"

She put it up to her and twirled around the sewing room. She felt like Cinderella after being given her dress by her fairy godmother. "This is the gown my mother's wearing in her portrait."

"I thought your grandfather burned it."

"That was the story I heard. But Mother's gown was obviously one of my grandmother's secrets."

"It looks like it would fit you."

"Hmm. I think I just found *my* wedding dress."

45

Olivia and Travis breezed through the dining room door like a swarm of bees were after them. Meg and Uncle Lionel had already started eating.

"You're never going to guess what we found," said Olivia breathlessly.

Meg's sandwich was half way to her mouth when she looked up. "It wasn't in the cemetery, because I went there looking for you."

"We never made it outside. Instead we went . . ."

"I looked everywhere. Finally, I gave up and sat in one of the chairs down by the river. I figured I'd catch you on your way back from wherever you went. Can you believe the weather here? It must be seventy degrees out there—in April."

"The attic," Olivia said before Meg could get another word in.

Uncle Lionel scooped up a forkful of potato salad. "Why did you spend the morning in the attic? It looks like a beautiful day outside."

Olivia followed Travis over to the sideboard. "Don't you know what's hidden in the attic? You seem to know everything about this house—and Grandmother." Olivia picked up a plate. "Yum. Sarah's famous chicken salad."

"I don't know everything. I only came here once. What's up there besides a lot of dust?"

Yeah. Sure, Uncle Lionel. Like how you arranged for all the security equipment upstairs and probably everything in that little room in the basement. The only thing missing is machinegun mounts on the roof.

"We found my mother's childhood, that's what. And my grandmother's most cherished thoughts." Olivia glanced across the table. "Uncle Lionel, do you remember Grandmother's note you gave me the day I accepted the inheritance? It said I would find the answers well hidden in the valley."

"I remember. I told you that I wasn't aware of any valley on the property."

"Everyone I asked said the same thing—except Travis found the valley . . . inside."

"Roof valleys." Travis demonstrated by putting the base of his palms together making a V shape. "Olivia's grandmother hid everything that belonged to Maureen behind the wall. It's amazing."

Sarah pushed open the swinging door to the kitchen. "Can I get you anything? I have lemon meringue pie for desert. There's also some cheesecake leftover from last night."

Olivia pulled out her chair and placed her plate on the table. "Travis and I found the secret room in the attic."

"More like a secret closet," said Travis while getting situated at the table.

"What secret room?" asked Sarah.

"Can you have Benjamin come in here?" Olivia started in on her chicken salad.

"Sure. Hold on." Sarah left the room and came back a minute later with Benjamin.

Olivia looked up as Benjamin entered. "Travis and I found a secret space in the attic. Can you meet us up there after we finish lunch? Last room on the left—you'll need tools that can cut or pry out a plaster wall.

"Sure thing, Miz Olivia. I'll go get my stuff."

William arrived at six o'clock and met everyone in the library for cocktails before dinner. The topic of conversation, of course, was the afternoon's attic adventure. As soon as Benjamin and Travis had the wall removed, Olivia and Meg jumped in like scavengers on road-kill. Every toy was brought out and played with. Every trunk dragged into the sewing room and emptied. Each item of clothes examined. Benjamin returned to other chores after removing the debris, Uncle Lionel returned to his room and computer, and Travis finally left when the discussion turned to how children's clothes had changed since Maureen had worn them.

Olivia moved to William's side. "One of the most interesting finds was in a compartment in the largest of the trunks. Grandmother's diaries from the time Mom was born until she left are all there. I'm sure we'll know everything that happened during those years once I have a chance to read them."

"What do you hope to find?" asked William after taking a healthy swallow of bourbon.

"I don't know. It's looking like the hatred Grandmother felt toward her husband was all based on his treatment of my mother and disowning her. Yet what we've found at McLeod House shows that he wanted to reconcile. Even to the point of keeping her Packard. Perhaps I'll find out what really happened in the months leading up to her leaving."

"Where are the diaries now?"

"We left everything upstairs. The next two weeks are really busy for me. I may even ask Gertrude to come out here and work a few days. Those diaries have been hidden away all these years—they can wait a little longer."

"It was so exciting," Meg exclaimed before she took a sip of her Jack and Coke. "It took us all afternoon to go through everything. I wonder how long it took to hide and seal up the wall?"

Sarah stepped into the library. "Excuse me. Dinner will be served in half an hour."

Olivia turned around to face the doorway. "Sarah, I can't believe you and Benjamin didn't know about that room. Didn't Grandmother even hint that she'd hidden my mother's things in the attic?"

"No, ma'am. That must have been about forty years ago. I was living in New York then."

"I knowd."

Everyone looked past Sarah to see Miranda in her wheelchair.

"What do you know, Miranda?" asked Olivia

Miranda put her index finger to her lips. "Shhhh, it's a secret."

Sarah bent down to her mother's level. "It's okay. You can tell us."

"Bad things were gonna happen to Missus." Miranda tilted her head as if listening to another voice. "Hurry, Miranda. Hurry. We have to get everythin' down to the tunnels. He's comin' home. He'll burn it all. We have to save my babies things." Miranda nodded her head as if in agreement. "I promise, Missus. I won't tell anybody. It's our secret."

"Mamma, how did everything get from the tunnels to the attic?"

"He was terrible mad. Ran all over the place looking for Maureen's stuff. Yellin' the whole time. Sayin' she'd pay."

"Mamma, didn't he look in the tunnels?"

"Never went down. Missus knowd he wouldn't go there. Afraid of ghosts, he was."

"You helped move everything from the tunnels to the attic?"

"Yep. He left that day. And Missus and me moved everything to the attic. Pappy helped and made the wall."

"Whose Pappy," asked Travis.

"Miranda's husband—my father," said Sarah.

Olivia went over to Miranda and crouched down beside her. "Miranda, why didn't you tell me? Did you forget that all my toys were up there?" Olivia looked up at Sarah and winked. She had to stay in character as Maureen.

"You didn't ask. It's a secret. Sides, yur too old for that stuff."
She looked up at Sarah. "Why are we here? It's time for my dinner."
Miranda stroked the arm of her wheelchair. "Missus gave me her
chair when she passed." Then her hand moved the control turning
the chair and with a whir went back down the hall.

"I'm sorry, Ma'am. Her mind isn't right. I can't say if any of what
she said is true." Sarah turned to leave. "Give me half an hour and
I'll have your dinner ready."

Could Miranda actually have remembered what happened the
day everything was hidden from Angus, or was it just her mind
creating a story based on our excitement? Her tale of anger and
threats didn't mesh with what had been found at McLeod House.
Her grandfather had kept his daughter's Packard for Christ's sake.
The answer must be in the diaries. If Miranda's recollection of the
events were accurate, then surely her grandmother would have
poured her heart out in the diary. The real story was out there—she
just had to know where to look.

Meg was the last to sit down after filling her plate from the array of
food that tested the strength of the sideboard. "Sarah outdid herself.
This is like Thanksgiving in April." She took her time spreading the
napkin across her lap. "Livy, Fairfield and McLeod House are wonderful. I hope you're beginning to think about staying here. I mean
now that you've found your family and they're not nearly as bad as
you thought. Well, maybe your grandfather was a bit skitzo. But other
than Miranda freaking out, I had a wonderful day. I love living here."

Olivia glanced at Travis expecting him to protest. After all, his
reason for coming to Fairfield was to help her sell off the properties and move back to Marblehead. The only indication that he had
even heard Meg was a raised eyebrow. "So, Meg, you're hoping I'll
stay here at Fairfield on a more permanent basis. And as my assistant you would be close by."

Sarah came in and checked the coffee urn and pot of tea. "I'll
be right back with more coffee."

"Sarah, Fairfield is beginning to grow on me. If Travis is willing, I'd like to call this old farm home."

"Whatever's best for you ma'am," Sarah gave a tight-lipped smile then left through the swinging door.

Travis put down his fork. "I have to admit this place is beginning to grow on me too. What about the old Captain's house? What about our life in Marblehead?"

Sarah's reaction wasn't what Olivia had expected. She thought Fairfield's housekeeper would be happy. They'd developed a good relationship. Olivia had been eating with them in the kitchen. Was it what Miranda had said about knowing what was in the attic? Was something else bothering her?

"Livy?" Travis waved in Olivia's direction. "Livy?"

"Oh, sorry. Yeah. Emily has been keeping me up-to-date on the house's progress. Your cousin Nick has added extra guys to his crew. The house should be completely finished by August. It'll be a welcome change when the heat and humidity of summer in Virginia drives us North. And it'll give us a place to stay when we visit your family."

William got up and headed to the buffet for seconds. "This all sounds wonderful. I'm glad you're planning for the future, but if Lionel and I don't find where this money trail leads and who killed your grandmother, there may not be a rosy future."

"I know. Believe me, I know, and I think of little else." Olivia leaned back in her chair. "Maybe, it was just wishful thinking that there could be a somewhat normal life out there for me."

"I was waiting for the right time to tell you. I guess it's now." Uncle Lionel shook his head in frustration. "Someone tried to run Jefferson off the bridge on Friday afternoon."

"Oh no, Livy!" Meg's hand flew to her heart. "I had you scheduled to attend that fundraiser at the children's center. When you couldn't go, I sent Jefferson with the painting you were donating for the auction."

Olivia's blood turned to ice. "Someone thought I was in the car."

"Livy, only Gertrude and I knew your schedule that day. Could it have been an accident?" Meg asked.

Uncle Lionel got up and refilled his coffee cup at the sideboard. "It wasn't an accident. Jefferson noticed an older sedan that appeared to be following him. He was on guard and ready when it happened. He's positive that it wasn't a professional behind the wheel or he wouldn't have gotten away with just a fender-bender. Someone wants you out of the way."

Olivia spent the evening propped up against a mountain of pillows with her grandmother's latest journal, the one that ended six months after her mother ran off with her father. There were too many questions that needed answers. Like why did her grandfather seem to have two personalities? He could be a generous father and husband, and then a raving lunatic. There didn't seem to be any reference to his violent side until her mother ran off. Okay, but what fueled his fire after she was gone? What set him off? Why eliminate all traces of his daughter then keep her car? Assuming her grandmother was killed over her not bending to the wishes of the Morrison brothers, then why was Jefferson run off the road? Why had she been poisoned? The past was somehow connected to the present. She just needed to find out how.

Olivia sensed Travis in the room before she heard him. She sniffed, but her eyes never left the diary. "You smell like cigars."

"Can we shift these pillows around a little so I have at least a portion of my side of the bed?" Travis didn't wait for an answer. He tossed two of the pillows on the floor and slid between the covers. He leaned over and kissed her.

Olivia ran her tongue over her lips. "You taste like whiskey."

His hand glided over her stomach to rest on her hip. "William just left. We had a guys' night around the pool table. Lionel even set his reports aside to join us."

"That's nice," Olivia said and went back to reading.

"Are you ready to call it a night? How interesting can your grand-mother's journal be?"

"I'm beginning to see a pattern. It's all beginning to make sense."

Travis reached over and removed the book from her hand and set it aside, then reached for her pajama top.

Olivia slid down under the covers. "Travis, you're naked."

"Uh-huh," he mumbled before covering her mouth with his.

Olivia and Meg looked up from the week's calendar spread out before them on the desk. The mid-morning sun bathed her office in bright light. Olivia smiled at the sight of the man standing in the doorway. William's presence always gave her the reassurance and confidence that she was in the right place. That she belonged here. Maybe it was the understated suits that screamed designer, or the faint scent of expensive aftershave, or the thick head of styled hair, or maybe it was just the aura that you could almost touch—the aura that said he was in control of himself and everyone around him. The man her mother had trusted with her life.

"William, you're just the person I wanted to see. Meg, we'll check out the first floor of the power plant later this afternoon. That man wouldn't dare say no to *me*."

Meg crossed the room and closed the office door behind her.

"Wilson caught Meg exploring the old power plant to see whether it would be possible to set up a day care center in the building. He claimed she was trespassing and kicked her out."

"I told you this plan of yours wouldn't be easy."

"I know, but those two have to realize that I won't back down. In fact, Clive and Wilson are what I wanted to talk to you about." Olivia pushed the calendar aside. "But that isn't why you're here. What's up?"

"Lionel thinks he's on to something. We're going to my office in DC this afternoon to review my copies of the government contracts

over the last ten years. Tomorrow morning, I have a meeting with
Casper Weinberger, the Secretary of Defense. We could be gone
three or four days. Lionel will be staying at the house with me."

"Wow, bringing in the big guns."

"It's just a hunch, but Lionel's confident enough to make the
trip. I'll fill you in if there's anything to it."

"In that case it's even more important that you and I talk. I think
I'm on to something as well. But we can't discuss it here." Olivia
got up and walked around to the front of her desk. "How about I
buy you lunch? I know this fabulous chef at a charming house on
Freemason Street."

William frowned and glanced at his Rolex. "Okay, but it's already
after eleven. Should you check in with Nathaniel first?"

"It's all arranged for noon."

"Not knowing my plans for the day, that was pretty bold of you.
I might not have been available."

"I guarantee you would have changed your plans for what I have
to tell you, and we need somewhere I'm sure isn't bugged."

Nathaniel ushered Olivia and William into the dinning room.
Their meal was already on the table. After they were seated, Olivia
spread her napkin in her lap. "This looks delicious, and I'm truly
sorry about the short notice."

"It's not a problem, Mrs. Bentley. I always keep enough on hand.
Now, if you and Mr. Morrison don't mind, I have a couple errands
to run. I should be back in an hour or so. There's chocolate mousse
in the fridge for dessert."

Olivia twirled a few strands of angel hair pasta around her fork
then stabbed a piece of shrimp. Giving William her news wasn't going
to be easy. Would he even believe her when she was finished? He was
a man who lived by facts. She needed to keep her facts straight.

She swallowed and put her fork down. "I guess I should begin
while we have the house to ourselves. Believe me, this isn't going to
be easy."

"Just spit it out, Olivia, I have a good idea of what's coming."

"I began reading Grandmother's journals. The ones Travis and I found in the attic. I don't know how often you went to the house after my mother left, but it turns out that your father and brothers were pretty regular visitors."

"I was tied to the Pentagon. Although I was still in the Navy, my father forced me into a position that kept me in Washington. I guess you could say that we weren't on the best of terms. I was happy to keep my distance."

"Well, my grandmother didn't like Clive and Wilson even as young boys. For that matter, neither did my mother. Anyway, one day my grandmother was on her way to the parlor, to get as far away from the meeting between Angus and your father as possible, when the closet door in the passage opened. Out stumbled your brothers looking more than a little guilty. They said they were just playing hide-and-seek, but my grandmother was sure they had just come up from the tunnel."

William nodded. "Maureen never liked them. I can imagine her showing them the tunnels just to keep them occupied and out of her hair."

"Grandmother wrote that your brothers were two mischievous boys who weren't to be trusted and Lord help us all if they ever got control of McLeod and Morrison. She found them a few minutes later opening the door to the closet across from the office, which also leads down to the tunnels. She took each boy by an arm and marched them into the library and made it very clear to Angus and your father that Clive and Wilson were no longer welcome at Fairfield."

"She never attempted to hide her dislike of them. After Angus died, she made sure Clive and Wilson understood she was watching their every move. She picked apart budgets and outwardly opposed and blocked their ideas of Western expansion. I agreed with her on that one. Although she trusted me on many things, I was still a Morrison."

"I imagine they were getting pretty desperate," Olivia said as she stabbed another shrimp.

"Lionel has found the money that should have been going to your grandmother was actually being used to fund the California land deals. Your grandmother and I had successfully stopped or at least tabled Clive and Wilson's plans. What we didn't know was they were already committed. We have signed contracts making my brothers financially responsible if McLeod and Morrison didn't build. The West Coast contractors were pushing and pushing hard."

Olivia pushed her plate aside and turned toward William, resting her arm on the table. "I believe they were desperate enough to do something that would eliminate the only threat that stood in their way."

"But they still needed my . . ."

Olivia raised a hand to stop him from going further. "My grandmother had a regular schedule and routine. I found out from Gertrude that she kept a tin of Sarah's special tea in the office. Horatio had it tested, and it, too, contained a very high amount of potassium. Clive and Wilson both had the opportunity to take care of that detail, forcing Grandmother to spend more time at Fairfield because she was coming down with some mysterious illness. Then, at her doctor's request, you hired the live-in nurse to take care of Grandmother. She started getting better without her daily four o'clock pot of tea, so your brothers bribed the nurse with enough money to keep her comfortable for the rest of her years in the Caribbean or South America."

"And you think the nurse added the potassium to the tin at Fairfield."

"I think they contacted her somehow and made the deal. Possibly even using the tunnels to get into the house undetected. The nurse could easily have gotten enough potassium to provide the lethal mixture of tea. Sarah said the nurse was often in the kitchen and could easily put it in the tin. The nurse would have known that only my grandmother drank Sarah's special tea. The rest of the household drank coffee."

William rested both elbows on the table. "And you're sure they could have gotten in through the tunnels?"

"Yes. There are no cameras in the tunnels because the entrance, down by the dock, is protected by an electronic eye. An alarm goes off if the beam is broken. All the nurse would have to do is flip the switch in the kitchen to disarm it and later turn it back on again. Benjamin does it all the time."

"We still need proof."

"I know, but I wanted to fill you in on what I've found. Both my grandparents' journals and the letters we found here clearly indicate that your father kept the hatred against my mother alive. I'm sure Clive and Wilson were aware of that."

William had the face of a man defeated, a man who had just been dragged through the gutter.

"I'm sorry, William, but you had to know. Maybe I should have waited until you returned."

"No, this is perfect timing. I checked Clive and Wilson's whereabouts on Friday afternoon when Jefferson was forced off the road. Wilson was at the old powerhouse meeting with the sales rep from the company that will be supplying the fitness equipment for the gym. Clive was out running errands. He could have picked up an old car from anyone on the street and paid handsomely for the use of it for the afternoon. I'm sure it's in some scrap heap by now."

William hesitated, and Olivia knew there was more to come.

"I'm worried about your safety. I have a buddy at the CIA who has arranged for me to pick up a car to use until this is all over. Lionel and I will drive it back."

Thoughts raced through her head of the kinds of car one would get from the CIA. Maybe a James Bond type with machine guns mounted in the trunk. "Must be some special car."

"It was designed to protect the President."

46

Two weeks later Olivia sat on the screened-in porch that ran along the river side of the hallway from the library to what they were now calling the family room. It was the small parlor most often used by her grandmother. The room where the TV resided, and once upon a time had been her mother's playroom. Benjamin had brought out a table so Olivia could bring her work and enjoy the outdoors. The morning sun had burned off the dew, filling the yard with the fresh sent of flowering trees, boxwood, and newly mowed lawn. Yes. She could be very happy living here. Fairfield was the perfect place to raise a family, and she was willing to bet that Sarah and Benjamin would love having little ones running around and getting into mischief—just as her mother had.

Olivia reached for the tall glass of iced tea. Sarah did make the best tea, complete with a wedge of lemon and a sprig of mint. She took a sip and leaned back in her chair, her gaze following a sailboat heading toward Newport News. William and Uncle Lionel's trip to Washington lasted a full week. Uncle Lionel came back with a new energy and determination that bordered on obsession. He couldn't stop talking about everything from working in William's impressive office just blocks from the Pentagon to their meeting with Casper Weinberger. How come neither of them would give her any details? What about the meeting with Casper Weinberger?

She wanted details. She had a right to know. She'd get him alone and demand to know. William seemed to be keeping a low profile, and what was that about? All she did know was that Jefferson had taken to handling the armor-plated Lincoln they'd driven back like a duck to water.

"Here you are, Livy," said Meg as she opened the porch door. "You're not going to believe this. You know those cute little houses beyond the wall? Well, Benjamin showed me one. He said it was built for the farm manager back in 1929." Meg flopped down in a wicker chair. "It's perfect for me. Well, not perfect. It's really dirty. But the lights and everything work." Meg leaned toward Olivia. "Livy, can I live there? It has two bedrooms. I can set one up as an office and work from there." She grabbed Olivia's hand. "Please. I love living here. I'm your assistant. I need to be close by."

Olivia hadn't seen Meg this happy since they were kids staying at their families' cottages on Sandusky Bay. And she was doing a phenomenal job at sorting through the charities. "Okay. You'll have to show it to me later this afternoon."

Meg jumped up and kissed Olivia on the cheek. "Thank you. I won't let you down." She glanced over her shoulder as she headed out the door. "Sarah has a stack of Sears catalogs for me to look at. It'll be so cute."

"Hmmm, looks like I'm the last to know," Olivia murmured, then took another sip of tea. She set the glass back on the table and picked up her grandmother's journal she'd been reading.

Travis opened the door from the library and poked his head in. "Want some company?"

"Sure. Why not? Meg just left. She wants to move into one of the bungalows."

"Yeah. I heard her talking about it to Sarah." Travis settled into the wicker chair next to Olivia and stretched his legs out in front of him. "You've been holed-up out here for hours. Find anything new?"

"Not really. Just a lot that reinforces my belief that a lack of communication can ruin a perfectly good relationship. Grandmother's hatred simmered over the years until it boiled over, causing her to actually plot against her husband. Angus wanted to end it all and get his daughter back, but old man Morrison squelched those plans as soon as they surfaced. I guess it was Grandfather's Scottish pride that wouldn't let him confide in his wife—or perhaps her hatred of him was already keeping him at a distance. But the bottom line is that it didn't need to be. It was all just a horrible tragedy.

Travis reached over and took Olivia's hand. "Well, from where I sit, it appears that somebody has let go of the anger toward her grandparents."

Olivia pulled his hand up to her lips and kissed it. "I'm seeing both sides as they did, in their own words and thoughts. Neither hated my mother, they were just reacting to outside influences. I have to admit that if my mother had tried harder, it may have had a totally different outcome. Maybe she was just too late."

"What do you mean?" asked Travis as he released Olivia's hand.

"When we were in New York, Daisy told me that Mother had decided it was time I knew about her past. She arranged for us, my brothers included, to use the suite at the Waldorf before taking the Queen Mary to England. Grandmother was going to contact our relatives, and we were to have a fabulous vacation, meeting cousins Mother hadn't seen since before the war. That could have been just what was needed to get my grandparents talking again. You see, Grandmother was planning on a huge surprise when we got back to New York . . . she was going to be at the Waldorf to meet us."

Travis leaned forward, resting his forearms on his knees. "Wouldn't she have lost everything and been cut out of the will?"

"It's right here in black and white. She was going to walk away from Angus. She still owned the Waldorf suite and a small fortune of her own, not to mention her shares in Uncle Lionel's company. She wanted to spend her remaining years with her daughter and grand-children, regardless of what it would mean to Angus. Knowing this, I believe he would have re-written his will and welcomed his daughter back. Mother died less than a year before this trip was to take place."

"Wow!"

"Imagine this." Olivia scooted forward in her chair. "We know Grandfather kept his daughter's car. Nathaniel told me that Angus maintained the Packard and several times a year would take it for a drive along the James. What if on one of those trips he just happened to turn onto the lane to Fairfield? He pulls up to the door and Grandmother steps onto the stoop. He tells her to hop in and they go for a spin. Do you see?"

"Yeah. He'd kept the Packard. He didn't need to say a word. In that moment your grandmother would have known her husband never stopped loving his daughter. History would have been rewritten."

"Like I said, it was a huge tragedy. I've grown to love them both. And I want more than ever to avenge my grandmother's death."

William called Olivia the following Saturday to say he would be there for the usual Sunday dinner. He asked her to have everyone present, including Sarah and Benjamin.

He arrived a little before one. He entered the library carrying a black garbage bag and set it on the floor near the door. He looked older to Olivia, as if he carried the problems of the world on his shoulders.

"That looks heavy. What's in the bag?" asked Olivia.

"That's for a little after dinner demonstration." William smoothed his suit jacket and tugged at his cuffs. "Sarah asked me to let you know that dinner is ready."

The dinner conversation revolved around everyone filling in William on what had transpired in the past two weeks since he and Uncle Lionel got back from DC. Meg let everyone know of Olivia's approval for her to move into the bungalow. Uncle Lionel put a stop to that idea real quick, saying that it wasn't safe for her to be outside the walls at this time. Meg pouted, but agreed to spend her free time browsing stacks of magazines for decorating ideas.

"So, William, what have you been up to? I was beginning to think you were bailing on us," Olivia asked.

William took his time placing his fork across the plate.

Interesting. It appears the question caught him off guard. Was he stalling? Deciding what—or how much—to tell? Well, she had a right to know. Now. "William?"

William inhaled deeply then let it out slowly. "Over the last few months, I've been staying in my apartment at Sheffield Court. Actually, I've been there more than I have in the last ten years. I guess it's been a combination of spending most of my time in DC and just not wanting to be in that museum my family calls home. I remember Maureen questioning me about the tremendous expense of keeping an estate as large as Sheffield Court, and the enormous staff needed. It wasn't so much the cost to maintain the house and grounds, but my father needed it to be ready to entertain everyone from European royalty to Hollywood stars. Father lorded over his own little kingdom, and that took the majority of his expendable wealth. When he died, there was comparatively little money for the three of us to inherit. I wanted to sell everything that related to the past, but Clive and Wilson had learned well from our father and insisted on keeping Sheffield Court. Clive and Wilson both live there with their families. I created an apartment for myself in the guest wing."

"That pretty much falls in line with what Olivia has read in the journals and what I have found at the yard. Your father kept the feud going so that Maureen wouldn't be able to inherit half the shares of the company, thereby keeping it all intact for his sons," said Travis.

"My brothers waited for your grandmother to die, leaving them total control of McLeod and Morrison. But she was taking an active interest and questioned every project that was put on the table, not to mention that her health was amazingly good for a woman of her age. They had made commitments and needed to move forward on the California deals," said William.

"I've found the blueprints and operational plans for the West Coast site," Uncle Lionel said. "Your brothers were planning to move the corporate offices West as they expanded into military planes, there was even mention of building cruise ships."

Olivia placed her napkin on the table. "We've figured out that it was total control of the company that motivated the two, regardless of how William felt. But we still need the evidence that will put them away."

The door to the kitchen wing opened, and Sarah stepped into the room. "Does anyone need anything before I serve dessert?"

William pushed his chair back and stood. "Actually, I would like you to hold off on dessert. I have something I want to show everyone, including you and Benjamin. I'll need everyone to follow me to the library. Oh, and you'd better bring Jefferson."

Sarah went back to the kitchen to get Benjamin and Jefferson. They arrived in the library just as everyone had taken a seat and William opened the garbage bag.

"I figured that if Clive and Wilson were behind the murder then any evidence would be at the house rather than the yard where dozens of eyes might notice. I've been using my time wisely, searching likely hiding places. Olivia, after you mentioned the story about Clive and Wilson knowing about the tunnels here. I remembered how they liked to play in the tunnel at Sheffield Court. So I went down and searched the boiler room and the various utility rooms that run along both sides of the tunnel. Father was very particular that none of his guests would ever see tradesmen or deliveries, so the tunnel was built connecting the garages to the house. An elevator went from the tunnel, just outside the wine cellar, to the kitchen hall and on up to the attic."

William reached down into the bag and pulled out several black rubber items, then held up the largest.

"A wetsuit!" said Olivia and Travis in unison.

William dropped the suit and held up a hood, gloves and thin rubber boots. The last item he pulled out of the bag was a black mask. "I suspect the person wearing these came by boat to the river entrance. The nurse could have turned off the electronic eye, giving him access without tripping the alarm."

"I'll be damned," said Travis

Olivia reached down for the rubber suit. "Are you sure about this?"

William handed everything to Travis. "You look to be about the right size. Would you please put these on, and wait until I give you the word to come back into the room. Sarah, I'd like you to go and get your mother. She needs to be here."

A few minutes later, footsteps along with the whirr of Miranda's wheelchair could be heard coming down the hallway.

Miranda glanced around the room. "Are we goin' to have a party? I'd like a little nip of bourbon, please."

Sarah stood at her mother's side, placing her hand on Miranda's shoulder. Then she nodded to William.

"Ok, you can enter," William said in a raised voice.

Everyone turned toward the door at the sound of shuffling and rubber chaffing against rubber. Suddenly, Miranda turned in horror toward the door.

She grabbed the handles of her chair and tried to get out. "The black demon!" Then she settled back in her chair and tweaked the controls. The chair came to life heading toward the large Palladian window. She reached out her hands to some invisible form. "Stop! Don't you hurt my Missus Olivia!" Miranda leaned forward. "I seen you before! Go away!" she shouted.

Travis left the room as quickly as the rubber suit would allow.

Olivia ran to Miranda's side. "It's okay, he's gone."

"My missus. . . my missus . . . did he hurt her?"

"No, she's fine." Olivia wrapped her arms around Miranda. "You protected her. The demon is gone."

Sarah turned Miranda back toward the center of the room. William walked over and crouched next to the wheelchair. He took Miranda's hand. "I'm sorry, but this was the only way to determine if my hunch was right." He looked up at Olivia and Sarah. "I think one, or both, of my brothers used the tunnel to gain access to the house and get the potassium to the nurse."

"Potassium is common. Every store that sells vitamins has it. Maybe the nurse brought it with her," Olivia said as she moved away from the wheelchair.

"It would need to be a large amount," said Sarah.

William stood and moved to Olivia's side. "What I think happened is, when your grandmother came back from the hospital feeling fine and the nurse was long gone, my brothers had to take matters into their own hands. They used the wetsuit as a means of disguise on the slight chance that someone would be awake in the middle of the night. They wouldn't have known that Miranda had taken it upon herself to watch over her precious Missus Olivia. She slept on the cot that Benjamin had brought down from the attic. There was no way for Clive and Wilson to know Miranda rarely left her side and would certainly see them."

Olivia shook her head. Fairfield had state of the art security. Uncle Lionel said so. Maybe they weren't so safe after all. "I don't understand how your theory is possible if it was the nurse who turned off the alarm. She was long gone by then. The alarm would have gone off the moment Clive or Wilson entered the tunnel."

Benjamin cleared his throat. "Well, maybe it was already turned off . . . by accident. I'm always turning it off when I work on the river side of the property. It's just a lot faster getting around especially if it's raining. Sometimes I forget to turn it back on."

Sarah folded her arms under her breasts. "That nurse was always in the kitchen, making herself at home with the coffee and food, and smoking. She would have heard plenty of times when I chewed-out Benjamin for forgetting to turn the tunnel alarm back on."

Olivia reached for her throat. "Then it seems likely they knew there was a good chance the alarm would be off. Do you think one of them actually killed my grandmother because the potassium laden tea wasn't working fast enough?"

"Miranda's probably the only one that saw what happened. She may never remember something that horrible."

"We're not safe here." Meg grabbed Olivia's arm. "Those assholes can come after us. They'll just wait until the alarm is off."

"No they won't," said Jefferson from where he'd been leaning against the fireplace. "I watch the monitors upstairs and make sure the alarms are activated." He paused a beat. "And I walk the property, especially along the river. Everyone is safe here."

"Oh. I thought you just liked taking walks." Meg released Olivia's arm. "I trust you. We all trust you."

"I don't *just* take walks. The only time I'm not watching out for you is when I'm sleeping. And that isn't much."

Olivia smiled. She liked Jefferson. She liked him a lot. What he wanted to say was that he spent all day, every day watching our sorry asses, while we ran around in circles looking for a killer with no proof of a killing, and searched a Fortune 500 company for missing money.

"Jefferson's right. We're safe here, and he's with us when we're at the yard. But we still need proof that they murdered Grandmother," said Olivia. "Not just that they own a wetsuit."

William reached into his pocket then held out his hand in front of Olivia. "I found this in the secret compartment in the library desk at Sheffield Court."

Olivia turned up her palm as William dropped the object into her palm.

"My grandmother's signet ring."

Olivia slipped the ring on her finger as Travis entered the room.

"I can't believe my brothers were so stupid. They took something everyone knew she always wore," said William "This is our evidence. It could only have been removed from her finger the night she died. We can finally go to the Sheriff."

Travis put his arm around Olivia's waist. "It was their trophy— even if they could never put it on display."

47

The following morning, Captain Malloy of the Charles City Sheriffs office arrived. Everyone except William was present to offer what information they could about the events surrounding Olivia Maureen McLeod's death.

"I'm sorry, Mrs. Bentley, but I need to take the ring," said Captain Malloy.

Olivia slipped her grandmother's signet ring off her finger. The gold glistened in the morning sun streaming in through the Palladian window. She ran her thumb over the McLeod crest. "This ring has been worn by McLeod wives for generations. I have no idea how old it is, but my great-grandmother is wearing it in her portrait upstairs. Even after her husband's death, Grandmother still wore it." Olivia held it just above the Captain's palm. "I've been searching for it since I arrived back in January."

"Don't worry, Mrs. Bentley, we'll take good care of it. Unfortunately, this is the only piece of hard evidence we have that ties Clive and Wilson Morrison to the death of your grandmother." He placed the ring in a small envelope and tucked it into his pocket. "I'm sorry, but it could be months before you get this back."

"I understand. At least this whole nightmare will all be over soon and I can relax. Just knowing what happened is good enough for now."

Captain Malloy lifted the black garbage bag containing the wet suit and carried it out to the driveway. Despite the warmth of the late morning sun, a chill raced through Olivia as the Captain hoisted the bag into the trunk of the Sheriff's car. "I'll be in touch with William Montgomery later this afternoon. Now that I have statements from everyone here and the evidence, we'll be able to arrest Clive and Wilson."

Olivia wrapped her arms tightly around her waist in some vain attempt to ward off the chill. "I'm afraid they'll be able to get off somehow. How many men in their social class actually go to prison?"

"They do if they commit murder, and it appears that Miranda may have actually seen him do it. Whichever one of them that may be."

Captain Malloy reached out his hand to shake Olivia's. "I wish we had more concrete evidence to go on."

The Captain didn't speak with much conviction. Grandmother's death had been brushed off as an old lady dying in her sleep. Her doctor and the coroner didn't see anything suspicious. Now, five months later we claim it was murder. And all we have is a ring, a wetsuit, and a deranged mind.

"I know," sighed Olivia.

Captain Malloy had suggested Olivia work from home until Clive and Wilson were safely behind bars. She wasn't putting any money on that happening anytime soon. So that evening Olivia gathered everyone, including Jefferson, into the library for cocktails before dinner.

Olivia poured herself a glass of wine and moved to the center of the library. "I've spent the day working out a plan for how we can get through the next few weeks with me working from here. William will be taking over the duties of CEO until a replacement can be found. Uncle Lionel, if you can prolong your visit a little longer, William would like you to become the interim CFO. He'll provide you with a company car so you can move back to McLeod House on Freemason Street."

"Sure. I would be happy to. Maybe William would like to move there as well. I'm sure it would be preferable to living at Sheffield Court."

She glanced at Jefferson. "Do you see a problem with Uncle Lionel coming and going on his own?"

"I don't like it, but he isn't the target. It would be a whole lot better if Mr. William was staying there too," said Jefferson.

"Meg wants to move into one of the bungalows out front. My only concern is the security until we get out from under this threat. My grandmother was paranoid about kidnapping—and I'm not saying I've inherited that as well—but Meg is my right hand. I need to consider it, especially since she wants to begin redecorating the cottage. Jefferson, can you and Benjamin tie in her house to our security system?"

Benjamin and Jefferson exchanged looks. "Sure thing, Miz Olivia. May take two or three days," said Benjamin.

"What about me?" Travis asked.

"That's easy . . . you stay with me." Olivia slipped her arm through his. "Now, let's eat."

Sunday dinner had become a routine that Olivia looked forward to each week. Everyone was sure to show up including William. It was the pivot point that ended one week's activities and heralded in the next with either excitement or dread. It had only been a week since Captain Malloy's visit, but it felt like a month to Olivia.

"I can't help but notice, Olivia, that you're looking rather glum. You haven't had more than two words to share since we sat down." Uncle Lionel said with a frown that showed his concern. "I can assure you that McLeod and Morrison's finances are in good hands. In fact, I could easily take over as the permanent CFO and be more effective than Wilson ever was."

"I'm not worried about your ability, Uncle Lionel, and I've actually been enjoying my days here. It's given me a chance to study the history and read the accounts put down by the various overseers. This land has played a significant role in local history since settlers moved into the area. Back then the threat was Indians."

Travis leaned toward Olivia and took her hand in his. "What can I do to help?"

"I'm afraid you can't do anything. The problem is *us*. I'm trapped here, and we can't acknowledge that we even *like* each other. We can't hold hands unless we're sure Miranda isn't lurking in the shadows."

The whoosh of the swinging door ended any further sharing of Olivia's thoughts. "I've got apple raisin pie for dessert, and I'll bring more coffee."

"Sarah, I have an important request for you after we finish with dessert," William said as he picked up his fork. "I want you and Benjamin to bring Miranda to the parlor. She has too many bad memories associated with the library, so I think the ladies parlor would be better for what I have to say."

Olivia glanced up at William but he only shook his head. Except for puzzled glances at each other and shrugs, no one in the dining room uttered a word.

Olivia had had enough surprises lately to last a lifetime. She hoped this wasn't going to be another bad one. But why include Miranda?

William and Travis huddled in the far corner of the parlor discussing something that obviously wasn't going to be shared with the rest of the group. Olivia's head turned toward the door as the faint whirr of the wheelchair could be heard.

"I'll be back in a moment," Travis said and left the room.

All this cloak-and-dagger stuff was beginning to wear on Olivia. Her life had not been even a smidgen of what could be considered normal since she'd left Marblehead. Yes, her time in New York with Daisy had been more than a little exciting, and she had grown to love Fairfield. But she couldn't let down her guard until Clive and Wilson were safely behind bars.

Miranda came flying through the door as fast as her chair would allow. "What's going on here? I wasn't finished with my dinner and didn't get my dessert. William, you should be ashamed of yurself callin' for me in a rush like this!" She glanced around the room. "How come everbody's in the parlor?"

William bent down and took her hand. "I have something important to tell you."

Miranda looked up at her daughter, then back at William. Her face suddenly filled with happiness, as if a wonderful message had been delivered from heaven. "You came back and now yur gonna marry my Lily."

"Miranda, you must understand that I loved Maureen enough to let her go and marry the man of her dreams." William took both of her hands in his. "And I love your Lily as if she were my daughter. She will always be a part of my life." He motioned to Travis who stepped into the room.

William stood and reached out for Olivia and Travis to join him. Then William took Olivia's hand and placed it in Travis's. "Miranda, Lily is in love with Travis. He is the man who will make her happy. Can you understand that?"

Miranda's tear-filled eyes held fast to Olivia's, then she nodded her consent.

Travis got down on one knee before Olivia while still holding her hand. "I know you wanted time to find your family and their past and most-of-all yourself. You're not the same person that gave me back my ring before coming here, but I loved you then and I love you now." Travis pulled Olivia's engagement ring from his pocket and continued. "Olivia, will you marry me and let us walk into the future together, whatever that may be?"

Olivia placed her right hand over her heart. She reached out her left hand to Travis. He slid the ring onto her finger then stood and took her in his arms.

"I've missed this, and my love for you has grown stronger with each passing day." She wrapped her arms around his neck. "I've found the love of my family, the history that is mine and the only thing that I want now is to be your wife and raise our children here at Fairfield."

Olivia turned and bent down to kiss Miranda's cheek. "Will you continue to watch over us and our children?"

Miranda pulled the handkerchief from her sleeve and dabbed her eyes. "I will, for as long as the good Lord lets me."

Olivia stood and glanced around the room. "You are all my family. And that makes me very happy." Everyone rushed over and embraced her. She felt their love. She'd finally found the family she'd been searching for since she was fifteen. And it was *her* family, her ancestors, and her family's home. Her heart was filled with happiness—and the room was filled with the scent of roses.

"Well this has been one of my more memorable days at Fairfield," Olivia said as she pulled the sheet up to her waist and rested on one elbow. "I don't know who was more surprised by your proposal, me or Miranda. I have to say the old girl took it pretty well."

Travis shifted to his back with his hands tucked under his head. "Yeah, until the first time she loses it and flips back forty years. William and I have been discussing how to do this for some time now. It was all in the timing and that just never seemed right. Of course I had to be pretty sure that you would say yes."

Olivia ran her hand over his bare chest. "I'm happy, and I know in my heart that everything will work out in the end."

"Which ending are you talking about? Don't forget about Clive and Wilson. Their trial could take years."

"I trust William to take care of his brothers and watch over me." Olivia glanced up toward the painting over the mantle. "And Great-Grandmother Alexandra."

"You still believe she watches over you from the grave?"

"Absolutely." Olivia tossed the sheet aside and rolled over onto Travis.

"Don't you find making love in front of *her* a little kinky?"

Olivia chuckled. "Nothing she hasn't seen before."

48

"They're out?" Olivia slammed her hand down hard on the arm of the chair. "How is that possible? How do you get out on a murder charge?"

Captain Malloy spread his hands in a helpless gesture. "That's just it. We have a ring that ties them to your grandmother's killer, but no one saw the act. All we could charge them with was theft."

"What about the tea?" Olivia paused a beat. "That was supposed to kill her."

"Potassium. It's not like it was rat poison or cyanide. Sarah even said your grandmother took Potassium supplements on her own—against her doctor's orders. And there's no proof that Wilson or Clive put it in her tin of tea."

"Where the hell is William?"

Olivia's attention turned toward the sound of someone at the library door.

"Right here, and I have Sheriff Gentry with me," said William.

The Sheriff stood every bit of six feet. His black uniform fit an erect frame as if it had been custom made. Olivia guessed he fell somewhere in the mid-fifties range. He had a long, easy stride that kept pace with William.

Olivia and the Captain stood and waited for them in the center of the room.

"Malloy." Sheriff Gentry did a quick tip of his head in the Captain's direction. "Mrs. Bentley, I'm so sorry for the loss of your grandmother. She was an amazing woman."

His gaze quickly took in the entire room. Not long enough to study for the first time, more like checking to see what might be different. His steel-blue eyes returned to Olivia. He's been here before. How much did he know about her grandmother?

"What's going on? I thought this was over," Olivia demanded of William.

"Let me explain."

"You don't need to. Your brothers go free and I'm as good as dead." Olivia's raised voice couldn't hide her fear and anger.

Captain Gentry stepped forward. "Mrs. Bentley, we had no choice but to let them go. They claim they found the ring under the desk when they cleaned out your grandmother's office at the yard. Wilson put the ring in the library desk at Sheffield Court for safe keeping then forgot about it."

"And you believe them?" Olivia shouted.

"No, of course not. None of us believe that. But they've hired the best criminal attorney that money can buy," Sheriff Gentry said while shifting the hat tucked under his left arm.

"Fine, so now I'm supposed to throw up my arms and turn over my shares that my grandmother ruined her life to protect. And then what? Crawl back to Marblehead so Clive and Wilson live happily ever after?" Olivia slammed her hand on the table causing framed photographs to topple like dominos. "Well, I won't, damn it! I'm a McLeod and I won't back down!"

William took her hand and guided her to the sofa. "Sit down and listen to me. I know this appears hopeless, but I know my brothers. They're their own worst enemies. They feed off each other like piranhas. I held an emergency meeting of the Board, and Clive and Wilson have been relieved of their positions with McLeod and Morrison until this is over. They won't even be allowed on the property, and that alone will kill them. Or at least start the feuding."

"I don't understand, won't they just spend all this free time conjuring up a way to do me in?"

Sheriff Gentry sat down in the chair opposite Olivia. "We don't believe they'll try anything. They know we're watching them, and William and Captain Malloy both assure me security measures here are state-of-the-art. Jefferson will drive you anywhere you need to go, and Benjamin has people watching the property."

"My brothers were driven to this because of their need for control of the company. They've lost that now, so it will only be a matter of time before they turn on each other. One of them wore that wetsuit and entered this house. Sooner-or-later the other one will spill his guts in the hopes of getting his position back. He can then return to the hallowed grounds of McLeod and Morrison."

"And how many years do you think that will take? I could end up like my mother . . . a prisoner behind these high walls."

"It won't be that long. I know my brothers, and believe me I've spent my whole life manipulating them. I'll be at Sheffield Court as much as I can to hurry the process along."

Olivia gazed out the library window over the heavy boat traffic. Summer had arrived on the James with a wall of heat and humidity. It had been nearly a month since the meeting with Sheriff Gentry and Captain Malloy. Olivia had fallen into a pattern that she could at least live with. Meg had finished the renovations on the bungalow, but Chief Gentry wanted her to remain inside the high serpentine brick walls until there was no chance of her becoming a target. Meetings and personal appearances with the various charities were scheduled with no advanced publicity, and Jefferson was always at her side.

"Here you are. I've been looking everywhere for you. I thought for sure you would be in the rose garden curled up on a bench with a book."

Olivia turned her head to see Travis weaving his way between sofas and chairs as he crossed the library with a manila envelope in his hand. "What have you got there?"

"This just arrived. It's from Emily Elfin. Looked important."

"Ah, yes. I just talked to her for the fourth time this week. The Captain's house is finished, and she sent photos. Let's take a look."

Travis took Olivia's hand and guided her toward the sofa. She nestled down beside him, resting her head on his shoulder. She slipped her hand inside the envelope and pulled out a handful of photos. "It looks like she took a picture of every room in the house."

"Wow! Look at this one of the new five-car garage."

Olivia glanced at the photo. "Your cousin, Nick, said it would look just like a carriage house that had always been there. He did a nice job replicating the gingerbread on the house. It looks like they were built at the same time."

Travis handed her another photo. "Take a look at your new back-yard. Just beautiful sweeping green lawn right down to the water. There's no evidence that the boat slip and cave was ever there. And there's a new stone patio where the old garage used to be."

After reviewing and commenting on each photo, Olivia set them on the coffee table. "Emily's done a wonderful job of oversee-ing the project. I can see why she wants us to come for a visit. You know she's going to try her darnedest to convince us that that's where we belong."

Travis wrapped his arm around her shoulder. "What do you think? You know you can't leave here for a while."

Olivia fingered her engagement ring. "Travis, I really want to go back for a visit, but I'm feeling that this is home now. As much as I love the old Captain's house and your family in Marblehead, I just don't feel the need to live there on a fulltime basis. But I worry about you and your business in Port Clinton and Cleveland. You need to be there, and this is your busy season."

"Thank you for your concern, but I've been talking to my cousin almost every day. He's handling both locations and is talking to a friend of ours about managing the Port Clinton office." Travis kissed the top of Olivia's head. "And speaking of family, have you given any thought about our wedding?"

"Thanks to Emily and Meg, I've had little time to think of anything else!"

Travis scooted sideways so he could see her face. "Well, don't keep me in suspense. What have you decided?"

"I'd like to keep it small with just family and close friends and get married in Marblehead."

Travis chuckled. "My family isn't small."

"I know, but I thought we could use the house for out-of-town guests. Emily assures me there is more than enough room, and she can hire temporary staff locally."

"And I can go and organize the whole thing with Emily's help," came a voice from the doorway.

Travis and Olivia sat up with a start. "Meg, how long have you been standing there?" Olivia asked.

Meg entered the room and sat in the chair opposite the sofa. "Long enough to hear that you were discussing wedding plans. I think Marblehead is a wonderful idea, but what about the people here?"

"I want to keep it small so I was thinking about just inviting William, Uncle Lionel, Gertrude, Sarah, and Benjamin. Oh, and I can't forget Horatio and Daisy."

Meg crossed her legs and leaned back in the chair. "They can all stay at the house. We'll use your Gulfstream to fly everyone there. You can stay in the apartment over the new garage. It's so cool. It looks just like a carriage house. It's huge, even has a fireplace."

"Yes, Meg, we've just looked at the photos Emily sent."

Travis cleared his throat. "I hate to put a damper on all these plans, but we don't even have a date yet. And it could be quite some time before Olivia can resume anything close to a normal life."

"Emily suggested Christmas." Meg uncrossed her legs and sat forward. "It's perfect. I love it."

Olivia chuckled. "So it's beginning to sound like you, too, have been talking to Emily on a regular basis."

"Well, just trying to keep up on things for you. After all I am your assistant. You have to agree there isn't much happening now with you hidden away behind these walls. So how about if I go back to Marblehead and arrange your wedding?"

49

"Excuse me, Miz Olivia. Daisy is on the house line for you."

Olivia reached over for the phone. "Hello, Daisy. What a wonderful surprise. Where are you? Sarah mentioned that you'd gone back to Montana."

"I'm here, at the Landing. I arrived late last night. Mo and her kids will be here in a few days. We packed her car full of what they'll need on the trip and shipped the rest."

"I don't understand. Why are they bringing so much?"

"My daughter, Maureen Olivia, has been going through some rough times. Her husband has had a difficult time dealing with their youngest son who was diagnosed early on with cerebral palsy. It finally led to a divorce last year. Finding qualified people to help her with that is hard to come by in the wilds of Montana."

"I'm so sorry to hear this. Won't it be difficult for your daughter to adjust?"

"Mo always loved the summers spent here with her grandmother. When it came time for college she chose The University of Virginia in Charlottesville. She came home to Montana for June, July and August, but the rest of the time she called the Landing home. I'm going to suggest she and the kids move here permanently. It will be a better environment with less friction. And there is adequate professional help. Mo already has many friends in Virginia, more than she has in Montana."

"What can I do to help?"

"You're only six months apart in age. Just be there for her. She's going to need a lot of help and someone close-by she trusts."

"So you're there alone for a couple days?" Olivia asked.

"I don't mind. There's a ton of stuff I want to do before the kids arrive. I need a supply of food in the house—the cupboard's rather bare."

Olivia would have liked nothing more than to be at the Landing helping, but leaving Fairfield wasn't possible. "How about if you stay here? We can have some girl-time and Sarah loves cooking for guests. There's no point in both of us being alone."

"Where are Travis and Meg?"

"Travis is in Port Clinton working with a new manager he hired for his company. Meg's in Marblehead working with Emily Elfin on our wedding arrangements."

"Are you okay with that?" Daisy was silent for a moment. "I know this isn't your first marriage, but don't you want to be there, choosing colors and flowers and menus and all that important stuff?"

Olivia let out a long sigh. "Of course I would like to be there, but I can't. And besides, Meg calls me nearly every hour with a question, and she's sending pictures of floral arrangements and cake designs."

"Okay, you've convinced me. I'll be there around noon."

"That was a fabulous lunch, Sarah. I just may not go back to the Landing. Mo and the kids need to learn to fend for themselves."

"There's always a plate for you in my kitchen, Miz Daisy. And speaking of meals and such, I'm putting you in the Queen Ann room while you're staying with us. Meg's using Maureen's old room."

"That's fine. Would you mind if I take a peek in her room? I spent a lot of time there as a kid."

Olivia pushed back her chair and stood. "I think that's a wonderful idea. Let's go on up and take a look. I think I left Moms diaries piled up on a table."

Daisy hesitated at the bottom of the stairs. "I see the portrait is back in its place. It just didn't look right over the fireplace." She then took the stairs two at a time.

Daisy sat on the bed. "You know that Maureen never felt like a prisoner. I get the impression that's how you see it. But the fact is she had a wonderful life here and was happy, right up until she left."

Olivia carried several books to the closet and placed them on the top shelf. "The pieces of Mom's life are beginning to come together, but there are still a lot of holes."

Daisy moved to the side window. "We had our ponies and would dress up in costumes we found in the attic and ride across lawns, down the lane past the old cottages and out-buildings slaying dragons and pirates or whoever the villain of the day was. In later years we swam in the pool and took Sinatra to horse shows. Then we really sprouted wings when Maureen got the Packard convertible. It was all wonderful until Maureen chose love."

Olivia put the rest of the books next to the others on the shelf. "It sounds like you didn't approve of Dad."

"Our lives followed a script planned by our parents." Daisy turned to face Olivia. "And that was okay until the war came and changed everything. Life became very fragile and emotions took control. Your mother and father would never have met if it hadn't been for the war, and your mother's sense of responsibility to help with the various drives and USO activities. We all helped and did what we could, from rationing and selling war bonds to entertaining the servicemen. Maureen and William would have married and lived their lives as planned and probably been happy enough. But the war sent me off to the safety of Montana's mountains and Maureen into the arms of your father. Nothing was ever the same again."

"I don't think it was for anyone," Olivia said just as the phone rang. "Excuse me while I get that." She walked over to the desk and answered the phone. "Hello?" Olivia mouthed to Daisy that Meg was on the line.

Olivia rolled her eyes at what she was hearing. "Yes, red roses and white Poinsettias would be lovely. Just keep my bouquet simple. It's all about the dress. Yep, I'll talk to you later."

Olivia put the handset back in the cradle. "She wants to keep me in the loop. Christmas wedding, Christmas theme. I'm sure it's going to be beautiful."

"It's all about the dress. So I assume you've already picked out a dress? And without my help?" asked Daisy with raised eyebrows.

"Ah, you don't know about our little find. Remember me telling you about the note Grandmother left me with the little keys? The one where we are to look for answers hidden in the valley. Well, we solved the mystery. Actually, Travis figured it out. Come with me. I think you'll like my dress, and I didn't even have to pay New York prices."

"Like paying New York prices would be a problem." Daisy exclaimed and followed Olivia across the hall to her bedroom.

"Can I help you?" asked Daisy from her perch on the edge of the bed.

"No. Stay right where you are." Olivia said breathlessly. "Wow. Lots of little buttons. Oh, forget it." Olivia laughed. "You are going to be so surprised. Just another minute."

"Are you sure I can't help? Sounds like you're having trouble."

"Don't move. Yikes, this is big."

"This reminds me of our shopping adventure in New York. How many times did you make me wait, while you struggled into one outfit after another?"

"Okay, I'm ready. Close your eyes, and don't open them until I tell you." Olivia held the skirt of the ball gown up and hurried into the bedroom. She stood in the middle of the room with her arms outstretched. "Open your eyes."

"Oh my God!" Daisy gasped. Her hands covered her mouth. "Maureen. It can't be. It isn't possible."

"Seen a ghost?" Olivia twirled around.

Yards and yards of white silk billowed out in a cloud of memories. "Olivia? I don't understand. This dress was destroyed. Your grandfather had it burned after Maureen left. Just the thought of it broke your mother's heart. I was with her in New York when your grandmother had it designed. Do you have any idea how difficult it was to obtain silk after the ban was lifted? She was a princess that night, slowly descending the staircase to her waiting prince who then slipped a ring on her finger. It was the story of fairytales . . . too bad it didn't have a happy ending."

Olivia stopped and posed in front of the fireplace. "It's my wedding dress."

Daisy brushed the tears from each cheek. "Maureen would be very proud. You look just like her. You've become your mother."

Olivia rushed over to the bed. She took Daisy in her arms. "Thank you. It's a magical dress, and I feel like a princess. I'm going to take the tiara that Mom would have worn for her wedding and have a simple veil added. I found it under the false-bottom of the trunk."

Daisy shook her head in disbelief. "But how? Where has this been all these years?"

"Grandmother had a secret room upstairs!" Olivia turned around with her back to Daisy. "Help me out of this thing and I'll show you."

After slipping on jeans and a tank top, Olivia took Daisy's hand and dragged her up to the attic. The door to the last room stood open. Afternoon sun streamed in through the window in the sewing room. "Travis found the valley *and* my mother's childhood."

Olivia stopped Daisy at the door. "All this stuff was hidden behind that wall over there. We pulled it out and looked at everything." Olivia gasped and rushed into the sewing room. She stood before the largest trunk. "This isn't right! This isn't the way we left it. Someone's been in here!"

"How can you tell?"

"The lid's ajar. The hinges are loose. You have to jiggle it to make it fit." Olivia searched the contents of the trunk. "The tissue paper that Mom's gown was wrapped in is on the floor and the door to the lid compartment is open. I remember closing it."

"Travis, please listen to me. Everything is okay." Olivia paced back and forth at the foot of her bed. "You don't need to come back yet." Olivia motioned for Daisy to close the bedroom door.

"It doesn't sound like everything is okay. Even if nothing is missing, someone got into the house and searched that room," Travis argued.

"It was only the trunks that were moved. Only the one containing photos and the journals was rummaged through. But you and I had already moved all the journals and letters to my room."

"You're not safe there. I want you back to Marblehead," Travis demanded.

"Travis, I'm perfectly safe. Benjamin, Jefferson, and the two security guards that were hired assured me that no one other than those authorized have entered the grounds."

Maybe she shouldn't have called him. She knew Fairfield was secure. She had professionals watching over her. Now she was going to worry about what and how she talked to Travis so he didn't overreact.

"Fine, but I need you to schedule Phillips to pick me up."

"Uncle Lionel took the plane to San Diego. He's investigating the deal Clive and Wilson were making to purchase that aerospace company. He can swing by and pick you up in a couple of days."

"I don't like this, Olivia."

"Gotta go. I hear the doorbell. Gertrude is coming by with some important documents for my review. Talk to you later. Love you," Olivia said as she ended the call.

Olivia jumped onto the bed with Daisy. "That didn't go well. But I'm really okay with all this. Maybe Benjamin moved the trunks when he was working on the wall, and I forgot to close the lid tight."

"So who are you trying to convince? You wouldn't leave an antique trunk lid cocked like that. Would you?"

"No, I wouldn't." Olivia said. "Gertrude. . . Gertrude. . . Gertrude. She's been here," mumbled Olivia under her breath.

Olivia finished signing the stack of letters and pushed them across the desk to where Gertrude sat facing her.

She picked up the pile and began setting them in her briefcase.

"What were you looking for in the trunks?" asked Olivia.

"Just old . . ." Gertrude's eyes opened wide as they met Olivia's.

"Just old what?"

"I'm sorry, Olivia. I should have asked permission first. But I was just curious if there were any old letters or paperwork from Angus. He never talked much about the years just after his daughter left."

"And did you find anything?"

"No. But I should have talked to you first."

Olivia got to her feet. "Thanks for coming by. That will be all for now."

Gertrude removed an envelope from her briefcase before closing it with a snap. She stood, handed it to Olivia, and waited.

It only took Olivia a minute to scan the letter. "Your resignation?"

"I've been with the company for thirty years." Gertrude hesitated and took a deep breath before continuing. "This last year has just been too much. Loyalty to one's employer should only go so far, and ever since your grandmother started getting sick nothing has been the same."

"What are you trying to say, Gertrude?"

"I know you walked into a hornets nest the moment you entered the doors of McLeod and Morrison. Right from the beginning you've been honest with me. You trusted me when you had no reason to, and I respect that. Your grandparents would both be proud of you."

"Thank you." Olivia glanced down at the last paragraph. "You know this doesn't have to be effective immediately."

"I'm moving out of the area. I've nearly finished packing, and I've chosen a temporary replacement until you can find someone from the outside."

Olivia set the letter on her desk then looked at Gertrude with a frown. "I shouldn't hire from within?"

"No." Gertrude walked toward the door then stopped. She turned to look at Olivia with pursed lips. "Don't trust anyone." She paused and took a deep breath. "Wilson told me to search the trunk for any letters that Angus had written."

"Wilson? But he's not permitted on company property."

"No, he's not." Gertrude turned and headed down the hall.

Olivia caught up with her at the door. "Gertrude, did Wilson kill my grandmother?"

"I don't know for sure. But I'm moving where no one will ever find me."

50

Olivia and Daisy had just sat down to breakfast when Sarah pushed open the swinging door. "Excuse me, Miss Olivia, but Travis is just coming through the gate driving a white Bronco."

Daisy set her fork down. "Sounds like the Calvary has arrived."

"Yeah, so much for me telling him that we're fine. Unless he thinks the enemy is going to storm the walls or attack by sea."

"Go easy on him. He loves you."

Sarah came through the door with a plate stacked high with blueberry pancakes and a thick slice of ham. She set the plate and silverware down at the place Travis always liked to sit. "I see a hungry man about to descend upon us."

They all turned toward the door as Travis entered.

"Good morning." He glanced over at the table. "Thank God for Sarah and her amazing breakfasts. I'm starving. And hold the coffee, I've had enough to last me two full days."

Olivia stood, rushed over to him and threw her arms around his neck. His kiss was long and hungry. Olivia felt the stirrings of desire grabbing at her self-control. "This is a wonderful surprise. I've missed you."

"I drove all night. I figured you'd be pissed if I told you I wasn't waiting for the plane, so I didn't call."

Olivia glanced over to Daisy who gave her a sly smile and a wink.

"I love surprises. Now sit down before your breakfast gets cold."

Travis was already sawing away at the thick slab of ham when Sarah came into the room with a tall frosty glass of orange juice. "Thanks. I have a fresh supply of maple syrup, honey, and jams in the car. I guess the Paterson family doesn't realize we have fruit trees in Virginia. I'm to tell you this was an especially good year for the maple trees and you'll have all the syrup you want for the rest of the year."

"Who are the Paterson's?" asked Sarah.

"My Aunt and Uncle own a farm and orchards on the Marblehead peninsula. They have a large fruit stand and market. We have fresh produce all summer."

"Very nice. Please thank them for me. I'll get it unloaded before the sun starts heating up and turns that fancy vehicle of yours into an oven," Sarah said as she left the room.

Travis was on his second stack of pancakes when Sarah returned to remove Olivia's and Daisy's plates and refilled their coffees. "So what's been happening around here? Anything new since I talked to you yesterday?"

Olivia set the dainty floral-patterned cup on its saucer. "Nothing. Except Gertrude resigned. She believes it was Wilson that killed Grandmother. And she's going to move where no one can find her."

Travis yawned. "Very funny, Olivia, but you shouldn't joke about murder. So would you mind if I took a little nap, like for four or five hours?"

The next day Daisy packed her things and moved back to the Landing. Her daughter and grandchildren had arrived. She promised to bring them by once they were settled.

Late that afternoon Sheriff Gentry called to say he was on his way with an important development. At four o'clock, William arrived saying that Sheriff Gentry had asked him to meet him at Fairfield. They had no more than gotten settled in the library when

Horatio arrived, also saying that he'd received a call from Gentry. Fifteen minutes went by with each speculating on what the news could be when Sarah ushered Sheriff Gentry into the room.

Everyone crowded around the sheriff while he opened his brief-case and removed an envelope containing several colorful, foreign looking stamps. "I received this last week, but I didn't want to get your hopes up until I checked it out." He set the envelope on the table. "It's a letter from the nurse, postmarked from Amsterdam, explaining how Wilson had offered her a million dollars if she would add the entire bottle of potassium he left just inside the farm gate, to the tin of specially-blended tea that was kept in the kitchen pantry. We know the tin of Sarah's tea that Gertrude kept in her office also contained a high amount of potassium."

"Gertrude knew about this?" Olivia asked.

"No. I believe Wilson added it himself. He had plenty of opportunity."

William stepped forward and took the letter. "Your Grandmother's illness began slowly over a period of several months." William shook his head and snapped his fingers against the letter. "I was the one to insist on the nurse. If I hadn't, she might still be alive."

Sheriff Gentry held up his hand. "Don't blame yourself. Wilson would have found another way. He transferred half the money into her bank account and promised the rest when the job was done. I have the documentation from the bank. He left a plastic bag containing the bottle just inside the farm gate behind the boxwood with instructions to dump the contents into the tin and then shake the box every time she had the opportunity to keep it well mixed." He looked up when Sarah entered the room with a tray of iced tea and a plate of cookies. "Apparently the nurse went on daily walks and would check behind the bush to see if Wilson had left anything."

Sarah placed the tray on a side table. "Excuse me, but the nurse did go on walks every day. Once in the morning and again in the evening, weather permitting. She always went the same way. I noticed because her white uniform stood out. If she wasn't outside, then she was with me in the kitchen. Liked to help out. I thought she should be spending more time with her patient, but then my mother was often in the library watching over her beloved Missus."

"Did the nurse ever go into the pantry?" Travis asked.

"Oh, sure. She was always getting stuff for me."

"Did she ever make the tea?"

Sarah thought for a minute. "Now that you mention it, she did. She'd show up about the time I was boiling the water. She'd get the tea and put it in the pot."

Olivia reached for a glass from the tray. "But do we know for sure the tea killed her?"

"No, and that was also explained." Sheriff Gentry lifted a second envelope from his briefcase. "Two days ago, I received this second letter postmarked from Rome." He opened it with a frown. "Now let me see here. Olivia, do you know where we would find the Hemingway book, *For Whom the Bell Tolls*?"

"I think it would be in with the more recent fiction. And that would be within this century." Olivia walked to the far end of the library and, after a few moments, returned with the book and handed it to Sheriff Gentry.

Horatio chuckled. "So our nurse is seeing the world."

"There's a warrant out for her arrest. A million dollars will allow her to travel the world several times over. She can blend in anywhere as a tourist. Eventually, she'll be caught." Sheriff Gentry fanned the pages. "Here it is, just as she said it would be." He lifted a folded sheet of paper from between the pages and carefully opened it and scanned the contents. "Evidently, she has a conscience." He handed the paper to William. "It's a typewritten note telling the nurse to turn off the tunnel alarm after everyone goes to bed and then turn it back on before dawn. She's to leave an extra pillow at the foot of the bed and make sure it's in the same position in the morning. The letter is signed with a *W*."

Olivia reached over for the note and read with a frown. "But she was already gone when Grandmother died. She must not have followed these instructions, or something went wrong." Olivia handed the note back to the Sheriff. "It's typed. How can we nail Wilson on this without more proof?"

"We match the type on the note to the typewriter. It's an older one." Sheriff Gentry said. "See how some of the letters didn't strike evenly? We'll also check for fingerprints."

William nodded his head in agreement. "There's an old type-writer in the library at Sheffield Court. Tomorrow, I'll get you a sample."

Olivia wasn't convinced the nightmare could be over. "This doesn't seem like enough evidence. If he gets out on some techni-cality, he could just disappear."

"There's more. Gertrude stopped by yesterday. She gave a state-ment of everything she knew about Wilson and Clive since before Angus died. There's enough information here to point several fin-gers in their direction, and if the type matches we'll pick Wilson up on murder charges. Hopefully, he wasn't smart enough to wear gloves and we'll have some nice prints."

"I hope you can tie this up quickly." Olivia shook her head. "My grandmother's later years seemed to be one big tragedy."

"Not as far as I'm concerned. There are many families in this county that owe a great deal to her."

"I don't understand, Sheriff."

"Whenever there was a family in need, all I had to do was call her." Sheriff Gentry's face lit up. "There were two families who would have lost their homes through no wrong doing. Your grandmother paid off the loans. Whenever there was hardship she stepped up, and always helped anonymously."

"Jerome Gentry. Right?" Olivia thought for a moment. "I found a file with your name. I set it aside because the documents inside didn't make sense. There were receipts in large amounts from banks, invoices from toy stores, grocers, clothing stores, and con-struction companies. And copies of checks made out to you."

"Yes. She would often send me the money and I would disperse it. That way no one knew she was their benefactor." He brushed at a tear. "She was a great lady. The whole county will miss her."

"I'm happy to continue her work." Olivia put her hand out to shake the Sheriff's. "Please feel free to call on me anytime."

"It's Jerry to you, ma'am."

"Olivia." She paused. "Just call me Olivia."

The atmosphere was far too quiet for the usual gang including Meg at Sunday dinner. "Come on, guys. We should be celebrating," Olivia said enthusiastically. "William matched the typewritten note to the machine at Sheffield Court and Wilson's prints are all over it. And he found a large, empty bottle of potassium under the sink in Wilson's private bathroom in his office. Wilson's officially been charged with the murder of Olivia McLeod—my worries are over."

But were they over? She'd been doing a good job of convincing those around her that she felt safe behind the high walls and security at Fairfield. But the truth was, she wondered if she would ever feel safe again. Maybe it was just part of life on this plane. She remembered all the references her mother had made in her diaries, and all the measures taken to ensure her safety. Maybe her mother was not merely running into the arms of the man she loved, maybe she had run into the arms of a simpler life. A life far removed from power and social responsibility.

"I'm looking forward to getting everyone back to the yard. We have a lot to clean up, and Gentry's confident we've seen the last of Wilson," said William.

"You're not agreeing, Livy?" Travis leaned over and took Olivia's hand. "I thought you'd be cheering over the return of your freedom."

"I'm having a tough time believing it's really over."

William rested his elbows on the table and leaned forward. "You're worried about Clive and what role he played. I can't give you guarantees, but I do know he's been following Wilson's lead since they were toddlers. He's the weak link in this chain, but if I thought for one moment that he could be a threat, I'd tell you."

"I know. Maybe it's as simple as just easing back into my old routine."

"And I'm here to help you with that." Meg said with a mouthful of raspberry cobbler.

"I appreciate you getting here so quickly. I know it was probably hard to leave Marblehead and the wedding plans."

"Nonsense. I just called Phillips and hitched a ride with Lionel on their way back from San Diego. Emily can carry on without me."

"Speaking of California, what news do you have, Uncle Lionel?"

"I thought I'd leave the best for last. As you know, I went out there to investigate what the boys were really up to. Norton Industries is working on the development of a high tech B-2 bomber. It has a wing design like nothing you've ever seen before. You can imagine the pentagon was all over this and Wilson got wind of a potential deal for ten of these babies at a cost of around seven hundred and forty million each. Norton dumped all their resources into the project and then Congress got cold feet once they looked at the total costs. Norton was ripe for a takeover, and Wilson and Clive jumped on it."

"But why? The Pentagon scrapped the project," William asked.

"True. Except that Wilson has some very powerful golfing buddies. The Air Force wants this plane. In order to take over Norton, the deal had to be made before Norton got wind that the government was taking another serious look. Wilson and Clive pooled their money and started the wheels in motion. They even bought a house in the area—a big one—and joined a very exclusive country club."

"I get it now. They needed McLeod and Morrison's Board to agree to the Western expansion and the purchase of Norton Industries." Olivia sat back in her chair. "Grandmother stood in their way. And old as she was, it didn't look like she was going to die anytime soon."

"Word on the Hill, is that this administration wants that plane." William set his napkin on the table. "Money could start rolling into

Norton Industries and save the company. Wilson is running out of time to finalize his deal."

"And he needs McLeod and Morrison on board now to come up with the rest of the money for the takeover." Uncle Lionel leaned forward placing his forearms on the table. "From what I've been able to find, Wilson and Clive don't have more than three million between them."

"Huh . . . so . . . my brothers are virtually broke."

"At least I know now why Grandmother had to die."

"Too bad my brothers weren't upfront about what they were doing. Sounds like just the kind of exciting project your grandmother would have jumped on. But they saw a gold mine and didn't want to share. Greed never wins in the end."

Travis turned in his chair facing Olivia. He took her hands in his. "Livy, we need to talk about . . . well, about me."

"This sounds private. I think we should give these two some space," said William as he got up and headed toward the door.

Oh, my God. Now what is happening? His words struck fear in her breast. Maybe her lifestyle is too much for him to handle. What if he wants to go back to the slow pace of Marblehead, Ohio? Did he want out of their relationship?

"Please, don't drag this out, you're scaring me. Are you ill? Are you unhappy? Do you want to go back to Marblehead? Just tell me what's wrong."

Travis took a deep breath. "There's nothing left for me to do here. Between you and William, you've figured out Clive and Wilson's plan for the re-structure of McLeod and Morrison. I think there are some strong candidates for the brothers' positions. Lionel is willing to stay on for as long as you need him. I'm just hanging around taking up space."

"But you're not just taking up space. I need you."

"I love you, but this isn't me. I need a project, something to create—something that *I* need. And I've found it . . . or it found me."

"This sounds exciting. Tell me. I'm all ears."

"Livy, I've been talking to Mo over at the Landing. She has a wonderful idea of taking some of her unused land and creating a therapeutic riding camp. Her son just blossoms when he's around horses. This would not only help him but other kids with disabilities as well. A camp is needed in this area, and she asked if I would help her. I really want to do this. It will mean traveling to successful organizations across the country, and possibly England, to see how they are set up. We want this to be done right, and I'm willing to do whatever it takes for these kids."

Olivia leaned toward Travis, wrapping her arms around his neck. "I think this is a wonderful idea. And it certainly falls within the mission statement of the Hampton Roads Charitable Children's Trust. Have Mo submit a business plan. I bet I can get the Board to fund the entire project. I believe there are some unused acres of Fairfield that border the Landing that could be included if needed."

"Livy, I love you." He wrapped her in his arms for a long kiss.

51

Meg settled into the chair across from Olivia's desk at McLeod and Morrison. "I had to move your schedule around this week. Caspar Weinberger has requested that you join him in a meeting on Thursday. William will be attending as well and will give you the details later today. You'll need to leave for Washington on Wednesday and return on Friday. I've scheduled Phillips for the trip."

Olivia turned her head toward the door at the echo of heels on the terrazzo floor. "Excuse me, Mrs. Bentley. I have those letters ready for your review and signature." She set the stack on the corner of the desk and turned to leave. "If you don't have anything else for me to take care of right now, I'll run over to the new Employee Center and make sure everything is in place for the ribbon cutting later.

Olivia's eyes followed the tall blonde dressed in a black pencil-slim skirt and yellow jacket with a lace camisole peeking out between the black lapels. "I can't believe my luck in nabbing Lynette away from the executive offices of NBC. She just screams the glamour of Rockefeller Center and has an amazing amount of experience with the new office machines. There was no way Gertrude would even consider giving up her IBM Selectric."

"Well, it's not just that she wanted to come back to Norfolk to take care of her ailing mother. Lynette mentioned yesterday that there's talk of major changes coming at NBC. It was a good time to get out."

"Whatever the reasons, we need to make sure she's happy. I've never seen this office running so smoothly, maybe some of her energy will rub off on the other staff on this floor."

"What is that supposed to mean?" asked Meg with a touch of sarcasm.

"I didn't mean you, Meg. Now, don't you have something to do?"

"That reminds me. Word on the floor is that Wilson's secretary, Candy was fired."

"Too bad. Under that bimbette façade is a real person. She has a pleasant voice," Olivia said.

"Vivian Dumbarton is looking for someone to answer phones and help her with the dozens of calls she gets everyday. I can track down Candy and see if she'd be interested," offered Meg.

"Sounds like a great idea. See what you can do." Olivia picked up the pile of letters and had just read the first one when William walked in and took the seat that Meg had just vacated.

"Congratulations, Olivia, you've managed to get what you want. Wilson will be spitting mad when he finds out what you've done to his gym."

"You're sure he'll be put away for good?"

"No question about it. You can relax. And by the schedule you've been keeping for the last two months, I'd say you believe it deep in your gut. It's over."

"This gym is an important project for the employees. I just wish we could have put it in the old administration building along with the day care center. I don't think that building is safe with those old generators still on the first floor." Olivia shivered with a sudden chill. "I have a really bad feeling."

William turned at the sound of Meg coming through the door. "Hey, Livy, ready for the big day? I've gotten confirmation that there will be plenty of media coverage. The grand opening of the Employee Family Health Center is a big deal. And it was all your idea."

"Thanks, but you made it all happen while I was in hiding. I can't tell you how good it feels to be back in this office again."

"Livy, shouldn't you be thinking about changing? We need to be downstairs in a little over an hour? You'll start with the ribbon cutting at the powerhouse for the gym." Meg glanced at the clipboard she held. "Then everyone will walk over to the Employee Center for the second cutting. I have refreshments set up in the meeting room in the Center for everyone after the Day Care tour."

"Hey, this day calls for champagne!" Travis walked in holding two bottles over his head. "Meg, can you find us some glasses?"

Meg took the bottles from Travis and carried them to a bar tucked in an alcove adjacent to the bathroom and closet. "Livy, your black Chanel suit is hanging on the bathroom door. Are you really planning on wearing that today?"

"Of course. I always wear it for funerals or when I need a boost of courage. Today is the latter. Where's Uncle Lionel? He should be here for this."

Travis took her hand in his and raised it to his lips. "He was on the phone when I walked past his office. I motioned for him to join us."

Meg set the five flutes of champagne on a round tray and walked toward the three standing at the windows. "Lionel is going to miss the toast."

"No, I'm not."

Meg turned toward Lionel. He took one more step and collided with the tray. The five full glasses fell toward Meg as the tray flew into the air. Meg jumped back, but not in time.

"Oh, my God! Meg, I'm sorry. I didn't see the tray in time. I've ruined your dress," said Uncle Lionel.

Meg brushed the still dripping champagne from her skirt as it puddled on the oriental rug. "I'm fine, just a little soggy."

Olivia ran toward the bathroom and returned with a towel. "Here, you take the towel and I'll get the tray and glasses."

Meg soaked up as much liquid as she could. "This is never going to dry, but there isn't enough time for me to go home and change. What the hell am I going to do?"

Olivia got down on her hands and knees. She reached for the towel and began sopping up the puddle. "Wear something of mine. There should be several things to choose from in the closet."

"You keep clothes in your office?" asked Travis

"Of course. Being two hours away from home, I need a second wardrobe here."

"I want to wear the Chanel."

Was she kidding? How could she even ask? Olivia wondered as she continued soaking up the champagne. "No! I'm wearing that. Pick anything else."

"But I've always wanted to wear that suit. Besides you need to break out of your old habits. You've become far too predictable. Please, Livy, at least let me try it on to see if it fits," Meg pleaded as she headed for the bathroom.

Travis reached down to help Olivia up then took the wet towel and put it in the bar sink. "She's right. You do have a tendency to wear that suit whenever you need a boost of confidence. How about wearing the white one with the black lapels and wide, black shiny belt? That is if it's here."

Meg appeared a few minutes later. "I think that would be fabulous. We would be the black and white-sisters." She twirled around. "How do I look?"

"It's a little short. And don't take any deep breaths—you'll pop a few buttons," Olivia pursed her lips and nodded. "Okay, just don't spill anything on it."

Meg ran over and gave Olivia a hug. "Thanks Livy, can I wear the hat too? I just love wide brim, floppy hats!"

"I was going to wear that."

"You're too short to wear big hats. How about that darling little fedora? It would be perfect with the black and white."

Just then the phone rang. "I'll get it," said Meg as she reached over the desk for the phone. "Lynette is working with the caterers." A frown creased Meg's brow as she listened to the caller. "Are you sure? What did you say your name is? Are you sure that it has to be now? We're right in the middle of . . ." Meg paused for just a moment. "Okay, I'll have Mrs. Bentley meet you in a couple minutes." Meg slowly put the phone down. "That's strange. Something's wrong over in the gym. They want you to see it before we can begin the tour."

"What can possibly be wrong? Everything was fine when I left there earlier. I'll go over," said Travis.

"No, he said that Olivia needed to make a decision on something."

Meg grabbed the hat from the desk and placed it on her head, checking the placement in the mirror. "Livy, there isn't time. You get dressed, and I'll go, I know every inch of that place."

"Who called?" asked Olivia

"I'm not sure. He had a husky voice, but I think he said Benny."

Olivia shrugged her shoulders. "Benny. I don't know a . . . Oh, could it have been Lenny? Lenny Sinclair, the plumber?"

Meg pulled the brim down a little in front. "Do I look like you?"

Olivia chuckled. "Maybe, if you were about six inches shorter."

Meg winked and headed toward the door. "Whatever's wrong, I'll fix it. I don't know why Lenny didn't just ask for me in the first place."

Olivia grabbed the black and white suit from the closet and headed to the bathroom. It smelled like roses. Lynette must be using a new air-freshener. Olivia wove the wide black patent leather belt through the loops of her suit jacket. The shoulder pads accentuated her tiny waist, and the black and white suit shouted designer. Yes, Meg was right. It was time to start her new life. In fact, she would give the black Chanel to Meg. She didn't need the suit as a mental crutch anymore. She was ready to take over the helm of McLeod and Morrison. She cinched the belt tighter as she smiled at her reflection in the full-length mirror attached to the bathroom door. The media would love her. She looked the part of a powerful executive. Now she was ready to prove it.

Boom! The building shook. Olivia fell against the bathroom counter. She braced herself and looked up at the mirror. It was a spider web of cracks. Her hip hurt. She was shook up, but probably nothing more than a bruise or two. What happened? Were the guys okay? Olivia opened the door. A cloud of dust filled the room. "What the hell is happening?" She yelled as she came around the corner.

William and Travis lay under a pile of glass and metal framing. Uncle Lionel was closer to the desk. No one was moving.

"Travis," Olivia shouted. No. No. No. He can't be dead. Why isn't he moving? "Uncle Lionel? William?" Olivia coughed. She frantically made her way through the debris strewn over every inch of the office. Glass crunched beneath her feet. Good thing she was wearing comfortable pumps and not stilettos. She bent down and grabbed the large piece of twisted metal covering Travis and lifted. She pushed it aside as Travis coughed.

"Oh, my God, Travis! You're bleeding." He put out his hand for Olivia. She helped him to stand. "It's your head." Blood streamed down his cheek. He pulled a handkerchief from his pocket while his other hand found the gash just above his hairline. The square of white quickly filled with blood.

William moaned. Olivia and Travis lifted a section of window frame off of his shoulder. She helped him stand. He held his upper arm against his body. "I'm okay." William stepped over the debris. "Lionel. You okay?"

Uncle Lionel was the furthest from the windows. He got up on his own, brushing glass from his hair. "What happened? Looks like a bomb . . ."

Blaring sirens echoed around the room.

Olivia covered her ears and followed Travis as he skirted the largest debris and headed toward the opening in the wall. "It's the powerhouse," Travis shouted. "There's been an explosion."

"Oh, my God. Meg's in there!" Olivia shouted.

Two of the yard's firemen stood where the rear entrance to the powerhouse had been just minutes before. The older gentleman stepped forward preventing Olivia, Travis, William and Uncle Lionel from getting any closer.

"Meg's in there." Olivia shouted. "Get out of my way."

"Someone was in that building? Are you sure, Mrs. Bentley?"

"Megan O'Brien was meeting someone there. She was on her way when it exploded."

"So, she might not have gotten inside yet."

Meg would have taken the stairs outside the office. Down four flights, even in heels, she would have made it in less than five minutes. Then across the road . . . yeah she would have made it inside. "Why are you just standing here? Do something!" Olivia shouted.

"She would be here, standing with us if she wasn't inside," Uncle Lionel assured the fireman.

The fireman put a radio to his mouth and pushed a button. "Call in the city. There may be victims inside. We're going to search. Better get the doc here just in case."

Jefferson and Lynette came running from the Employee Center with Jefferson a few strides ahead. "Olivia, what happened?"

"Meg may be inside. The firemen are going in to look for her." Olivia glanced around. The yard security force was keeping onlookers at a safe distance. From the sound of the city fire trucks, they were just outside the gates. "Lynette, start making phone calls to cancel today's event. *No* press on the premises—and I mean *none*."

"Yes, ma'am. I'll be in the office."

Olivia grabbed Lynette's arm. "The office is destroyed. Get what you need from your desk and use William's."

William winced as he reached into his pocket and handed Travis his handkerchief. "Here's a fresh one. Looks like the bleeding's almost stopped." William turned toward Olivia and Jefferson. "We're in emergency lock-down. No one in or out unless authorized."

"I checked this building not an hour ago." Jefferson said glancing at his watch. "More like half. It was secure. No one was inside. I moved on to the Employee Center to check it for any possible security issues."

The two firemen climbed amongst what had been the front half of the powerhouse.

"I see a clipboard," shouted one of the firemen.

"That's Meg's," shouted Olivia. "She was carrying a clipboard."

"It could have been you under all that brick and concrete," said Travis.

Olivia shuddered. "It was *supposed* to be me."

Two more firemen that were working the other end of the building joined the search. They started tossing chunks of concrete and bricks aside. One of the men began shouting. "I see something."

Large slabs of roofing were being carefully lifted and heaved to the other side. Olivia's heart raced. Why couldn't they work faster? She prayed they'd find her alive. She and Meg had finally resolved their differences. Meg had become the sister she'd never had. Olivia wasn't ready to lose her now.

One of the firemen disappeared down what looked like a hole.

"We've found her!" The firemen cried out.

"Is she alive?" Olivia shouted over the noise of the approaching city fire truck.

"Don't know yet," said the fireman in charge as he climbed down from the pile of rubble. He ran to the fire-truck. "We've found the woman. She's pinned under a steel beam. We need jacks to lift it while we pull her out."

"Anyone else in there?" asked the Norfolk Fire Chief.

"It doesn't look like it. Although she was supposed to be meeting someone there."

"Who was she meeting?" asked Jefferson "No one was supposed to be in there until after the ribbon cutting."

"I got a call from Lenny Sinclair, the plumber," said Olivia. "Meg talked to him on the phone and wanted to handle the problem."

"Strange." Jefferson scratched his head.

"Okay, we start with the jacks," the Chief yelled over his shoulder to his men unloading equipment. "Bring the jacks . . . and the board!"

The yard's doctor approached. "Mr. Morrison, I'll need each of you to follow me over to the ambulance." He removed the handkerchief from Travis's forehead. The bleeding had stopped. "We'll start with you." He motioned for Olivia and Uncle Lionel to follow.

"I'm fine. I wasn't even in the room at the time of the explosion," said Olivia. "I can't leave until they get Meg out."

The doctor nodded his agreement then ushered the men to the rear of the ambulance.

Olivia kept her eyes on the firemen working to get Meg out. She nudged Jefferson. "Go. I know you want to be with Uncle Lionel."

It wasn't long before Jefferson returned. "Travis's wound was cleaned out and the top of his head bandaged. It looked worse than it was. William got a sling. He has a dislocated shoulder. It'll mean a trip to the hospital. I'll take him later. Lionel's cuts to his hands and face were cleaned and treated. He'll be fine."

"Look." Olivia pointed to at least a dozen men in bulky rescue attire climbing over and down into the heart of the powerhouse. "Meg has to be alive. She just has to be."

"I don't know what was so urgent that Lenny needed to see you," said Jefferson shaking his head.

"Maybe it was one of the old boilers or a generator. I had a bad feeling about those."

"William said it's been thirty years since those machines were used. There's never been any reason to think them unsafe."

"Well, Lenny thought there was a problem and called me. Why can't they get her out? What's taking so long?"

Cheers were suddenly heard from inside the rubble. Several men climbed out and crouched at the hole. Then, slowly, Meg was lifted out. She was strapped to a wooden backboard. Once out, they placed the board into a metal basket-like apparatus.

Four firemen carried Meg across the mound of debris and down to the waiting doctor and ambulance.

"She's unconscious, but alive. That big hat protected her face," The chief called over to Olivia and Jefferson "We'll continue searching for the man."

A thick blanket of dust covered Meg as she was lifted into the ambulance. The doctor climbed in the back with her.

"I'm riding with her," demanded Olivia. "And I want to the see the rest of you at the hospital to get checked out," she said over her shoulder as she climbed into the ambulance.

The vehicle drove off with lights flashing and sirens blaring. Jefferson stood at Lionel's side. "I'll get the car when you're ready to go to the hospital. This rescue effort should be winding down soon. I don't expect that there was anyone else in there. That call was probably made from another location. The fire department will remain until they have the site contained.

William adjusted the sling. "Go ahead and get the car. I think we all want to get to the hospital to be with Meg."

Jefferson turned to leave when one of the firemen shouted from the far side of the powerhouse.

"Over here! I have a body!"

The body was located just inside the door on the opposite side of the powerhouse from where Meg was found. The damage to that side of the building was minimal—there were still walls standing. Jefferson kept everyone back while the firemen prepared to remove a large piece of the roof that had caved in. Jacks were used to lift the slab high enough to get the forklift under it, and pull it out of the way.

The Chief motioned for William, Lionel and Travis to come over to the site. "This isn't pretty. Do any of you recognize this man?"

"Clive!" they all said in unison.

52

The hospital conference room had been turned over to the executives of McLeod and Morrison, at least for now. Their wounds had been treated in the emergency room. Now they could only wait.

"I feel terrible," exclaimed Olivia. "You're all hurt because of me. And poor Meg could be in there dying because of spilled champagne."

"He was my brother, and I swear I didn't see this coming," William shook his head. "I don't even know how he got on the property. He had to have started planning this when the Employee Center ribbon cutting was announced. Clive grew up in the yard. He would have known where explosives were stored, and how to set it so it would appear as if an old faulty boiler blew."

"But I checked the building. There wasn't anyone there," assured Jefferson.

"The power plant was a favorite play area for my brothers. Clive could have been hiding behind those big generators or up on the catwalk, and you wouldn't have noticed. Why would you? You had no reason to suspect foul play."

"He probably lit some kind of fuse when he was sure you were coming. At that point Meg looked like you," Travis ran his fingers across his bandaged head. "He must have misjudged how long it would take him to get out of the building, since he was found just inside the door."

"Clive was never good at planning things. He was the follower. Wilson made all the decisions. I'm not surprised that he botched this," William leaned back in his chair. "I wonder if Wilson put him up to it."

"I guess we'll have some answers after we see the reports from the fire department," Olivia stood and began pacing back and forth. "What's taking so long? Did the nurses forget we're in here waiting?"

"I'm demanding a full report from the head of security," William added.

Everyone turned toward the door as the doctor knocked and entered the room. "Good news. We're hopeful that Megan will make a full recovery. However, at the moment she remains in a coma. This is necessary and will allow her body to begin the healing process. She's going to be one sore lady for a while."

Once they were convinced that staying holed up in the conference room wouldn't help Meg, they left for the night. Uncle Lionel and William headed to McLeod House while Jefferson drove Olivia and Travis to Fairfield. After a quick dinner of sandwiches and pasta salad in the kitchen, they went to bed.

Travis rolled over, taking Olivia in his arms. "Meg will be okay, thank God. You have to stop blaming yourself."

Olivia's gaze burned into the portrait over the fireplace. "I should have known. Great-Grandmother was trying to tell me I was in danger. I just ignored her. It's my fault. I should have been more careful."

"Livy, honey, don't beat yourself up like this. There's nothing anyone could have done."

"Every night for three nights, I woke up in a sweat. I'd look up at Alexandra, and her face would be glowing. She was trying to warn me. It was a sign," Olivia sat up in bed. "And how can you explain that slab of concrete falling on Clive? It was the only thing disturbed on that side of the building—just fell out of the ceiling and killed him as neat as can be."

"You can't really believe in messages from the grave, honey. Alexandra's painting wasn't glowing. Just bad dreams and moon light coming through the window."

"Believe what you want to, but Meg's in a coma. She nearly died because she was wearing my clothes. That explosion was meant for me. Clive tried to kill me and my great-grandmother saved me."

"I believe it was spilled champagne that saved you."

"And I believe it was Great-Grandmother who caused Uncle Lionel to walk in front of Meg causing that rather wet disaster."

"Nonsense." Travis pulled Olivia back down, cradling her against his chest. "There's nothing we can do for Meg until her doctors bring her out of the coma. Nothing's going to happen at the yard until a full investigation is completed, and it could be weeks before you can get back into your office," Travis kissed her forehead. "How about we sneak away for awhile. Let William and Lynette handle the mess."

"Hmm. I think that's an excellent idea." Olivia's eyes met those of the man she loved with all her heart. "How would you like to experience *my* New York?"

"Sounds exciting," Travis ran his lips across hers. "I bet it's not too late to give Phillips a heads-up."

"I'll call Clarence," said Olivia as she reached over and turned out the light.

EPILOGUE

December 21, 1985

Olivia and Uncle Lionel waited at the back of the church in Marblehead, Ohio for the last guest to be seated.

"I thought you said this shindig was for family and close friends only. It's standing room only in there," he whispered to Olivia.

"Travis has a rather large family."

"We should have set up roadblocks out on Route 163 that say Town Closed; Wedding Traffic Only."

"Oh, Uncle Lionel, it isn't that bad."

"I bet the mayor, police chief and fire chief are all here, and you might as well throw in the Coast Guard," Uncle Lionel paused. "For the last twenty years I've watched you search for a family that could replace the one that was taken from you." He nodded toward the church's sanctuary. "Looks like you found one."

A swish of red satin announced Meg's arrival at Olivia's side. "It's time to line up."

Travis's cousin, Patsy, was already in place. She clutched her small bouquet of white rose buds at the waist of her pencil-slim gown of red satin. Meg handed Olivia her bouquet of red rose buds and white poinsettias, then made one last adjustment to the heavy diamond tiara.

Olivia inhaled the sweet scent of roses and looked into the eyes of a tearful William as he approached from a side door.

He glanced at the tiara Olivia and Travis had found in the trunk along with the gown. "This is how your mother would have looked on our wedding day." He bent down and kissed her cheek. "That was for Maureen," he whispered. Then he stood brushing any tell-tale sign of tears from his eyes and smoothed the front of his tux. "I'd better get up front. Daisy is saving me a seat."

"Meg, I need to tell you . . . I need to tell you how much you mean to me and . . ." Olivia swallowed the emotions ready to erupt. "I don't know what I would have done if . . ."

"I know . . . and please don't cry. There's no time to fix your makeup again."

Meg took her place behind Patsy as the music began.

Patsy glanced back to give Olivia a wink before taking her first step down the aisle.

"I'm so proud of you and what you have achieved. I feel that I have finally fulfilled my promise to your father," Uncle Lionel took Olivia's hand, resting it on his arm. "Travis is a good man."

Olivia's gaze took in the sea of happy faces. The sanctuary was packed. Not another person could have been crammed in. They were all there for her and Travis. She would never have to feel the tremendous weight of loneliness again. Looking beyond Patsy she could see Travis waiting for her. His radiant smile was enough to guide her to his side. His strength would carry her through the uncertain years ahead. She knew there would be many of those. It was just part of life, and some lives had more than others. But that was okay now because she not only had Travis . . . she had a family.

Olivia mingled amongst their guests at the reception. They had taken over the entire first floor of the Island House in Port Clinton. The Cleveland branch of the Tanner family all had rooms upstairs. "William, I would like you to meet my dear friend, Emily Elfin. She is the one responsible for introducing me to the Captain's house and has overseen the renovations. Without her the project would have come to a screeching halt. She and Meg have allowed me to be in two places at once."

William shook Emily's hand. "It's wonderful to meet you and be able to put such an enchanting face to the name that I have heard so often."

"You don't want to get too close to Emily . . . she's psychic." Olivia patted his hand. "But in the event you should suddenly find yourself on the receiving end of a premonition, remember to ask questions. Ask lots of questions!"

Travis suddenly appeared at Olivia's side. "Sorry for the intrusion, but I must steal my bride for a few minutes. Family is waiting and all that stuff." Nick Tanner intercepted Olivia and Travis on their way across the room. He was pulling at his very wide red cummerbund—his face was equally as red. "Are you in pursuit of my wife for the next dance, or just stretching that thing?"

Nick twisted his neck from side to side and ran a finger inside his collar. "I'll tell you one thing, Travis. I hope this is the last time I have to wear a tux, I'm just about ready to bust outta this thing!"

"Sorry, old boy, it won't be much longer. Why don't you take off the jacket and cummerbund and ditch the bowtie? You'll be a lot more comfortable."

"Wow! Can I?"

"Yes, of course you can," Olivia said. "And I want to thank you for the magnificent job you did on the Captain's house. The carriage house looks like it's been there forever. The workmanship is amazing."

"I'm glad you're happy with it. Of course, having an endless supply of money helped it along."

Olivia followed Travis as he headed in the direction of a table abuzz with chatter. Nick was already out of his jacket and whipping off the tie. Aunt Mavis and Sarah had their heads together, no doubt in some culinary conspiracy, while Miranda dozed in her wheelchair.

Mavis was the first to look up. "Ahhh, the happy couple! Sarah and I have been talking food."

"Guess what Miz Olivia? Here I've been fixing you all these fancy meals, and I hear from Mavis that I could have just thrown a couple burgers and hot dogs on the grill and you would have been just as happy!"

Olivia gave Sarah a sheepish shrug. "Oh, well. Sorry. I didn't want to upset you."

"Not to worry. Nick is coming down in the spring and put in a new patio, complete with a gas grill and plenty of room for outdoor entertaining."

"And I should come down and help Sarah with new barbecue recipes," Mavis said with a wink.

"And I'll teach you a seafood chowder to die for," exclaimed Sarah.

Olivia put her arm around Travis. "Oh boy! I'm beginning to understand family dynamics. I think it's time I had another dance with my husband."

An hour later William placed his hand on Olivia's arm and gave a gentle squeeze. "Sorry to interrupt, but I haven't had a chance to dance with the bride. I hope you don't mind, but I requested a special song that was a favorite of your mother's. Olivia recognized *We'll Meet Again* by Vera Lynn. It was a well-worn record in her mother's collection.

She was soon carried along in the gentle waves of a bygone era.

Emily stood off to the side watching the scene before her. Olivia moved with an unaccustomed grace in William's arms. Her mother's diamond tiara began to fade away until it was no more, and a wide pearl choker slowly wrapped its many rows around the young woman's neck. Her face was younger, her back straighter and William held her tighter. She slowly raised her head until their eyes met. Their auras quivered becoming one and both were enveloped in a cloud of pure love.

The colors of the aura grew more brilliant as a voice smoothly sang the lilting lyrics. *We'll meet again, don't know where, don't know when, but I know we'll meet again, some sunny day.* Emily watched as William danced with the woman in the portrait that hung above the fireplace in Olivia's parlor. Emily had never felt psychic heat this intense nor love so strong that it bridged decades. So why had Maureen walked away from her true love and soul mate? Or was she pushed? The pearl choker began to fade. The diamonds of the tiara once again showed their brilliance. The song came to an end. Olivia's steps faltered and William steadied her. His eyes caught Emily's with a question. How could Emily explain what her gift had allowed her to see? She saw the love, the passion, the emotions that defied death. William's eyes pleaded for confirmation. Still feeling the love that had spilled over into her being, Emily smiled at him and nodded.

Olivia held onto William as if she were coming out of a trance. Her hand went to her head to stop the spinning of the room. "What happened to the music? Why did it stop?"

"It's over, Livy. The song is over."

"Huh, must be low blood sugar." She shook her head. "I think I need cake."

Travis walked over to them. "Hey, William, that was some dance you had with my wife. Looked like you were both swept back in time with that song. I didn't know Livy could dance that well." Travis put his arm around Olivia's waist in a rather possessive manner. "Actually, you look more like father and daughter."

William gazed at Olivia with a slight tilt of his head and a frown. "I've grown to love Olivia like the daughter she should have been. The dance and music brought back memories of her mother." William glanced around the room with a puzzled look. "Excuse me, I need to find Emily. She was just standing over by the window, and now she's gone."

"Can't help you there. Livy and I are heading over to the cake."

An hour later, Olivia watched Emily heading toward her wearing a scowl on her face. She knew it meant trouble. She raised her glass in one hand and a plate in the other. "Cake and champagne are a rather unusual combination . . . but good."

Emily took the glass of champagne and replaced it with the glass in her hand. Olivia shrugged her shoulders and took a sip. "*Really*, Emily? Sparkling water? You've been taking away my glasses all evening!"

"It appears I may have missed more than a few."

"This is my wedding. I can have as much champagne as I want!" Olivia reached for her glass of the bubbly, but Emily held it high above her head. "What's with you?"

"It's not good for the babies," Emily said calmly.

Olivia frowned and looked around the room. "I don't see any babies."

"Your babies."

"Come on, Emily! I don't have any babies!"

"Yes, you do."

"No, that isn't possible. I would know if I were pregnant with a . . . babies? More than one?"

Emily smiled and looked down at Olivia's stomach. "If my vision is correct? You have two boys in there, duking it out."

The snow fell beyond the large bay window in the apartment over the garages. Olivia clutched the front of her white satin negligee tightly across her chest. The Marblehead lighthouse stood strong and proud before her. Her life seemed balanced when in its shadow. She was looking forward to a month alone with Travis on a private Caribbean island. It would be a honeymoon free of decisions, problems and complications—a normal kind of life—if there were such a thing. Should she tell Travis about her possible pregnancy tonight or wait until after their honeymoon? How would he take the news that he was about to become a father? He'd said he wanted kids. But that was a year ago when they first got engaged. A lot had happened since then. She couldn't stress about it now. This was her wedding night.

They had come back to the carriage house early, leaving the younger crowd to dance until dawn to the heavy-metal music they preferred. Making love had been amazing.

"I'll close the drapes if the light bothers you," Travis said as he wrapped his arms around her, pulling her to his chest. She snuggled back to feel the warmth radiating from his body.

The rhythmic arc of light reached far out into the lake. "That beacon has always been the light of safety and warning. It guides our weary sailors home, protecting all who fall within its rays. It gives us hope for a new day."

Travis kissed the top of her head. "And it will always be here to guide our family home."

ACKNOWLEDGEMENTS

I must thank my editors, Diane Taylor and Polly Sue Poppy, who work tirelessly to clean up my drafts. And the amazing ladies in my critique group who pushed me to dig deeper into my characters' heads, expand my scenes, and never forget the importance of choreography.

When looking for an historic house to use as a model for McLeod House in Norfolk, Virginia, I stumbled on the *Moses Myers House*. The guides took the time to give me a private tour and a thorough understanding of life during the 1700s. I hope they don't mind that I made changes to the house and expanded the grounds to include a gazebo and a carriage house.

Thank you to everyone at *Shirley Plantation* who made plantation life come alive and who sent me on a mission to find Judy Ledbetter at the Charles City County History Center. Thank you, Judy, for the time you spent with me. I hope our paths cross again for another book set along the *James*.

Although I only had access to the grounds, *Westover* was truly a wonderful inspiration for Fairfield. I spent two lovely afternoons taking in the sights and sounds and imagining what lies beyond the rosy brick walls. I sat on a bench along the *James River* and watched dragonflies dance across the lawn and inhaled the scent of box-woods. Of course, as a mystery/suspense writer, my mind went crazy with the plot. I hope the owners of *Westover* can chuckle over what I've done to their magnificent home. I would love to set future books there.

My travels also took me to Manhattan and a tour of the *Waldorf Astoria*. I enjoyed exploring everything from the ballroom to the kitchen. It was easy to let my mind wander and imagine the magical world of the Waldorf.

I'm looking forward to where Olivia takes me next time.

AUTHOR BIO

Pamela Ann Cleverly is a novelist and member of Romance Writers of America and Sisters in Crime. She lives in northeastern Ohio where she is finishing her third book, *It Started With Besse.*

Pamela is the Executive Director for CANTER Ohio—a non-profit organization dedicated to providing Thoroughbred ex-racehorses the opportunity for a new life, home and career through rehabilitation, retraining and rehoming.

Made in the USA
Columbia, SC
01 February 2019